IN THE DARK

THE UNBOUND FATE
BOOK 1

C.J. BLAIRE

Katie Wolfe: Developmental and Copy Editor

Jay Aheer: Cover Design

For the ones who act first & ask questions later

AUTHOR NOTE

Dear Readers,

My goal for this novel was solely for no one to read it, truly. I had no intention of ever publishing this book, and wanted to keep it for myself.

But then I kept writing and my family pushed for me to publish. And the more I thought about it, the more I wanted others to read the story that got me into writing.

Before you read, just know that Isa's story is a little bit of an unraveling—where you learn things the moment she does which leaves her a little... panicky.

I feel like there's a point in all our lives where we think, *who the fuck am I?*, so we do what we think is best given our circumstances.

That's who Isa is in this book, someone who discovers who she is or could be beyond her training. Someone who also has a hard time asking for help even though she knows she should. She's fiercely independent and when someone offers help, she thinks she can just do it herself. Isa makes mistakes and that's okay, but sometimes our mistakes get us into a whirl of trouble.

Enjoy the ride and the twists!

Thank you for purchasing and taking the time to read this book. I cried many tears in the process, so enjoy my sorrow.

CONTENT & TRIGGER WARNINGS

In The Dark is an adult romance fantasy with explicit content, intended for audiences 18+. There is on and off page violence, and the romance is explicit. The trigger warnings below are solely to prepare readers for what they'll be reading. I trust you as a reader, know what you can or cannot handle. May contain minor spoilers.

- Explicit sexual activity (all consensual)
- Explicit language
- Parental loss/abandonment
- Violence and assassination (on and off page.)
- Memory loss and identity manipulation (central to her arc, with psychological and emotional consequences.)
- Psychological trauma: PTSD-like symptoms, dissociation, and emotional numbness.
- Captivity/Forced Loyalty
- Child abuse/neglect, exploitation, kidnapping: Taken as a child and raised as a weapon for the crown.

- Political Oppression: Power struggles between realms; children and civilians caught in the crossfire.

PLAYLIST

Bury A Friend - Billie Eilish
Lovely - Billie Eilish
Nightmare - Halsey
Control - Halsey
Chokehold - Sleep Token
Dangerous - Sleep Token
The Death of Peace of Mind - Bad Omens
Like A Villian - Bad Omens
Just Pretend - Bad Omens
Renascence - The Pretty Wild
Living Ded - The Pretty Wild
I'm the Sinner - Jared Benjamin
Against All Odds - Micah Ariss

<u>**MAGIC SYSTEM**</u>

Realm of Elderheim
*All Aetheri can use elemental magic, leaf whisper, and
communicate with animals.*

Aetheri Magic
*Siphons
Crystal Scrying
Stone Shaping
Herb Weavers
Healers*

Realm of Aurelia
*All Shadovar can use elemental magic, enter the Veil, and shift
their appearances.*

Shadovar Magic
*Seers
Shadow Shaping
Vision Walkers
Shadow Mending
Death Whispers*

1

———

What if I never come back?

What if I lock this door and disappear?

The knob warms beneath my fingers in the dead of summer, locking runes flickering up the frame in a glow of sigils. I stand just outside my chamber door with an impossible decision and a grind to my teeth.

Go out tonight, or disappear? Would the king even care?

Either way I'll be searching for them again—my parents. The ones I'm not supposed to care about, but I do. No one knows, and if the king found out, I doubt I'd ever leave the castle again.

And losing my freedom by death is the last thing I need.

I force my shoulders to relax despite the questions. Despite the severed heads flashing across my vision from my most recent mission. I keep telling myself: just one more, and I'll be free to search for the ones who abandoned me so long ago.

Would I actually be free? Probably not.

Yet I know this feeling will pass, as it always does. It's just the mission—nothing more than another disappointment. I'm sure I'll feel better after I go out tonight.

I let out a defeated sigh as my boots smack against the stone steps of my stairwell, strands of my hair fluttering from the warm air coming in from the arched entryway.

If it weren't for the back-to-back missions, I probably would have found an escape sooner than I have, but the king has kept us busy running his errands. That's what I call them—errands—because it feels like I'm taking care of something for him he'd rather not do himself.

The bloody parts. The cruel, gruesome killings he likes so much, leaving me to wear one of the many metaphorical masks he's trained us to develop in the Veiled Brotherhood—masks of personality and disguise. Something we're all good at.

Masking my expressions is like second nature now—hiding my emotions from everyone like it's always been a part of who I was meant to be.

Except for when I'm around Ezra.

"That's what you're wearing?" Ezra throws me a teasing scowl the moment my boots touch the gravel.

"What do you mean?" I glance down, pinching my brows: loose black pants and a matching tunic draped off my shoulders.

"I figured you would have worn something more... accessible." He chuckles like he can't believe what I chose to wear. I scoff and roll my eyes, tossing my braid back over my shoulder.

We're on our way to the Painted Bird, the finest brothel in Alvonia. One with strict rules that, if broken, get you thrown out by your hair. It's typically where I go after completing a grueling mission, and the anticipation of going ate at me all day. Though their rules can be quite annoying at times, I love the place so much, I don't dare break one.

Tonight is the only night Ezra and I can escape after weeks of nonstop missions. I just need a damn breather, but Ezra's incessant pestering isn't going to help me relax.

"What would you like for me to wear?" I ask.

"You're wearing pants. You look like one of the males," he

says, his hazel eyes throwing me a sideways glance as we exit the stone rise of the castle.

"Were you expecting me to wear one of the king's ball gowns when all I'd do is get it dirty? You're wearing pants. What's the difference?" I grumble.

His pants are paired with a fitted tunic that sits snug around his chest, showing off years' worth of our training in the Brotherhood, though he's all rough edges and hard lines.

A hardness that I believe has made him an unshakeable tool for King Elion to use—forged by combat and killing. But I'm not glaring at a honed weapon. I'm glaring at my best friend.

He snorts, walking past me with a quick glance over his shoulder. "I didn't say that. Just something, you know, less masculine."

I quicken my pace. "This is not masculine. Besides, pants *are* easily accessible. All they would have to do is—"

"Oh, come on, Isa. You look like you might fight someone for no reason. I'll honestly be shocked if they let you in with all the weapons you're wearing," he interrupts, and I fall into step beside him with another glare.

"It wouldn't be for *no* reason—there's always a reason." I shrug, a small grin tugging at my lips. "I'm not headed to the brothel for one of the males anyway, so I think I'm fine. Did you bring your mask to get in?"

Our boots crunch against the gravel, the only sound at this hour, and even though it's only mid-evening, most are inside their homes by now. Castle Alvonia sits just outside the city, surrounded by a field of lush grass with oak trees lining the gravel roads.

Ezra flicks his wrist, summoning a glowing orb of light with the elemental magic of Elderheim, illuminating our walk.

All Fae of Elderheim possess the elemental magic of the realm, but only the Aetheri—high Fae of the light realm—have specialized powers that make them unique. Ezra is a halfling like me, with only the ability to form basic magic. My abilities are limited to light orbs the size of marbles, and occasionally, my heightened sense of smell.

"Yes, did you? And did you hide your color?" He arches a brow, attempting to peek around to scan my hair. But my lip curls as I dart out of his line of sight, immediately knowing what he means by *color*.

"Of course," I grind out. "You make it sound so dirty."

I reach around to ensure that the auburn streak behind my right ear is still neatly pinned in place. I was born with a birthmark directly in my hair, and with the rest of my hair black, the lighter color can be spotted if you look hard enough.

I've never seen anyone else in the realm with a streak like mine, which is why the king insists I keep it hidden to protect my identity during one of my missions—in case I fail. Which I never do.

"Good. Just making sure. I'd hate for King Elion to throw a fit over it." He smirks, but I ignore his remark as we continue our walk into the city, an easy silence falling between us.

Ezra and I were recruited from the orphanage at five, trained into the Veiled Brotherhood—the king's hidden assassins, though the realm believes we're a part of the royal guard.

The king created the Brotherhood himself, favoring Aetheri Fae and halflings like us. Siphons were his primary weapon of choice, but after they grew scarce, he began handpicking orphans to eliminate threats to the crown.

Orange lamps shine in the distance, lighting the outskirts of Alvonia. The city clings to the southern side of Mount Ravenrock, carved into the mountain and surrounded by oak and rowan trees. As we step onto the cobbled streets, vined shops and lit homes line our path, orbs of light drifting lazily through the air.

A mother and her child pass in front of us, and for a few moments, all I can do is watch as they reach the edge of the shop to our left. A sense of longing washes over me—something that's been more frequent lately.

I've never had proof that they're alive—my parents—but I need to know.

Over the last year, my mind has constantly pulled me back to who I was before, or who I could be outside of being a king's assassin. And for the last several months, I've taken that time to search for my parents—if they exist—after my assigned missions.

As much as I want to inform Ezra about my activities, I unfortunately know how that conversation will go as I've had it a couple of times with some of our brethren in passing. It always leads to them explaining that they're most likely dead or gave me up willingly. Yet I find myself wanting the truth—and to close that door on my own—despite what they say, and despite the fact that I know nothing about where I come from.

Because all their words do is leave me to search for them on my own, forcing me to keep my whereabouts to myself during my missions for fear of King Elion withholding the high-profile targets I receive. It's my only escape to other cities, and I've been taking advantage of it when I can.

Even if that means keeping it from Ezra.

My eyes land on the Painted Bird as it comes into view, spotting the dark red door as groups continue to weave between us.

"Are you looking forward to seeing anyone in particular tonight?" Ezra asks as the wind picks up, blowing his sandy brown hair over his set brow.

"Maybe Bess, if she's there. I haven't seen her in a while. What about you, anyone special you want to see?" I ask, knowing his type is typically large-breasted blondes.

It's been a couple weeks since I've enjoyed Bess's company last, and I grin, remembering her curvy features, long brown hair, and green eyes. I enjoy both males and females, but tonight

I'm eager to see Bess. But liking her isn't the only reason I'm visiting the brothel tonight.

She was the reason I was eager for my mission near Nymara —a four-day trip—having told me about a secluded orphanage and a contact for me to speak to, but that was a dead end. Again.

Ezra chuckles, scratching his jaw. "Not really. I'm just ready to have a night off."

"You didn't even want to come!" I exclaim, throwing him an annoyed sideways glance. "Will you relax?"

He's scanned the area five times now. Ezra specializes in tracking, known for his observational and awareness skills. It's why he struggles with taking time away from the castle—when we do get it—as he can't seem to shut it off no matter the distance.

And it drives me insane.

It took all afternoon to convince him to join me at the brothel, Ezra claiming that one of the local taverns was better than having mediocre conversation in a pleasure house. We came to an agreement that he'll accompany me first before he splits off to find a tavern.

He frowns, furrowing his brows. "Sorry, old habits. I'll relax when we get there." Then he smirks, playfully bumping into my shoulder as a bark of laughter escapes me.

"Oh, I'm sure you will."

After a few minutes of walking, we finally ascend the stairs to the second level, arriving outside the red doors of the Painted Bird. Ezra bangs on it three times as we begin to put on our masks.

The popular brothel requires that you always wear a mask, apart from the courtesans. They claim that guests visit for pleasure, and to ensure their privacy without being the subject of city gossip, everyone is required to wear one. Whether you're mated, own a business, or have a family—it's non-negotiable.

Gods, I love this brothel. For no reason other than that it allows me to be free of my obligations.

A screen slides open, two dark eyes peeking out at us when the door creaks open a moment later. A large male steps to the side.

"Shoes and weapons in the corner, coins in the bowl," he grumbles—one of the rules—and then shuts the door.

Walking in, I blink as my eyes adjust to the brothel's dim interior. Oil lamps bathe the red walls in a golden glow, rugs scattering across the creaky wooden floor beneath a gilded chandelier.

I instinctively scan the area. Two long curtains to the left close off access to the rooms, which I'm now hearing all sorts of noises coming from. Another large male stands nearby.

After abiding by their rules, I quickly nod to the male in the doorway and drop a few coins into the bowl with a clink as Ezra quietly trails behind me.

We're greeted by those loitering in the hall, recognizing familiar faces along with a few new ones, but I scan the area for Bess. No luck.

Then my steps falter when I shoot a glance over my shoulder, finding Ezra grabbing hands with two females—blonde females—and entering one of the chambers behind me. A knowing grin tugs at my lips with a shake to my head.

I guess he'll be busy for a while.

A quiet chuckle escapes me as I break off to find Bess, reveling in the thought of seeing her familiar face and eager to hear what else she might have for me. I walk through the grand pleasure room, heading to the back where her chamber resides. Multiple couples enjoy their caresses, taking turns touching and kissing while others watch.

No matter how many times I've been here, I can't help but smirk at the way guests watch each other—blatant and unashamed. I walk slowly against the far right wall, not to hide, but to observe. The warm lighting softens the edges of the room as I take in the details.

The room is large with many settees surrounding the main fireplace. On the far left wall are smaller rooms curtained off for privacy, and toward the back is a mantel that goes up three stories. Each level is lined with wooden railings and private apartments, but only the top floor has windows. I've always been curious to know what sits on the top floor.

I turn right, heading toward the private quarters where guests sometimes go to have business meetings and do... other things.

Stopping just outside the room she frequents, I find the curtains to be down but partially opened in the middle. With a glance through the curtains, I raise my brows at Bess enjoying herself with a male. Though I can't see his face.

She's on her back, brows furrowed, dark hair spilling onto the pillows behind her as the male's head works between her thighs. I grin. It's been too long since I've seen her, and I can't help but admire how beautiful she is.

But she may have another lead—another name, or perhaps something about my past. Just one step closer to finding the truth about who I am.

I make a mental note to come back, but before I can make it two steps to leave, my body comes to an immediate halt—smacking right into someone's hard chest.

____

2

"Oof!" I cry out, my mask sliding across my face.

Was that a brick fucking wall? The male grips my shoulders, holding me at arm's length as we face each other. Only now I'm annoyed, because why didn't he see me?

"I'm sorry," I grunt. "I didn't see you, but surely *you* saw me standing here."

I fix my mask and look up, finding that he's very tall. With a large step back, I attempt to view the stealthy guest—his features mostly hidden by a large hood reaching past his forehead. *Go figure.*

I mentally kick myself for not knowing that someone was behind me—almost like he appeared from nowhere—and quickly scan the corridor only to find us completely alone. My fingers twitch, itching to grab the missing daggers that are typically secured to my waist as I size him up. My teeth grind.

That's the only rule I hate.

"And who are you?" His voice comes out low and resonant as he glares down at me from behind his dark red mask.

"No names, remember?" I flash him an annoyed smile, reminding him of one of the rules, and dust off my tunic.

"Right, I almost forgot," he says, his lips tipping up as he glances past me, nodding in Bess's direction. "Are you enjoying the view?"

Heat sears my face when I glance behind me, seeing Bess. *Gods.* "Oh, no, it's not what it—"

"You were watching, weren't you?"

My eyes narrow. "I was seeing if my friend was… I wasn't…" *Good gods, why am I flustered?* I take a deep breath, composing myself. "I don't think it's your place to ask me what I was or wasn't doing. Who are *you* anyway, or are you just sneaking around making others feel uncomfortable? Are you with anyone?"

I crane my neck to peer around him, the corridor still shadowed and empty, before flicking my eyes back. Although dark, I can make out *some* of his features. The mask conceals from his brows to the bottom of his nose, which I see is pointed from our height difference—he's perhaps six foot three.

His hood remains up, but shadows dance across his face from the lanterns hanging off the walls, accentuating his jawline. Something shiny sits across his top lip—a scar, maybe— and he's noticeably attractive regardless of what I can't fully see.

But I don't recognize him. No. I would have remembered his voice if we had crossed paths before.

"Did I make you feel uncomfortable?" He chuckles quietly. "I'm not here with anyone. I do have a meeting, though." He nods to one of the private rooms nearby, but the way his eyes meet mine leaves me to believe he's rethinking his own plans. "Are you waiting on the male?"

My eyes dart past to the empty wall behind him as a small grin pulls at my mouth. "I was waiting for the female."

Then an odd wave of familiarity skitters across my skin when the faint earthy scent of him drifts by. I can't quite place why when he—very noticeably—scans me with his eyes.

"You're waiting on the female?" he asks.

"Females know how to please better." Nothing could convince me that males are better lovers when females know exactly what you need.

His eyes track the way I cross my arms, staring at me in a way that makes me feel like he can see me without my mask. My neck flushes, and I find myself unsure of my movements, which is unlike me.

His mouth slowly rises into a cocky smirk. "Is that so? Well, if you're going in there with her, I want to watch."

Words fail me, my cheeks flushing. No one's ever wanted to watch before. His words are arrogant—even a little ridiculous— but the way he says them has my core heating and my head tilting to the side. A sudden curiosity blooms in my chest, and it takes me a few breaths to gather my thoughts before I offer him a slow, curious grin.

"You're bold," I say.

He only chuckles, casually placing his hands in his pockets. "Maybe a little. You must not have much experience if you think females are the only ones capable of giving adequate pleasure," he says with a lazy grin, but then it falls, a serious- ness coating his tone for a breath. "Would you like for me to change your mind? I'd love to show you what real pleasure is like." He leans down, whispering inches from me, "We *are* in a brothel."

Oh, he *is* bold. And very cocky, it seems. Yet my eyes narrow as I step back again, giving him another casual once-over.

"Maybe some other time," I say, his eyes flicking to my lips. My breath hitches, and I'm unable to stop my tongue from grazing my bottom lip. Like I can't help myself.

A lingering silence hangs between us, my pulse skyrocketing as his intense stare meets mine. My eyes dart across the sharp lines of his mask, trying to decide if he's toying with me or if he actually wants to follow through with that promise.

A promise that's enticing to me the longer I stand here. He

has an enthralling, commanding energy, and I find myself wondering what a male like him is doing at the Painted Bird.

Lips parting, I eye the faint scar rising on the right side of his lip, realizing that he must feel the charged space between us too. His chest heaves. His mouth hovers over mine, inches from me.

But why do I want to brush my lips across his? What an odd, unfamiliar feeling...

My fingers twitch as the wild thoughts whirl in my head, and I find myself wanting to touch him. Without a second thought, I reach up to graze his scar with my fingers, closing the distance.

I suck in a sharp breath, my stomach dipping when his hand shoots out with a low growl, catching mine before I can graze my fingers along the hard lines of his face.

With a small tug, I attempt to pull back, but our hands remain frozen in the air, our eyes locking with challenge.

Is he angry or curious? It's hard to tell with these damn masks, but my brow arches at his refusal to let me go. Without warning, he backs me against a wall, bracing a hand beside my face with a low, heated hum.

My breath catches in my throat when my hand goes cold—icy, almost—forcing my gaze to his chest. Then my brows pinch, my eyes landing on what look to be shadows skimming my—

"And you said I was bold," he mumbles, forcing my gaze back up. "I really want to see where this goes, but I'm late for my meeting. What are you doing tomorrow night? I'm in town for a few days."

He wants to meet tomorrow? A low chuckle escapes me as I study him, my eyes raking over his masked face. I'm unsure about this exchange. Not only do I *not* linger after visiting the brothel, but relationships outside of the Brotherhood are strictly forbidden. We aren't even allowed sexual relationships *within* the Brotherhood. King Elion doesn't like distractions—anything that pulls our focus away from his missions—so if we have needs, the brothel is where we go. But it's clear that this male doesn't work here, as he's also wearing a mask.

"I have… things to do," I quip.

"Things… like what?"

"Not *you*," I reply sarcastically, adding emphasis to the *you* part, but I can tell he doesn't believe me. "There's no need to come back for someone's sloppy seconds. I'm sure you could find someone else to satisfy you tomorrow, so why don't you do that instead?"

"I know I could, but I don't want to. And I can assure you, nothing I give is ever *sloppy*." His gaze lands on my lips. "What can I say? I'm… curious."

I chuckle. "What could you be curious about, exactly? You've spoken to me for what… a few minutes? I'm not a courtesan."

"I know you're not a courtesan. But I am curious to know what your mouth tastes like… and that's not the only reason." He pulls back to look at me, his voice dipping low. "You look like you like it rough."

A low heat travels down my body, settling at the apex of my thighs, and I'm forced to swallow the breath caught in my throat at how right that assumption is. I do like that, but how did he read me so well?

"I'd prefer you on your knees with your head between my legs." I grin, throwing him a teasing wink. "I won't be here tomorrow, but you're more than welcome to think about me later."

He exhales, the sound amusing as he assesses me, as if figuring out a way to change my mind. Then his attention shifts to the wall behind me. His head tilts, eyes narrowing almost like he's listening to something and causing a whirl of unease to curl my stomach. With a quick glance around, I know we're the only ones in this hall when his gaze lands on mine again.

"What if I said please? Are you going to make me beg for it?" he asks, almost breathlessly.

"You don't look like the begging type."

"I'm not." He throws me a lazy half grin, so close to me that I catch the faint oakmoss that lingers on his skin. Then my eyes narrow as I actually begin to think about the request.

If he's only in town for a few days, perhaps I wouldn't have to see him all the time, meaning I wouldn't be breaking any rules within the Brotherhood. He also looks as if he has connections in the realm—he could help me discreetly search for my parents.

Another silent minute passes before I give him a small smirk, my eyes lingering on his lips.

"Fine. I'd hate to see you on your knees, *begging*. Tomorrow night, then," I say.

A blur of someone walks past, but I don't take my eyes off the mysterious male, searching his face. Then a throat clears in the doorway—Bess.

I glance to my left, meeting her gaze. She studies me with a raised brow, brown hair spilling over her shoulders, wearing loose linen clothes. A smirk slowly lines her mouth, and I realize that the male she was with was the one who walked by.

"Bess, hi!" I exclaim. The male in front of me steps away, leaving me feeling alone and cold against the wall.

"Tomorrow." He nods to me, smirking as he turns away, then disappears into the private room across from us.

I shoot a quick glance at Bess with a small grin, brows raised as we exchange similar looks.

"Who was *that*?" she whispers with a wide grin, as if she wants to taste him as much as I do. "I've never seen *him* before, and he was fully dressed. I don't think he works here." It's not uncommon for guests to find pleasure with each other, but it's usually the courtesans willingly offering the service.

"That is a good question..." I mumble.

"Oh, join me, please. I haven't seen you in ages, and I need all the details of what that male did that has you looking like... that." She points to my face, leaving me to chuckle after her.

I stride through the curtains and flop down, sinking into the lush pillows that rest on the large circular bed settled in the center. She secures her curtain with a hard flick, then hands me a glass of wine, a grin on her face.

"How was your trip to Nymara? Did you find anything?" she asks, her green eyes holding mine as she sits on my left, and I prop an elbow.

I shake my head, sipping. "Not yet, but I feel like I'm getting close. Turns out, not many know much about who my parents could be. Either one could have been human, but there's really no way to know which one—or if my name is actually my own."

Since I came from the orphanage, it's impossible to know if my name was given to me by my parents or those at the orphanage. And without names to give them, searching for my parents has become... a challenge.

Dim light flickers in the room, casting streaks of orange along the walls as I silently sit with my words. Bess remains unaware of my real name as a part of the brothel's rules, frequently calling me by common pet names like *darling*.

The names don't bother me, but I find myself wishing I could tell her more, as she only knows slivers of my life. Since the brothel rules only apply to masks, names, and weapons, Bess knows that I work for King Elion. Only I've told her that I remain in the castle as a house-maiden as a way to keep my identity a secret.

Her brows pinch, as if not finding my parents is as painful for her as it is for me.

She frowns. "I'm sorry. I wish I could do more. Have you tried searching further north? I hear there are a few orphanages along the way to Eldryn."

I shrug, taking another sip. "I'm not sure King Elion would allow me to leave for so long."

Which is partially true. King Elion hasn't sent me that far north yet, and Eldryn is almost two weeks away. The terrain is harsh, as it's settled beyond Mount Pyre, but you have to travel through the two mountain peaks to arrive.

And there are only a few weeks out of the year when the weather is decent enough to make the trip there safely, as it's coated in burning ice. It's why Kiev and Selphira Blackwyth—the duke and duchess of Eldryn—hardly visit. It's too much of a risk. But not only is the journey there rough, the Twin Valley sits between Eldryn and Alvonia. A valley that comes with its own difficulties when traveling.

"Maybe you can ask the king if you can take a temporary leave," Bess says with an arched brow. I know she tries to offer whatever help she can, frequently suggesting more options.

I huff with a shake of my head, knowing that King Elion would never allow me to leave to search for my parents. Not unless he intentionally sends me north on a mission for fear of said distractions.

Luke, Malrik, and Ren are typically the ones sent on missions that long, since they're some of the few full Aetheri in the Brotherhood. Their tracking capabilities are superior as two Healers and a Stone Shaper, but they haven't been on missions that long recently.

"I know what the king would say if I asked. Plus I need the money. I can't be gone for that long without work." I shrug.

"You're right. Even if you are a house-maiden, I'm sure he'd deny your request just because he could and then withhold your pay," she says with a disgruntled huff.

Money's never been a problem, as King Elion requires hefty payments for his services. But I know why he pays us so well—he craves information. And as long as the Brotherhood exists, he'll continue to collect secrets and requests from the realm's most elite.

The dukes and duchesses of Elderheim are the same high-ranking families on Elion's council. They help run the cities, but when it comes to dirty work, they keep their hands clean by paying Elion to send his *guards*. Though none of them have actually met us or knows who he sends—it's always private. And because of that, King Elion has become the greatest threat to Elderheim.

Bess sets her glass down with a clink, facing me as she settles herself deeper into the pillows.

"Here's what I think," she says, tucking a pillow beneath her as a devious grin lines her mouth. "I think we should set this aside for a while so you can relax and take your mind off it, because I want to know who that male was in the hall."

A carefree laugh bubbles out of me as I playfully nudge her even though I know just as much as she does. "How much detail do you want?"

She chuckles. "All of it."

A few hours go by with what feels like only a blink when I finally bid her goodbye. The wine's buzz courses through me, head heavy, feet stumbling as I exit Bess's chambers with a small giggle while she waves.

I only make it a few steps before something dark and shiny catches my attention on the floor. My eyes flick to the ground. A black coin, looking as if it might have belonged to the male that was with me earlier as it rests right where we were lingering.

I bend to pick it up.

The coin feels solid in my grasp—perhaps heavier than it should be—made of a heavy material similar to stone. Though I've never seen a coin quite like this one, it almost feels warm to the touch. Like an energy is imbued within the material itself.

I stride down the hall and flip it through my fingers a couple of times before mindlessly placing it in my pocket.

3

———

A tired groan escapes me, eyes squinting as they open. Streaks of light stream through the arched windows just a little after dawn, and I realize that I forgot to close the drapes before flopping on the bed last night.

Running my hands over my breasts, I glance to find I'm still wearing the outfit from the brothel. Another groan. My head is pounding and I throw an arm over my face to shield myself from the beams of light. I arrived a few hours before sunrise, sauntering back to the castle drunk off wine, without Ezra. I find myself wondering where he ended up.

Sitting upright, I rub my eyes and instinctively glance at the door, spotting the white envelope shoved under it. I grind my teeth, knowing exactly what it is as I climb out of bed and snatch it up.

The king's golden seal rests in the center—another mission, and with as little information as possible. There are two rules to the missions we receive: eliminate the threat and ask nothing.

My target is to be taken care of tonight at the Silver Lily—an inn for high-ranking families from all over the realm, including wealthy merchants.

A place where they can conduct business and socialize without having to mingle with the common folk, making them feel superior. But I scoff, knowing the real reason King Elion has the inn: to keep the elite in one centralized location where their movements can be observed and watched closely. A private location, meaning I'll have to find a way in.

Target: *Alec Thorne.*

For tonight only, and I'm to end the mission *dirty.*

And by dirty, I know he means bloody and not to find a place to bury or burn him like we typically do. He must be a high priority if it needs to be done on such short notice, as I'm usually given a few days to get it done. But not this one.

My eyes close on a long breath. Requests are being placed at an all-time high, seeming like Elion accepts all of them.

Of course it's tonight, the one night I want to sneak back to the Painted Bird, but it looks like I'll be occupied for the evening.

I bite my lip. Thinking back on the male last night has my stomach turning in the most exhilarating way. It's almost tempting to stroll straight to the brothel instead, interested to discover what that male is like between my legs.

But I know how that would end—a beating handed out by Theron, King Elion's personal guard.

Perhaps I can visit after eliminating my new target. I'll be in the city after all. The thought runs through my head as I toss the order on the table.

After bathing and dressing with every weapon I own, I leave my quarters in search of Ezra, who's most likely still sleeping.

The commons isn't far, through the door just around the corner of my stairwell, separated from everyone else. It's where the brethren meet with training just beyond the arena doors. If we don't have missions, we're responsible for training the new orphans.

When recruiting, the orphans are lined up and forced to

hold two rune-inscribed stones to measure their magical capabilities. If the runes glow brightly, they are full Aetheri, and if the runes stall but emit a faint glow, they're a Halfling that possesses a sliver of magic. It's possible for Halflings to not possess any, but the king wants some magical capability, often discovered around the age of five.

The Brotherhood is separated into three groups of ten based on our best skills: combat, tracking, and infiltration. We're all skilled, but each brother has a specialty. Mine is disguise and infiltration.

The commons is large, easily holding all thirty of us, and is surrounded with tables and chairs. Similar to a tavern but less fun.

Boots scuff on stone as I walk toward the table of fresh food, my eyes landing on Malrik and Luke eating with a group of others before landing on Ren, who stands nearby.

"Morning, Ren." I nod, grabbing a few pieces of fruit, not bothering to get myself utensils.

"Isa," he grumbles back.

My brows rise, as he doesn't typically acknowledge me. As a precaution for myself, I choose not to have relationships with many of the males here, though I do my best to be cordial toward them when I'm around... sometimes.

Ren is the exception.

A six-foot-six Stone Shaper with medium length black hair and a scar across his left brow—sliced at the tail. He wears linen around his wrists, and I have yet to figure out why.

He's thirty-one and has been in the Brotherhood a few years longer than me, becoming my instructor at only sixteen when I was ten. He looks the same as he did at twenty-eight though: tall, strong, and lean.

Now, he seems to hold a grudge against me—for what, I don't know. I don't particularly care, but I've learned to ignore him, and he hates that even more.

Though I can't resist teasing him when the opportunity presents itself. And now, he seems to be in a rare enough mood to tolerate me, so it looks like I'll be taking it upon myself to piss him off this morning.

"Strange that you're talking to me today. Did you finally get another target, or are you just bored?" My voice drips with sarcasm, and I hear Malrik snort a laugh nearby.

I know Ren doesn't typically get a lot of missions—not anymore, at least. I don't know the reason for it because I haven't cared enough to ask. I just figure King Elion withholds them or gives missions to the others.

His feet remain planted a foot away as he faces me, dropping his plate to the table. A sneer twists his face.

"How is it that someone so small can be so insufferable?" he asks.

"Am I though?" I chuckle, craning my neck to meet his glare, then drag my gaze over him, ending with a faint smile. "I personally think you're losing your edge, or maybe the king just feels sorry for you. Keeping you around even though you're aging out of usefulness. How long has it been since you had a decent mission?"

His jaw tightens, hands curling into fists at his side. For someone who always thinks he's in control, he sure is easy to unravel. Then he lunges at me, but I dodge effortlessly.

"Oh, come on, Ren. Don't be so predictable," I taunt and step out of his reach. "You're no fun when you're angry."

For a moment I think he's going to try again. When he doesn't, I throw him a final look over my shoulder and dart for the stairs, snagging some fruit off the table for Ezra. My pulse thrums—not from fear, but from the satisfaction of watching him seethe.

I reach Ezra's door and knock. A minute passes, but he doesn't answer, so I try the door only to find three runes preventing entry. I scribble on a temporary counter rune, feeling the magic warm at my fingertip as I infiltrate his chamber.

Counter runes are used to divert the energy away from the original ones and into the one that I write, effectively canceling it out. This will allow me to gain access into any location for a short amount of time before it disappears, leaving the area protected once more, but they don't require a lot of magic.

It takes all of five seconds for me to gain entrance and step in. He's sprawled out with his face buried in the pillows—shirtless. At least he had the forethought to shut his curtains, unlike me, so I fling them open, earning a groan.

"Whoever the fuck is in my room better shut those before I kick your ass," he mumbles groggily.

Looks like he stayed up late too. Ignoring him, I grin and rip the quilts from his grip, receiving a slew of curses.

"Ugh, I'm going to kill you," he growls.

I snort. "I brought you food… well, fruit. You'll have to get a plate of the fresh food downstairs. Be careful though. I pissed Ren off."

"Great, just what we need for the day. A pissed-off Stone Shaper with a stick up his ass." He chuckles, pushing himself up to greet me with a wide, teasing grin. I toss him an apple and sit.

"How was your night? Those blondes looked nice." I wink just as he takes a bite of his apple.

He hums. "Much needed, but I found myself at a tavern after that. How was yours?"

"Ah, there's so much to tell. Where do I start?" I grin, looking out the window. "I found Bess, but not before I met a new mysterious male in the hallway."

He snorts, lifting a brow. "Was he any good?"

"He was… something," is all I can say because I don't know how else to explain it. Although he never touched me, he quite literally took my breath away. I found myself thinking about him the remainder of my time with Bess, eager for tonight.

"*Oh,*" Ezra says, his brows shooting up as he straightens. "He was really good, wasn't he? Are you going back to see the courtesan?"

Courtesan. Ezra thinks he works there. A quiet laugh escapes me with a shake of my head, but then my smile quickly falters as I remember my orders from the king earlier. Another target slid right under my door just like every other week.

"I actually *did* want to go back tonight, but I got another target this morning."

He stops chewing. "Another one?"

I nod. "King Elion gave me clear orders that it needs to be done tonight."

He glances out the window. "He's been keeping us busy these last few weeks."

We're both tired, having had multiple targets over the last few weeks, and tracking them has been exhausting and unusual. Having these targets isn't uncommon, but the number of targets we've had is. It leaves me wondering who's placing these requests or if it's the king's doing. I silently thank the Fates that I know where my target will be tonight, so hopefully it will be a quick mission.

I nod, standing with a teasing grin. "Well, let's get going. We need to spar because you need practice. You're becoming slow."

I turn for the door and almost make it to the knob when he chucks his apple at my head, forcing me to duck.

"Missed!" I laugh and wait in the hallway.

Ezra exits after a few minutes, buttoning the top of his tunic, paired with matching black pants. His hair is damp, and once his tunic is secure, he falls into step beside me. Our boots thud against the stairs as we descend into the commons, only stopping to eat before our intense training session.

We walk in silence and enter the arena, which opens into a huge sphere with an intricate glass ceiling that reminds me of the greenhouses the Herb Weavers work in. We're immediately welcomed by warm air as the sun shines through the large windows above us.

A grin lines my mouth when I spot the weapons rack at the edge and stride over to grab my favorite—the staff. Simple but effective in taking down an opponent.

Ezra and I typically do morning training sessions, as they're a requirement from the king to maintain our stealth and combat skills.

It's noon by the time we take a break, our shirts thoroughly soaked as we drip with sweat. My attention shifts to the arena doors when they creak open, spotting Ren and a few others striding toward us. A sneer creeps up Ren's face the moment he sees me, no doubt from our exchange earlier this morning. After taking a drink out of my flask, I wipe my mouth with the back of my hand.

"Taking my advice and training your endurance, Ren?" I nod to the arena just as Luke chuckles beside him.

"Don't fight, Isa," Luke says with a lazy grin. "If you land a blow, I'm afraid you'll ruin his charming good looks."

Ren instantly silences him with an icy glare. Luke is around Ezra's height with short dark brown hair with bronzed skin, eyes a shade of amber. A Healer and the biggest gossip in the Brotherhood. My eyes instinctively flick to the weapons strapped beneath his thick cloak.

"Don't," Ezra mutters to me.

Ren steps forward with a growl. "You sure do know how to push my buttons, don't you?"

Luke and Malrik quickly shut their mouths once the other males stride to the weapons to begin their training, ignoring us, as they already know where this is going.

A grin tugs at my lips as I lean against my staff with my elbow, crossing my ankles.

"You make it too easy. You wear your emotions on your face," I say, and his gray eyes flick over me before he huffs.

"Whatever. I have training to do, wench. Get out of my way." He stalks past, boots thudding heavily against the floor.

"Mm, yes, you do. Go train like a good dog," I mutter when he stops, slowly pivoting in my direction.

"What did you say?"

"I thought we were name calling," I remark with a blank expression even though I fight the smile that's begging to come out.

Before I can blink, he throws his right fist in my direction, and I dodge it with ease. Amusement glints in my eyes, and I smile.

"You missed, you slow bastard," I say.

He throws another fist, leaving me to jolt to the right, kicking him hard in the hip. He stumbles back with a grunt. My punches may be hard, but my kicks are harder—he should know. He trained me.

Then Ezra steps in.

"She's not worth the fight," Ezra growls. "Let's continue with training. We'll be out of your way in a few min—"

"Let him fight me." I point my staff at Ren. "He thinks he can win? Let's fight."

"Isa," Ezra warns with another low growl.

"He's right. You're not worth it," Ren snarls, sharply turning on his heel without another word.

I snort, facing Ezra. "You just ruined my fun, you know that?"

"What do you mean? I just saved you from an unnecessary fight. No need to use all your energy when you have a mission later," Ezra says, taking my staff from me.

I shake my head and chuckle, grabbing my flask. "I hate it when you use logic, but I'll see you later. I need to get ready for tonight."

"Bye!" Ezra calls out just as I reach the doors.

4

———

It didn't take long for the guard at the Silver Lily to show his true intentions. After leading me to a dark room filled with chairs, he lunged for my hair as soon as the door clicked shut.

I anticipated the move, sidestepped, and then slid the dagger into his throat, backing him into a chair.

Now, my dagger swipes clean across the slumped guard's tunic, his eyes open. I'd feel sorry for having him believe I was a courtesan if he hadn't been so aggressive. But I don't.

King Elion doesn't care how I complete a mission, just as long as it's done, and I've never had any complaints about it. Unfortunately, this has allowed me to complete my missions at a much faster rate because males have no common sense.

As soon as a female bats an eyelash, all the blood drains from their face and into their member.

I hate doing it though, becoming this person, as it's what I do when I want to finish a mission quickly. To be alluring and convincing enough to get these males to spill or allow me access into a private building. It's what works—luring them to their death with a simple flirtatious grin.

Not always but sometimes.

If my life were different, I'd imagine a quiet one. One without killing and manipulation. One where I could live peacefully by myself.

It definitely wouldn't be *this*.

Luckily for me, this will be an easy mission if this is how the rest of the night is going to be.

Blowing the hair out of my face, I fix my dress and check for blood, turning to the vanity behind me.

All clean, not a single drop.

My hair is a mess, leaving me to ensure my auburn mark remains hidden as I stare at my reflection in this frilly olive-green dress. Although similar to what the innkeepers wear, this one hugs tight around my chest, accentuating my muscled figure.

I didn't choose to be an assassin—a weapon. *Smile and be grateful,* I was told. But I scoff at the thought.

Given? More like forced into. It's not like I had a choice, not really. Especially not at five years old, needing to survive, be fed and housed.

I could disappear if I wanted to since money isn't an issue, but where would I go—north or south? A city or a town? The quiet conflict of leaving or staying pulls at me, and no matter how hard I try, it's one I never can seem to explain.

Still I remain at the castle, unable to find the courage to leave as my duty to King Elion trumps my urge to leave.

I pat myself, feeling for my daggers before turning the crystal knob with a sigh, looking over my shoulder one last time to scan the chamber behind me.

Finally, the door creaks open and I scan the corridor. Still empty.

I quickly note where everything is, having passed by in a blur to follow the guard. The ledger desk sits straight ahead, and across the desk is the guest corridor, leading back into the building. It's a little after ten but not very many are up, and thankfully, the inn isn't busy.

On silent feet, I rush down the hall, reaching the front desk for the names on the inn's ledger.

"No," I mutter, flipping the thick pages. "No, not him. No—" I stop flipping and grin as I tap the only name in red with a finger.

Alec Thorne, room eleven. *Just who I'm looking for.*

Quickly grabbing extra rags, I stuff them in my arms to blend in as an innkeeper. My pace is slow and controlled as I casually walk down the hall.

Since the Silver Lily is a private inn, we use Helga, the innkeeper, as one of our informants. She's the one who relays information to the king, usually by a leaf message, which is Elderheim's quickest way of communicating. After scribbling on a leaf, you light it with the intention of sending it to who you want, vanishing only to arrive next to the recipient. Helga is how we knew about Alec in the first place.

My steps come to a halt at room eleven and I knock, looking down as I wait. "Sir Thorne, I have towels for you!"

It doesn't take long before shuffling emerges from behind the door. At last, the door clicks open, and I glance up.

The Fae male towers over me, his large frame taking up the entirety of the doorway. His pointed ears peek out from beneath his perfectly tousled auburn hair, as if he just rolled out of bed. I scan him, noticing his strong jaw, light-colored eyes, and a faint scar across the right side of his upper lip.

My eyes narrow at the scar, the familiarity of it, though he's the most striking Fae I've ever seen.

He looks down, then back up in a deliberate once-over, tilting his head to the side with a squint. I shift my gaze down and sheepishly extend the rags—feigning innocence—but he doesn't take them.

"Who are you? I didn't ask for these." His voice is low and smooth but seemingly annoyed.

Then my stomach drops at the sound of his voice. I recognize it. It's the male from the brothel last night. Now that I can see him without a mask, I almost groan. Why does he have to be attractive?

It's too bad I have to kill him, but now I find myself wanting to bolt in the opposite direction. Instead, I stand with lethal composure, giving him a soft, convincing smirk right before I lunge.

In a whirl of movement, I toss the rags in his face. My dagger slices through the air to swiftly swipe across his neck, but before the blade makes contact, he sharply pivots to the side, movements precise and fluid. His body twists, quickly darting back into the room, leaving me no choice but to follow him in.

I grunt and lunge again, and the faint hiss of my blade grazes past as I swipe, but I don't make contact. Instead of him retreating like I expected, he steps into me, his arm deflecting my strike with ease, and before I can recover, his fist drives into the side of my ribs.

Crying out, I stumble back as the impact knocks the air from me, his counterattack catching me off guard. I dart out of his range when the door clicks shut, but my eyes focus on him slowly circling like a predator.

"Who are you?" he growls, icy rage sliding into place.

My eyes flick to the daggers in his hands, dark as night, as if they're swirling in shadow. He twirls them, widening his stance with a knowing grin, circling the chair near the wall.

I quickly scan the room. The area is spacious—the bed rests against the windows, and there's enough room for a chair and a small fireplace. I'll have to work around the furniture, but I can do it.

"I'm Isa Valedara," I get out, tilting my head. "Here by order of King Elion."

I catch a flash of surprise before it vanishes, and I smirk, eyeing my new threat. Maybe he recognizes me. Or perhaps he's heard about the king's specially trained *guards*. Whatever it is, he ignores it, easily keeping his pace with mine as he assesses my footwork. He's clearly skilled.

He throws me a menacing grin. "Just who I wanted to see. Couldn't wait to see me again, darling? You know, I was just thinking about you and what I wanted to do right between those legs." *Ah, so he does recognize me.*

"Don't flatter yourself. I wasn't going back," I say, but I know that's a lie, especially with how quick a heat settled low in my core. I had every intention of going back tonight, but my mission is more important than a quick release. I fling the chair to the side, allowing more space as we continue to dance around each other, waiting for someone to make a move.

"How did you know it was me?" I ask.

He grins. "Oh, I'd recognize your sultry voice anywhere, but I think you were going to go back." He glances down at my breasts, and I realize the mask I tucked between them has begun to fall out. *Shit.* "Tell me, did you think of me while you were with Bess?"

"No!" I grunt, lunging again as I attempt to swipe across his middle.

But he's fast—so fast that his movements blur in the dim light and I barely see him move. One moment he's in front of me, and the next, he's behind. I blink, and an eerie chill scurries down my spine as I realize he's no longer where I thought he was. My muscles tense as his arm comes across my neck, the other holding my arms down to prevent me from stabbing him.

Normally, I'd be able to get out of this maneuver, but he is... really fucking strong, and I grunt against his hold. His grip is firm but not tight enough to cut off my air. I pant beneath him, squirming to get free.

Usually, killing Fae is easy—a slice to the throat, the head, or even the heart, but this one knows how to fight and fight *well*.

"I bet you did think of me," he whispers low in my ear, causing a shudder to run through me. "But how would you feel if I told you I've been looking for you? And I'm not speaking about the Painted Bird. *You* are Isa, the only female in the Veiled Brotherhood. Tell me if I'm right..." he murmurs, his breath hot against my cheek. "Let's see, you're best friends with Ezra, instructed by Ren Demaris, and *captured* at five... years... old."

I squirm, using all my strength to break free, but he doesn't budge. "What do you mean?" I grit my teeth. "Who are you, and how do you know who I am?"

My head spins, wondering who King Elion sent me to kill if he's this skilled in combat and has been looking for me—*how* does he know that about me? He shouldn't know anything about me, and I know that some of my targets can fight, but not like this. This is years' worth of skill—centuries, even.

His mouth moves against my temple as if rising in a smirk when he whispers, "I'm your past, present, and future."

My frustration bubbles, and I cry out right before my head snaps back, connecting with his nose. He releases me, and in an instant, I whirl around with my blade. He quickly ducks, flicking his tongue over the blood dripping down to his perfectly scarred lip.

"Mm," he says, eyes gleaming with amusement. "I like when they're mean."

My eyes narrow. "Well, pretty soon, you won't like anything."

He twirls his daggers. "King Elion loves sending his assassins to do his dirty work, doesn't he? You would know. You've been doing it since you were..." His auburn hair falls to his brow as he tilts his head to the side. "At what age does he give out missions? I'm guessing twelve."

My face blanches. "How do you know that?"

No one knows specifics about the Brotherhood, so how does he? I continue to watch his feet, calculating his movements, and notice how he hasn't tried to hurt me. He's made no swift strikes—no attempt at cutting me. Instead, he's focused on dodging my blades, but every move of his is precise and calculated.

"I know all about you, darling," he says, but his eyes go dark. "King Elion isn't who you think he is, but I do think you should know who you're killing."

"And who's that?" I snap.

Anger flashes in his eyes. He growls, "Innocents."

A noise drifts by, causing his attention to briefly flick to the door, when I take advantage of the distraction and lunge. His eyes snap to me as he dodges, but I predict his move. And before I can question the sudden need to hesitate, I throw out a dagger.

The blade instantly hits its mark—his heart.

He grunts, holding his chest as his eyes go wide with shock, and takes a staggering step back, bracing a bloody hand on the wall behind him with a gasp. His breathing becomes labored as he holds my gaze and slowly slides down the wall. I stalk forward, a small smile creeping up the corners of my mouth.

"It's a shame," I mutter, looking down my nose. "I actually liked you."

He chuckles despite a knife being lodged in his chest. "You put up... a good fight." He breathes. "I'm impressed."

I crouch down and let out a soft laugh, then gently slide the knife out of his chest. Blood drips from his mouth while he stares at me. Killing isn't something I particularly enjoy, but I'm good at it.

"You should be. I'm the best," I mutter, and intently scan his face again, committing his striking features to memory. Up close, I realize his blue eyes remind me of an ocean sunset, especially with the hint of gold in the middle.

I admit, killing the male that made me want to come on his

face the previous night isn't what I was expecting, but I kill who King Elion orders—no questions asked.

Even if they are beautiful.

"You're going to… regret this in the morning." He chuckles but it comes out rattled, and then he winces. "I really… hate dying."

My brows knit as I frown, watching his face pale, and an unexpected sadness creeps in. And something else that's a little hard to name. Guilt, maybe.

My eyes flare at the realization. Do I feel… guilty for killing my target? Since when do I feel guilty?

Before I can question the unexpected emotion, his head slumps forward and his hands go limp, dropping to his sides. I wait a moment before checking his pulse—nothing. I exhale, eyeing the blood pooling on the floor.

Dirty indeed. Just like King Elion asked.

With a quick wipe of my dagger on his tunic, I sheathe my blades and glance down, spotting the edges of my jeweled mask tucked between my breasts. A swift tug pulls it free, and I toss it on his lap as a final farewell.

Smoothing out my dress, I make my way to the door. Luckily, there isn't a single drop of blood on it again. With my ear against the wood, I check for any signs of the innkeepers this late. If I wait any longer to leave, they'll find the guard I left behind.

The door lets out a creak before I quietly shut it with a soft click. After scanning my surroundings, I quietly reach the end of the hallway, exiting the back of the inn.

In my twenty-five years, I've found that walking is the best way to leave a mission, otherwise you risk alerting everyone in the area. So I keep my pace slow and controlled, bunching up the ends of my dress as I turn toward the main street.

Humans and Fae litter the city, but it's a quiet walk. Inns are filled and taverns are busy. A few tipsy females huddle in a group, clearly giggling from too much drink. It used to not be like this—everyone getting along.

When Elderheim and Aurelia were at war, humans couldn't walk around without being beaten half to death. Aetheri and Halflings were constantly battling, causing brawls in the middle of the streets. Taverns were segregated for Fae and humans.

Until we closed our borders after the War of the Veilstone, distancing ourselves from Aurelia—the realm of the Shadovar, the dark Fae, known for their manipulation. Two realms share one continent, and although different, our powers only weaken when crossing into their land, never fully disappearing.

A warm breeze brushes across my skin as my boots crunch the familiar gravel leading to the castle. Sweeping my hair out of my face, I find myself thinking about what Alec said.

He knew a lot about me, including the king. Knew that I was trained in the Brotherhood—trained by Ren—and how first missions are given at twelve. He knew about *Ezra*.

My stomach twists at the thought.

King Elion wouldn't send me to kill innocents, would he? I've known from the beginning that my targets are criminals, paid to be eliminated by the elite.

But Alec wasn't innocent.

Not with how he fought. A male like that had to have had blood on his hands. My thoughts swirl, hating how my target has made me question the king I serve.

And regardless of knowing that Alec was probably wrong, I nervously thumb the inside of my wrist where a small scar sits. It's almost too faint to notice by anyone other than me and a habit I picked up when I'm anxious or lost in thought.

A faint scar shaped into a vine, curling into a circle with an intricate center—colorless. I'm unable to recall the memory, but Ezra reminded me that we branded ourselves after the Painted Bird one night as a dare, drunk off wine. I smile at the thought, thinking of Ezra and how close we've gotten over the last few years.

The entrance to the castle gleams under the soft glow of the moon. Walls crafted of white stone, its towers reaching into the sky. I finally reach the gates, the scent of smoke filling the air. A fire is lit.

It doesn't take long before I pass through the castle walls after greeting Silas at the gates. He's one of the few human guards I actually like. Even though he likes to effortlessly flirt with me when he gets the chance, I sometimes come outside to chat with him when I can't sleep and show him my magic.

The staircase to my left leads me to my chambers, but if I were to take the door on the right, it opens into the courtyard—a vast, enclosed space surrounded on all sides of the castle. It's not open to outer lands like normal courtyards, as every inner wall is visible from within.

I'm unsure if it was out of convenience or favoritism, but the king placed me at the edge of the castle—a location with easy access to leave if I need to run one of his errands.

Reaching the top of the stairs, I twist the knob to my chambers and enter with a deep breath. My eyes close as I savor the familiarity of it.

I instinctively inhale the scent of the mantel and fresh air that floats in. Three arched windows come to a point across from the door, and next to that is a stone mantel that's surrounded by settees. Farther in and to the left is my four-poster bed and bathing chamber.

I'm treated better than the majority of my brethren, as none of them have a chamber quite as grand as this one, but I believe that maybe it's because I'm the only female.

I glance down and sigh. There's not much on my dress, but I feel ridiculous and filthy, especially after the way tonight ended. I kick my boots off and stride into the bathing chamber.

After quickly washing my night away, I slide into bed, my

eyes landing on the black coin resting on the table next to me. The coin I found at the brothel the previous night.

I find myself thinking of Alec again and what my plans were supposed to be. The random pang of sadness I felt as I slid the knife out of his chest. It was odd—I've never felt that on a mission before.

Questions bounce around in my head as I stare at the ceiling, exhaustion tugging at me as I revisit Alec's last words. Then a sliver of unease curls in my stomach—I brushed past it in the moment, too focused on ending him. But now, as the quiet settles in, it hits me.

Did he say he hated dying?

5

———

The pounding at my door startles me awake, forcing me to jolt upright. My heart thrums wildly in my chest, adrenaline pumping as I calm my breathing.

"Isa Valedara!"

The incessant banging pulls me to the door in utter confusion, hair a mess and strung in all directions. Opening it in nothing but a sheer slip, I find Theron standing on the other side and appearing annoyed. Like I just spit in his breakfast.

Like always.

Out of all the personal guards he has, I particularly hate that one. Pompous and cruel, but the king seems to like him for some reason. I've had my fair share of Theron's wrath a few times due to my mouth, but I know better than to open it now.

"Yes?" I attempt to hide the sneer creeping up my face, but I'm not convinced it's working.

"You're needed at a briefing with the king."

"I'll be right out." The door slams in his face.

It's a little after sunrise, casting the open land in a soft orange glow. Perhaps King Elion wants an update on the mission from last night.

I quickly dress, securing my weapons at my thighs and ribs, hair woven into two braids going down the sides of my head. Then I throw on my hooded cloak.

In the span of a couple of minutes, I'm out the door, shuffling down the stairs only to find Ezra waiting for me again. He must have already been awake, but I frown at the sight of him.

When the king calls for a briefing or a summons, it's usually only one of us. Most of the time, it's an update on our most recent mission, but Ezra's here.

"What's going on?" I clasp the top of my cloak as we begin our walk to the throne room.

He's dressed in black, hair catching in the morning light, giving it a warm tone. He's cut short on the sides again and claims that he doesn't like it when it's in his face, but I always try to convince him to grow it out.

He's armed in a black leather harness, his silver sword secured on his back. Then his eyes graze mine, and he gives me a small smile.

"Something important, I guess. He's called for both of us. Do you know what it's about?" he asks.

"I'm assuming he wants an update about how my mission went last night," I say, throwing him a sideways glance.

"That would be important. How did it go?"

"As good as killing anyone goes. Do you want filthy details or a summary?" I exhale with a smirk, knowing damn well that I don't want to repeat last night's events if I can help it.

"I think I can fill in my own details, thanks." He glares but it's lighthearted, and I'm thankful he doesn't force me to relive it.

Striding down the front of the castle, shaded by the floor above, we walk in silence the rest of the way. We enter the grand hallway that leads to the throne room when two of the king's personal guards immediately open the doors for us. We stroll through, meeting the king, who's already sitting on his throne looking utterly pissed. *This can't be good.*

I refrain from glancing at Ezra as we finally come to a stop at the base of his obnoxious chair—*throne*. It's tall and made of a dark steel. He claims that it's the rarest steel in Elderheim, so rare he's required to sit on it.

Theron stands behind his right shoulder when King Elion's stare blazes into me, his jaw set with anger. Fury pours out of him in waves of power, something I've only seen him use one other time.

It shocked me even then, seeing whips of golden white light lash out like extra hands, pouring out of him like fog. And as bright as the sun. Stunning yet terrifying.

"Your Majesty," we say in unison, bowing at the waist.

His deep voice echoes through the chamber. "I called a briefing for both of you this morning. Do you know why? No? Good, I'll tell you," he growls, not waiting for either of us to answer.

King Elion is a large, angry, stern male, fit to be a king with his emerald-golden crown resting on his head. With silver hair and a long, full beard, he looks to be in his fifties, although I know he's much older than that, around 375. Aging begins to slow when Fae, Aetheri, or Shadovar reach maturity around the age of twenty-eight. We call it the Stilling, and though Halflings age slowly, our lifespan is about half of theirs.

King Elion glares at me with his deep amber-colored eyes, like mine but darker. And angrier.

"At first, I wanted an update on Isa's mission last night. Then I received an update from Helga first thing this morning." He pauses long enough to hold up a leaf as proof, showing us the message. "About how her son was killed and was left in one of the back rooms. Luckily for you, she thinks it was the Fae male she gave us information on. Isa's mission."

The blood drains from my face as my heart skips. The son? He was a guard. I was certain of it. The room feels too small as I remain frozen by his words. Air escapes me as the weight of them settles in my chest, and a chill snakes down my spine. I didn't just kill an aggressive male who got too handsy with me.

I killed Helga's son.

King Elion continues. "He relieved the guard at the door so he could take a quick break on duty. The original guard found him after a few hours. Do you care to explain what happened last night, Isa?" He strokes his long white beard, piercing me with his steely gaze.

Well, that answers my question.

My posture remains taut as I hold his stare, trying not to visibly tremble at the news. "It was a mistake, Your Majesty. He was a casualty. I had no knowledge of who he was. He was guarding the door, and I needed to gain entrance—"

He calmly points a finger at me. "Not only that... The target you were originally there for was not taken care of and his room was empty. Not a single drop of blood in the room as I requested," he says with a calmness that has my entire being screaming to make a run for it.

Don't run, don't run, don't run.

My stomach coils at the thought. It's not possible—Fae can't return after dying, and now King Elion thinks I didn't complete my mission.

This is bad. My head spins for an excuse—anything to explain what happened—only to come up blank. Perhaps I didn't check his pulse long enough, but I know I did. Alec had no pulse. I'm sure of it.

My head shakes. "I completed my—"

"Apparently not when he's missing!" he bellows, furiously looking away. His oily hair falls to his brow in his fit of rage. "This just tells me that you tracked the wrong male. You failed. And now the crown pays the price. The Silver Lily is an important part of how we receive information. I wanted to use his death as a message, but Helga told me he was nowhere to be found when she inspected his room this morning," he states calmly, looking out the windows. "You have become quite comfortable here, have you not?"

I nod, chin high, while my panic climbs up my spine as I recall every detail from last night—anything to determine where the mistake was. I fight the urge to reach for my wrist out of habit. This target was incredibly important and I failed. *I fucking failed?*

"I asked you a question, Isa." He leans forward, stroking his beard. "You have become quite comfortable... have you not? Living in your chambers, eating fine food, coming and going whenever you please."

"Yes, Your Majesty." My hands clasp behind my back with nothing left to do but agree.

King Elion can be incredibly frightening when he becomes calm. I can take his wrath. It's when he's quiet that I worry, wondering what my punishment is going to be. Ezra stands beside me and attempts to step forward when the king lifts his hand in warning.

Theron steps into view and grins.

Ezra doesn't typically step in, but he stops when the king glares at him, forcing him to hold his position. He hasn't so much as breathed a word and would never dare interrupt the king at anyone's expense. But I can see that he's nervous with the way he's started to shift on his feet, clearly wanting to do something for me. We were trained not to make mistakes, and I've apparently made a huge one.

Elion slides his eyes back to me with a calmness. "That ends now. You are to complete this mission and find your target, is that understood?"

"Yes." I exhale, relieved and hoping I'm not sent to Theron after this conversation. I glance up to find him smiling down his nose at me, and I inwardly shudder.

"Good. Ezra is to accompany you since you can't seem to complete a mission by yourself without failing. He's an excellent tracker. You'll find your target and finish it quickly with him by your side under his command."

My eyes snap up in confusion. Ezra's command? I've trained my whole life for this, and he's having someone watch me like a child. There's a reason I get the high priority targets, and because of *one* mistake, he's having someone accompany me? Why go to Theron when this is clearly my punishment?

My teeth grind, my calm composure slipping. "Your Majesty, I don't need Ezra to complete this mission—"

"This is not up for discussion! Get the job done and do it quickly. We cannot afford to have this target out in the open for much longer. It was why I needed it taken care of last night, which you *failed* to do. You have three days, and that's all you will receive." He dismisses us with a wave of his hand. "Find him and get out of my sight."

I nod and we bow, quickly making our exit. Leaving the castle grounds, we look at each other, sharing the same exact expression and at a complete loss for words. I'm embarrassed... and then I'm *fuming*. I storm off into the direction of my chambers.

"Where are you going?" Ezra asks, hurrying to follow me across the front of the castle and down the gravel path.

"As much as I love having you around, Ezra, I don't need you to accompany me. Just stay behind and let me do this alone. I can track him myself," I get out, refusing to have someone watch me.

"Absolutely not," he says, catching up. "You heard the king— he'll have my head if I don't go. If we both track him, we can find him faster. You will need me there. Who else would keep you company?"

I spin around, almost having him run into me, my hair barely missing his chest.

This is not the first time we've had an argument where I storm off in a fit of rage while he tries to calm me down. I admire his ability to maintain his composure, but I hate feeling as if I can't complete a mission by myself.

I gaze up to look at him, but he grips my shoulders with a small smile. He softens a little, palming my cheek.

"It's not your fault. It could've happened to anyone." He glances at my hair and thumbs the braid with my birthmark, and I frown, my eyes darting away.

"But it didn't. This is our job, and I failed my mission. I don't *fail*, Ezra, and now he's having you watch me like I'm a child. I'm no better than the newly trained orphans at this point!"

"We'll find the target, but it'll be faster if we both go. Plus, I miss working with you. You know we haven't had a mission together since we were fifteen. It'll be fun." He smirks and softly tugs my braid as he studies me, patiently waiting for an answer. Rolling my eyes, I look at him and grin.

"It's been that long?" I ask and he nods, hope gleaming in his eyes that maybe I'll allow him to join me without a fight. "Fine. Maybe it'll be fun."

We quickly decide to meet at the stables after grabbing a few extra clothes before heading to Alvonia with the horses to scout the inn. I enter my chambers, shutting the door on a click, and bang my head against it with a defeated sigh.

I swallow the panic that threatens to rise at the thought of my failure. Yet there's one question that sears my mind: what just happened?

Alec Thorne died by *my* hands. I know this because I watched him bleed out as he took his last breath, even checking his pulse. It doesn't make sense. Biting my lip, I replay every detail down to the scent only to come to the terms that maybe Helga is wrong.

Now the only thing we can do is investigate the Silver Lily and find out where this Alec disappeared to.

6

With my lucky coin in my pocket, I arrive at the stables to find Ezra gathering the packs and adjusting the saddle on his horse, Freya, a gray mare with a silver mane. I rub the side of her face and watch as he ties off the saddle from underneath, cinching it at the waist.

Mulling over our conversation with the king and everything that happened this morning, I can't bear the thought of making a mistake. It's not in my nature to overlook details like accidentally killing the wrong person and not my target, which I swear I did.

Maybe the king is right—I am too comfortable. I rub my wrist, an effort to bury my emotions, but they've been surfacing a lot recently. The feeling of being lost and alone, like there's more to life than mindlessly killing.

Yet my pulse climbs to my temples, the pressure building behind my eyes and forcing me to close them with a deep breath. I hate feeling out of control, and worse, I hate being a failure.

"Isa," Ezra calls out. My eyes fly open, catching him staring at me. "Are you okay? I said your name three times." He reaches for me but catches himself, lowering his hand with a conflicted expression.

We kill for the king, so showing any emotion other than cold indifference is something we all struggle with. He's better than he used to be though. It took me almost a full year to get him to smile at one of my awful jokes, but I'm glad that I'm the one who gets to see that side of him.

"I'm fine," I say with a tight smile. "Let's get going."

"Okay, your saddle is hanging on the stall over there." He gestures over his shoulder to where Bjorn stands. "Bjorn is ready to go. He just needs to be saddled."

I approach my horse and gently rub his face. "Fates, you're beautiful."

And massive, around sixteen hands and ebony in color—dark and rich as a blackened sky.

The Aetheri Fae can speak with animals as a part of being a light Fae, the ability to form deep connections. But I have yet to feel that connection with any animal, assuming it's due to my magic not being strong enough. Unlike me, Ezra can speak to them and understand what they want. With quiet strides down the length of Bjorn, I run my hand down his side.

"Do you think we'll find anything at the inn?" I ask Ezra while checking Bjorn's form and coat, ensuring he's in the best condition for our travels in case we need to track Alec outside of the city. Which is likely.

"I'm not sure. I'm hoping Helga can offer us more information."

"I know I killed him. I watched him crumple to the ground, choking on his own blood." I face him with my arms crossed.

He walks over, intently scanning my face. "I believe you."

"Do you? Because the last time I checked, you can't exactly survive a plunge to the heart, but I watched him bleed out. I even checked his pulse." My hand casually pats Bjorn's shoulder.

Ezra walks back to Freya, looking over his shoulder. "We'll

find answers, I promise. I wouldn't think much of it. It's already almost noon, and we need to get to the city."

With a hesitant nod, I heed Ezra's advice and walk toward Bjorn's saddle. The creaking of the stable doors near the back forces my head to whip up just as Ren walks through with a shit-eating grin.

"What are you doing here? On a mission?" Ezra asks casually, throwing me a sideways glance.

"Yeah, yours." Ren crosses his arms, directing his smile in my direction. Ezra and I straighten, halting our tasks.

"What do you mean?" I ask.

Ren grabs another saddle to mount on a third horse. "King Elion has ordered me to accompany you on your journey to ensure it gets done. I'll be there every step of the way." He's wearing a full grin now.

Gods, I hate him. Not only did I piss him off yesterday, he knows that I failed my mission and is set to accompany us.

"Great, a watchdog," I mutter.

He only chuckles, the sound low and dark as he cinches the saddle on his horse, clearly not falling for my trap like yesterday. The king sent someone to keep an eye on me as a warning. Though I thought that was what Ezra was for, I guess I was wrong.

I throw Ezra a wary glance as Ren finishes up, and we share the same concerned expression because *what the fuck?*

Mentally throwing a slew of curses around in my head, I finally grab my pack to secure it to the saddle and mount Bjorn.

"You ready?" I ask and pat myself, ensuring all my weapons are where they need to be—daggers, short swords, and a bow at my thighs, waist, and back. The weapons are familiar beneath my fingers.

Ren mounts his horse with another menacing grin, and I catch the way his brow quirks at me as he settles into the saddle. My teeth grind as I face Ezra.

Ezra nods. "First stop is the Silver Lily. We need to know what happened last night."

Driving their heels into the horses, they both exit the stables and take off into a gallop. Doing the same, I'm not too far behind, going at a steady trot, heading for Alvonia.

Approaching the city doesn't take long as we come to a slow gait on the cobblestone. The Silver Lily sits just north of entering.

Locals enter a market to our right, lining the road in such a way that we need to squeeze our horses through, their hooves beating against the stone. It's clear that some are visitors while the others seem to be selling off items from their crops. Animals, food, drinks, and handcrafted items are surrounding the area, filling the needs of everyone in the city.

I've come to realize that I've never actually been in the city during the day. Most of my missions are done at night when there aren't many people around.

Fae and humans barter, laugh, and haggle gold in the heat while children chase goats. On my right, couples dance to the music that spills in from the square. I look down, finding merchants holding out intricate pendants as we ride by. The bustle of the city makes me realize how much I didn't know existed—how much people are enjoying each other's company.

"Do you see something you like?" Ezra grins, catching my attention. Ren rides behind us as we take the lead.

"No." I shift my gaze to Ezra on my left. "I just never realized they did stuff like this. Is it a market?" Ren stiffens out of the corner of my eye, surely annoyed that I began speaking, but Ezra's brow arches.

"Yes. It's the Fae market. They do it every week to offer leftover food from their crops after their weekly tithe to the castle. Animals and clothing are also offered to trade," Ezra says.

"I like it," I mumble, watching children run by. But after a moment, I pull my hood up to block out the afternoon sun and

Ezra's inquisitive glances. Midday in late summer is always unbearable this time of year, but winter quickly approaches.

"We don't go out much during the day," Ezra says after a couple of minutes. "We should though. If we have time later, maybe we can come back."

He must feel bad if he's offering to take me to the local market, but I hold back a mocking scoff and nod.

"If we have time. The mission comes first," I say and trot ahead.

After arriving at the inn, we tie the horses and reach the door, Ezra knocking. Helga answers with broken sobs, her face puffy from grief.

Yet I can't help but not feel guilty.

I feel guilty for failing my mission and taking a mother away from her son, but not for his death. He was the type of male that hurt others, and I have a feeling I wasn't the first.

"Helga," Ezra says. "We were notified about the incident last night, here to investigate what happened, by order of the king. May we come in?"

I glance at him. He's formal, wearing a composed mask just like mine to gain information. She sniffles and eases the door open while Ren stays behind, checking for evidence of the target leaving.

Helga doesn't know what happens with the information that she gives to the king. All she knows is that whatever she gives, she gets paid for it. She has no recollection as to who we are other than we are the king's royal guards, here to investigate. She doesn't even know that I was here last night, having snuck in when the Silver Lily was practically empty.

Coming into the inn, I recall the desk is to the right of entering, where I retrieved the information on Alec's room.

"May I look at your ledger to see if anyone of importance came at the same time your son was killed?" I touch her arm, and she nods, still crying.

Ezra privately escorts her down the hall as I go through the rooms again, looking through the heavy book while I hold my lucky coin. I wasn't mistaken. Alec *was* here last night, and he even signed out? *That can't be accurate.*

I glance up to find Ezra still chatting with Helga, her frantic whispers echoing in the air, nervously glancing around. "If conversing with the king puts my family in danger, I am not sure I can continue giving away information about my guests!"

Hearing no more of her argument, I walk to Alec's previous room. After stepping inside, I stop at the back wall where he died and crouch to find that there isn't a single drop of blood—just like King Elion said. My brows knit.

"I told you that you'd regret it."

I gasp, my head snapping up. *That was... strange.*

The words echoed in my head as if they were my own thoughts, yet that voice wasn't mine. I glance around, searching for anyone in the area, but no one else is here but me.

"I'm going insane," I mutter to myself and search the room.

I step toward the table near the window. Faint scratch marks are etched on the surface, looking as if something was written. Opening the drawers, I move things around. The subtle clatter of items breaks the silence while I try to find parchment and charcoal to write with. Then I pull out a black jeweled mask—my mask from the brothel.

Shit. I quickly look around before tucking it into the pocket of my cloak. I shut the drawer and lay the parchment on top of the scratches, scribbling frantically to reveal what was written—a note and a location.

I found her and she won't be alone. I'm headed to Sylvanor. Meet at dusk. - A

My breath catches, remembering what he said when we fought. Is he talking about me? Despite my unease and the shiver coursing down my spine, I pocket the parchment.

If he's headed north to Sylvanor, that means we'll have to

travel through the Twin Valley to track him. Despite my failed mission, a thought rises.

Perhaps I could drop in at some of the orphanages while we're gone and ask questions. It would be tricky, but I bet I could sneak around Ezra and Ren to do it.

I finish looking through drawers, lifting the mattress, and touching the curtains but find nothing substantial to use. Exiting the room, I stride down the hall to find Ren next to Ezra as he finishes up his conversation with Helga.

"Did she show you where her son died?" I ask, barely above a whisper. Ren falls into step beside me with a glower as we head toward the son's room.

"I thought you were quick with your killings?" Ren asks, indicating that he scented what I left behind—a crumpled and bloody male slumped in a chair. Surely they've cleaned it by now.

"I am," I say casually, continuing forward.

"I guess having fun first doesn't count?"

I ignore him but my brow arches, as he must think I slept with Helga's son, leaving me to wonder if he scented the male's lingering scent of arousal. It didn't quite get that far, but he doesn't know that.

He stops and grips my arm, yanking me back. "Stop fucking your targets. You left a mess, and Helga shouldn't have had to see that," Ren grinds out, as if he has any right to judge me on how I follow through with my missions.

I rip my arm back, craning my neck to hold his stare. I'm so close to his face I can feel his breath on my skin. "Do you think that was fun for me? You have *no* idea. Since when do you care about inn owners?"

Ren's brows lower. "Since they're an important part of our crown, that's when."

"Fuck the crown."

A dark chuckle shivers at the edge of my mind, and my breathing picks up. Yet I somehow manage to maintain my composure while I stubbornly hold Ren's gaze.

Is... that Alec's voice? My irritation spikes, realizing that it *is* his voice I heard and that I must be going insane if I'm hearing him in my head.

Ren's eyes intently scan my face, almost curiously, before his attention shifts behind me. Ezra walks up while Helga strides toward the front of the inn.

"Stop arguing, both of you," Ezra clips, a flicker of frustration crossing his face when his eyes land on me. "And keep your voice down."

I know that voicing my hatred for the crown out loud is close to crossing a line with both of them. Speaking so boldly about it is good enough to get me hanged or beaten.

Yet over these last few months, I've realized how much I want to leave this life behind. I can't help but feel that if I knew more about my mission, we could have avoided this altogether. Because most of the time, Elion gives us the bare minimum.

Ezra steps closer as Ren huffs, walking down the hall a moment later.

"You need to watch what you say around him," Ezra mumbles. "Ren will run straight to the king to report you for that. Don't cross him anymore than you have. I'd hate to see you beaten for it."

"Because we both know you wouldn't stop it?" The cruel words leave me before I can stop them, unable to hold back my frustration. I know it's not his fault, and I can't blame him for not stepping in since Elion would most likely punish him for it.

"Seriously?" Ezra says.

Alec's voice growls, forcing me to rub a hand over my face in an attempt to control my breathing and subtly scan the area. *Gods, what's happening?*

Alec's accusations had me fighting sleep last night. Perhaps that's what I need—sleep. Though a prickle of awareness crawls down my spine because that's not what the evidence shows. Alec isn't here, and he signed out. So is the voice in my head made-up or real?

Ezra's brows furrow before he shifts his attention down the hall, eyeing Helga from a distance. As if he's ensuring she didn't overhear what I blurted out.

He rubs a hand over his jaw. "Did you get anything from the target's room?"

I remain quiet as I hand him the written note, letting him take a moment to read it. "I think we can track him once we get there and find the exact meeting spot."

He nods. "I agree. Let's check out the son's room one last time and then check the target's room again. I'll have Ren inspect it and see if he can pick up a scent through the stone."

Stone Shapers have the ability to create weapons of stone by pulling them out of the environment, but they can also pull lingering magical signatures from it as well. So if there's anything left behind, Ren will find it.

For the rest of the time at the inn, there's nothing but silence as we search for more information about the male in room eleven. Ren inspects the room after Ezra did a thorough examination while we continue to chat with Helga.

She hasn't stopped crying, but I give her my sympathies as she talks about her son between tears. We placed blame on Alec, as it made the most sense. Ezra and I excuse ourselves and step outside after saying our goodbyes, waiting for Ren near the horses.

Merchant chatter fills the air as I take one last look around the city, and I can't help but think of the Fae market. A small part of me wishes to see it, but not when Alec is missing.

Ren steps out, his dark brows lowering as he meets us,

looking as if he just found the most disturbing news. He glances over his shoulder one last time before turning back to us.

"What is it?" I ask.

"We're tracking a Shadovar."

7

Shadovar, the dark Fae.

Unease coiled in my stomach over Ren's muttered words earlier and at the realization that Alec is Shadovar.

That must be why he felt so... pushy. Demanding. But even as he showed all of that during our initial introduction, I never felt threatened—I liked it. He never even attempted to kill me when I attacked him at the inn.

A wave of frustration and shame jolts into my chest. Not only did I engage with him at the brothel, I failed to kill him as well.

But that doesn't explain why he didn't die.

Because no matter the realm, all Fae die the same. Yet Ren and Ezra fully believe it's because I killed the wrong person, not that he evaded death by my blade, as there wasn't a single drop of blood on the carpets.

As if someone cleaned it before we arrived.

We asked Helga about it, but she said no one had come in before us, though I had a feeling she was lying. There wasn't a single trace of evidence that I was there either—neither Ren nor Ezra picked up my scent, which I find odd.

I also find myself wondering how Alec is in our realm, as King Elion decided years ago that it was best to keep our borders closed for the safety of Elderheim.

He created strict laws that allowed every race to live in peace, but he banned the discussion or the harboring of the Shadovar. No one is allowed in or out of our borders, and King Elion enforces it, as it's our only measure of protection to keep citizens safe from their dark magic.

All Fae have the capability to wield elemental magic, but the Shadovar have their own unique power specific to their realm.

Like Elderheim. Our realms are two sides of the same coin—equal in power and long-term rivals.

But I'm not familiar with their magic or their capabilities, as I never bothered to learn since the border was sealed long before I was born.

"We need to stop soon. The horses need rest, and I need to dip in a stream somewhere before I end up melting." I squint at the sun, hoping it will stop beating down on my face and cool down.

Even though it's much cooler in the mountains, the afternoon sun bathes me in my sweat. I'm eager for dusk when the temperature drops thirty degrees.

We entered the Twin Valley a couple of hours ago, but we plan on pushing through in order to make it to Sylvanor by tomorrow afternoon. It's a valley I've only been in one other time and although beautiful, it's a bad place to get stuck in with only two exits—forward and where you came.

Luckily for me, I haven't had any more intrusive thoughts of Alec's voice in my head since Alvonia, having chalked it up to stress and failure over this mission.

Large intimidating trees surround the area, offering heavy coverage other than the frequently traveled path that we're currently on. Ren travels ahead to ensure nothing is lying in wait, acting like bait if anything wants to come out of hiding.

"I think we can make it. We don't need to stop in the valley this close to the town," Ezra says, looking completely unfazed in this heat, which is ridiculous. How can he look like that on a horse in midday and not be sweating profusely?

"Well, I won't." I glare at him. "We can handle ourselves. If we don't rest soon, you're going to get a boot right up your—"

Bjorn halts, shuffling his feet only for Freya to mimic his movements half a second later. Both horses are huffing in agitation, swinging their heads. Ezra and I share a quick glance while Ren continues to ride ahead about half a mile.

We scan the surrounding area. The mountains and trees rest on either side of us, though there's nothing for miles, but I can sense it. It's one of those rare cases where I can hone in on the feeling. My body begins to hum with energy.

I glance at Ezra, putting a finger to my lips, when he looks down and motions at the footprints below us.

"Grokees," he whispers.

"Fuck," I say. Just what we need in the smoldering heat—Grokees.

They're the most grotesque creature in our realm, which is pretty much how they got their name, typically found in the Twin Valley. Giant wolves that are five feet tall at the shoulder and missing fur and skin, with exposed bone. It makes me shudder just thinking about them.

We haven't figured out why they look that way or what happened, but we think it's a deformity or a sickness. Whatever they are, they become incredibly aggressive and will attack at any chance they get. And I'm definitely not in the mood to deal with withering, dying creatures.

The hair on my neck rises, and with a deep breath, I force my heart rate to slow despite the rush of adrenaline. My eyes lock with Ezra's as we slowly grab our bows and put our horses into walks. We begin to slowly move forward, but within a heartbeat, three Grokees launch at us on our right.

"Now!" Ezra shouts, both of us shooting an arrow at the same time and hitting the first one in each eye.

"Why do you always aim for mine?" I shout as our horses frantically trot in place.

"I saw it first!"

Ren swivels around, gripping the reins and turning his horse. He races toward us, grabbing his bow in the process.

Nocking another arrow, I aim for the next one as we both launch our horses forward. Trusting Bjorn to run straight, I pivot in the saddle and catch the second one in the shoulder. It doesn't go down. Ren's determined eyes lock onto one behind me just as he launches his arrow, hitting it before I can reload.

Thank the Fates his aim has always been great.

"Isa, behind you!" Ezra shouts.

Within seconds, the third one launches itself at me and latches onto my right shoulder. It throws me off Bjorn with such a force that the breath forcefully escapes my lungs.

Ezra's horse continues to gallop ahead when I land, smacking my head against the ground so hard that stars dance across my eyes. I fight to keep my eyes open and focused as its snapping jaws are inches from my face. I'm pinned by its feet with my forearm against its throat, preventing it from ripping my face off.

Gods, it's drooling on me.

Its beady eyes are glossed over, as if there's nothing there but aggression and hunger. I cry out as my right fist drives into its ribs, but when I pull it back, my hand is coated in fur and flesh. I gag.

It smells awful—like it's decaying.

The stench of it almost makes me retch, but I'm able to free my right hand enough to get it to my ribs and grip a dagger. I shove it in its chest with enough force that it instantly stops moving and lays all of its dead weight on me.

My eyes water from the smell as I turn my head, gasping for

air. But Ezra and Ren come running, shoving it off me a moment later.

"Are you okay?" Ezra breathes. He shields his face with his elbow in an attempt to stifle the smell. *At least he's finally sweating.* "I thought you were dead by the way that thing latched on. Let me see your shoulder."

I sit up with a cry of pain as my adrenaline fades, leaving my right shoulder burning. Luckily, whatever infection they carry isn't transmittable to Fae or humans, so their bites—though nasty—are harmless.

Still, it fucking hurts.

"Not dead. I'm okay though," I groan, tilting my right shoulder forward with a wince.

"You're lucky I came back—I almost took off without you," Ezra teases, throwing me a grin.

Ren remains silent as he nudges it with a boot. It's decaying in a heap of flesh and bone, beady eyes glazed over. Ezra looks at my shoulder, now blackened and slick with drool.

"Damn, that looks bad. I have some supplies in my pack. The horses got spooked and ran up the road. Let me gather them and we'll clean it up."

I nod, meeting his gaze just as I notice the sound of running water nearby and grin. "There's the stream I was wishing for."

Ezra barks a laugh. "I guess this is our stop then." He throws me a wide grin over his shoulder, taking off at a run to round up the horses.

"You're definitely bathing. I refuse to catch a whiff of you on the saddle." Ren's face is twisted in disgust and scans my face, now splattered in a sticky drool.

Normally, I'd argue just to argue, but I have to agree with him. A quick dip in the stream is exactly what I need to erase this awful smell, so I walk in the direction of the moving water.

Nestled in the middle of the mountains, Sylvanor is tucked away at the edge of the valley instead of in the mountain itself. Trees and sharp-edged peaks surround it for miles, leaving us fresh air and a cool breeze.

We only got a few hours of sleep outside of Dryborn before waking again, leaving just before dawn to arrive with enough time to track Alec. Thankfully, Ezra picked up his scent on the trail earlier, confirming that we were headed in the right direction.

Ren's remarks throughout the day had me wanting to throw an apple at his head, but not before Ezra reached over to snatch it from my hand.

But finally, I breathe.

The quaint little town comes into view early afternoon. With the sun shifting down, we only have a few hours left before dusk settles on this side of the mountain.

Sylvanor is quiet and small, surrounded by tall lampposts that line the cobblestone road. The horses' hooves click against them at a steady pace. Flanking both sides of the main road, bushes and vines snake up the structures.

I could cry with relief. The heat was excruciating, leaving me slick with sweat, head pounding, shoulder throbbing from yesterday's bite. And although I rinsed the wound in the stream and kept it clean, it's begun to burn again.

"I could go for a cold bath and an ale right about now." I wipe my forehead with the back of my hand. Even though I'm not a huge fan of ale, the heat of summer is the only reason I ever want one. I glance at Ezra, both of us dripping in sweat as the afternoon sun continues to beat down on us.

"You and me both." Ezra chuckles, Ren grunting in agreement behind us. "But let's find a local inn and ask around about where our target could be. We still have a few hours before dusk, so I think we still have time. How's your shoulder?"

"It's fine." I keep my voice steady, but in truth, six hours of sweating on top of a large horse hasn't done me any favors.

The salve helped at first—numbing the area and dulling the sting—but in this heat, it's already been sweat off. I didn't want to say anything earlier and risk slowing us down. I try not to let it show.

Ren rides up, glaring at me from atop his horse, and clips, "Let him apply more salve. We can't afford you being injured when we have to finish this mission by tomorrow night."

My teeth grind. "I'm *fine*."

"You're wincing," Ezra argues and I huff, attempting to wave him off. "Stop being stubborn and let me apply some to your shoulder after we get to the inn. Can you continue tonight?"

I give him a quick nod. "Fine. We'll apply more when we arrive, but we're going out tonight for answers."

Going into a light trot, we enter the town after a few short minutes. We finally dismount and hand the horses off to Ren to find a nearby stable. We agreed on an inn called the Golden Oak —secluded from the rest of the town but close enough to the horses should we need to leave quickly.

"I'll stand watch while you arrange the rooms." I lean against the outside wall of the inn and sigh.

Groups weave between the crowds, walking toward the local taverns. I begin to wonder if it's where everyone will be, silently wishing that I were one of them right now.

But the Silver Lily tugs at my thoughts—thinking of everything I encountered over the last two days and the note in Alec's room.

I found her and she won't be alone, it said.

What does that mean and who did he find? He must be important if the king is set on finishing the mission, leaving me to wonder what Helga might have relayed to him. When Ezra asked, she refused to discuss it, insisting that it was meant for the king's ears only. The inn's wooden door creaks open, leaving me to swivel my head.

Ezra steps out. "We got two rooms."

"*Two* rooms? Who's sharing?" I blink, mouth falling open on a retort—because I clearly misheard—when I'm interrupted.

"Excuse me, miss!"

A boy no older than eight, with auburn hair and freckles, stares up at me. I scan the area, searching for his mother, then glance back down, wondering where he just came from.

"Do you have any coins?" He eagerly extends his shirt like he's expecting me to drop some in. I blankly stare, as a sense of familiarity washes over me. My blood prickles, as if the magic beneath my skin is itching to crawl out. An odd feeling, and something that's never happened before.

"Have we met?" I ask.

He only gives a quick shake of his head, holding out his shirt again. A small, tight smile lines my mouth as I study him, dropping a coin anyway. He saunters down the road at a slow pace, inspecting the new coin in his fingers. Ezra raises his eyes back to me, caught off guard as well.

"Room, yes," he says after a minute. "We have to share because they're booked for the night."

"Oh, please. This town is tiny, and *this* inn is booked for the night? I get my own room. I refuse to share with either of you," I demand, not believing a word he says.

"If I have to share a room with anyone, I'm killing someone tonight, and it won't be our target."

Ren walks down the road, carrying his pack over his shoulder, clearly annoyed at the situation. He gives me a once-over, as if I'm the last person he wants to share a room with.

"Are you sure you don't want to share with me?" I taunt with a menacing grin. "I bet you haven't had a female sleep next to you in years." He scans my face in silence, clenching his jaw.

Ezra fights a grin, failing before quickly trying to recover with a cough.

"Don't worry, I'll share with Isa." Ezra waves his hand, gesturing us to follow and throwing Ren a glance over his shoulder. "We need to get ready before the day is gone. By the way, we'll need to split up tonight—cover more ground. The innkeeper told me that she might have seen a newcomer earlier today that fits his description. There's a couple of taverns here, and she thinks he'll be in one of them. I'm hoping to pick up a scent. There's also free breakfast in the morning." He winks, leaving Ren to grumble and take his key.

We all take a right on the side of the building, the inn's rooms lining up off the corner of the road, accessed outside. Ezra halts in front of the third door, slides a key into the lock, and swings it open.

"After you." He smirks, bowing dramatically, hair brushing his forehead as he gestures for me to go in. I chuckle and walk through.

After a couple of hours of settling in and applying fresh salve, I finally lace up my boots. I head to the chamber, adjusting my hair in the mirror.

Even though I opt to leave it down for a more approachable look, I braid the auburn patch behind my ear and pin it. To avoid being overly noticeable—especially if Alec is here—I weave it into a braid, tucking it into the wavy strands.

It vanishes entirely.

Ezra's reflection stares at me from the doorway, an arm resting on the frame as he gives me a subtle once-over.

"You'll pass." He shrugs.

I throw an unimpressed glare at him through the mirror. I'm wearing all black except for my cream-colored tunic. Still, I pinch my cheeks, summoning a little color as I know flirting might be a part of tonight's plan, pulling every advantage I can get as I question the locals.

"Careful, I might take that as a compliment," I say, raising a brow when his eyes meet mine in the mirror.

He snorts, shooting a glance toward the mantel as he flicks his wrist, lighting a fire. "I'm hoping you don't scare anyone off before we find our target. We're a little pressed for time."

I pivot, huffing through my nose as my back leans against the basin, crossing my arms with a teasing grin. "I don't think it's me you should be worrying about with Ren next door."

"I actually agree with you on that." He chuckles, scratching the scruff on his face before turning, leaving me to grin after him and exit the bathing chamber.

It's always been easy with him. Arguments between us are typically short-lived, dropped almost as soon as they start, as he's the one who keeps me in check. But when it comes to the king's orders, Ezra follows through no matter what, and I admire his loyalty for it, which is usually why I let it go most of the time.

"Are you ready? Do you remember the plan?" He grabs his cloak and mine off the back of the settee in the bedchamber, then extends it to me.

"Yes. You'll be at the Wytches Brew, Ren will be somewhere unimportant, and I'll be at the Cauldron all night getting drunk and flirting with strangers," I repeat for the third time, tone dripping with sarcasm as I secure my cloak.

"Flirting? Yes, always. Drunk? No. You need to stay alert. Let's all meet here at the end of the night to report back."

"You kill dreams for a living, Ezra," I mutter.

"You hurt me." He places his hand on his chest like I've truly wounded him with an incredulous look on his face, grinning as we walk out.

Ezra pivots to knock on Ren's door, raising him from his slumber. He stumbles out of his room with nothing more than a pissed off look and a grunt, clearly waking up. Rolling my eyes, I turn and head in the opposite direction.

Dusk has arrived, bringing life to the seemingly small town. Walking down the cobblestone, we see the lights line the road, an orange glow reflecting off the stone as people gather hand in hand.

I spot the Cauldron—one street south of the inn—under a few orange lamp lights and a sign hanging on a metal post. Turning the corner, I finally reach a tiny arched door.

Something that was clearly made for a child.

My brows pinch with a glance around, and I bend to peek inside, unsure of where to start. This must be a cruel joke.

"You must not be from around here," a little voice says, and I whirl to find the same boy from earlier. How does he do that? I scan the area again, utterly confused.

"No." The word comes out unsure, my eyes warily locked on him. "Is this the Cauldron?"

"Yes, but that door is for pixies. The Fae door is around the corner." He tilts his head with a toothy grin. "You should see the inside. Looks can be... deceiving."

My hands land on my hips. "Okay then. I guess I'll try to go in."

"Thank you," he quietly blurts, and I stop. "For the coin. I've been asking all day, and you are the first to give me something," he says in such an innocent way that it squeezes my heart.

I know what it's like being an orphan—hungry with people shooing you away like you're nothing more than a stray. At a loss for words, I watch him retreat down the path, vanishing around the corner.

After a quiet minute on the street, I decide to follow him, finding the doors he mentioned, and let out a huff of disbelief. I almost forced myself through those tiny doors without a second thought.

How embarrassing would that have been?

I pull the large oak doors open, revealing the most exquisite tavern I've ever seen. Having frequented a lot of taverns, I'm shocked that this one escaped my notice.

Looking around, I now understand why the Golden Oak is booked. It looks like I'll be apologizing to Ezra for assuming he lied about the rooms with how busy it is. I chuckle to myself, knowing that I definitely won't be apologizing.

The tavern is spacious, and I think of what that boy said, about how looks can be deceiving. The tavern is mesmerizing.

A large skylight rests on the ceiling, bathing the tavern in a soft moonlight glow. Candles and lanterns litter wooden tables while Fae, human, and Halflings of every kind sit at them. Bookshelves line the walls from floor to ceiling, Fae sprawled out across the room. Some read, some sit with company, and others are drinking.

A mantel with a roaring fire sits to the right, complete with settees. The tavern fills my nostrils with ale, cedar, and incense.

With a grin, I stride to the large bar near the back that's bustling with guests. I slowly scan the room and sit, looking for anyone familiar.

"What would you like, miss?" a scruffy male asks from behind the bar, kind eyes and a wide grin. There's hardly an empty seat at the tall bar, surrounded by groups of two chatting and laughing. Intricate melodies drift by when my eyes land on the floating violins playing themselves.

"An ale, please, and stew if you have it," I say.

I find myself staring at the instruments magically playing when the male nods, and I slide a few coins across the bar. After a moment, he comes back with my ale, a friendly grin spread across his face.

"You're not from around here, are you?"

"No, just passing through." I grin, though my eyes go wide, the small sip of ale shocking me as the taste of crisp apples touches my tongue.

"I can see that." He grins. "My name's Donny. Holler if you

need anything." He pats the bar, parting to take orders from the other guests.

I make my way around the room, beginning my investigation by chatting with a few of the locals, subtly trying to identify those who are not from the area. I'm careful not to reveal the real reason I'm here to avoid raising suspicions.

Yet I find myself easily laughing, sitting on laps, and becoming one of the locals for a few hours, meeting a slew of new people. And as grateful as I am for the company, I eventually find myself walking to the darkened corner of the tavern toward the mantel, too dim to be noticed. With an exhale and a large grin on my face, I rest my head on the back of the settee and close my eyes.

After a moment, someone settles in on my right.

Assuming it's one of the males that I was flirting with earlier, I'm greeted by the familiar scent of tobacco and oakmoss.

"I think you forgot this." His voice is deep and smooth—a voice I recognize.

My eyes slowly peel open, my gaze immediately locking with Alec Thorne.

8

The blood drains from my face, and within seconds, I'm palming my dagger, aiming it straight at his groin. My left hand clamps down on his forearm, locking him in place from elbow to wrist. But a small, devious smile plays on his face when he lets out a chuckle, his breath brushing my cheeks.

"You should be dead," I growl, digging my nails into his skin.

He sighs. "The chase was getting quite boring. Turns out, you're not as good of a tracker as I thought," he chuckles, meeting my gaze. "Any more noise from you and you'll disturb the entire tavern."

"I don't care," I snap, a little louder than I intended, but no one seems to pay us any attention.

"Well, I do," he mutters quietly, then slowly drags his gaze down to our forearms. A menacing smirk lifts the corners of his mouth. "You're going to regret that. Again."

"How am I—"

Before I can finish my thought, I'm whirled from reality and thrust from the tavern. Dark shadows swarm behind my eyes, too fast to comprehend. My stomach lurches, flipping around like I'm falling with no solid ground. My ears begin to ring.

Then with a sharp jolt and a solid thud, everything stops.

I stumble forward, gasping for air when my knees buckle beneath me. My palms hit the ground, and dizziness floods my senses as I try to grasp my new reality. Nausea consumes me as my head spins, pulse pounding so loudly in my ears, it's deafening.

Then I'm retching in the leaves. I'm heaving when I slowly come to my senses, feeling around with my hands.

Leaves. Dirt. Rock. Gods, I'm outside, but how could I—

"I should have warned you, but this is much more enjoyable," Alec says casually.

"Where… am I?" My voice comes out in a rasp.

"No worries, we're just on the outskirts of Sylvanor, away from prying ears should you decide to *scream*." His voice drips with sarcasm. "Or run. But just remember, I'm faster."

Rage consumes me, and the next thing I know, my vision clears and I'm palming my daggers again.

"I'm going to kill you." An angry growl tears through me. At lightning speed, I spin on my right heel, catching my dagger by the blade to throw it straight at his disgustingly beautiful face. Then he tilts his head to the side and catches it.

My eyes go wide. *What the fuck?*

"You tried that, remember?" he retorts with a grin. "Didn't work out so well for you, now did it?"

A frustrated shout brushes the air as I flick my right arm out, aiming a dagger for his ribs. But he sweeps that same arm down and catches that one too. I'm grappling for more weapons when he disappears, forcing me to halt and scan the area, searching for him. *How did he do that?*

"You're a feisty little thing, aren't you?" He chuckles from everywhere and nowhere, but I can't see him. Where is he?

Fury consumes me, yet I somehow manage to rein it in long enough to scan my surroundings. With a deep breath, I quickly realize that I'm two blocks south of the inn off the main road. I slowly pivot in a circle, calculating my movements as adrenaline courses through me.

"You're a coward! Come out and talk. Or are you too afraid I'll kill you again?" I shove my hair off my face, grateful for the partial coverage to hide my shock, but now I'm wishing that I braided it all so I could fight more accurately.

"You can't kill me. And not if you're going to be throwing daggers at my head all night. Will you be nice?" he asks with a hint of amusement.

I realize very quickly that he's teasing me, and it's really fucking *annoying*.

"Fine," I muster through clenched teeth and forcefully sheathe my daggers, holding my palms up. "No sharp things."

"Good," he whispers, appearing right in front of my face seconds later. "Because I'm not your enemy."

Startled, I stumble back and reach for my ribs.

"Don't do that," he warns. "You said you'd be nice. I'm much harder to kill when you can't see me, so I suggest you put them away." He arches a brow.

"Who the fuck are you, and how did you do that?" I snarl, giving him a quick once-over.

His dark auburn hair settles just above his brows as a cocky grin smears across his face, his cloak flaring out as he crosses his arms. It takes everything for me not to fling my daggers as he eyes me from three feet away.

"I know you've already figured it out." His tone is annoyingly casual. "Your little friend seemed to catch on pretty quick."

He's right of course, since Ren already discovered he was Shadovar. Still, my eyes narrow—assessing him. Perhaps Ren was wrong. But how would he know Ren figured it out? Alec continues to casually stand with his hands in his pockets, as if our little conversation is the same as any other day.

He scratches his jaw. "Your realm did a really good job of

wiping us from your books *and* your head." He grins, tilting his head to the side. *"Who do you think I am, darling?"*

"Get out of my head," I grind out.

My heart races as I realize that the voice I thought I imagined is real, very real—it *is* him. Entering my head and into my thoughts like a whisper in the wind.

"You're not supposed to be in this realm. The Shadovar are banned here. What do you want with me?" I ask quietly.

"I want a lot of things." He pushes the thought out.

"I said get out of my head!" I growl, but his words linger, leaving me to wonder what he meant by wiping them from my head. I step toward him. "How did you vanish like that? And how did I end up here?"

"I'm a Veil Walker. Just like everyone else in Aurelia."

"I don't know what that means," I clip.

"You would if you'd give me a chance to explain it," he says as a grin tugs at his lips.

With a huff of air, I urge him to continue with a wave of my hand, wishing he wasn't holding my other daggers. The small clench to his jaw tells me that he must still be angry about me killing him a few days ago. But I didn't kill him... clearly.

"A Veil Walker means that I can walk in the Veil, and that allows me to move undetected, but I can see *you* just fine. It also allows me to travel great distances while still being able to hold a conversation. I'm able to touch and bring others with me, like I did with you."

"What's a Veil?" I ask, my shoulders tensing, hating how curious I sound. But I know nothing of their magic.

He sighs. "It's hard to explain, but the Veil is like a thin layer between realms that exists outside the physical world but overlaps it."

I shake my head. "Either way, *you* being here shouldn't be possible—we sealed the border years ago, but that doesn't explain how you've been tracking—"

His form ripples, shifting his appearance right in front of me, back into the... young boy from earlier?

I blink as a boy with round cheeks, shaggy auburn hair, and light freckles stares up at me. His face appears younger, like he instantly reversed the clock. I stumble back before he quickly shifts into the male he was seconds ago. *What the fuck?*

"It's the magic from my realm, similar to yours here. All Shadovar can walk in the Veil and manipulate their appearances. I can do it for a short time," he says, exaggerating a wave of his hand. "From someone who is alive or has been alive, but it helps me meet someone discreetly without being noticed."

Words seem to have escaped me when a disbelieving chuckle bubbles out, but I quickly compose myself. Yet I can't help the confusion surfacing in my chest. What does a Shadovar want with me? He shouldn't be here, but curiosity gnaws at me, and I find myself wanting to know more.

"Why would you want to meet someone discreetly? Can't you just, I don't know, meet them like a regular person?"

He gives a soft chuckle. "Because I want to assess what type of person they may be. When I want to see someone's true character, I'll appear in my child form to gauge how I can approach them. Turns out you can really tell who someone is by showing up as a homeless boy. From what I gather, the crown hasn't completely destroyed your character yet."

He offers my daggers to me like a peace offering. My eyes lock with his for a moment before I take them with a shake of my head and cross my arms. Little does he know, giving me my daggers back is a mistake.

"Who was the boy from earlier, since you steal appearances?" I ask.

He scoffs. "I don't *steal* appearances—I adopt them for a short amount of time." *Like there's a difference.* He hesitates, as if debating his words, and he throws me a soft grin. "It was me as a boy, which is why there is no scar on his face."

A breeze flutters my hair as he walks past to a nearby oak tree, leaning against it and crossing his arms, leaving me to trail behind.

My frustration rises. "Well, thanks for the useless information, but I have orders to kill you. As far as I'm concerned, you should already be dead. The Shadovar are banned here."

He lets out a loud guffaw with a shake of his head. "Good luck. I'll just come back, and then King Elion will punish you… *again.*" I growl this time, palming my daggers, but he just eyes me with a raised brow. "I told you—you can't kill me *because* I'm not from this realm, and a couple of other things that are unimportant at the moment. You do remember leaving me to bleed out?"

"I'm sure I can find a way to make it permanent."

His smile falters, as if he can't help his rising frustration. It flickers across his features momentarily when he clenches his jaw. "Your life is a lie."

"Nice try."

"Do you ever ask yourself who you're assigned to kill? Have you asked why you're killing them?"

"Why would I care? I take orders from the king. It's not my position to question him, and I wouldn't dare to. Not unless I want to be beaten for it."

"You truly don't know." He stills as shock flashes across his face, nostrils flaring. "You've been killing my people."

"*Your* people? What do you mean, *your* people?"

He straightens, towering over me, and he points to his chest with a snarl. "*My* people. I have been sending my people into this realm to track *you.* King Elion is cruel and hateful. Do not let him make you think otherwise. He has you killing innocents," he says, exasperated—sad and tired, it seems. "There is so much you don't know."

"Then tell *me.*" My hands clench around my daggers. "Even if they are *your* people, they don't belong here. King Elion has his reasons, and it's not my position to question him," I repeat. "Why have you been tracking me? How do you even know who I am?"

He shakes his head, looking off while he rubs the back of his head. "Oh, but you will care, trust me…" He halts, turning his head as if he's heard something in the distance before turning back to me with a sigh. "I wish we had more time to discuss this tonight, but Ezra and Ren are headed back to the inn, and we can't risk getting caught. They'll come looking for you if you don't show up with an update. There's too much to tell you, but we can talk again tomorrow," he says dismissively, ignoring my questions.

And I realize that he knows too much.

"We will discuss it now!" I hiss, my voice shaking with anger. "You brought me out here for what? To taunt me?"

He spins back to me, his tone sharpening. "No, darling, you don't understand. We *don't* have time. If they find us here—together—this entire thing falls apart, and I can't risk that. I *won't* risk that." His words come out fast, almost rushed. "Meet me tomorrow night. I'll explain everything then, but you need to go back before they notice."

"Do you think I'm going to let some Shadovar convince me to meet with him in private, again? No. I won't do that because my loyalty isn't with *you*," I say firmly.

His brows lower as he steps closer. "No? Who is it with, then? Because I don't think it's with King Elion. Deep down you must know he's hiding something just like everyone else in the Brotherhood. I have answers about your past that you didn't even know existed," he breathes, scanning my face. "I know your parents and where you come from."

"I'm from Elderheim," I say, but my breath catches in my throat. I hold his gaze, searching for any sign that he's lying to me. *Is he lying to me?*

"Are you?" he asks quietly, challenging me.

He claims to know my parents? How—how is that possible? I've been an orphan since I was five, but my memories don't extend beyond that. Yet over the last several months, I've been digging for information regarding who my parents are. Information I want and desperately need for my own sake.

I hate to admit that I want those answers—answers that trump lying to my brethren. I've already been keeping my search to myself for almost a year, so this would be no different.

I groan in frustration, turning away to pace. I'm conflicted between meeting with him for answers and reporting back to Ezra about what happened tonight.

My pacing finally halts when I face him, only to find him standing with his arms crossed, but a flicker of desperation crosses his features before he looks away. He makes it impossible to say no.

"Fine!" I huff, giving in. "How am I going to distract the other two? I have to tell them something."

He growls, turning from me. "Don't trust them. You don't know everything yet, so please, don't say anything until you hear it all so you can make that decision for yourself."

"Of course I trust them. Honestly, you could probably kill Ren, and I wouldn't say a word about it. I might even help you." I chuckle at the thought. "Besides, I have to tell them something tonight. I don't have a choice."

He turns back around. "Just tell them you might have a lead from tonight and need to go to the Cauldron again, but nothing more or they'll question it."

My brows knit at his words as I realize he's been following us for a while. How could I have not noticed it?

"What, do you think I've only had eyes on you?" Alec says with a smug grin.

"You're fucking annoying."

He laughs, deep and loud. "That's a new one. I've never been called annoying before."

But I ignore him and look away, trying to decipher everything that was revealed, as confusing as it is. I'm unsure if I should trust this stranger or stab him. Though my training tells me to lunge at him, my mind somehow forces me to hesitate. *Why am I hesitating?*

"Isa," he says, snapping me back to reality. "Be careful, and don't let them think you're questioning the crown. They're loyal."

I find myself nodding because I know exactly what he means, but then I frown, realizing I just chose to trust this stranger over my own realm—my family—within seconds of hesitating.

Alec doesn't belong here, yet I couldn't bring myself to kill him, and the thought bothers me. I've trained my whole life for this—becoming a weapon. But as far as I'm concerned, I did kill him. It's not my fault he came back.

"Tomorrow," he confirms and begins to walk away, then pauses for a moment to turn around one last time. "Oh, I meant to thank you earlier," he quips with a grin. Now I'm really confused.

"Thank me for what?" I ask.

"For paying for my ale." His grin is so wide it looks like his face could split in half. It's breathtaking and annoying all at once.

My head shakes. "I didn't pay for your al—"

Then I stop, my eyes narrowing into a glare realizing that I did, in fact, pay for his drink. I gave him money in his boy form. That weasel.

"You owe me a drink!" I call after him as he continues to walk away, disappearing in the Veil.

He chuckles. "Looking forward to it."

I wait a few moments under the branches before making my way down the road, my steps light and cautious as I walk to the inn.

It's late, only a few hours left until sunrise, when I realize how exhausted I am. It's only been a day and a half since I was sent to kill Alec, and I've barely had any sleep and now... Now I have to keep secrets. Something I'm not sure I want to do.

The inn door opens on a soft creak. I shut it and kick off my boots only to find Ezra waiting in complete darkness. My eyes barely make out his shape as he stands.

"How was your night?" I ask. I'm curious to hear what he might have discovered. "Did you find anything useful?"

"No, not really. I made conversation with some locals but didn't gain anything of use. I found myself chatting with the innkeeper for most of the night. What about you?" he asks, hopeful and eyeing me.

"I might have found a lead with a local here but I'm unsure how credible it is. This mission is odd," I lie, already mentally kicking myself for it. "I think we need to stay another day or so to see where this goes."

He nods. "I feel the same. The scent I picked up at the Silver Lily is spotty—I'll catch a trail, and then all of a sudden it drops off. I'll send Ren with you tomorrow." He turns and kicks off his boots when he bangs on the wall connecting to Ren's room.

"I heard!" Ren calls out from the other side.

"No," I blurt, leaving Ezra to glance at me with an arched brow. "I don't need Ren. He's the last person I want ruining it. I don't want to spook the lead and need to go back to the tavern tomorrow night. Let's do what we did earlier and meet up again to report back. It seemed to work great in my favor tonight." I smirk, hoping he doesn't catch the lie.

Ezra holds my gaze, then nods. "I agree, but we need eyes everywhere. Ren can drink at the bar while you meet with your lead. He can keep an eye out." The words instantly snuff out any relief I had just seconds ago.

"Are you sending the brute to babysit me?" I ask, anger and annoyance present in my tone, not caring if he overhears me.

"He won't be in the way. We'll stay another night because we only have a day left, but Ren's going with you."

The decision is clearly not up for discussion, so I give him a short nod, biting my tongue. It looks like I need to figure out a way to distract Ren.

"I'm going to wash up," I mumble.

When I come back after a few minutes, he's already sprawled out on the bed, an arm resting above his head and lightly snoring.

Exhaling, I crawl in next to Ezra, who's quietly dozing beside me. My thoughts whirl from earlier, stuck on what exactly Alec knows and what he could be hiding.

I find it hard to believe everything that was spoken tonight was truthful. I've known Ezra and Ren my entire life—since childhood—but I find myself at odds with the conversation I had with Alec. If I should be worried about anyone, it would be Ren.

9

───────

Daytime comes in a blink with only a few hours of sleep, leaving us to head to the front of the inn to retrieve our breakfasts. The bell rings above as we walk through the wooden door, and a dark-skinned female with wild, curly hair peeks out from the back.

"One moment!" she hollers, bright and cheerful as the morning sun, like she didn't just spend the night chatting with Ezra.

I admire her cheerfulness, but I'll never understand morning people. My blank stare lands on Ezra and I groan, sliding into a seat at one of the wooden tables, and rub my temples. Ren sits beside me.

"Good morning, dearies!" she says, pouring us three mugs of their morning brew. I grin, sipping. "Would you like our breakfast pie to start your day?" She looks at us expectantly. Ezra only nods, drinking out of his mug, clearly not a morning person either.

"That would be great, thank you," I say.

Twenty minutes go by. We're inhaling our food at an

impressive speed when she comes back with another round. Whatever it is, it's delightful.

"Eat up, we have plenty," she says.

Ezra eats in silence while Ren practically moans into his food, inhaling his fourth serving. Both have been quiet for most of the morning, leaving me to spark a conversation inspired by the one I had with Alec.

And my favorite way of gaining information.

"You know, I was thinking about the orphanage yesterday—how I still don't know anything about my parents." I take a bite, hoping my words sound casual. "I was hoping that once we complete this mission, the king would grant me leave to start my search."

"We've already had this discussion before. They're most likely dead. It would be a waste of time," Ezra says, chewing his food as he looks up at me, mouth full. Ren briefly side-eyes him, the utensil halfway to his mouth, furrowing his brows, but he remains silent.

Ezra casually waves his fork in the air, continuing. "If King Elion took you in from the orphanage, it would be a waste of time to look for your parents. You know that, otherwise you wouldn't have been at the orphanage." He holds my gaze as if it's obvious, which it is. "King Elion would be disappointed if you left. Besides, he's practically a father to you."

"*Father* is a bit of a stretch, but he's right," Ren says, talking around his mouthful. "Most of us have never even tried searching for our kin, and the ones who do often come back with a grave marker."

His gaze drops, a brief sadness creeping in. I realize that I've never actually thought about Ren's family much. He came from the orphanage as well, bringing insight to the early Brotherhood days. I chew my food and nod, as if thinking about it.

"I could see how it might be a waste of my time. Best not to get my hopes up." I chuckle.

"Exactly," Ezra replies with a grin, going back to his food in silence.

I brush off the previous conversation and lean against the chair. Ezra sips, and I begin to wonder what put him in such a quiet mood, assuming it might be because of Ren tagging along. The two hardly get along.

"You seem tired," I point out.

"I am. Isn't it obvious?" Ezra huffs a laugh.

A devious grin tilts my mouth. "How can you be tired when you didn't even cuddle me last night? I walked into the chamber after washing up and you were already asleep."

"Probably because you suck the life out of everyone," Ren mumbles, and I go to stab his hand with my fork. He dodges it with a menacing grin as it makes contact with the table, utensils trembling.

Ezra huffs sarcastically. "I was too busy waiting for you to cuddle."

"So, what are our plans today?" I chuckle but throw Ren a glare, ripping my fork back out of the wood. Throwing my napkin on the table, I ignore Ren again, trying not to cringe the moment he begins to breathe into his food.

"I thought about heading to the local apothecary to restock our healing salve. How's your shoulder?" Ezra asks.

My shoulder—right. I actually forgot and haven't checked it since he put more salve on it yesterday.

"Surprisingly well, it seems, since I forgot I had an injury," I mutter with a casual shrug. "The salve helped."

"Good," he says. "Still, I'll head down a few blocks to restock since we're running low. We'll need it for the journey."

"I also need salve. Myst told me she cut her leg yesterday," Ren says, mentioning his red mare. I admire the fact that he can talk with her about such things.

"We'll go together," I say, and Ezra nods as we rise.

I drop a few coins for the innkeeper, turning to follow Ezra and Ren out the door, when someone grips my arm. I whirl around to the innkeeper, who's an inch from my face.

"You startled me," I exhale, palming my dagger.

"Trust him," she says quietly, anxiously glancing toward the exit. My eyes flick across her expression—an attempt to read her face—when her gaze meets mine. "Looks can be deceiving, dear, but trust him."

Her brown eyes remain serious, nothing like the cheerful demeanor she had when we walked in. She releases me just as Ezra peeks his head inside.

"Isa, are you ready?" His eyes immediately land on the innkeeper, his brow arching, as if he's unsure about what's happening between us.

My expression remains neutral when she gives me a light pat on my arm, accompanied with the same bright smile from earlier.

"Thank you for my coin, dear! I am very grateful for your kindness." Nodding and turning away, she walks back to where she came from.

Is she speaking of Alec? How does she know I met with him? I quickly brush off the strange interaction and exit the inn to find myself back on the cobblestone street. Ezra's already scanning the area with the face of an assassin—always calculating and looking for threats.

"Excuse me, sir!" a little boy says. "Please, do you have any coins?" The boy holds out his shirt as Ren stands on the edge of the street.

No, not any little boy. *The* little boy. Alec.

Auburn hair and freckle-faced just like yesterday, but I can clearly see the color of the boy's eyes today, a deep blue with a hint of gold. How I didn't notice them the first time is a mystery —they pierce your soul.

My eyes narrow, but he's clearly set on getting Ren's attention. I'm quickly reminded of what Alec said about testing someone's character. I'm curious how it unfolds, letting it play out, knowing Ren will probably kick the boy for fun.

A grin tugs at my lips.

Just then, Ren leans down to give the boy a gentle pat, tossing a coin into the shirt, and begins walking in our direction with a faint grin on his face. Which is unlike him.

My face scrunches in shock and confusion. What the fuck?

The boy makes brief eye contact with me as if to say, *I told you*. So does that mean Ren is decent? I almost turn nauseous at the thought.

Alec quickly passes by when Ezra tosses in a couple of coins before he scurries down the path without so much as a second glance toward us. Ezra remains silent as he scans the town, though his jaw is slightly tense.

"Are you okay?" I ask.

"What?" His tone is a little sharper than usual but nothing out of the ordinary as his attention shifts to me. I raise my hands in mock defense when he sighs with a half grin, the tension easing. "Sorry. I didn't mean to be rude. I didn't sleep well last night, and it has me on edge this morning. I'm ready for this mission to be over, and we only have tonight to finish the job. We're cutting it too close," Ezra says quietly.

I nod, understanding exactly what he means, but remain quiet the rest of the walk to the apothecary. We're cutting it way too close. Walking in after Ren, we're instantly greeted by an Herb Weaver.

Herb Weavers have the power to manipulate plants with a simple touch, allowing them to obtain the knowledge they need to create potions, tinctures, and salves—a direct connection to the land. Plants extend from every surface, hanging from the ceiling and cascading off the shelves, tables, and counters. The male touches them, silently muttering nice words to each leaf as he passes by.

Old and frail, he greets us with a smile and shows us his best healing salves off to the side. Ezra and Ren search for what they need as I walk near the front of the small shop in silence, Ren filling the space with how large he is. The shop smells wonderful though, like an earthy incense supplied for every ailment under the sun. I pick up a few jars and sniff.

"Careful," the male says. "You don't want to sniff those unless you want babies."

Scowling, I slowly set them down, shooting him a sideways glance. He chuckles, eyes crinkling. It's not uncommon for Fae to conceive naturally but most take the special drafts created by Herb Weavers, giving them an extra aid in fertility.

"I'm Edwin. Who are you, my dear?" he asks tenderly, taking my hand in his.

"I'm Isa."

"What can I do for you? Or are you here for the same thing as those grumpy males over there?" He arches a gray brow, gesturing over his shoulder where Ezra and Ren currently browse.

Ren bumps into a table, knocking over a jar, and he lunges to catch it. A grin tugs at my mouth as I secure a loose strand of hair behind my ear.

"Actually, no, but you may be able to help me," I say softly, recalling what's supposed to happen tonight with Ren accompanying me to the Cauldron. Now is my chance to hopefully find something to put him to sleep for a few hours. "Do you happen to have anything for... sleep?" I ask warily. "I've been having some trouble sleeping lately and need something a little stronger than my usual tonic." I'm hoping he understands what I'm asking as my gaze flicks behind him again.

"Oh yes!" he hollers loudly, like he didn't catch anything I was hinting at. It takes everything in me not to silence him with my hand when both males look over their shoulders in our direction. "I have just what you need for your monthly affliction. Follow me!"

Ezra and Ren grumble behind him, and I hear them shuffle deeper into the far corner, cowering away as if I'm something gross.

Oh wait—hah! Clever little weaver. I grin and follow him through the large curtains in the back. Looks like I underestimated him and he did catch on after all.

I'm greeted with the warm touch of the room as the sun streams in through the windows that line the ceiling, casting streams of light on the red-and-orange brick floor. Vines from various plants line the shelves in search of the sun, but surrounding the creeping vines are hundreds of jars resting on the surface. Below them lies a wooden working space resting against the wall. He gestures to a little jar on the table.

"This right here would do the trick for you. You'd get plenty of sleep and might even sleep for an extra..." He shrugs. "Half a day. You won't even taste it." Winking, he grabs a jar off the shelf in front of us—no questions asked. Edwin places it in my hand, closing my fingers around the jar. "Take it. I'm not sure what you might need it for, but it should accomplish what you need," he says gently and lifts his brows with a stern expression.

But I find myself hesitating for a breath. Not because I would feel guilty putting Ren into a deep sleep, but because of how much I want those answers from Alec. I want the truth about my parents—and it terrifies me how far I'm willing to go to get it.

I glance over my shoulder in search of Ezra or Ren when I finally face Edwin with a small nod, placing it in the hidden pocket of my cloak.

"Thank you," I mutter as he gestures to the curtains behind me. I sigh and walk through, finding Ezra and Ren paying for their items with Edwin's wife.

I smile at Ezra, my heart pounding against the glass jar in the pocket of my cloak. "You ready?"

10

—————

The sound of blood rushing against my temples has me fighting the urge to squeeze my eyes shut. A pounding headache has begun, and I haven't even left the inn yet.

I clasp my sheath to my thigh, securing my favorite dagger before tucking my pants into my boots. My fingers graze my hair, reaching around to ensure my auburn mark is securely pinned, when Ezra opens the door to the bathing chamber. He walks out with a small grin, reaching for his short sword off the side table.

"Let's regroup in a few hours. I picked up a scent trail earlier a few blocks north of the inn. I intended on tracking it tonight after one of the taverns. But if he's not here, we'll all follow it tonight," Ezra says, securing the silver blade to his hip. "Plus, I think I found the inn he's staying at. I'm going to try to get in."

"A few hours. Sounds good," I say.

I wanted to spend the evening obtaining more information from Alec without being interrupted by Ren, so I stopped by his room earlier. I slipped him the sleeping draft when we shared a glass of whiskey and hoped that he didn't become suspicious of the gesture.

Or worse, scent it.

He eyed me as I made quiet conversation and apologized for my behavior at breakfast. I grinned when he threw his head back, swallowing the amber liquid in one gulp.

Now looking at Ezra in front of me, I want to do the same but know that if I do, they would both end up suspicious. Clearing my thoughts, I return to the room and nod to the door.

"We should get going before it gets too late. I need to get Ren."

"Okay. See you later." He grins.

We quickly exit the room together, and I watch as he strides down the road, throwing me one last glance over his shoulder. A minute goes by before Ezra finally turns the corner, and I slip into Ren's chamber behind me. Ren remains seated in the chair that I left him in.

Head back, eyes closed, and breathing softly—asleep.

Taking advantage of what little time I have, I swing my cloak over my shoulders and shut the door behind me, locking it. I pat myself, feeling for the herbs secured in my cloak just in case Ren wakes up confused. There's no need for him to dig through my things if he's suspicious. Which, I gather, he will be.

My walk toward the Cauldron is quiet except for the sound of my feet lightly grazing against the stone. I stick to the shadows and wonder how I plan on finding Alec. Then a light breeze drifts by, carrying the scent of oakmoss... his scent.

I guess I won't be needing to find him since he already found me. My brows pinch as I whirl around, scanning the area for him, but he's not there, causing my teeth to grind.

"Are you alone?" Alec pushes the thought to me, quiet and barely there.

"Yes, I'm alone," I say. He doesn't respond, leaving me to face the Cauldron only to come to an immediate halt. Alec stands in front of me with a devious grin.

"Good," he says, pivoting on his heel toward the tavern

without another word, and I quietly trail behind him. The entrance to the Cauldron comes into view after a short minute, and I throw him a nasty glare. He quickly opens the massive oak door for me.

"After you." He grins.

Laughter fills my ears as incense drifts by, rich and earthy. The tavern is full of Fae and humans like the previous night, everyone gathered around tables. Finding a secluded table off to the side, we both slide into the chairs as a golden-haired waitress approaches us. My eyes break away from her to glance at Alec, but he's already studying me.

"Two ales, please. I owe her a drink," he says, finally breaking our gaze long enough to acknowledge the waitress. He smiles, leaving her to giggle and scurry back to the bar, looking over her shoulder as if he hung the moon himself.

"Where are Ren and Ezra tonight?" he asks, quickly scanning the room, then faces me.

"Ren is…" I calculate my answer. "Sleeping, but we should be good for three or four hours until we regroup at the inn. Ezra is at the other tavern working the locals again. I'm afraid they'll come find me, so we need to be quick." *Before I kill you,* I want to add, but not until I get answers.

The waitress strides back with our drinks, and he flashes her a charming grin—one I know he's probably used a thousand times to get what he wants. Yet I can't help but stare as he holds her gaze.

I can't blame her flustered response though. His eyes immediately draw you in, being a deep, vivid shade of blue.

"Now that you bought me my ale, are you finally going to tell me why you've been tracking me?" I get out and force down a scowl and sip the ale, realizing it's not the same as the previous night. Little does he know, I'm not typically a fan of ale except on rare occasions. "What do you know about my parents?"

His glass is halfway to his lips when he halts, setting it back down with furrowed brows. He leans back and uncomfortably rubs the back of his neck—or maybe that's just in my head, but I track the movement anyway.

"You wouldn't believe me even if I told you," he mutters, not quite meeting my gaze when there's a pause, like he's searching for the right words—or perhaps he's just stalling. "That's why I haven't told you everything yet. You already... startle so easily. I don't want to frighten you any more than you are. You're like a little fawn." He chuckles and crosses his arms, but I can't tell if he's uncomfortable or just being an ass.

Regardless, my temper flares at the comment—little fawn. Good to know this is a joke to him. After all, he should be dead. The ale in my hand meets the table with a hard thud, my patience thinning the longer I sit here.

"Are you going to tell me anything, or are you just going to keep avoiding answering my questions?" I grit my teeth.

The silence stretches as he holds my gaze, the air thick with tension, but he doesn't look angry, almost as if my quiet outburst is expected. He sighs, hands splaying like he's bracing himself.

"Isa," he says quietly, but then his brows pinch as if he's having a hard time finding the right words. "You've been missing for twenty years, but I haven't seen you in fifteen. My name is not Alec... It's Rydian."

I bark a laugh of disbelief, the sound sharp, before taking another sip of my ale, shaking my head in annoyance at the untimely humor. Then discomfort coils deep into the pit of my stomach as the ale slides down my throat. My eyes flick up, stomach dropping to the floor when I catch his serious expression. *He's serious?*

"That's not... possible. We've never met. I don't know you," I say, the words tumbling out.

Alec—*Rydian's* calm exterior falters just enough for me to catch the brief flicker of panic in his eyes before he composes himself. He remains seated though, hands calmly resting on the table like he's trying not to spook me.

Missing for twenty years? What does that mean, exactly? Does he think I'm from Aurelia?

My pulse rises as his words play in my head over and over. I slowly shake my head, rubbing the inside of my wrist until it aches. He's Shadovar—he could be manipulating me, right? It's in their nature. So he *has* to be lying.

"You know me," he says confidently.

"Twenty years?" My voice wavers, and I hate how unsteady it sounds as I process his words. "You're lying. That's not—that's not me. It's not possible. I was born *here*, in Elderheim. You're mistaken." But even as I say it, doubt squeezes its way in. *What if he's not?*

"I found you once before when you were ten," he says calmly. "It's not a mistake. I knew your parents. Your father was—"

"I would have *known*," I growl, my mind racing with all the possibilities. Bracing my hands on the table, I stand with a deep breath, closing my eyes. Alec mimics the movement in anticipation, earning a few glances from guests nearby, I assume, given the quietness that just settled over the tavern.

And just like that, I flee from the table, away from *this*, leaving my ale and Alec—Rydian, or whoever he is—behind as I bolt for the doors.

"Isa, wait!" he calls out, but I'm already out the door, heading to where we met under the trees. A minute passes before he finally catches up, my pulse thrumming in my veins when he reaches for me.

My eyes flare when I whirl around. "How? How is it possible that I could have been missing for twenty years? It doesn't make sense! This is my *home*."

"This is not your home!" His eyes frantically scan mine as if searching for any sort of recognition, but I come up blank.

Frustration grips me, because I know he's wrong—he has to

be. I've always been an orphan, no sign of my parents or knowledge of where I came from even after searching for them.

But what if I've been searching in the wrong realm? Doubt
pushes its way in just as he takes two large steps forward,
extending a hand as if to prevent me from running. Only I step
back with a glare, instantly palming my daggers.

"Isa, please," he says calmly, his hand still outstretched.
"Please don't run. It's much easier to show you than it is to
explain it to you."

He quickly darts forward and grabs my face with a heavy
exhale. Yet for some reason, my daggers fall to the ground the
moment a shudder races down my body from his touch. He's
the only thing keeping me in place as his eyes dart across my
face, lips parting.

"How can you show me? I can't leave with you," I mutter.

"I can show you in a different way. Let me show you," he
says, and a strained exhale escapes me when I slowly and hesi-
tantly nod "You have to say yes, Isa." His voice is low, carefully
exhaling in relief.

"Yes," I breathe.

"You're going to take a breath and close your eyes." He
guides my head back in his hands. "Then you're going to feel my
presence in your mind. When you do, you're going to search for
me and let me in."

I do as he suggests, searching for him behind closed eyelids
—something I've never done before, but I feel him.

It's faint, but his presence rests against the forefront of my
mind, cool and heavy, right between my eyes. It's as if he's
wrapping me in a comforting embrace, yet there's an undeniable power in his presence, steady and unwavering. I inhale,
catching the earthy scent of oakmoss, something that's
grounding and ancient. I mentally reach out to touch his
presence.

He shudders. "Let me in."

Just then, my head is thrown back in a series of images as they flood my mind, launching me into another world.

Not a world... *his memories.*

11

RYDIAN

I attempt to reach her through the Veil again, but she's not responding. The usual steady connection has gone cold, which can only mean one thing: she's injured. My heart pounds as I sprint, my magic already too drained to travel in the Veil.

Aurelia was breached unexpectedly, catching us off guard, when King Andre told me to run. As his second-in-command, I knew I needed to find them, even though I didn't want to leave his side.

"Find Elynor and Isa!" King Andre had shouted at me as he withdrew his sword, holding the front line with his men. We were ambushed at the border, not too far from the castle, but even as I took off, I was sprinting past our enemy to find Queen Elynor.

The realms were supposed to have peace—a treaty created by the kings in an agreement, the first time in history where we were granted such a luxury.

Elderheim arrived so quickly that the whole realm was caught off guard.

As I run through the trees near the back of the castle, my

eyes land on Elynor in the gardens fighting her way down the stone path with Isa on her hip. Two of her personal guards continue to cut through the chaos, heading toward the castle.

"Elynor!" My feet quicken their pace when I notice the gash on her ribs, deep and dripping down her side.

She's a force of power—cutting, ducking, and dodging, even when she served as an informant for the king. But now, with a crown that rests on her head, she commands a presence that's hard to ignore.

She's fair-skinned with dark emerald eyes and black hair, though a blonde mark rests in the center of her head. Varethin marks are often acquired in your hair—the bond between souls, connecting you to someone in your realm like a mate.

Elynor received hers while on a mission in Elderheim, marrying King Andre. The two have been inseparable since her arrival back five years ago.

With heavy, panting breaths, I finally reach them just as she cuts down the last of the soldiers surrounding her. Isa grips Elynor's tunic—uncontrollable tears streaming—when she glances at me. She just turned five.

"I… I'm scared, Mommy," Isa says between sniffles.

"I know, baby," she mutters, then turns to me, breathless and clutching her ribs. "Rydian, what happened?"

"Are you okay?" I ask, inspecting her as she winces in pain. "Why aren't you healing?"

"I—I don't know."

"There's been a breach from Elderheim. King Andre's at the border. We need to get you and Isa below the castle."

"No." She shakes her head. "I'm not leaving Andre, *my mate,* to fight alone."

"Please don't fight me, Elynor. Queen or not, I've been ordered to get you to safety. We need to get you and Isa below the castle. Your safety comes first," I press.

She pivots, looking to the side with a heavy exhale before finally turning to me with a quick, defeated nod. "Okay."

"We need to be quick. There are more coming," I say, commanding orders to her personal guards. "Give me Isa," I demand, but Elynor shakes her head.

"No, I'll be fine. Focus on fighting." She grips Isa tighter, as if afraid to let her go. We race toward the castle, a sword already in her hand as I follow close behind.

My sword is withdrawn, but we're quickly ambushed by those who have already reached the castle's back entrance seeing her two guards fighting up ahead. Glancing over my shoulder, I see hundreds of soldiers race toward us, and panic crawls up my chest.

I kick out, catching a soldier in the hip before slashing down, slicing him across his midsection. I continue to fight our way up the stairs and into the castle. We're almost there—if we can just make it inside, we can get to safety.

My sword slashes down when Elynor's screams tear through the air, leaving me to discover her bringing her own sword down in a wide arc.

In a race to protect Isa, she's ambushed by four soldiers from Elderheim. She's struggling to keep Isa in her hold when she's struck across the back of her head.

They lunge to grab her, one of them grabbing Isa. But Isa's screaming and kicking to be released, thrashing her wild black hair as she claws at the soldier's face.

"Rydian!" Her small screams reach me before they're muffled by a soldier's hand, her eyes wide with panic.

"No!" I slice and kick the nearest soldier, struggling to fight my way to her when something hard hits my skull.

The sun beats down on my face, the harsh light revealing the destruction of the battle we just faced as my eyes peel open.

A battle we clearly lost.

The burn from the gash on my lip forces me to wince and groan in pain. My hand flies to my ribs, pulling back to eye the blood coating my fingers—a stab wound, my armor stiff with dried blood.

The battle must have just ended, and I recall Elynor and Isa being taken by the soldiers from Elderheim.

Panic races through me as I force myself upright, crying out in pain as I brace myself on my arm, clutching my ribs. I hope to find Elynor but know deep down that they're already gone. My hope is fleeting as I search the castle, calling out as I check the hidden sanctuary below to find it empty. No one was able to make it inside, and defeat sits on my chest.

In my search for survivors, I find Ivy—a dark-skinned female soldier—also bloody and bruised. She lifts injured soldiers, doctoring their wounds when she turns in my direction.

"Ivy, what's the update?" I get out with a wince, clutching my ribs.

"Rydian, I'm so sorry," she chokes out, tears welling, streaking through the dust on her face. A cold dread settles in my stomach.

"Tell me!" I demand, gripping her face.

The destruction is undeniable. They obliterated everything we had—women and children are scattered amongst the bodies as fires continue to burn the homes of the people who lived in Vyria.

"They took them. They took them back with them, Elynor and Isa. We couldn't stop it. After they took them, everyone stopped fighting, retreating to where they came, and the king... They sent his second-in-command," she says quietly.

"What do you mean? Where is Andre?"

"They had the blade." She shakes her head, grief palpable beneath my fingertips. My hands leave her as I step away.

They found the blade. How did they find it? The Blade of the Veil. One that has been missing for hundreds of years. The only blade capable of killing a king or queen of Aurelia.

"I have a few soldiers down there with him until we can move his body," she whispers.

My feet pull me into a run, and I ignore the sharp pain in my side—I need to see him. I search for Andre near the large vale where the water meets the shore, coming to an abrupt halt as I spot him lying on his back.

Lifeless.

The air feels heavy, pressing down as I move forward. Ten others kneel near his body with their heads bowed. Soldiers immediately stand as I approach, parting wordlessly as their gazes avoid mine.

I take a step, then another, until my feet refuse to move, my knees weakening. I shake my head with disbelief.

My vision blurs as I stumble forward, landing on my knees just as an angry growl escapes me. I can't breathe. My heart slams against my ribs as he slowly comes into focus.

His blonde hair is dark from the thick coat of blood except for the black mate mark at the crown of his head. His face is pale, but his hands lie resting on his chest with his eyes closed, as if the soldiers knew I was coming. They leave us in silence, one by one.

I reach for him and cradle his head in my lap, moving hair away from his face as I hold the one male who was with me for the duration of my life.

Our memories together come flooding back. We didn't always get along, but he was my king.

The loyalty and the bond we built over the years is something I'll never forget. I loved him—admired him as if he were a brother. He was the kind of king that encouraged you to be better.

But Elynor made him better somehow. Their bond was something to be sought after, and I yearned for that. I was envious of what they shared, seeing how amazing they were, and with Isa, the girl I saw only moments ago. And it was gone in a matter of minutes.

My only job was to protect them.

And I failed.

My eyes flick to Ivy walking into the king's study as I'm going through scrolls—curly hair controlled in tight braids going down the sides of her head. She halts a few feet away, clasping her hands together.

"Sir, we need a king," she states.

"It will not be me. I won't do it." I shake my head, continuing to rummage through the scrolls, but she presses.

"It must be you, Rydian. With Elynor and Isa missing, the laws of succession are that if there are no royals left, the second-in-command is to take the throne—the decree of the Fates."

"A second-in-command has never taken the throne before, Ivy."

"But now there has to be. You *are* the second-in-command, and we need to do the ritual. We've already pulled Andre's blood for the essence. We just need to complete—"

"No, I don't want it!" I shout, slamming my hands on the table as I stand, the items on the desk rattling from my outburst.

"We need you!" she shouts back, knowing me well enough to confront me on the issue. "We need someone on the throne. It's been three weeks. I know you're not royalty, a Vaelborne, but the people need a king, and that is you. It has to be you—we have no other choice. I understand that you're grieving Andre and that you want to find Elynor and Isa, but we can't do that without a realm or a king. We can't do that without you."

Stepping back, I shove my hands through my hair, now touching the tips of my ears from the growth. Looking out the window from the castle, I see the depths of the ocean come into view amongst the city of Vyria, the realm's capital.

I try to come to terms with the issue at hand, but I know deep down that it has to be me. Pain grips me, squeezing tight in my chest. I will never stop grieving the loss of him.

"I know," I say finally, pacing the length of the window as I rub a hand over my jaw. My steps halt and I face her, my eyes closing on an exhale. "Let's get it over with, then. We'll do it tomorrow, and I'll appoint you as my second-in-command."

"Sir?" she asks, her eyes wide.

"You're not afraid to confront me, and I need that by my side when times are tough. I want you as my second. You can choose my third if you want, but I want you in control of the army and strategizing. I watched you even before the battle and wanted to raise you up the ranks then. From the recent informants that I've sent out, King Elion believes that there is no Aurelia left and no royal on the throne. Let's lie low for a while. I don't want him suspecting that we survived."

"Yes, my king. Thank you," is all she says before leaving.

"I have something for you," Ivy says.

We walk up the grand stairwell leading to the council chamber as I take the scroll from her.

"This just came in from our messenger hawk. They found Isa," she says. I halt on a breath and turn with disbelief. It's been five years since they were taken with no lead in sight.

"Are you sure?" I ask.

She stops with me. "Yes, but they think King Elion is wiping her memories somehow. We aren't sure how they're doing it, but Isa had a brief conversation with Orin a week ago. She doesn't remember our realm, claiming that she's an orphan of Elderheim and was raised amongst her friend Ezra. We found out that they keep moving her location, which is why it has been so difficult for us to track her. They're hiding her somehow. Orin wants you to meet him in Arcan to talk to her. She's ten and should still be able to Vision Walk. Maybe you can refresh her while you're there."

If she can Vision Walk, it would make it possible to refresh her memories. If I can get my hands on her face, it should be able to work. Shadovar tend to gain their unique capability at a young age, and hers was Vision Walking at age three. We didn't know what her power was until she started talking, giving us insight to our own memories when we touched her face, revealing hidden truths. I remember that Elynor would flush in embarrassment over it.

We finally arrive in the council chamber with a swing of the doors to discuss what's to happen while I am gone. Ivy, being second-in-command, will be in control of the armies. Should I not come back, we strategize my departure and come up with a solid plan.

I leave the chamber to ready myself for the long journey by grabbing a few of my weapons and Veil to the edge of the Elderheim border near a hole that allows me to make my way inside.

It takes me a moment to adjust as Elderheim's power surges through me. Even though I can still access my magic, it's not as strong as it is in my own realm, my reserves draining so much faster here.

Both realms have their own wards against the other, and right now, Elion has a border up, but there's a crack in it near Red Hollow. And although we're still able to access the realm and our magic, it's muted upon entering, only allowing me to shift or walk in the Veil. Anything stronger and my power drains at a much faster rate.

With a glance down, I watch as the shadows on my fingertips disappear, feeling it settle beneath my skin. Once across the border, I visualize Arcan and take a step, quickly arriving at our meeting spot—a local tavern—while shifting my appearance. I have been to Arcan once before, but that was years ago, having met with a few discreet locals before the journey to find Isa began.

Orin is my third in command that Ivy appointed a few years ago. He offered to go in place of the other informant that I wanted to send, claiming that he was more skilled in tracking and was confident he could find Isa. Rightfully so.

Originally a large dark-haired male, Orin has also shifted into a new appearance. Only this time he's shifted into a frail older male, and I'm assuming it's to not scare Isa away.

"Orin." I push the thought out, speaking in the Veil. His eyes lift as I slide into the chair across from him. *"What have you found out?"*

"She's living at one of the orphanages here in Arcan. She's become close to a boy named Ezra and has a young instructor of sorts named Ren. I'm not sure who Ren is, but he's near her a lot. She doesn't remember anything, not even the battle when she was taken with Elynor. I had to talk with her at a local archive just to get her alone. I believe they're wiping her memories with a Siphon."

"A Siphon? You're sure? They haven't been around for years. What makes you think that?" I ask.

Orin is also educated when it comes to each realm, having studied as a scholar prior to becoming a soldier for King Andre and now me.

"Siphons are able to pull energy from the land. It's been said that they can do the same to a Fae's memories as well, though it is not common knowledge. It could be possible, and from what I've gathered, she has some of her essence but not much. I can sense it, but she doesn't

know that she can wield. She thinks she's a halfling and knows her name, but she doesn't remember anything else. If they're siphoning her memories, they're pulling her essence out as well. Whether it's intentional or not is hard to say."

I exhale, speaking aloud. "It's going to be hard convincing her."

"Mm, I agree," Orin grunts.

An hour passes as I finally arrive outside the orphanage and watch Isa from a distance. My heart clenches as the sight of her —identical to Elynor with her black hair, except for her bright amber-colored eyes. More yellow than orange. She belongs in Aurelia, and I can't stand the thought of her being here any longer. We're so close to bringing her home—I can't fail this time.

She's gathered around a few of her friends when I make my approach near the trees of the orphanage's courtyard, disguised as someone much younger than my current self.

"Hello." I grin.

She briefly turns my way when she waves her friends off, walking up to me with a soft smile. A solo freckle sits under her right eye while the others are splashed across her nose.

"Hello, do I know you?" Her voice softens, but I hesitate before answering, unsure how she'll respond.

"You met my friend at the archives about a week ago," I say casually.

She stills, her eyes widening. "No, I don't know you." She anxiously looks over her shoulder, continuing in a hushed tone, "I'll tell you what I told that old man last week. You have the wrong girl. I'm an orphan, and I'm from Elderheim."

"No, Isa, you're not," I mumble, her eyes somehow widening even more.

"How do you know my name? Who are you?" she asks, her voice trembling.

I quickly reach for her face just as I shift into my true form as Rydian, but the hope I had for her vision capabilities dissipates when my fingertips graze her temples—her essence is dark.

It barely brushes my mind when she pushes me off, shouting and frightened. I shouldn't have grabbed her.

"No! I don't know you! Please, leave me alone!" she screams, backing up as tears stream down her face. "Guards! Ren!"

No, not again. I groan, and my eyes flick behind her, looking to see if anyone heard her yelling, before lunging for her arm. She can travel with me through the Veil. I just need to touch her. My fingers graze her when she reels back and slaps me, bolting in the direction of the orphanage.

Whether it's instinct or fear of failing, I chase after her, and she runs right into the arms of a light-haired boy near the back entrance. My steps halt as I realize that he must be the younger kid, Ezra.

An older one follows him around the corner—sixteen or seventeen, maybe. He glances behind Isa and meets my gaze, spotting me near the trees in my true form. *Fuck.*

The massive kid, Ren, I think, shouts for guards who are now heading in my direction, leaving me no choice but to step into the Veil as they swarm me. I arrive at the border within seconds, my power already feeling depleted, realizing that I can't go back. I'm left with no choice but to leave Isa behind.

Ice coats my veins as a guttural, angry shout tears through me. But the moment I cross the ward between realms, my shadows explode from my palms, shattering the trees in a cloud of darkness.

Ivy sits to my right as other members sit across from us in the council chamber. We're discussing the future of sending more trackers and informants to Elderheim in search of Isa.

Ever since I made an appearance to retrieve her, they've successfully kept her hidden from us. *But how are they doing it?* The thought has plagued me since I left fifteen years ago, but every time we catch a lead, they vanish without a trace.

"We need to move forward, Your Majesty. We can't do this forever, and we've lost too many informants as it is. They're tired and scared of never returning. We have fewer and fewer informants willing to travel to Elderheim to track her. We're chasing a ghost," Ivy explains, earning a few nods from the remaining members.

She's not a ghost. She's alive.

Yet it's been fifteen years, and I can't sleep—I can't eat or function. The thought of her in that realm turns my stomach, and I refuse to give up because she's the last royal of this realm since we're still unable to locate Elynor. Kaeda hasn't even been able to find her as a Death Whisper within the Veil, speaking to the dead—Elynor's essence simply can't be found, leaving me to believe she's still alive.

King Elion's motive for their capture remains unknown, even after all these years. We've dug through every inch of our archives and informants' notes for any information. Not even the council knows. If Elynor were here, she would have been able to add some input to this mystery—but she's not. *And I need to live with it.*

I nod, acknowledging Ivy's concern, and pull at my long beard. I refuse to give up on either of them, but I know that I need to. For my sanity and the future of Aurelia. Yet I've spent most of my years as a king in search of both of them.

Maybe I am chasing a ghost. Maybe focusing on this realm is what I need to do. I could marry and create new heirs if I really wanted to, but ever since I got my mark a few years ago, I wanted to wait.

Orin storms through the double doors, leaving us to all

swivel our heads in his direction, spotting the scroll clutched in his hand.

"A scroll has arrived. Our last informant has sent word back," Orin says.

I stand, bracing my hands at the head of the table, my shaggy auburn hair falling to my brows. "And?"

Orin continues. "They found her. Again. She's alive and is living at the king's castle."

"Are you sure?" I ask, hope rising in my chest.

"Yes, you need to go back. She lives near Alvonia," he says.

Leaving the council members, I rush into the corridor and fall into step besides Orin toward my living quarters, Ivy trailing closely behind. Grabbing my pack, I toss it on the bed and begin throwing items in there for the journey.

"Ivy, I need you to lead the armies and informants similar to the last time I left. We're not leaving that realm without her. If there's a war, so be it, but I expect you to prepare them for what lies ahead. After that, I want you to meet me in Sylvanor in a few days to discuss strategy and to meet with my contact from Eldryn. I'm hoping to reach her through the Veil if it's possible." I grab a few of the Veil coins, hoping to somehow find a way to give her one or reach her when we sleep.

"Of course." She turns on her heel, exiting a second later.

I grip Orin's shoulder. "Thank you for standing by me when I needed you."

"It's been my pleasure, Your Majesty. I'll see you both in a few days. Be careful," he says with a curt nod.

Walking into the bathing chamber, I reach for my straight blade and watch as the hair falls off my face, uncovering the sharp lines of my jaw. My reflection reveals the hope in my eyes for the first time in years, and a declaration to come back with Isa or die trying.

Arriving in Elderheim the next day, I check into a local inn located in Alvonia after making my travels from Arcan and meet with the informant the same night at the Painted Bird—a local brothel, but masks are required.

As I slip through the dimly lit corridors, my eyes land on a figure down the hall. Yet the moment I see her in the dim light, she feels… familiar.

She turns in my direction, slamming into my chest, but the way she studies me—though masked—feels as if she holds my soul in her palms, her eyes as entrancing as her voice. Then we part ways.

The next evening comes at the inn when someone knocks at my door, and I open it only to see—

Isa.

12

Pulling myself away from his memories and the flood of emotions, his hands gently cup my face as I firmly grip the realm I'm in. *Elderheim.*

"Isa," Rydian says softly, though my eyes remain closed as quick breaths fill the space between us. "Isa, come back to me."

"Rydian." My wide eyes finally open, fixed on him.

He exhales, relief evident as his thumbs swipe across my face. He was never Alec but always the king of Aurelia. *Oh gods.*

"That—that was me? How...?" My head shakes, words tumbling out in a mess.

Even though I saw his memories, I don't remember anything. The young girl certainly looked like me with black hair and golden-amber eyes. And the resemblance between myself and Elynor was too similar to ignore. Yet... my doubt creeps in.

"King Elion captured you and your mother, Elynor, a few years after the War of the Veilstone. We were supposed to have a treaty, which was why we weren't expecting the attack. It didn't make sense. Then they killed your father, King Andre, with the Veilblade during that battle."

My chest heaves as I'm taking in the information, but he firmly grips my shoulders, peering down at me.

His eyes soften. "I searched for you. I never gave up. I truly believed you still lived, regardless of not finding your mother. And I sent the best trackers through the border near Nymara, but King Elion kept you hidden. They somehow knew that I was sending people across the border. But once I saw you for myself, I knew then that they were siphoning your memories. I couldn't even feel your essence, and if I didn't find you and bring you back, you would be lost forever." He paces, his hand waving in explanation. "Earlier this year, an informant told me that Elion had a secret Brotherhood who were killing my men, and after a while, he, too, stopped sending letters. After the most recent informant sent word that he found you, I wanted to come to Elderheim myself to bring you home. I wanted to try again, despite the last unsuccessful mission when you were ten." His brows pinch, and he drags a hand down his face.

"I didn't know," I whisper, but doubt settles itself at the back of my head because I don't remember him at all. *Is this another trick? Could he be manipulating his own memories in to convince me?*

"It wasn't your fault. I didn't know they were taking your memories and should have tried harder. I only suspected it, but I *should* have tried harder. I never should have left you the first time," he says.

The guilt lining his features is palpable as he paces, and quick breaths escape me as I realize that he *is* telling the truth. Oh gods, I find myself believing the words tumbling from him as he continues his explanation.

"We tracked you to Alvonia, and I stopped at the Silver Lily to plan the mission. Little did I know you would show up right to my door. Luckily for me, Helga didn't know who I was, so your regular killing didn't go as planned. I was at the Silver Lily when you arrived with Ezra and Ren and knew it would be hard to get you alone after seeing you arrive, so I left you that note. I only hoped you would check the table. It's been a long twenty years, and so much has happened since they took you." He glances at me, hope sparking in his eyes. "But I'm here now, and I want to take you home. Please come home with me."

"I don't remember you," I get out, not quite ready to give up what I've called home for the past twenty years. Because that's what it is, home, and I hate that I still feel this way. *Why do I feel this way?*

"I know, and I'm sorry I failed you. You and your mother," he mutters. It's clear that he's tired of searching for me after so many years. Yet they were sending me to kill his men. I killed his men.

Our men, and... oh gods.

My stomach churns. I'm going to be sick.

I whirl around, bracing myself against the tree with my hand, and vomit, overwhelmed by the information and realization of what King Elion had me doing all these years. Using me to erase his past—my family—while mocking me.

This is the true punishment.

I'm bent over, wiping my face with the back of my hand. Rydian strides to me, attempting to rest his hand on my lower back, but I swat it away.

"Don't touch me," I croak, straightening to look at him just as my eyes flare.

I'm feeling nauseous again, the realization of being a princess of Aurelia sweeping in, stealing my breath. Dread seeps through, my stomach sinking and coating my entire body like ice in my veins. I can't breathe. A princess of Aurelia?

And the king of Aurelia has been tracking me to take me home, to claim the realm as my own for the past twenty years. Oh gods, I'm definitely going to be sick again. The color drains from my face, my breaths quick as saliva coats my tongue.

"I'm—I'm a princess," I get out.

His eyes widen as he realizes where my thoughts have gone.

"Yes... you are, but nothing needs to happen yet. I'm only here to bring you back, that's all."

My hand settles on my stomach as I close my eyes, trying to force down the bile that's rising again, and take a few deep breaths. The memories, the confusion—it's too much. I'm unsure if that's something I even *want*. I'm no princess, and I'm definitely not a queen.

Silence stretches as my thoughts continue to whirl. He's here to bring me back to Aurelia, but what if I don't want to go? Would he let me stay if I asked? But then again... *do* I want to stay in Elderheim?

It's been my home here for the last twenty years, but I've always felt like there's more to life than serving King Elion. Yet my father is dead and my mother... well, she's most likely dead too after what I saw in Rydian's memories. So what I have now is a duty to rule Aurelia? It's a responsibility I'm not sure I want.

"And what if... what if I don't want it?" I mumble.

His jaw clenches slightly. "We can discuss it later—"

"Isa!" Our conversation is cut short by a guttural shout of my name. We exchange a glance, panic swiftly crossing our faces.

"Ren," I whisper, realizing whose voice that is.

How is that possible? I slipped him the sleeping tonic in his drink earlier, but it's only been a few hours. He should still be asleep. Glancing over my shoulder, I hear him coming up the road and my breathing picks up. Panic thrums in my veins.

After knowing the truth, I realize that Ren must have been a really good liar all these years if he possibly knows where I'm from, but there's no sure way to know, and I don't want to be near him right now.

"Isa." Rydian's voice is a quiet, urgent shout now, trying to snap me out of my thoughts. I'm still glancing over my shoulder when he grabs my hand, pulling me deeper into the shadows of the trees. "Look at me," he whispers, gripping my face and forcing me to meet his gaze. "You need to slow your breathing, do you understand?"

I nod, struggling to focus, but the fear of Ren arriving gnaws at me—he's almost here. Rydian quickly puts his hand into my cloak and pulls out the sleeping draft, then tosses it further into the forest. He's hiding the evidence. *How did he know that was there?*

Ren's voice calls out in the distance. "Isa! I went searching for you at the Cauldron, but you weren't there." He's closer now and tracking me somehow, and a sharp pain shoots up my wrist.

Rydian's eyes shift behind me and then lock on to mine again. "Listen to me, we can't run right now. You need to finish your mission, and if he sees me in this form, he will know exactly who I am. We don't know who the Siphon is, but Ren saw me when you were ten. He knows I'm here for you. This isn't what I had planned, but this is what we're going to do. I'm going to shift into someone else and pretend to be Alec Thorne." He pauses briefly, his voice steady but firm. "You're going to kill me again. Do you understand?"

"What—no!" My shock cuts through the air.

"You have to. You can't kill me, remember?" He throws me a menacing grin, and I grit my teeth.

"It's Ren. I'm sure he'll sniff it out and find a way to make it happen. I know him. Don't do this."

"You will do it. And you will tell him that you need to bury me. Tell me you understand." His tone is now serious, but he sees my doubt. "I'll be fine, I promise. I'm the king of Aurelia. I can't die by a simple blade, and I'm not alone. I brought another with me and will not leave without you again. I promise." He glances behind me again, hearing Ren just around the corner. "He's almost here—put that mask back on," he says, and I know exactly what he's asking of me.

My mouth falls open, but before I can protest further, his form ripples, shifting into a completely different person—Alec

Thorne. A much shorter male with shaggy auburn hair, features resembling someone a little older.

Then Ren's behind me.

Quickly masking my panic, I adopt the facade of the lethal assassin and slowly turn in the direction of Ren with my daggers outstretched. A smug grin tugs at my lips.

"Look who I found, Ren. Looks like the note at the Silver Lily was right. Alec *was* here after all." My gaze flicks up and down as a snarl escapes me. "Did you take a nap, brute? I needed help."

He turns to me with a glare—a lethal calmness. If looks could kill, I would be dead right now. His eyes curiously dart between us as I hold my composure, using every ounce of confidence I have left so as to not make him any more suspicious than he probably already is.

"Please, I didn't do anything," Alec gets out.

Our attention shifts to Alec with his palms up, appearing confused as he backs up in surrender. Ren chuckles, a low, menacing sound, stalking to where Alec stands.

"Look what we have here." Ren tilts his head, his black hair falling to the side. "The king will be pleased that we found our target, won't he?"

My understanding of why King Elion has Ren in the Brotherhood jolts through me as I watch him. His brows lower as he strides forward with a steady calmness, gray eyes sharp and calculating, as if he's looking right through Alec. His wide shoulders steadily sway with each step, like he's the hunter and Alec is his prey.

He's absolutely terrifying.

Alec glances at me just as Ren lunges, swiping with his blade. Alec lifts his arm to protect his face with a loud cry, only to be sliced from his wrist to his elbow. My breath stalls as I watch it play out before me.

Ren darts behind him and kicks his knees in, forcing Alec to fall to the ground. He catches himself with his hands, blood dripping, when Ren comes up from behind him to grab a fistful of auburn hair, exposing his neck with a knife to his throat.

"Are you going to tell me how you're alive, or did Isa really fail this time?" Ren grinds out, his mouth grazing his ear while meeting my gaze.

"I'm not sure what you mean." Alec growls in pain, wincing as the knife nicks his throat, blood dripping to his collarbone.

Ren snarls, gripping tighter. "Back at the Silver Lily. How are you alive?"

"I-I don't know what you're talking about," Alec stutters, tears streaming down his face. "I-I'm just a simple businessman in the area to visit my niece."

He's so persuasive that, for a moment, I almost forget who he really is, especially with him gasping for air as Ren tugs his hair.

"I've never seen either of you before, I swear!" Alec pleads.

"Well, it looks like Isa really did fail then. Too busy with her own affairs, it seems." Ren sneers, and I know what he's implying by what was found at the Silver Lily. His assumption of me. "The king will be thrilled to learn that tidbit, won't he?" Ren's words are sharp, but I maintain my composure with a small grin.

"He's lying," I interject softly, stepping forward to stand in front of Alec as he kneels on the ground, a sneer plastered to my face. "It doesn't matter now, does it? We'll be finishing the job tonight and then bury you after," I say, keeping my tone icy.

Ren chuckles menacingly low in agreement, dark hair falling over his brow. My gaze locks on Alec as I look down my nose, noticing a hint of pride shining through his blue eyes. Resignation settles in my chest when Ren gives me a small nod, exposing Alec's neck to me. My lip curls, and within a second, I sweep my dagger across his throat with a sudden movement of my right arm. Life drains from Alec's face, so similar to the inn, leaving him slumping forward into the leaves as Ren steps off to the side. Then I let my fury build, my eyes swiveling to Ren.

I whirl to him. "Where were you?"

He shoves a hand through his dark hair, slicking it back. Anger shines beneath his gaze as he takes a step forward. I can't help but step back out of caution, recalling Rydian's memories. Then I shove him—hard. He stumbles back with a growl, his hair falling to his brow once again.

"I thought you were supposed to be my watchdog tonight, but you didn't show, and I was left to handle this myself," I growl, and the accusation is sharp in my tone as I tilt my head to the side.

I do my best to have him believe it's his fault that he wasn't here when I needed him. That he abandoned me to do it all on my own. And despite the anger still etched on his face, something unreadable crosses his features before he turns to me. He strokes his jaw, dismissively replying in a calmer tone, "Since when do you need help, wench?" His eyes flash with anger. "You know what? Whatever. It doesn't matter now—the job is done. We're leaving at dawn."

He strides over and nudges Alec in the ribs with a boot, ensuring he is truly dead. My breath catches, and I can't help but flinch, but he doesn't seem to notice.

"I say we leave him here for the Grokees to devour," he mutters, spitting on Alec's lifeless body.

"We need to bury him like we usually do, or the town will come searching for us," I say.

"Let them. We'll take care of whoever gets in our way."

"Ren," I press, undeterred.

He glances at me, giving me a final once-over. "Fine, find a shovel and bury him yourself. I don't care. I'm heading back to the inn to clean up," he says, signaling an end to the conversation.

Ignoring his dismissal, I close the distance with precision, my head tilting up with my dagger pressed against his chest.

"If you tell King Elion I neglected my duties because I was preoccupied…" I scan his face, a small grin tugging at my lips. "I'll tell him you slept through yours, since I'm assuming that's what you were doing."

He growls, eyes flicking over my face, knowing that what I threaten will get him fewer and fewer missions as a result. He only nods, something unreadable briefly crossing his face before it's gone.

Then he leaves me alone to bury Alec in the dark. Ren strides down the path toward our inn, and when he's finally out of sight, I lose what little composure I have left.

Quick breaths escape me. I feel something close to the panic I felt earlier before collapsing against the trunk of a nearby tree. With a few more long breaths, I close my eyes, focusing on controlling my breathing. Adrenaline still runs through my veins.

My eyes flick open to Alec's lifeless body before I muster enough strength to meet him at his side and flip him over, not convinced that he's alive. I find myself lifting his head to cradle him, sitting in the shadows for a few minutes as my breathing finally slows. What the fuck just happened?

"He'll be fine." A female voice echoes deep within the shadows of the trees. My head whips up as someone approaches on soft leaves, twenty feet away with her hood up.

"Who are you?" I demand.

Reaching over Alec's body, I grip the dagger that fell. She strides forward, slow and steady as she approaches, before gripping the edges of her hood to reveal her face.

She's beautiful, with dark skin that's smooth and rich with almond-shaped eyes—expressive and deep, framed by her long lashes. Her black hair is wild and curly, cascading around her shoulders. The white streak lining the crown of her head makes her overall appearance noteworthy, if it wasn't for the air of confidence she radiated. I briefly recall seeing her from Rydian's memories.

"I'm Ivy," she says, hands resting on the hilts of her swords peeking out from beneath her cloak. "I'm his second-in-command."

She's captivating, and it's easy to see why Rydian chose her as his second, standing with a fierceness that commands attention. With wide eyes I glance down at Alec, who remains lifeless, noting a faint pink mark indicating that the cut is already healing.

"I can take him from here if you need to rest."

"No, I need to stay," I insist, shaking my head. "Just until he wakes up, please. I don't want to go back."

She looks at me with understanding, a flicker of compassion passing through her eyes when she finally nods. "It won't be much longer. He's already healing. To us it would be fatal, but to him, it's a minor wound. He'll be fine," she says.

"I'm Isa."

She gives me a soft smile. "I know. We've met."

"We have?" My brows knit.

"Yes, at the inn. I tried to speak to you."

My interactions at the inn run through me, and I realize that she must have been the innkeeper who grabbed my arm at breakfast.

"You can change your form like Rydian?" I ask.

She nods. "Yes. In Aurelia anyone from the realm can shift and enter the Veil, but the Shadovar have their own unique abilities like the Aetheri."

"Like what?" I always knew they did. I just never bothered to learn the specifics considering speaking of the Shadovar was forbidden. Now I realize I just might need to, especially if I'm a princess. My pulse climbs at the thought.

Before she can answer me, movement rustles my lap, forcing my gaze to shift down.

Alec breathes. His form ripples, mindlessly changing back into the male I saw before Ren arrived—the king of Aurelia—and my eyes go wide. His auburn hair rests on his brow, though dark swirls of ink appear down the left side of his neck. Something I must have missed before.

"Rydian, can you hear me?"

He opens his eyes, a small smirk forming. "I hate dying. But if this is how I wake, I might not mind doing it again," he mumbles, leaving me to groan at the untimely humor.

"Welcome back, Your Majesty." Ivy grins, stifling a laugh as she bows at the waist.

"Stop that." He sits up, angling his body toward me. "You stayed."

"Well, I can't go back now."

"No, you can't," he agrees.

"Well..." Ivy says, holding up her finger.

Rydian whips his head in her direction, rising to his full height, as if he didn't just lose his life for the second time in three days. He's in her face now, and I draw my knees up to stand, confused as to where this is going.

"No, she is *not* going back with them." His eyes grow hot with fury. "We've already discussed this. She stays with us, and that's final."

"She's our only way in." Ivy pushes, leaving him to growl.

My brows draw close together. "What do you mean—your only way in?"

"Ivy." Rydian glares so intensely, as if warning her to remain quiet. Ivy only throws him an apologetic glance, knowing she is probably going to be punished later, and steps forward. Her hands rest on her hilts. She speaks in a way that any commander would relay information. As if I have sway. *Do I have sway?*

"We still don't know where Elynor is. We don't even know if she's alive *or* dead. We've had no leads since you two were taken twenty years ago," she manages to get out, lowering her eyes. "If you can go back with your brethren, maybe we can find something regarding her location."

My mother. *She could be alive?* Knowing Elion, she's probably already dead, but there's really no way to know that.

"This is not up for discussion. She stays with us, and that's final. She needs to be in Aurelia. We can keep searching for Elynor as soon as we get back," he grinds out.

"We're already here, Rydian," she counters again.

"No, she's right," I say, their gazes swiveling to me. "I can help. It makes sense. They have no idea that I know anything and don't suspect it because technically, we completed our mission. I could resume my life and gain information from the castle about her whereabouts… if she's still alive."

Rydian growls in frustration and starts to pace. Ivy and I watch him as he's clearly at odds with the situation, watching him scratch the back of his head in agitation. He finally halts with hands on his hips and then looks up with a decision.

"No. I can't risk you being near anyone who can Siphon your memories again. I can't do it—I *won't* do it again. It's too much of a risk. I lost you twice already. There's no way around it, and your safety comes first. We will get you back to Aurelia as soon as possible," he says as if it's final. Like he's *my* king.

"No," I say, my words hanging between us. I'm deciding for myself this time.

Ivy stiffens when he whips his head in my direction, but I hold his gaze, lifting my chin as he steps forward. The silence hangs in the air when he stops a few inches from me to slowly, firmly grip my chin. He's not aggressive with the movement but stern as he searches my face.

Our gazes lock while he holds me in place. A challenge.

My words come out a quiet whisper. "Let me do this, Rydian.

Let me be your informant. I am no more important than my mother—the queen."

"You are the queen, Isa. I won't risk you again," he whispers back.

"Not yet. Not until a ritual is done from what I gathered from your memories. For right now, I am still Isa Valedara, bound to the Veiled Brotherhood."

He knows that I'm right. I'm not the queen of Aurelia yet, and I live here, in Elderheim, and I have a choice—my choice is to stay.

Rydian holds my stare, like he's calling my bluff. His gaze is so intense it would bring anyone to their knees in submission, but I stand my ground in a silent challenge. There's an anger in his eyes as he studies me, and a quiet minute passes before a look of resignation flicks across his face.

His scent of oakmoss fills my senses as I steadily breathe in, willing my heart rate to slow. I never thought I would like the earthy scent, but the more that I'm around him, the more I find myself searching for it.

He finally nods and releases me, folding his arms across his chest. "Fine, that's what we'll do, then. First, we'll need to strategize a plan before they notice your absence."

And I look at Ivy, who was already watching me, catching her staring, her eyes darting back and forth between me and Rydian. Her brow slowly arches as if she's just realizing something.

Her face reflects awe of the scene that just unfolded, her gaze flicking to Rydian, who is now rubbing his forehead back and forth with his thumb and forefinger. She swings her gaze back to me and throws me an inquisitive glance, curiosity written across her face.

Like how I just convinced him to let me go.

Again.

13

I spent no more than an hour with Ivy and Rydian in his room, strategizing what lies ahead. They didn't have to voice their tension in order to feel how high it was over the anxiousness of Ezra and Ren discovering my absence.

Thankfully, when I returned to the inn, I discovered Ren's door was locked and Ezra was sleeping with an arm over his face. Both seemed unaware of where I was the rest of the evening, especially if they didn't come looking for me. Ren must have filled Ezra in on the turn of events.

But our plan is simple. I'll travel with Ezra and Ren, behaving like I normally would with the two of them. Friendly with Ezra, continue to hate Ren—easy.

Rydian will follow us to Dryborn through the Veil, ready to assist me if needed, while shifting his form between stops to remain hidden. Though he was adamant about coming, it's clear he's anxious about the journey.

His abilities have limitations, as he can't remain in the Veil for long without consequences. Any extended time in the Veil drains his power at a much faster rate and could even cause him to emerge in an entirely different location, leaving him stranded until he recovers. Shifting is similar, only he can't hold it as long, which is why they choose to use the Veil more.

So, to manage their reserves, Rydian and Ivy will take turns following us. Ivy left immediately after our conversation to meet Rydian in Dryborn, which is our halfway point, but I'm going to push to keep our stops consistent. If we coordinate around their abilities, they should remain undetected in the Veil.

We then turned our attention to what awaits at the castle regarding my mother. We suspect Elynor, if she's alive, might be hidden below. My task is to gather information on her whereabouts and to find the Siphon—if there is one—and relay everything back to Rydian.

We agreed to meet at the Painted Bird to avoid raising suspicion, though Rydian wasn't thrilled with the choice, given its reputation, but I convinced him that it was the only location that I could go without tipping anyone off. My thoughts whirl as I revisit our conversation earlier, hours before dawn.

"Why can't you just walk right into the castle from the Veil?" I questioned.

"Because in the Veil, I can only appear at a location that I've previously been in. Plus I have to be invited inside King Elion's castle. He has wards protecting against Shadovar. I need to be invited in by a resident, as I've never been invited into the castle of Elderheim," he said. "I would only be able to appear right outside the castle walls, so if you can invite me in when we arrive, we'll be able to search together when given the chance."

Now, I'm sitting by the fire, too anxious to sleep and ready for the day as my thoughts have been racing all morning. Ezra stirs in the bed across from me, lightly rustling the sheets. I watch him by the window, stretched out as he becomes aware of his surroundings.

"Isa?" His voice is husky from sleep.

"Yes, I'm here." I stand, grabbing his shirt off the floor.

He yawns. "Did you sleep?"

"Some. You stole the bed though. I couldn't get comfortable," I say, trying not to look directly at him as I toss him his tunic. "We need to get going. We have a long journey today."

He catches it effortlessly and uses his hands to sit up, slightly leaning back on them. He blinks a few times, as if doing so will wake him up faster.

"You're in a rush," he quips, his tone playful as he pulls on the tunic.

"I'm just ready to be back." My words are sharper than I intended, but I can't help but find myself hyperaware of everything now that I *know* what the king's doing.

"Are you sure that's all it is?" He tilts his head, his tone teasing, but it's enough to make me glance at him with a small grin, hoping it's enough to convince him. He's really good at reading me.

"Yes," I say, walking to the wall that separates ours from Ren's and pounding on it. A loud grumble sounds from the other side, letting me know I successfully woke the brute.

"I heard about last night," Ezra says.

"What about it?" I ask, pouring water into two glasses from the porcelain vase off the table, then stretching my arm out to hand him one.

"How did it go?"

"I'm pretty sure Ren slept through it when he should have been with me. He appeared at the last minute and held him down for me," I say.

"Well, he left that out from what he told me last night. The bastard was sleeping?"

"I heard that!" Ren calls from the other side of the wall, leaving me to share a grin and a small chuckle with Ezra.

"I'm sure he did, and yes, but it's taken care of," I say. Though my smile falters slightly when I remember that someone is in the castle siphoning memories. It pulls at me to know that I don't recall any of my own from Aurelia, having had to relive them through Rydian.

Which I found out was my own ability to Vision Walk, something that I've had since childhood, apparently. It was a brief moment, but I was able to do it with Rydian coaching me through the process. I go back to what Rydian said just hours ago.

"You have the ability to wield your power. It's a small kernel, but it's there and it's growing. I can feel it." Rydian rubbed his jaw, lost in thought. He paced up and down the small room barely holding him in the space. A fire flares beneath the mantel.

"If your memories are being siphoned, it may have pulled your essence out with it, and if that's the case, I'm concerned. Why do they need to siphon at all? I understand why they would hide your memories but if they are using this on others, that's a concern," he said, talking out loud as he walked to the window and opened it.

"What do you mean growing? I can barely even leaf-whisper, and I can't talk to animals. The most I can do is form orbs," I said, crossing my arms. I leaned back, remembering the tingling sensation I get in my hands when I wield my magic.

"You're from our realm, so you'll have Aurelia's magic, not Elderheim's. Maybe you've just been trying to wield the wrong one. Try to practice the basic folk magic on your journey— elemental magic since all Fae can do that. Eventually, you should be able to Veil Walk and shift at some point, but that takes a lot of energy. Stick with the basics for now," he said, leaning against the window, when a large hawk landed on his shoulder, causing a gasp to slip from me.

"What is that?" I gaped.

The hawk was massive with a white chest and brown wings. Dark eyes landed on mine before he chirped, gently rubbing his beak on Rydian's hand. Rydian took a knuckle and gave him a small scratch.

"This is Ire, my messenger hawk," he said with a smile and handed him a scroll right before he flew from the window again.

My eyes followed him out before I shook my head and returned to the conversation. "That's easy for you to say. I have a hard enough time feeling my magic, but what is a Vision Walker?" I asked finally.

"Vision Walkers have the ability to see the memories or future outcomes of the person who touches their face with both hands. Though from what I know, it doesn't always happen if someone touches you. It's something you need to focus on in order to see them, like what I did with you last night." He stopped pacing. "You didn't happen to pick up a coin that night at the brothel, did you?"

A coin? A quizzical look grew on my face. What did that have to do with anything? But thinking back on the night, I did. The black one. My lucky coin, I called it and kept it with me.

"You mean this one?" I asked, pulling out the black coin with a diamond-shaped emblem etched on to the front.

"Yes, one just like that," he mumbled, grabbing it from my fingers. "Do you know what this is?"

"Of course I know what it is," I snapped, snatching it from his hands in annoyance. "It's money, a coin that I just happened to pick up. Why, is it yours? Don't you have enough money already, King?" My voice dripped with sarcasm.

He barked a laugh. "It's not mine, but it's a coin made from the Veil crafted by your Herb Weavers. There are only a few left, but it can help you enter the Veil or communicate through it if you are not familiar with our magic," he explained.

"What does that mean exactly?"

"As you know, Shadovar are the only ones capable of entering the Veil, so it means that Aetheri can enter the Veil or communicate through it if they have one of these coins. I brought them in preparation for you not having your abilities as a precaution. You should be able to push a thought out to the person you want to communicate with, like leaf-whispering."

"What?" I gasped.

"Isa?" Ezra is in front of me, touching my shoulder and pulling me from the memory.

"I'll gather the horses and lead them down to the inn," I get out. "My pack is ready to go. I'm just waiting on you two old bastards." I throw him a light chuckle and rush out the door, taking my bag with me.

Feet thud against the cobblestone as I walk down the path, my attention shifting to the auburn-haired boy across the street —Rydian. I scowl just as someone walks past, causing me to lose sight of him, and he vanishes through the Veil within seconds of her passing. *How convenient.*

Quietly entering the stables, I shut the doors and stride to Bjorn. I saddle him when I hear Rydian appear behind me in a *whoosh*.

"You're risking getting caught, you know," I mumble, throwing a look over my shoulder to find that he's shifted back into his usual form. Yet for some reason, my stomach flips at the sight of him.

Ignoring that, I turn and continue to saddle Bjorn. Rydian strides up beside me, helping with the saddle and grabbing the second buckle from underneath.

"I know, but Ivy has them distracted. She offered them breakfast and will keep them busy with conversation at the inn." He gives me a tight smile and then drops it, the conversation turning more serious. "Be careful."

I nod, leaning against Bjorn. "I'll be fine. Just worry about yourself."

"I know you want to trust them, but you can't mention anything until we know for sure who's siphoning your memories, and I don't want you getting hurt in the process. I've waited twenty years for this moment. I'd hate to lose you again after only just getting you."

I scoff. "You do not have me, let's make that perfectly clear."

He steps forward, the movement forcing my head back to meet his gaze. His eyes pierce me, searching my face with an intensity that makes him hard to ignore.

Regardless, my eyes narrow, and I take a cautious step back, the moment thrusting me back to the Painted Bird where we initially met. Did he know that was me? He seemed shocked at the Silver Lily when I came to kill him, so perhaps not.

He opens his mouth to say something before closing it again, looking off to the side. Then, as if sensing my discomfort, he steps back with a quiet sigh.

"I'm going to try to communicate with you through the Veil today, so try to keep the coin on you at all times if you want to respond," he says.

"I'll be prepared," I reply, turning to the other two horses to finish their saddles.

But before I can take another step, he grips my arm as if reluctant to let me go. He quietly studies me for a moment with an expression I can't quite name. Something that sends a shiver down my spine. My lips part in surprise, as it's something I don't expect to feel.

There's a quiet intensity in his stare that catches my breath, but all I can do is stand there, trying to ignore the heat beneath my skin and the skipping of my pulse. And he hasn't said a word.

Then he steps into the Veil, leaving me to blink at the space he was just occupying.

Whatever I felt a moment ago left nothing but a world of confusion as I finish up with the horses. Conflicted feelings continue to rise—I'm still unsure who to fully trust, regardless of the memories he shared with me.

Regardless of knowing that I'm the princess of Aurelia. All it does is urge me to search for the truth as one question bounces around in my head.

Who am I?

14

Once done gathering the horses, I tie them off at the front of the inn. Ezra and Ren open the door to the building, saying their goodbyes to the innkeeper, who I now know is Ivy in disguise. Giving them a happy, glowing smile, she waves them off, meeting my gaze with a firm nod before slowly shutting the door.

"I see you did something useful for once," Ren quips as he strides up to pat Myst, his smirk more menacing than it is friendly.

Of all the males in the Brotherhood King Elion could send, it's him. My temper has gotten the best of me recently, the weight of the current events bearing down, so I try not let him get under my skin. Yet I find myself snapping at him.

"Why do you do that?" The sharp words leave my lips before I can stop them. I don't know what it is about Ren that makes me snap, my calm facade shattering with only a few words.

He halts mid-stride, scarred brow lifting in confusion. "Do what?"

"Are you so bored that you have to constantly undermine people to make yourself feel better? Or is there a deeper reason you're such an ass?" I take a step toward him, eyes narrowing as my frustration bubbles over. "You know, I think you do it so you don't have to face how sad and lonely you are, like a shield. A protective barrier to hide who you truly are, and it comes out in snide remarks," I mutter, now standing a foot away. I'm not sure why I say it, but I can't stop myself. "Am I right, brute?"

His smirk falters for a moment, eyeing me, the cocky mask slipping just enough to reveal that I've hit my mark. It's rare to catch him off guard, but he tears his gaze away from me and places his hands in his pockets. He takes a deep breath, letting out a steady exhale, almost like he's centering himself.

I watch as he carefully pieces his composure back together, smoothing his face out like a mask slipping into place. Still, I catch the tight clench of his jaw, the only indication that I've struck a nerve.

Then he scoffs with a shake of his head, giving me one last glance before turning his attention back to Myst, mounting her without another word.

After last night, I'm not quite sure where my loyalties lie at the moment. I want to do well for the king—be who he created me to be. But after seeing Rydian's memories, I can't help but question the king I serve.

I served King Elion all those years like he could do no wrong. Perhaps deep down, I knew something was going on and I chose to overlook it. It's easier to justify killing someone when you choose to remain hidden from the truth.

"Are you ladies finally ready to go?" I tease.

"You're not going to eat?" Ezra asks from beside Freya, hazel eyes shimmering in the golden morning light.

"I already ate. I want to arrive in Dryborn this afternoon." The lie rolls off my tongue. I'm desperate to search for answers within the castle of Alvonia.

Grabbing the pommel, I swing my leg over Bjorn. Rydian's young gaze catches mine from across the road, and then he nods at me. Silent understanding passes between us, even if I still feel as though I'm betraying my brethren. As though I'm being pulled in two directions—two lives.

After I give Bjorn a gentle nudge, we take off at a gallop as Sylvanor fades behind us. Rough wind whips at my face, the shops passing by in a blur as he leads me through the heart of the town.

I begin to wonder how Rydian keeps up with the speed of our horses, figuring it has to do with Veil Walking. He told me it was similar to wearing a cloak—hidden with the ability to jump from one place to another if he wished. The Veil's time is different from that of the realm, allowing you to walk alongside someone unseen, making them the best spies.

I close my eyes, inhaling the cold, brisk air straight into my lungs. My cloak dances behind me as Bjorn picks up speed, shooting us further into the valley.

After a few hours of pushing the horses, we finally slow our pace to a steady walk on the mountainside, overlooking the hills and rocky terrain. What was sunny earlier is now a darkened sky, the air coated in a soft mist as water dews on the shoulders of my cloak. High into the altitude, Dryborn comes into view, but we're still hours away from arriving.

Something brushes against the edges of my mind, similarly to when I experienced Rydian's memories. This time, it catches me off guard, as it's sharp and jolting, like ice across my forehead. As if someone is pushing my head into a frozen river.

"I really wish I had a horse right now," Rydian groans, appearing in the depths of my mind. A gasp slips from my lips at the sudden intrusion, causing Ezra to turn around with pinched brows.

"A branch hit me," I say with a small smile. He mindlessly faces forward again, Ren a couple hundred feet ahead.

Just as Ezra faces forward, my eyes narrow, darting them across the valley. Searching for anything to tell me where

Rydian is, only to come up empty. A huff of frustration leaves me.

I attempt to concentrate, palming the black coin he told me to keep as it warms in my grasp. Its energy spikes.

"Try feeling my presence and then push your thoughts out," he explains, which just annoys me even further.

I search my mind for what I felt the previous night when a tingling sensation forms between my eyes—warm and inviting, yet unfamiliar. This must be the Veil. I grasp on to the feeling, using my energy to push the thought his way.

"Your timing is admirable," I retort, sending it out with as much sarcasm as I can muster. *"I was almost caught."*

Rydian's presence flickers with amusement, a faint echo of laughter brushing the edges of my mind. Despite myself, a smirk tugs free, having figured out how to talk in the Veil. It almost feels as if I'm talking to myself.

"Consider it as motivation to control your noises," he says.

My teeth grind. *"Where are you anyway?"*

"I'm right beside you."

A faint touch brushes against my knee, down the length of my calf, and I swat him away, making contact with what I think could be his hand. A loud smack hitting the air forces Ezra to pivot around, pinching his brows again.

"Bugs," I explain, giving him a tight smile. *"Stop doing that!"*

Even though I can't see him, Rydian can see my annoyed expression flickering across my face as I glance down. I find myself wondering if he haunts people for entertainment like a spirit of the woods.

His laughter echoes across my mind, and I realize then that he's toying with me. The king of Aurelia has untimely humor, especially with Ren and Ezra nearby.

"Keep talking like that and I'll start to think that you like me," he teases.

I ignore him as I'm enjoying the ride on Bjorn, listening to the sounds of the horses trudging down the dirt path. A few silent minutes go by when the Ashen River comes into view, a mile ahead where the road meets the water's edge. Mountains reflect off the surface, water bright and clear, even from a distance.

"*Move over,*" Rydian says.

"*What?*" My eyes narrow, glancing down.

"*Let me on your saddle. Just slow down for a second and I'll slide in behind you,*" he grumbles, though amusement coats his tone, and my eyes widen with disbelief.

"*Are you joking?*" I let out a breath.

"*Do I sound like I'm joking?*"

"*I'm not sharing a horse with you—you won't fit,*" I stutter, but just as I'm about to send Bjorn into a trot, Rydian slides in behind me.

Bjorn shuffles at the weight a little, then continues walking, as if nothing happened. A gasp threatens to escape me when Rydian slaps his hand over my mouth, silencing me in seconds.

"Are you this noisy with lovers?" he whispers low in my ear, leaving me to think about that night at the brothel.

Despite myself, blood pounds in my ears, coating my face a deep shade of red as desire shoots through my veins. He slowly releases my mouth from his hold.

"You're going to get us caught," I whisper, but he quietly chuckles, the sound low and devious. The Ashen River fills the air—rushing water wild against the current. The same river that runs through the Twin Valley.

"The only thing that'll get us caught is your breathing. You're incredibly loud," he mutters, certainly too low for Ezra to hear now that the river fills the air.

Rydian is huge—too large to be sharing a saddle—and has squashed me forward, pushing my legs wider in a way that's pressing against a certain body part of mine. I'm too afraid to lean into him, feeling the hardness of his chest behind me as I sit perfectly between his legs.

My face flushes at his hands resting on my hips. Even though I can't see him, I can definitely feel him, sending shivers of need across my legs. The sound of him sniffing the air behind me has me stifling a groan.

"Are you… aroused?" he asks as if he's shocked.

"No. Stop it. You're distracting me," I frantically whisper, trying to hide what seems to be my body's betrayal, yet here I am, practically panting. My lip pulls between my teeth to refrain from saying anything else when he shifts behind me.

He chuckles. *"Are you that depraved?"*

Yes, I want to say but keep the thought to myself. In need of a distraction, my mind frantically drifts to the memories he shared with me last night—the former king of Aurelia being my father.

"How did you know my father?" I ask quickly, thankful for the sounds of the mountain water in the distance. I'm also itching to learn more about the former king across the continent I never knew.

"I was taken in at a young age by King Malvain, your grandfather. My father was his second-in-command when he…" He trails off, sighing. *"Let's just say something happened, and King Malvain felt an obligation to take me in. I was raised alongside Andre when I was only eleven. I became your father's second-in-command shortly after he took the throne."*

"Oh," I say. *"How old are you?"*

"Has anyone ever told you that it's rude to ask a Fae that?" he asks, and I can almost sense his teasing grin. *"I'm 229."*

"So you're old."

"I'm not old." He chuckles, low and throaty. A grin of my own tugs at the corners of my mouth. *"In human years, I would be somewhere between twenty-eight and thirty. As you know, the average lifespan of the Fae is around 750 years old."*

Knowing that I'm Shadovar, I realize that I'll be aging just as slowly. Having previously thought I was a halfling, I already came to terms that I had a much shorter life span by more than half.

Still long, just not almost a millennium long.

Ezra and Ren are spread a little more than hundred feet ahead of me in a single file line, making it almost impossible for them to hear at this distance. Even though Fae have heightened hearing, the stream we're riding beside makes it more difficult to hone in on.

Rydian brushes my braid off my shoulder, catching a few damp strands between his fingers as if inspecting them. Fingers lightly graze my neck where my birthmark sits.

I stiffen. Perhaps he didn't see the auburn birthmark that blends within my dark strands. Though I know it shouldn't matter, I'm so used to hiding it for fear of King Elion that it frightens me to think anyone besides Ezra might know it's there.

Then my skin heats as I realize how his fingers linger on my skin, and before I can think, I nervously shift my hips—rubbing against him. *Gods, why did I do that?*

We both freeze, breaths halting in our throats as we become aware of how little space sits between us. All sense of teasing is tossed aside, and for a moment, neither of us says a word as we ride further along the path.

The brothel pushes its way to the front of my mind despite my best effort. I may not fully trust him yet, but I find myself drawn to him, similarly to how shadows chase the light.

I can't see him, but I pivot as if I could. His breath grazes my temple, lips hovering near the side of my face. At this point, I really wish I could view his expression.

"Are you thinking about the brothel?" He grumbles the thought, then takes a deep breath, his chest sharply rising against my back as if at war with himself.

Heat sears my face because I am thinking about it—about how I planned on going back. To explore the feel of him...

"Are you?" I ask breathlessly, facing forward and ignoring the filthy thought that just plagued me.

"Do you want the answer to that?" he asks, moving his hand so that it rests on my hip again, awfully close to the edge of my pants. *"You know, I never got to thank you..."*

"For what?" My lips part, sucking in a sharp breath.

His fingers graze the rim of my pants, not fully touching me but almost... teasing. As if he's letting me know where his own thoughts currently linger. The same as mine, apparently.

"For not running... for trusting me."

"I don't trust you."

He hums, words slow and delicate. *"Maybe not yet... but I'd still like to thank you."*

His fingers brush my bare hip, leaving me panting as I know just how he plans on thanking me. I shouldn't want it, but I find myself eager to have his skin on mine, despite knowing that Ezra and Ren ride only a hundred feet ahead. The thought might be a little insane, but there's a sudden thrill in trying not to get caught.

"Would you like me to show you how grateful I am?" Rydian asks, my breath catching.

"It wouldn't mean anything," I say to him but mostly to myself because it wouldn't. It would be no different than going to a brothel. No emotions, just... pleasure. That's all it is.

"Of course not..." He trails off, leaning forward just as I feel the heat of him seeping into my cloak. *"This is just me showing you my gratitude."* His fingers ghost the edge of my pant line—a question—leaving me to focus on remaining quiet as I bite my lip, my blood heating in anticipation.

His chest heaves. *"And I'm very grateful—"*

"Isa!" Ezra calls from ahead, pivoting toward me, leaving Rydian to quickly pull his hand away.

My stomach drops at the sound of Ezra's voice, adrenaline shooting through me as I focus my attention on the path ahead. *Oh gods, did he see me?*

"What?" I call out, probably a little too quickly.

Shame washes over me, as I was about to let the king of Aurelia touch me and I was… enjoying it. Gods, something is seriously wrong with me.

Since it's clear Ezra wants to talk, I compose myself before riding to meet him near the water's edge. Rydian's tightly tucked behind me, my pulse climbing at the sudden realization.

"Slow your breathing. He can't see me," Rydian says, almost annoyed, leaving me to grind my teeth.

Ezra throws me a sideways glance when I approach. "We're doing well on time today. We should be arriving in Dryborn shortly. Ren and I wanted to keep going for a while."

"Keep going? I thought we were stopping in Dryborn?" I ask.

If we push through, the only thing in between Dryborn and Alvonia is the Twin Valley.

"We were, but I think we'd be able to camp right before we get to the Twin Valley so we don't get stuck in it tomorrow," he says, scratching his shoulder.

"Are you sure? What about the horses?"

"We talked with them already. They're okay to push through for a while." He chuckles, handing me a canteen.

Well, there goes that thought.

I sip, nodding. "Okay. We'll just camp outside the valley and wash up in the stream." Reaching over, I hand him the canteen.

I reluctantly agree, if only to keep him from becoming suspicious of me questioning our stops, despite knowing that Rydian will need to step out of the Veil and rest. I slow Bjorn, letting the distance stretch between us and the others.

"Ivy can still swap with me when we pass through. She'll just follow you out while I stay behind," he says, yet I can't help but feel disappointed.

But with that comes guilt.

Guilt for wanting more of his touch and enjoying the press of his body against mine, even though I know I shouldn't. Then thoughts of my missing mother come flooding back. I know that pretty soon, I'll be searching for answers inside the walls of Castle Alvonia.

Perhaps his touch was my own personal distraction to this newfound responsibility as a princess of Aurelia.

Something I'm not sure an assassin is worthy of.

My thoughts whirl, leaving the rest of our travels to be ridden in silence with no other touch toward me along the way.

15

We arrive in Dryborn a couple hours later, riding at a slow pace. Rydian hops off a mile from town, wanting to walk. He'll step out of the Veil, waiting until we're far enough so that he'll remain unnoticed, and Ivy will follow us out.

But Dryborn looks just as it sounds.

There's no charm to it like Alvonia or Sylvanor. Just a town that's simply caught in the middle of two beautiful locations, stranded on the flattest side of the mountain.

Finishing off a peach from my pack, I wipe my mouth, spotting Ren stretching his arms in the distance as we ride down the middle of the road. A small grin tugs at my lips as a glorious thought crosses my mind, knowing I'm about to ruin his brief moment of peace.

Chucking the peach, Ren's pained grunt cuts through the air, hitting him so hard on the back of the head that it throws him forward. Enough to know that it must hurt.

He whirls around, directing his narrowed eyes at me when I catch his gaze, throwing him a small shrug. I casually point to Ezra—completely oblivious to what just happened.

Ren curses at Ezra, rubbing the back of his head.

"What?" Ezra furrows his brows, throwing me a glance over his shoulder. I chuckle and ride up to his side just as we make it past the town, taking all of five minutes to ride through it.

"What's the plan for food tonight? We're getting low on what we brought with us," I say, needing something more substantial than fruit as we're getting low on our supply.

"I'll hunt. You and Ren can start a fire and tend to the horses. We'll set up camp in about an hour before we enter the Twin Valley," he says.

"I just pegged him with a peach, and now you're pairing him with me?" I ask.

Ezra swivels toward me with a glare as if realizing that Ren's outburst was because of me, then smirks a little. Teasing. "You can handle him. Just keep the hatred alive."

"Fine, but if you come back to a dead brute, that's on you."

A cool breeze passes through, the weather already better than when we came in a few days ago. Autumn is just around the corner with how quickly it gets cold in the evening.

"Hi, Isa," Ivy says, brushing the edges of my mind—softer and less invading than Rydian.

"How was your trip?" I ask.

"It was great. King Rydian has settled himself at one of the inns. I'll follow you to the campsite and join Ezra as he hunts in case he sends word back to the king."

"Thanks," I say.

I know she feels like she needs to track Ezra after telling them he was placed in charge of this mission. She quickly leaves me to my thoughts as we continue down the trail in search of our stopping point.

Another hour passes when we finally find a place to camp, just outside the Twin Valley. I slide off Bjorn, stretching my legs.

Aching from the long trip, I groan in relief and turn to scratch him behind the ear. He lets out a low chuff—a happy sound. Ezra grabs his bow off Freya, handing her to Ren after a moment.

"I'm going to start the hunt since we only have a few hours left of daylight," Ezra says, quickly making his departure between the trees, saying nothing more.

"I won't see you for a while, so reach out if you need me. You should be able to communicate even if I am a few miles out," Ivy says.

After unbuckling Bjorn's saddle from underneath, I place it on a nearby tree, escorting him to the field where the stream meets the grass. Freya and Myst are released shortly after.

Ren stops beside me while I watch the horses graze the field, listening to the grass sway in the light breeze. The forest fills my senses, a mix of cedar and crisp water.

"Bjorn says he appreciates the apples you give him," Ren says after a moment, his words barely brushing the air as if it's the most normal thing to say.

I blink, sliding my eyes to him. "He said that?"

Amusement flits across his face before he masks it, fighting a small grin. Then he clears his throat. "Unfortunately."

Is he joking with me, or did Bjorn actually say that? I attempt to push his shoulder at the insult when he catches my wrist, leaving me to glower at him with a small grin on my face. A challenge.

His gray eyes meet mine as he studies my face—only a few quiet seconds—before releasing me without another word. He just... lets me go. I stand frozen, watching him stride back to the campsite. His steps are soft but solid across the ground, broad shoulders swaying with each step.

The way he looked at me wasn't like before—it was different. Perhaps he's sick of arguing. Regardless, I'm exhausted from being on guard around him—holding my tongue more often than not. Maybe snapping at him in Sylvanor was what needed to happen between us.

After the horses are released, I stride across the forest in search of kindling, knowing the temperature will drop enough to chill our bones. My eyes graze the sky as the sun begins to set —an hour before setting completely behind the west side of the valley.

Dropping the wood to the ground, I notice that Ren has rounded up large boulders, placing them in a circle around the fire that's not yet lit. Waiting on the sunset, I suppose.

"This should last us the night." I wipe the sweat off my temple. "Has Ezra come back yet?"

"Not yet," he grumbles quietly. "He should be back soon. I saw some rabbits out in the field earlier."

The fire is lit with a quick flick of his wrist, and we sit in silence. It crackles—sharp pops and hisses as we settle in. Burning wood fills the area in a smoky haze, but I find it oddly comforting.

There's something about being in the woods late at night, sitting around a large fire, that brings me peace. I dance a couple of orbs across my fingertips, hands tingling as they light up my face.

Ren leans forward on his knees, a stone dagger firm in his grip as he carves into a block of wood. A gentle reminder that he couldn't be the Siphon since he's a Stone Shaper. He's quite skilled at creating his own weapons, never leaving without the knives he's created. They perfectly fit into his palm as he scrapes the sharp edge against the softness of the wood.

"What are you carving?" I ask, wondering why I even bother in the first place. He looks up, then lowers his brows, returning to his task, as if trying to ignore me.

"Myst," he mumbles after a few breaths. I continue to watch in silence for a few minutes as he makes the intricate slices, shavings falling to the ground. "We used to be friendly with each other, you know," he says.

A flicker of surprise crosses my face, orbs fluttering out over his mumbled words. Perhaps that's why he looked at me the way he did in the field.

Then I scoff, recalling my life and how we were raised. Nothing but weapons for King Elion—we were anything but friendly.

"We've never been friendly. You've always acted like I was a giant inconvenience to be around," I say with a scowl.

His eyes flick up with a confusing pinch to his brows, like he doesn't believe that. At any other point in my life, I might have liked him for his quick wit, but Ren's loyalty to the crown leaves me to believe I couldn't trust him. Even if I wanted to.

Yet I find myself hesitating on the thought, if only for a moment. After discovering my memories have been siphoned over the last few years, it forces me to question everything now. And I hate that.

I quickly recall Rydian's memories of how I called for Ren at the orphanage—like we were familiar. Perhaps we were at some point, and I just don't remember. That thought alone is infuriating.

After walking to grab Bjorn's saddle, I place it near the fire, unpacking my quilt. I'm careful not to say anything outright as I prod for more information, wanting to see if he lets anything slip.

"Friendly or friends?" I ask finally, airing out my quilt. "You've hated me from the moment we started to train. Just because you were forced to train me doesn't mean you know me."

He glances up, catching my gaze as the fire flicks between us, then glances to the right, watching the stream ahead. Shadows dance across his face as the sun sets behind the mountain, casting dark shadows amongst the forest.

I sit, sip from my canteen, and think of what words to say next as the orbs dance on my fingertips again.

"You're moody," he says into his carving—an attempt at a subject change. *Interesting.*

"Going back to the castle makes me moody... I feel like something is missing." I mutter the words even though it's risky, like I can't help myself. "You know, I used to imagine my life in a small town when I was younger. A place where I left all of this behind and just lived somewhere quiet. Maybe in a forest somewhere." Yet what I say is true.

I used to lie awake at night, dreaming of a small cabin in the woods to call my own. A place of escape where I could be free of the king's obligation, only killing out of necessity. And although I'm great at becoming a weapon, I wish my life had more meaning. Orbs play on my fingertips, and I roll them from finger to finger when my wrist begins to ache.

A groan of frustration leaves me as I thumb the inside of my wrist, the orbs fluttering out with the movement.

Ren straightens as if uncomfortable, adjusting his feet before crossing them at the ankles. Perhaps I shouldn't have said anything. He cautiously looks over his shoulder, then goes back to carving, ignoring me completely.

After another few minutes of silence, I find myself near the stream, tossing in rocks to pass the time. The stars stare back at me when movement to the right catches my attention, and I find Ren walking the horses back to the campsite. I quietly follow, overhearing his mumbled words to Bjorn as he grips the reins.

"No... I don't know," Ren says quietly against the wind, barely audible even for my ears. "Can't interfere, you know that... maybe one day... no, I don't wear it... how do you know that?"

My brows pinch in confusion just as a twig snaps beneath my boot, forcing me to freeze. Ren whips his head around, eyeing me from a few feet away before he huffs in frustration, then walks toward the fire. He quickly ties them off, sitting at the boulder he was occupying a few minutes ago while I stand across from him.

A sudden unease washes over me. Questions rest on the tip of my tongue. I'm curious what his conversation with Bjorn was about when leaves rustle behind him.

Within a second, I'm palming the dagger that was secured to my thigh when Ezra enters from the shadows, holding three rabbits by their back feet. Blood coats their faces, the only evidence of a quick kill.

My shoulders relax when Ivy gently grazes my mind but doesn't speak for the remainder of the night. We spend the rest of the evening preparing our meal, making quiet conversation. Ren throws me a few questionable glances throughout the night, but I ignore them, passing them off as curiosity about our conversation from earlier.

Now I turn over, resting my head on Bjorn's saddle with the quilt on my lap, thinking back on our previous conversation. I get the feeling that I'm missing vital information if Ren might have liked me at one point.

My thumb rubs the inside of my wrist as it begins to ache again, whirling thoughts preventing me from sleep. Stars shine down at me through the swaying branches, the light breeze brushing my cheeks. I've come to the conclusion that I'm missing more memories than we initially suspected.

And I'm determined to get them back.

16

———

After rising this morning, we quickly loaded up the horses and set off for Alvonia. Rydian walks—or travels the Veil—the rest of the way. I'm thankful for the reprieve, leaving me to sit with everything that's happened over the last few days as my trust wavers between realms.

Bjorn continues his leisurely pace now that we're only a few miles outside the city, the ride going by quickly. Ren and Ezra remain a few miles behind me, having slowed after a while.

There's currently too much going on in my head, happening at a pace I can't keep up with. My chest tightens as my thoughts settle on what's been revealed, a sense of overwhelm quick to follow. Both realms seem to pull me in, and I hate the fact that I feel at odds with it—that I don't know what direction to go in.

My eyes close on an inhale, and I breathe in the crisp mountain air. Yet I find myself stuck on *my* memories.

Or the ones I don't have, at least.

What relationships do I have that are real? What hasn't been stolen from me? And who can I trust? It's becoming harder to see past the blurred lines.

A sinking feeling settles in my stomach, something close to

144

the loss of air in my lungs. As if I'm drowning in a depthless lake with no bottom in sight and no way to push up. Especially now with the thought of me being a princess to a realm I know nothing of. That thought alone causes a shudder to run through me.

Finally riding into Alvonia, we're only a few minutes from the castle when Ezra and Ren ride up on either side of me. The sun shines bright as midday settles across the mountains, leaving us to shrug off our cloaks. Ezra lays it across his lap, rolling his sleeves up his well-muscled forearms.

"The king sent a message," Ren says. "He wants us to meet in the throne room after our arrival to update him on the mission as soon as we get in."

"And he sent word to *you?*" My brows knit.

If he did, it would be by a leaf message, and I didn't notice it. Realizing this turns my stomach to stone. It's hard to believe the king would communicate through Ren and not through the original person sent to kill our target—me. Or even Ezra since he was placed in command.

Ren was only supposed to accompany us to stay updated on the mission, and the fact that he's in communication with the king at all raises my suspicion. Realization prickles my skin— Ivy was keeping an eye on the wrong person for messages. I glance at him to my right, eyes narrowing.

"Does that bother you?" Ren smirks, resting his forearm on the pommel of his saddle.

"Why would that bother me?" I purr, fluttering my lashes with a smirk—cold sarcasm.

He chuckles to himself. Black hair ruffles in the breeze as he scans the road in front of us, watching a few mothers cross the street with their children being tugged behind them. The wind carries his scent of cedar and leather, forcing my nose to scrunch. Why does he smell good?

"Oh, I don't know. You seem to have this thought about

yourself that you're more important than you are," he mocks, giving me a noticeable once-over with a disgusted sneer on his face.

A tight smile lines my mouth as I ignore him, too exhausted to care. I blink and give him a hardened, flat stare.

"We need to stop." Rydian appears in my mind, but I don't startle this time. The tingle between my eyes has begun to feel normal. *"We need to meet up with Ivy at the Painted Bird and create a plan for the next few days."*

"No. I'm not stopping, and we already have a plan. I'll see you in a few days," I say, gripping the Veil coin.

A low growl reverberates across my mind. Hearing him growl in frustration would have normally sent a chill down my spine but right now, I don't really care.

The outskirts of Alvonia come into view, oak trees and the castle alive in the distance. Hitting the gravel path at a quick pace with a kick from my boot, I feel Rydian's connection fade, realizing that he must have not followed me out of the city. I'm slightly reprieved, hoping he decides to use the Painted Bird for himself—let off some steam.

The thought immediately sends an unwelcome pang through my chest. I clench my fists at the thought of him enjoying someone else's company. The mere idea of him touching someone has me biting my tongue.

It's none of my business, I remind myself, forcing my hands to loosen on the reins. *It's not like I care. Not really.*

We travel at a quick canter, eager to arrive at the castle, but I can't help the way my stomach tightens in knots at the thought of our upcoming approach.

Being at the castle with King Elion sets me on edge. If they were to find out that I know something is going on behind closed doors, they would either kill me or take my memories again.

But I still have my doubts.

It's something I need to see for myself to believe, but at this moment, I don't think the king will kill me. Not if he's spent his time wiping my memories. I must be an important part of his revenge against Aurelia if he's using me to kill off the Shadovar.

We finally slow the horses at the edge of the castle, making our way inside the gates as we ride further toward the throne room.

A headache forms, and I rub my temples, my wrist aching with the movement. My emotions seemed to have caused my body to throw itself into a turmoil, leaving me to take a deep breath. I soothe the inside of my wrist, hoping to ease the pain, but I catch Ren staring at me.

"What?" I say a little too harshly. He quickly flicks his gaze away, not saying a word as he trots ahead on the path. Wise choice.

Finally arriving outside the throne room, I dismount, following Ezra and Ren inside. The musk from the stone corridor fills my nose as we enter, reminding me of a damp cave. Light streams in from the windows, the massive floor shining in beams from the afternoon sun.

We arrive just below the dais where King Elion sits, Theron to his right. The king's white hair is slicked back, arms resting on either side of him as he strokes the throne. He doesn't look angry, but he doesn't look happy either. Almost annoyed.

"Your Majesty," we say, bowing in unison.

"Isa, what's the update?" he questions, amber eyes swiveling to me, and my stomach dips.

"We tracked our target to Sylvanor and quickly found him on the third night from a local lead. He was just outside of the town when Ren showed up and helped me finish the job. It was swift," I say, dipping my chin.

Ren's eyes flare as he glances my way as if he can't believe I acknowledged his presence that night. But I need the king to know that I wasn't alone, as long as Ren keeps to himself about what he thinks went on at the Silver Lily and Helga's son.

I don't think the king cares about how I finished the job, but if he thinks fraternizing was the reason I failed my mission, he may think otherwise. And I can't risk it.

With my face forward, I mask my features—a king's assassin trying to finish her mission. That's all.

"How did you dispose of him?" Elion asks.

"I buried him myself, just outside of Sylvanor, so we were not searched for after," I say.

"Ren, is this true?" he asks, stroking his beard.

"Yes, Your Majesty," Ren says.

"Where was Ezra during this?" Elion shifts his attention to Ezra, who nervously shuffles his feet.

"I was following a trail when the target was found. Ren beat me to the scene," Ezra explains.

The king grunts his understanding, looking out one of the windows before facing us again. A silent moment passes as he holds our gazes, as if he's thinking.

"Ren can clearly follow through on missions nicely," Elion says finally.

I refrain from furrowing my brows, stilling my features into neutrality, but my eyes flick to Ren.

Elion continues, "With this mission now complete, I'm placing Ren as captain of the Veiled Brotherhood. I need someone to give out targets for me as I am becoming quite busy with other... pressing matters. Matters that require my full attention, and with Ren being one of our most skilled and knowledgeable in the Brotherhood, he's the best fit for the job. Ren will ensure that the Brotherhood remains swift and silent in their duties, and I expect no less than absolute obedience in his command. Any who question him, question me."

Is this a joke? Most skilled? Now I *know* it's a joke.

With a brief glance at the king, I half expect him to huff a laugh at his own words. But it doesn't come, and I realize that he's serious, because he's always serious.

Captain of the Veiled Brotherhood?

Ren bows at the waist to King Elion, acknowledging his new position with a smug half smile on his face. Then he makes eye contact with me. A chill scurries down my spine at the look in his eyes, something unspoken shining beneath them.

Then my stomach sinks at the realization that finding my mother and the Siphon just became much harder.

After exiting the throne room with more questions, I'm striding back to my chambers, itching to bathe and sleep. Not getting any rest the last few days is finally catching up to me, deciding to process Ren becoming captain after I do that. I'll deal with it tomorrow.

I turn the corner to my arched entryway, running into what feels like an invisible brick wall.

"Fates!" I rub my face, frantically soothing the pain. Rydian must be patiently waiting for my return in the middle of the doorway. How does he know where my chambers are?

Just then, he steps out of the Veil right in front of me and blocks the only entrance to my stairs. In a panic, I glance over my shoulder, ensuring no one has spotted him right outside the castle walls.

"What are you doing? I think you broke my nose."

"Invite me in so we can start our search in the castle," he says.

I sigh, barely containing my exasperation as I step around him. His large frame fills the entryway, the space feeling smaller. He slowly turns to follow my movement, blue eyes tracking me like a predator. I'm already positioning myself with my back to the doorway, taking one large step inside the stairwell.

A thin smile spreads across my face.

"Invite you in?" My voice feigns sincerity. "Not yet."

My grin widens at the thought of him slamming into the barrier, briefly lifting my mood. I lean back against the stone banister, fully aware that he can't take another step closer.

"Good luck with the invite. I'll be in my room, bathing and sleeping—*alone*," I pointedly add, letting the word linger between us as I tilt my head to the side, dropping my voice. "We already have a plan. Let's meet in Alvonia in a few days. I'll come find you. How does that sound?" My tone is light, but my patience is thinning as my exhaustion settles in.

All I want is a few hours to myself—away from him and his demands. His presence gets under my skin, and my feelings toward him confuse me, especially with how my body responds. Something I'm not sure I want at the moment.

"Isa." His voice drops, and I catch the way his eyes narrow, dark and smoldering. I pull out the Veil coin and toss it to him, knowing that if I'm caught with one, someone is bound to ask questions. He catches it mid-air.

For a moment, his expression darkens, a flicker of frustration crossing his features as he clenches his jaw. If he weren't cut off at the entrance, I'm certain he would've crossed the space in a heartbeat.

Without waiting for a response, I stride up the stairs, taking the steps two at a time. His smoldering gaze burns into my back the whole way up, but I let him stew.

I need a bath, and more importantly, I need space.

17

"Isa, I know you can hear me. It's been a week," Rydian says in my head.

It's been more than a few days, and I had every intention of meeting with him, but for a reason I can't explain, I felt the need to stay put. I didn't want to raise suspicion for leaving the castle, and the extra space away from him hasn't hurt.

But I'm starting to really hate the fact that I tossed him the Veil coin, losing my only way of communicating. Not because I want to talk to him, but because I can't talk back. He's been in my head every single day since I arrived, and with my magic still coming in, I haven't quite figured out how to attach myself to the Veil just yet.

I can feel it. I just can't quite grasp it.

As for my other capabilities, I've successfully been able to light a fire and use my elemental magic. But why is it coming in now and not before?

"Isa," Rydian croons, exaggerating my name, and it takes everything in me not to scream. *Does he ever shut up?*

The constant badgering is starting to get to me and is impossible to ignore. It's not just his words, but the way his voice has started to echo in my head, overlapping my own thoughts until I can barely tell where his end and mine begin.

All week it's been, *"Ivy is headed back to Aurelia to take over for a while,"* or *"I know you miss me,"* followed by the ever persistent, *"Have you found anything yet?"* over and over again.

But I *haven't* found anything, and that's been annoying. Other than eavesdropping on a few guards with nothing substantial. Turns out, guards know just as much as I do, which is pretty close to nothing.

I clench my jaw, trying my best to focus on the task at hand, but his voice continues to loop back through as I take the steps in the commons two at a time. *It's like having someone constantly in your ear and you can't mute it.*

I stand outside Ezra's door and bang on it. It's around five in the morning, and we planned on going out to hunt today to do something. Hunting is not my favorite activity, but idle hands make me stir crazy because neither of us has had a mission since we've been back. At first I thought it was King Elion's doing, allowing us to rest, but that doesn't sound like something he'd do.

"I'll be out in a minute!" Ezra calls out from behind the door, groggy from sleep.

I step back and lean against the stone wall behind me when a door creaks open at the end of the hall. Ren halts, eyeing me down the corridor before he takes slow, deliberate steps toward me, boots echoing off the stone.

"What are you doing?" he asks, tone sharp.

I flick my eyes to Ezra's door, nodding toward it. "Waiting on Ezra to hunt. You?"

"Giving out orders," he grumbles, and I spot the white envelopes in his hand with the king's seal. So missions *are* happening. That's when I remember that Ren is captain, which I find odd, given we've never had a captain before.

My eyes narrow. "Why are you captain and not one of the others?" I ask, genuinely curious.

Because *why not* one of the others? What makes Ren so special that he was picked out of everyone here? I personally thought the king forgot about him.

"Are you questioning the king?" he says, crossing his arms. "You must have been too busy with yourself to notice me doing everything right."

I scoff, muttering under my breath, "I wouldn't count that as a good thing. If you're doing everything right in the eyes of the king, then you probably play just as dirty as he does."

Ren's eyes narrow slightly, and then he very, very slowly shakes his head in a subtle warning, eyes flicking across the hall just as Ezra opens the door. Ezra's hair is mostly dry other than a few damp strands at the top of his head, an indication of bathing.

"Stay out of my way," Ren growls at me, the sudden tone switch catching me by surprise. He quickly nods to Ezra, acknowledging him as he walks past, throwing me one last glance over his shoulder before descending the stairs.

"Gods, he really hates you. Are you ready?" Ezra chuckles, clasping his thick cloak at his collarbone.

In the last week, the weather has taken a substantial turn, giving us our first snow in the realm. The temperature has continued to drop more and more as the week has gone on.

"Yes, please," I groan, already itching to leave the walls of the castle and get away from Ren.

***

"Do you want to cook these now or at the castle?" I ask.

The snow lightly crunches beneath our boots on the walk back, still ten minutes from arriving. The snow made our hunt more difficult than usual given the noise, but we managed to catch three rabbits with our bows. Ezra looks around, scanning our surroundings before giving me a slight nod. We like to hunt in the woods behind the castle, still far enough away from the walls to light a fire.

"I can get a fire going. The biscuits we ate this morning weren't enough." He chuckles, tossing our catch to the ground with a wet smack. "Let's gather some wood."

After gathering some branches, we've successfully created a small fire, just enough for us to cook and eat while sitting on a couple of large logs. Sparks float in the air. I'm still too wary to use my elemental magic around Ezra for fear of him looking into it.

"Do you know why Ren was placed as captain?" I ask, tossing the remainder of the carcass on the ground.

He shakes his head, shoving a chunk of meat into his mouth. "No, I don't. I can see why the king wants him as captain though —he's ruthless. I've been with him on a couple of missions, and if you're a threat to him or the mission, he'll take you down without hesitating. I think King Elion loves that."

"You think that's enough to be a captain?" I huff.

He flicks his gaze to me, then squints. "Are you jealous of Ren?" Ezra asks, amusement flickering behind his warm eyes.

"What?" I scoff, rolling my eyes. "Why would I be jealous of Ren?"

Ezra chuckles, shaking his head while he grasps his meal, hands between his knees, the juicy meat dripping near his boots. "I wouldn't look into it too much or King Elion will look at it as questioning his decision. I think he's a good choice though. Don't take it personally."

I groan, sitting up. "Why would I take it personally?"

"Because you're Isa, and you always take it personally." I throw a bone at him with a grunt, and he laughs, dodging it. "What? You do! You probably see it as you not being good enough for the position, which you are, but Ren has more experience. He's a better fit. Plus I don't think you'd want that responsibility anyway."

"You're right. I don't." I huff and slump back. I've always known that Ren is ruthless. I just didn't think it was captain-worthy. But what do I know? I'm not jealous. I just don't understand why he would be chosen out of all of the males in the Brotherhood.

I glance at Ezra sitting across from me, now finishing his meal and wiping his hands on the outside of his pants. I notice how much his hair has grown over the last couple of weeks, brushing his forehead, and find myself wondering when he's going to cut it next. He always cuts it.

The cold wind bites at my eyes as I watch him stand and stomp out the remainder of the fire.

"Let's get going. I'm eager to see who went out for a mission today," Ezra says with a grin.

My breathing slows as I inch toward the stairs in the courtyard, steps quiet and nimble. The only light cascading down is the soft glow of the moon coming from the windows above. The courtyard looks like one you'd have outside with all its outdoor features, but a domed glass ceiling protects it from elements.

It's late, and for some reason, I decided that tonight would be a good time to explore the castle to try and find... well, anything regarding my mother.

But now, I've noticed a couple of extra guards walking in from across the courtyard, near the king's private archives. Two of them to be exact, and I'm afraid of getting caught as I know two more rest just inside those heavy wooden doors.

That archive stores every piece of information given to King Elion by the elite, holding valuable information of the castle and the realm. The only reason he has extra security guarding them.

Curiosity burns a hole through me as I think about every-thing that's in there, itching to get my hands on something.

I stick to the shadows, scurrying up the stairs, and pause against the stone wall, ensuring that I remain unseen. Guards stop in front of the doors and begin chatting.

I sigh. Looks like I'll be taking the long way back to my room, but I'll have to go down the corridor near the kitchens to get to the back of my stairwell. Especially if I want to get back without being questioned.

"I've sent you something, little fawn. Have you gotten it?" Rydian asks.

A warm tingle behind my eyes accompanies his soft-spoken words. I attempt to respond, still unable to grasp the Veil long enough to reach him, and it's infuriating.

But his voice causes my stomach to flip, and as annoying as he is, I enjoy the sound of him across my mind. Then I begin to wonder what he could have possibly sent me.

Heading down the hall near the throne room, I veer right. Luckily, the king doesn't require guards to stay on duty inside the castle, other than his precious archives and entry points to his wing. Most guards just stay planted outside the castle walls.

I reach the corner near the kitchens and immediately come to a halt, spotting someone exiting a door down the corridor. I remain quiet, inching myself closer to the wall behind me, melting into the stone.

But something shifts against my back, a rough scraping noise brushing the air. *Fuck.* My eyes widen as I realize that it's the wall that moved. Just as I attempt to dart around the corner, his head swivels in my direction.

I've been spotted.

"What are you doing?" Ren demands, his voice barely above a whisper. I hadn't seen him since our conversation in the commons five days ago.

I *knew* he was going to make it more difficult to find my

mother, especially if he's lurking in the halls late at night. I swallow my frustration, staring at him in silence.

He flicks his gaze down the hall near the courtyard, as if looking for the guards. An expression passes over his features—too quick for me to decipher.

With how the castle is laid out, the front is in the shape of a horseshoe with openings to the courtyard near the middle. The king's archives rest at the back and can be seen in any direction. Even though I took the long way, I still have to hide myself to arrive at my stairwell. But so does he.

And for some reason, I begin to think he doesn't want to get caught either.

"I could ask you the same thing," I counter, arching a brow when my eyes flick to his hands, a smirk tugging at my lips. "Are those tarts?"

He quickly hides the items, eyes narrowing.

"No," he says sharply, keeping his voice down. "And don't make me ask you again."

"I couldn't sleep," I lie, quietly moving toward him and stopping at the edge of his boots. "I didn't know I was confined to my room for eternity, Captain."

Since a lot of our missions are done at night, we don't necessarily have a curfew, which is why most of us like to visit Alvonia in our free time. But if we're caught running rampant around the castle late at night, you can guarantee we'll be questioned about it.

"Are you stealing from the kitchens?" I arch a brow. "I wonder what the punishment would be for that."

Silence stretches for a beat, and I notice the way he refuses to meet my gaze, as if wanting to avoid this conversation entirely. He glances down the hall once more before turning back to me.

"I won't say anything if you won't," he mutters, catching me by surprise. So he *is* stealing. A captain stealing from the kitchens? Well, this just got interesting.

"But I'm not stealing," I quip, giving him a menacing grin.

His eyes narrow as he scans me in silence before leaning down, muttering quietly under his breath.

"No, you're not," he admits. "But you're definitely not out here because you couldn't sleep." His eyes remain cold and uncaring, but I almost sense a hint of amusement within his gaze.

Dammit. I study him for a solid minute before carelessly shrugging—not wanting to question his reasoning for bypassing why I'm in this hall.

"Fine." I nod toward the courtyard, silently suggesting he take the lead, but only because I don't want to get caught. His scarred brow arches, and then I watch as he shifts his weight, stepping into the shadows on silent feet.

His movements are precise and utterly silent against the cold stone floor, and for a moment, admiration washes over me. Not that I'd ever admit that out loud.

The faint sound of armor clinks from the courtyard, forcing me to press myself against the cool stone, the scent of damp earth filling my senses. We wait, hearing the guards' voices drift in and out, one quietly laughing at something I can't quite make out from this distance.

Ren pauses a step ahead of me, his large frame barely visible once he reaches the edge of the hall. He peeks around the corner, raising a hand for me to wait, when I glance down, spotting the items hanging in his right hand.

Those *are* tarts. I knew it.

I smirk behind his back, quickly composing myself when he urges me to follow as we move left. I step forward, spotting the two guards perched outside the archives, deep in conversation.

We cross the threshold in an instant and out of sight,

remaining in the shadows near the entrance to my stairwell, making this little late-night adventure a success.

I shake my head. *These guards are awful.*

Now, I need to enter the door to my left while Ren needs to enter the one to his right, leading him down the hall where the rest of our brethren sleep on the first level.

He reaches the handle, then hesitates, only to glance over his shoulder to throw me a wry smirk before disappearing. And for some reason, I find myself giving him one of my own as we both go our separate ways. What an odd interaction.

I quickly race up my stairs and shut the door behind me as I enter and exhale. After shrugging off my cloak, I place it in my wardrobe and shut the doors with a soft click. With a flick of my wrist, I light the hearth and smile.

"Are you awake?" Rydian slides into my head, and I outwardly groan, instantly ruining my brief moment of joy. *"If you're awake, you'll see what I sent you."*

I kick off my boots with a huff and stride to my whiskey, then pour myself a glass. I catch myself wondering if I can find a way to get him to stop pestering me all day. It's not like I'm *not* doing anything.

I'm standing in front of the large arched windows, sipping, when a loud tapping noise beats against the glass. *What the...*

I carefully set down my whiskey and squint, attempting to look outside. After unlatching the window, I swing it open to reveal a large hawk perched on the edge of the window. *There's no way.* I recognize the large bird as Rydian's and groan.

"You've got to be kidding," I mutter. "I can't respond so he sends his damn bird to me?" I realize that this must be what he meant when he said he sent me something.

"I have a name," Ire says casually, and I gasp, my mouth falling open at the sound.

My eyes go wide, and for a moment, large hawk eyes blankly

stare at me, as if he didn't expect me to hear him. *Did I hear him?* His voice was low as it entered my mind.

"How long have you been there?" I ask.

"Only today. But I've been ordered to watch over you for a few days," he says.

"A few days? How long is a few days?" Annoyance coats my tone—Rydian doesn't trust me. "Why didn't you get my attention sooner?"

"I tried to earlier, but you didn't notice."

How could I have missed such a large bird outside my window? My eyes remain wide as I realize that my magic must be coming in a lot faster than I originally thought. It's odd considering I haven't progressed with any magic in years, so why now?

"Tell your king he's giving me a headache by talking to me so much. I can't think when all he does is badger me constantly," I say and hear a noise come out of him that sounds a lot like a chuckle.

I step away from the window as Ire hops onto the table, knocking over one of my glasses and causing me to lunge for it to keep from shattering. I huff, blowing hair out of my face.

"I can't. You have to tell him."

"Why do I have to tell him? Don't you talk to him?" I ask.

Ire blinks twice, then tucks his wings further into his sides. *"I talk to him. He just can't hear me, so you need to write a letter. He's becoming quite impatient,"* he adds and then takes a claw to scratch behind his ear while I stare at him.

"What?" I ask, brows pinching as a thought crosses my mind.

"Are you going to write something?" he presses.

"Yes. Okay, fine," I get out, quickly finding something to scribble a note, letting Rydian know how much of a headache he is and that I'm in fact searching the castle for Elynor.

I hand the note off to Ire, who flies off in a matter of

seconds. It doesn't take long for him to deliver my note, and Rydian's loud guffaw jolts in my head. So loud that I wince.

A sound I could easily get used to, it seems. His laughter is rich and warm, coating my insides like a thick quilt. Then he speaks, snuffing out the warm, fuzzy thoughts I was previously having.

"I do love that you're searching for Queen Elynor, but a headache is going to be the least of your worries if you don't meet me in Alvonia soon..." he warns, and I roll my eyes.

I wait a few minutes, thinking he's finished speaking, and begin changing my clothes into something to sleep in.

"I've found something, and I think you'd really want to know what I found," he says finally and I groan, my head slamming into the pillow just as I settle in bed.

18

It's just before dawn by the time I wake, tangled in my sheets. Even though I crawled into bed a little late, I feel rested. Cold winter air brushes against my skin, forcing me to roll over, eyes peeling open.

"Fates!" I call out, jolting upright. Ire perches on one of the settees. "What are you doing here?"

"King Rydian has ordered me to watch over you."

"And that requires you to be in my room?" I look over, realizing I left the window propped open last night, leaving the room incredibly chilly.

"Yes," he replies. *"Unless you meet with him. Then I won't need to be here."* His voice drips sarcasm.

"Who knew birds had sarcasm?" I mutter.

"I have a lot of things, but patience isn't one of them," he quips, and I groan.

"Well, it looks like you and the king have a lot in common then," I mutter.

It's been almost two weeks since I've arrived back at the castle, so I guess it's time I meet with him. But how exactly am I going to leave the castle without raising suspicion?

I haven't had a mission since I've been back, but someone is bound to look for me the moment I leave. Ezra got a mission shortly after our hunting trip and should be back by now, but I haven't checked.

Unfortunately, I believe Ren's purposely holding out on giving me missions now that he's captain. Not that I mind after finding out what the king had me doing for so long, but it does concern me—waking up to find nothing shoved under my door after weeks of getting missions back-to-back.

"I'll see if I can meet with him today. Hold on." I fling the quilts off, quickly writing another note before handing it off.

I watch as Ire exits through the middle window, leaving me alone with my swirling thoughts. The anticipation of seeing Rydian causes my pulse to race. I expect a quick response, but after a few minutes, nothing comes through.

It's strange how my stomach tightens at the thought of him, something I can't seem to easily shake. And here I thought putting space between us would help mend these unexpected feelings, yet here I am, realizing that it might've just made it worse. He stirs something in me that feels both exhilarating and terrifying, and I'm not sure I like it.

Why does he affect me this way when he's no different than any other male I've been around? Why does he seem to throw me off so easily?

My heart races, a part of me craving connection with someone, yet fear grips my chest, and I'm not sure he's what I need right now. Not when my mother could be alive, currently missing.

How do I search for someone I didn't even know existed until a few weeks ago? What happens if I find her—dead or alive? I chew my lip, too afraid to answer that.

Unaware of how I've zoned out standing near the windows, I look down to find myself tossing an orb in between my hands the size of my palm.

I stumble back, hitting the table behind me, when the orb sputters out. A groan escapes me, and I wipe my hands on my night slip, warmth settling in the middle of my palms as I stare in awe.

I still haven't said a word to Ezra about being able to wield more—too anxious about the Siphon. The knowledge of being Shadovar puts me at risk for being targeted, especially if they find out I can wield their magic. Still, it gnaws at me, keeping this information from him. *The secrets.*

I've trained with him almost every day since we arrived, seeing him for a couple of hours before being sent off. Then a thought crosses my mind as I push my hair away from my face.

Huffing, I stride to my wardrobe and dress, braiding my hair down my back, ensuring to tightly secure the auburn patch. Sheathing my weapons, I grab my cloak and scarf.

Wind whirls at my face as soon as the door opens, a flutter of snowflakes rushing up the stairs from the opening below. Winter has made its final appearance, and it feels as if it's approached much faster than the previous years. I squint against the wind, clasping my cloak under my chin. Boots thud on the icy stone as I descend, heading to the commons to find Ezra.

I swing the doors open, finding a few of my brethren eating at the tables, everyone pivoting to look at me before going back to eating. A fire blazes in the back, warding off the chill from the previous night, and I spot Ezra eating at a table with the group.

Ren accompanies them, briefly meeting my gaze before returning to his breakfast. After last night, I had hoped to have come to a truce, but he hardly lifted his head as I blazed through the doors. As if he knew it was me storming through.

I fix a plate and walk to where Ezra sits, then sit down myself. "How was your mission?"

"It was good. I just got back last night," Ezra says. "Were you sleeping in? You're usually the first one in the arena." The corners of his mouth lift as he takes another mouthful.

"I didn't sleep in—I just wasn't here," I reply, throwing a piece of biscuit. "Since when do I sleep in? You're the one I usually have to drag out of bed at the break of dawn."

"Because my nights are an absolute delight."

"You and I both know that's a lie when I have to beg you to join me at the Painted Bird." I chuckle, and then Luke pivots in our direction.

"Did you hear about the new weapons being forged?" Luke asks, his eyes eager. I meet his gaze, shaking my head at the information. New weapons are being forged?

"What new weapons?" I ask, meeting Ren's gaze from down the table.

Luke lowers his voice. "The king is forging weapons out of a new material. I'm not sure we're supposed to know, but I heard whispers about it on a mission a few weeks ago."

Ren clears his throat—almost in warning—about what Luke is willingly offering me, and I throw him a glare at the interruption. Ren stands and I follow as he tosses the remnants of his food away, striding toward the arena.

"Ren, wait!" I call out, meeting him within a few seconds. "Are there any new missions for me?"

"I'm not sure what you mean," he says.

"You know exactly what I mean. You seem to give Ezra and whoever else missions except for me. I haven't had one in almost two weeks. What's going on?"

His face remains forward, our pace even as we stride down the corridor, boots echoing off the stone. "That's none of your concern."

"King Elion has been absent since we came back. No new missions, and apparently new weapons are being forged..."

He halts his steps just outside the doors, facing me. "Keep your voice down and stop asking those questions before someone overhears you. What the king does in private is none of your concern. There haven't been any new missions open to our brethren either, so it's not just you. Just keep up with your training and do… whatever. I don't care," he clips, crossing his arms to stare at me.

"Fine." I narrow my eyes, then smirk. "How were your tarts?" I ask right before Ezra walks up. Ren's eyes narrow into menacing slits.

"Are you ready?" Ezra asks, glancing between the two of us.

"Yes, right behind you." I tilt my head up.

Ezra walks between us and taps my elbow, breaking my stare with Ren, forcing me to follow him as he pushes the door open. I throw Ren a quick glance over my shoulder as he stands there, watching me before the door shuts.

Grabbing my favorite staff, I approach the arena and twirl it in my hands a few times to warm up. But after a couple of hours training, we finish, leaving us sweaty regardless of the chilly air filling the arena.

"I'll be gone for a few days," Ezra says as we stride to the weapons rack.

"Again? How long?"

"I don't know. Four days—five? I can't be sure." He shakes his head. "King Elion has me tracking someone in Sylvanor again."

"Have you heard anything about what's going on with our missions? Ren refuses to discuss anything." I frown.

He runs a hand through his hair, exhaling. "Not really. Just what he's willing to offer, which isn't much. From what I know he's stalled the majority of our missions," he states, glancing at me with a soft smile.

"Except for you and a couple others," I point out. "Malrik has also gotten a few missions."

His brows furrow before he meets my gaze, knowing that over the last few years, I've received all high priority targets. But now, all of a sudden, those have stopped.

He winces. "I know. I'm sorry. I'll be leaving tomorrow morning. I won't be able to train with you this week," he adds softly, then changes the subject. "I haven't seen you wielding your orbs recently. Are you practicing?" he asks—a question that's not unusual since we frequently have conversations about it.

Regardless, my stomach drops. I know I have to lie. I nod. "Some. I still can't do anything more than my small orbs. I don't think I'll be able to do more than that." I shrug, the lie rolling off my tongue with ease.

Quickly grabbing my items by the door, I bid him goodbye with a small wave, walking down the corridor toward the exit. Pushing the doors open, I step into the cold courtyard.

My breath forms a cloud in front of me as a smile forms on my face. I knew Ren would unwillingly offer me information if I pestered him long enough. Ezra would feel bad enough to share tiny bits of information about his missions.

Ezra will be gone for a few more days, and Ren won't be giving me any new missions, giving me the opportunity to head to the Painted Bird without disturbing anyone. Or having anyone come looking for me. They won't need me, and it gives me time to sneak out and head to the city to talk with Bess. Perhaps I can rent a room from the brothel if Rydian is around. I'll have to figure out a way to find him.

The stable doors creak open, and I greet Bjorn with a wide smile, giving him the apple I snuck into my cloak, giving him a gentle pat. "Are you ready for a quick journey?"

"Anything for you," Bjorn says.

"You can talk to me?" I gasp.

"I always talk to you. You just can't hear me." He chuffs, practically repeating what Ire said about Rydian, and I chuckle. *"Where are we going?"*

"To Alvonia. We need to go to the Painted Bird," I say.

I waste no time and quickly mount Bjorn, leaving me to pull

my scarf over my nose as the cold wind hits my face. Shivering from the ride, I arrive just outside the Painted Bird, leaving Bjorn to rest just off the street.

"I'll be back." I pat him, and he quietly huffs.

Assuming that's him agreeing with me, I walk to the second level, now facing the large red door and knocking on it three times. I'm unsure if anyone will answer as it's midday and the brothel won't open for many hours still. After a few minutes, I knock again just as the small screen slides open, greeted by the large male from all the other nights. Dark eyes peer down at me.

He growls, "What do you want?"

"I'm here to see Bess."

"You can see her tonight when we open," he grumbles in annoyance and attempts to shut the screen. With it being so early in the day, the poor male was probably asleep.

"No, please! I need to see her. I don't want service. I just need to talk to her. I have extra coins for your troubles," I say with a persuading smile, jingling my coins. He shuts the window with a hard thud, leaving me to huff and turn to the street just as he opens the door.

"Hurry up," he says, shoving a mask in my hands. "Shoes and weapons off."

I quickly step inside when he holds out a hand, catching my gaze with a blank expression. I toss a few coins into his palm. He wiggles his fingers as if to indicate for more.

"This is all I brought." I throw him a glare.

He wiggles them again, and I huff, dumping the rest into his palm as a small smile slowly creeps up his face.

"Follow me," he grumbles.

I'm not sure what's worse—the brothel being dead silent in the middle of the day or hearing all the moaning at night. Regardless, both kind of set me on edge.

We walk through the grand pleasure room, eerily quiet and not a moan to be heard in the large building. Instead of veering to our right—toward Bess's chamber—he continues to walk straight.

To the back of the building.

"I need to see Bess," I say, only he ignores me, continuing his stroll in silence.

Opening a door that looks to be a large office, he steps to the left, allowing me passage. A brown-haired female in glasses sits behind a desk, sorting coins with her face pointed down in concentration. Two large wingback chairs sit across from the desk. Large enough to hide whoever sits in the chairs before her, as dark pants peek out from the side. She's not alone.

I feel as if I'm interrupting a meeting.

"I have Miss…" The grumbly male looks at me, expecting me to say something.

"No names, remember?" I shrug, and he grunts like I have the gall to remind him of one of *their* rules. He exits the room without another word.

"Isa?" Bess calls out.

My eyes flick to the female at the desk, who is in fact Bess. Confusion crosses my face as well as hers, like she wasn't expecting me to step through the door. How does she know my name? Then her jaw clenches as she eyes me, her gaze darting to the chair to the right of her desk. As if me strolling through set her on edge.

She's fully dressed, glasses sliding down her nose as she stares at the chair across from her. Her straight brown hair falls around her face, brushing the loose tunic that hangs off her shoulders.

"Bess? I—do you own the Painted Bird?" I stutter, my words spilling out, though a tight smile lines her mouth.

"I do. Please sit," she says, gesturing to the settee, but I'm frozen in place.

Of course, I knew someone had to own it, but Bess? All this

time she never mentioned it to me. My brows pinch, but I walk toward the empty seat anyway.

Just as I go to sit, I shoot a glance at the person occupying the settee next to me and pause. My head tilts, eyes narrowing as they shift from guest to Bess, when a sigh leaves my lips.

"Hello, little fawn. Nice to finally see you again," Rydian drawls with a smirk.

19

***

I stare at Bess, pointing my thumb at Rydian as irritation mars my face. "Why is he here?"

She only saw him once before—briefly and with a mask—when he visited as a guest, so her calm expression does nothing to quiet my growing confusion as to why he's sitting here.

"Is two weeks not long enough for you to be graced with my gorgeous face?" Rydian quips. His smirk is as entrancing as it is annoying, but his tone drips with mockery.

My gaze shifts to him, and the sight only deepens my frustration. Dark auburn hair slightly curls around his ears, only adding to his irritating charm. His eyes glint with a mixture of amusement and what appears to be annoyance.

Then I begin to notice the details, realizing he's not wearing a mask. His boots are still on and—*is that a weapon?* My eyes narrow, leaving me to rip off my mask. My scowl deepens, and Rydian raises his brow, the corners of his mouth twitching in quiet amusement.

"Did you finally sleep enough to venture out of your fancy little castle?" he asks, then relaxes into the settee, like he doesn't have his own castle in Aurelia.

His jab infuriates me though, and before I can stop myself, I somehow manage to summon an orb, hurling it at his smug face with a grunt of frustration. He dodges it, his grin widening as the orb sizzles against the back of the settee, eyes flaring with surprise. Frustration rises in my chest, irritated that he dodged it so easily, leaving me to throw another one.

Oh, I could get used to this.

"Those were expensive! No magic," Bess yells, her voice cutting through the air. She steps between us, leaning against the hard edge of her desk with her arms crossed.

"Maybe he should have thought about that before acting like an ass," I snap. "Do you know how annoying you've been these last two weeks?"

"I've missed you too," he says, his voice teasing, but his expression flickers with something a little deeper than amusement. "I forgot how much fun it is to watch you lose your temper. But if you didn't want to be annoyed for two weeks, perhaps you should have met with me like we planned. Though it brings me great joy knowing you couldn't respond."

I shift my attention to Bess, ignoring him as my temper flares.

"He keeps me company while we wait for you," she says.

"What about me?" I flick my eyes between the two of them, feeling like I'm trapped. "You know what? Never mind. I came to see how we could rent a room here as a private meeting location for that one." I point to Rydian. "But I guess you have it all figured out."

Rydian chimes in. "Well, yes, since you've been gallivanting at the castle for two weeks, I had to take it upon myself to find my own accommodations. Renting at the Silver Lily was not going to happen given my last... experience there. So yes, it's already taken care of. We were just waiting on you."

Our plan was to always meet here for meetings, but I didn't expect Rydian to rent a room at the brothel. If that's what he did. A heated shiver runs down my spine at the thought of all the brothel noises during those meetings.

"I haven't been gallivanting. I've been working," I say, and then my brows rise, curiosity spiking. "And already done? So does that mean we're good to meet here then?"

I look at Bess as she glances back and forth, like she's mentally cataloging every word. With a sharp turn, she uncrosses her arms and strides behind her desk, the picture of composure. She sits, her posture straight and authoritative, and I feel off as she glances at me.

She looks every inch like the shrewd brothel owner now—detached and professional. Nothing like the Bess I thought I knew, and a pang of sadness creeps in as I study her, realizing now that maybe I don't know her at all. The warmth she often offered me is gone: the easy smiles, the laughter.

"Yes." She sighs. "He's staying here, and you're welcome to meet whenever. Just keep it private. Also, Pete already knows of the arrangement, so he'll let you in when you come."

Pete. So that's the large male's name at the door. Wait…

I growl and exaggerate the jingle of my coin bag in front of my face, which is now empty, so it just sounds like shaking leather. "What do you mean he knows? He just took all my money."

My brows lower when Rydian attempts to hide his smirk from behind his hand. I throw him a stern look, warning him to shut up before I stab him with my… right. I don't have a weapon.

Bess smirks. "Well, you shouldn't have bribed him. He would've let you in regardless."

"So where is this meeting room?" I ask.

"She gave me the entire right side of the top floor," he says casually, offering me a shit-eating grin, as if he's also in disbelief.

My brows pinch. "How did that happen?"

I assume she doesn't know anything, and I wonder how he managed this. My eyes flick to Rydian, who's leaning back with his arms resting on the settee.

"Can I speak to you outside?" I ask him.

"She knows everything," he says, immediately catching on to what I want to ask. I peek at Bess, who's flipping pages in her ledger with her head down. Turning back to Rydian, I mouth the word, *everything?* And he nods.

"Would you... care to explain?" I ask Rydian out loud, but Bess looks up.

She shuts her ledger. "What would you like to know?"

"Everything."

She eyes Rydian as if asking permission, and he gives her a curt nod. "I knew of the Vaelborne family for many years, though I didn't know who Rydian was until he asked for my help two weeks ago."

"How?"

"Because I'm also Shadovar," she says. "And I support his cause... if that's what you want to call it. When the battle in Aurelia happened, it was when the treaty was in place, allowing everyone to travel to the realms. I ended up getting trapped here all those years when they closed off the borders, deciding that it was best I stayed."

"Did you know who she was?" I ask Rydian, but he shakes his head.

"No, but I suspected once I discovered that you found a Veil coin here at the brothel—one that wasn't mine. Being king gives me a certain ability to feel the magic of our own realm. I can't exactly pinpoint who it comes from, but I suspected it was her since we were just outside her chambers." He shoots me a smug grin, my face heating under his gaze as if his thoughts landed on what our plans were. "It was a risk I was willing to take given the secrecy her brothel provides."

"Bold risk." I pivot to Bess. "So the coin was yours?"

"Yes, it's mine," she says sharply. "I didn't want you to question me about it when I saw you pick it up in the hall, so I let you have it."

Oh. I have nothing left to say so I nod, studying her features. She appears unamused by today's turn of events, or perhaps it's something deeper she's not saying. But I don't miss the flicker of her eyes as she meets Rydian's gaze, and I can't help but think that I'm left out of a conversation I can't hear.

"Let me show you where we'll be meeting," Rydian says and stands.

He's at the door within seconds before I bolt from the settee. He takes long strides down the corridor, banking left for the back staircase that winds up all three stories.

I'm on his heels, doing my best to match his stride. We reach the top floor when Rydian takes another left, walking a few more steps before planting his feet in front of a large door.

It's astounding given that the space doesn't look like it should support how big the door is. After unlocking it without a word, he takes a step inside, pivoting to the right. Stepping in, I understand why the door is so big. The space is large and dark, not at all what I expected when he said "floor." It's a *loft*.

Brick stone lines the floor, partially hidden beneath scattered rugs, especially near the bed. Straight back is a spacious kitchenette tucked behind the wall where the bed sits. Still, it offers a view into the kitchen. Directly above that is a generous mezzanine with books lining the wall, and a spiral staircase to the left of the kitchen leads to the second floor.

Arched, textured windows reach the ceiling on the right, where I assume it looks into the grand pleasure room, accompanied by a four-poster bed. A stone mantel reaches the ceiling across from the bed, and the space is furnished with a long settee and a small table between them. There's no doubt the stone mantel comes from the mountain itself.

I finally turn to Rydian, letting my eyes drift over the space before settling on him. His glare is a small storm—arms crossed, jaw tight, and a heat in his eyes that feels like they could burn a hole through me. The air between us feels heavier—charged.

"Well, you're angry," I say casually, leaning against the door and refusing to let his anger rattle me.

"Angry?" he growls, voice sharp. "Angry doesn't even cover it. We had a deal, so what happened?"

He doesn't wait for me to answer, storming past, close enough to catch the faint oakmoss on his skin, and I find myself holding my breath. His presence is magnetic, and I hate how easily he pulls me in despite his anger.

I sigh, pushing away from the door to follow him as he strides up the staircase. When I reach the top level, he's already at the oak table, its surface scattered with scrolls and parchment. He whirls around to face me, and I cross my arms.

"Not that I need to explain myself to you, but I didn't want Ezra or Ren following me. I needed to make sure that I was clear before moving forward. It's not like I wasn't doing anything," I say.

His jaw tightens. "I have an entire realm to run. I can't just drop everything to chase after you when you decide to run away from your problems."

"Is that what you think?" I snarl as he strides closer, stopping inches from me when his eyes narrow into menacing slits. Eyes of a king.

"That's what it is, isn't it? Avoiding your problems—your responsibility. Or are you just avoiding me?" he asks, his breath warm across my cheeks.

Our gazes lock, seconds drifting by as we stare at each other, but his words hit me harder than he knows. But it's not just that. I'm still having a hard time trusting him and felt the need to search for Elynor on my own.

I tilt my chin up. "I didn't ask for *this*. I didn't ask for you to search for me, and in case you forgot, no one is forcing you to stay here. I've spent my whole life cleaning up other people's messes, so forgive me if I didn't consult with you fast enough, *King*."

"That's not how this works," he growls, voice low. "We're a team, and we do things *together*. We have the same goal here, do we not? No matter how long I have to wait, I'm not leaving without you. So whether it takes a few weeks, to a month, to a lifetime—I don't care. You will be coming home with me at the end of it. You can run if you want to, but I will find you no matter where you are."

Home. What does that even mean?

This clearly isn't the same male I met weeks prior in the hall at the Painted Bird. This is King Rydian. Protector of his realm and me, the heir of Aurelia, and he's putting me first like he has for the last twenty years. My stomach sours at the thought, and I'm unsure how to feel about that.

I hold his gaze, taking in his declaration to me. The intensity of it makes my chest tighten, and for a moment, it feels as if I can't breathe, the weight of it pressing in.

Loyalty is not something I've been able to count on from anyone except for myself, yet here he is, offering it to me without a second thought. The rhythm of my pulse betrays the composure I'm trying to hold as I stare up at him. I draw in an uneven breath, his scent filling my lungs, somehow grounding me and unraveling me all at once. Something I'm not used to.

"Okay," I mutter, blinking, though the words feel foreign on my tongue as I offer him the tiniest sliver of trust. Then something flickers across his face, softening the hard lines of his jaw.

His chest abruptly rises and falls, and I realize that he's close —too close—making my pulse thrum beneath my skin. Though it's not fear that causes it, but him. His presence leaves me unsteady—not in a way that sends me running, but in a way that leaves me feeling curious.

His pupils dilate as if he's sensing the sudden energy shift when he slowly steps back, turning to the table behind him with a heavy breath. I let out a shaky exhale, my body releasing the pent-up tension. *What was that?*

He returns to his notes, silently flipping pages while he rubs his jaw, eyeing the papers below him.

"So, what now?" I ask after composing myself.

He doesn't look up. "Now we plan. Sit," he says, his tone a little demanding.

He points to the chair across the table, and against my better judgment, I obey and sit down. He hands me notes and scrolls, research he's been doing over the last two weeks.

"What are these?"

"Records of the last few Siphons. There are three left and only two recorded. So whomever King Elion has, he's hiding. Bess, as you know, is Shadovar, but she's also a Seer," he says.

"A Seer—what is that?"

"She has visions like you, but unlike you, she doesn't need to touch someone to get snippets of information. It comes to her at odd times and is something she can't really control. She would be similar to a Scry in Elderheim but without having to use crystals. Being in Elderheim dampens her power quite significantly." I let his words sink in, a silence settling between us before he continues. "I told you that I found something last night. Bess was willing to give me information on one of the last Siphons who is apparently in hiding. So we need to visit with her soon."

"She's in hiding? From what?"

"*That* is a good question and is what we are going to find out. Maybe we can gain some insight as to what happened to your memories and see if they're something we can get back," he mumbles.

I exhale, eyes wide. "That would be amazing. When will we meet with her?"

"As soon as we can. For right now, I'm trying to find some

information on the castle's floor plan, but I have nothing of use." He leans on the table, arms stretched out in front of him as he leans forward. His stare sears a hole in me. "I could have been invited in a couple of weeks ago but was not. I would love for someone to help me on that end… I need to walk through the castle. We need the map."

"Yes, fine. I can do that," I mutter and look back down, feeling his stare beat down on me in my attempt to ignore him.

"That means sneaking into the king's private archives to steal it," he adds warily. "Can you do that?"

I freeze—*shit.*

As I know firsthand, the king's personal archives are heavily guarded, something that will need a lot of stealth to gain access to. I drag my eyes to his, scanning his heavily muscled arms in the process while he continues to lean forward.

"You do know that it's heavily guarded and gaining access to that is going to be… impossible. You said we would search the castle, not steal a map from his *archives.* We'll have to find the map, make a copy, *and* put it back without getting noticed. Do you know how much information is stored in his archives?" I shake my head. *There's no way.*

"That's why you need to invite me in." He throws me a blank stare.

I huff and sit back, resting my forearms against the chair. Realization rolls through me, and I know that I have no choice but to allow him access to the castle. I won't be able to steal that map alone—not with the guards stationed right outside those doors.

"Fine, fine! I'll get you in," I say, waving a hand to get him out of my face. "But you can't just show up whenever you want. You will knock on my door or I'm not agreeing to it."

He smirks. "Fine."

20

___

After rummaging through what scrolls Rydian had lying all over his table, we decided to wait until dusk before making our way back to the castle. It would be much easier to sneak him in as the sun started to set.

I was eager to leave the loft, not interested in staying any longer than necessary in order to avoid hearing the muffled moans as the brothel's activity began. I wasn't about to stick around long enough to find out how soundproof the windows actually were, no matter how many times Rydian insisted. The idea of sitting there, alone with Rydian, while that began below us? I bite the inside of my lip, forcing myself to focus, but my body heats at the thought.

Not because of him. Definitely not because of him.

Winter blasts me in the face, pulling me from my thoughts as I descend the steps to gather Bjorn.

"I'm sorry," I whisper as he huffs in annoyance.

"I'm getting hungry." He stomps his hoof.

"I know, I know. I'm sorry!" I whisper again.

"Your king follows you," Bjorn adds almost in warning, and I whirl around. My heart thumps frantically in my chest. I expect

to find King Elion behind me only to see Rydian securing his hood, descending the steps of the Painted Bird.

Right, he means King Rydian, not Elion. I groan, then frown, willing my heart rate to slow and realizing that he said *your king*.

"You're coming with me?" I ask, turning sharply to Rydian. "Can't you walk in the Veil, or better yet, meet me there?"

"I could… but I don't want to." He smirks, giving Bjorn an apple. "You're more interesting."

"You're walking." I grab the pommel, swinging myself over, when he grips my hand, catching me off guard.

My eyes widen, glancing down just as he releases me, though I recover quickly, tossing my braid over my shoulder, as if that will somehow settle the flood of heat rising in my face. Tugging the edges of my hood forward, I pull my scarf over my nose, creating a makeshift mask to shield myself.

Rydian smirks. "No, I'm not. He loves me. See? He doesn't mind."

I glance down, eyes narrowing as I watch him caress Bjorn's face, the dark horse leaning into him. The scene is ridiculous, with Rydian looking smug while Bjorn practically melts under his affection.

"Traitor." I push the thought out. Rydian's smirk deepens as though he's heard my thoughts loud and clear, eyes glinting with amusement.

"Well?" I ask Bjorn.

"It's true. I'm fond of the dark king."

I exhale, throwing my head back, and huff, my face heating from behind the thick scarf. "Fine, but if you even *think* about trying something, you're walking the rest of the way," I warn, my words coming out muffled. "And you need to conceal yourself. I don't need to be questioned about why there's a mysterious male riding behind me while we pass through."

Bjorn shuffles his feet, tossing his head as if in agreement, but Rydian doesn't move right away. Instead, his lips quirk into that maddening smirk of his.

"You'll be questioned regardless because of how loud you are, little fawn," he quips.

My hands tighten on the reins, his words quickly reminding me of our moment on the saddle a couple of weeks ago, my face burning hotter. It makes me want to throw something at him—preferably something sharp.

"Hurry up," I snap, losing my patience.

Rydian chuckles before swiftly swinging himself behind me in one swift motion. His movements are annoyingly graceful, and the shift in weight brings him closer than I'd like.

I stiffen slightly as his arm brushes against my waist. Then he Veils himself, his form disappearing into the shadows as if he were never there. Despite the lamp lights lining our path, the night remains dark enough to keep us both concealed.

"See?" His voice hums low in my ear. "Hidden. Just like you asked."

He adjusts his hips, shifting to get comfortable, and I let out a groan, knowing he's doing it just to get under my skin.

He chuckles again as we set off at an easy pace, and I can't help but bask in the warmth seeping in from the back of my cloak. He's the only thing keeping me from shivering as snow comes down in sheets above us, blanketing the realm in a soft, white pillowy cloud. The once-visible path slowly disappears beneath the swirling drifts, leaving Bjorn to navigate back to the castle by instinct. Each step he takes crunches softly beneath his hooves.

The cold air bites at my eyes, and I'm thankful for the fur-lined cloak and scarf that I brought with me. Rydian doesn't seem to shiver once, but his steady presence behind me makes the bitter chill of the night somewhat bearable.

"Is Ivy still in Aurelia?" I ask as we reach the edge of Alvonia, cloaked in darkness as we travel toward the castle's main entrance.

"Yes. She's taking care of the realm while I'm away. She and Orin will join us soon."

"And Orin is your third in command?"

"Yes, and he's brilliant. Why he's in my army, I'll never know. He would make an excellent scholar," he says casually.

His hands slip beneath my cloak, gripping my waist, fingers wrapping tight around my ribs. My lips part. The chill of his skin seeps through my tunic, yet his touch ignites a fire in me so low it's hard to ignore.

"Do you not listen?" My voice is sharp, but it's the only way to mask the way my breath catches as it sends a scorching heat across my skin.

He hums. "I'm curious as to what changed between now and two weeks ago when you were practically begging for me to put my hand in your pants on this very horse." His teasing words force me to release a groan. "I'm only warming my hands— they're freezing. Are you going to deny a king his *warmth?*" he murmurs, his voice dripping with sarcasm.

"You don't need to stick them there to stay warm," I mutter, yet I can't seem to shove him away.

He hums again, low and thoughtful, the sound far too amused. "I think this is the perfect spot since you always seem to be so flushed around me—like a furnace," he muses, somehow leaning closer. "Besides, I just can't seem to help myself."

"Do you practice this level of cockiness, or does it just come naturally for you?" I bite out.

"It's effortless, I assure you." He chuckles, flexing his fingers just to prove his point and causing me to bite my cheek.

I don't trust myself enough to respond, so I remain focused on the road, riding the rest of the way in silence. His hands remain where they are. Despite my mild irritation, I let them stay, finding the weight of his touch oddly comforting.

Arriving just outside the castle's gate, I spot Silas hovering around a small fire, bundled in a fur-lined cloak and puffing a pipe. Smoke billows around his face on an exhale.

He straightens, striding to the gate to prevent my entrance. A large grin spreads across my face, even though he can't see my mouth. Rydian stiffens behind me as he approaches, still hidden in the Veil.

"Who are you?" Silas questions. "Get off your horse so I can inspect you."

He freezes the moment my laugh pierces the air. Not from the chill of the cold night—but from the sound of my voice. I yank down my scarf to reveal my face just as his drains itself of all its color.

"Oh, Silas, questioning my whereabouts again?" I tease, chuckling as I pierce him with a playful glare, my eyes glinting as I peer down.

He pauses, his eyes sweeping over me in a slow once-over before a deep, booming laugh escapes him, reaching to pull me off Bjorn as if I weigh nothing. He wraps me in a large hug, squeezing the breath from me.

"And where have *you* been hiding?" he says, hands firmly resting on my shoulders as his gaze sweeps over me again, shining with mischief. He winks. "You look good. Better than good, actually."

"Oh, come on," Rydian grumbles in my head, his voice dripping with annoyance. I ignore him, focusing entirely on Silas.

I bat my lashes, feigning innocence. "What do you mean? I've been at the castle. It's only been a couple weeks. I couldn't have changed that much."

"Oh, but you *have*," he says, his tone playful. "You look ravishing. And here I thought that the cold has been unbearable —turns out, it's the lack of your company that's been the real challenge. You didn't think to visit me? It's been awfully cold without you." He runs a gloved hand down his face like he's being tormented.

I snort. "You're ridiculous."

"Don't tell me you've been saving all that charm for someone else," he accuses.

"Is this really necessary?" Rydian growls.

"I've just been… occupied." I exhale, unable to find the words to explain, knowing that I need to stay silent. Giving him a warm smile, I admire the full beard he's grown now that winter is here. He plants a gentle, friendly kiss on my left cheek.

Rydian's irritation flares again as another growl enters my thoughts, leaving me to refrain from rolling my eyes. Bjorn shuffles his feet, most likely agitated from Rydian's growing frustration, so I cut the interaction short.

"I need to get Bjorn to the stables. It was good to see you, Silas. I promise to visit, I swear," I say, squeezing his hand in farewell.

"It's good to see you. Stay warm for me, yeah? Wouldn't want someone as pretty as you to get cold." He grins.

Grabbing Bjorn's reins, I steer him to the left of the castle as I glance over my shoulder to Silas.

"That human is in love with you," Rydian grumbles the moment we're out of earshot. He appears from the Veil and hops off Bjorn once we reach the inside of the stables. He unclasps the saddle, flinging the straps like they annoy him.

I scoff. "No, he's not. Silas is just a good friend. He keeps me company at night sometimes." Taking the saddle from him, I toss it over the side of Bjorn's stall.

Rydian huffs a dry laugh. "You don't actually believe that, do you?"

I don't, but I won't tell him that. Silas has always flirted and has been very open about his affection toward me. That man wouldn't know what to do with someone like me though, so I've ignored it and pushed it aside as playful banter. I'd rather remain blissfully unaware than break his heart.

"How would you even be able to tell, anyway?"

"Because he reeks with it. I can smell it," he says, insinuating that his sense of smell can detect such a thing. "Plus, it's the way he looks at you. He wants you—he's infatuated."

I huff because Silas has always just been there for me late at night. Someone to talk to when I'm lonely. I feel nothing for the human other than the friendly conversation I offer him.

Tucking a strand of hair back behind my ear, I study Rydian a moment longer. He flicks an invisible piece of dust off his cloak and lifts his eyes, meeting my stare.

"You can't tell just by a look, Rydian."

"Trust me, I can."

"How?" I challenge him.

"Because I'm familiar with it, that's how," he mumbles and holds my gaze just long enough before walking past me. His boots thud, then crunch against the straw as he peeks out the back, scanning the area from side to side.

"Are you sweet on some lady back in Aurelia?" My tone is taunting, mocking him as he eyes me.

"Something like that," he mutters, and my stomach drops. I'm unable to stop myself from the stab of jealousy simmering up my spine. *Ugh, what is wrong with me? Why did I even ask?*

Rydian peeks out the back of the stables again and then gestures for me to follow, like he's the one who lives at the castle. I roll my eyes, following him out and veering to the right.

We walk a few steps before he disappears into the Veil again once we hit the corner of the stables. I continue forward, looking to my right to find Silas still near the gate, and pretend that I'm headed to my room as usual. I make it to my stairwell, but just as I'm about to ascend the steps, Rydian clears his throat. I halt, my foot halfway raised to the first step when I turn back around to face nothing but air. Right, because he's still in the Veil.

With a huff, I peek around the corner to check Silas's position, tucking myself into the shadows so he doesn't see me, and drop my voice to a whisper.

"How does this… permission thing work?"

"Orin gave me a few different options when he looked into it," he says in a way that leaves me to believe he's not exactly sure it's going to work.

"You should know how to get in, right?" I ask.

Silence lingers. "I've never been invited to Castle Alvonia, so no. Just… grab my hand. Orin mentioned something about a resident letting you in that way, but you need to grant them access by speaking the words."

"Fine," I say with a sigh, thrusting my hand into the space where I assume he's standing. Only a quiet grunt of pain reaches my ears. I blink, tilting my head. "Did I just—"

"You hit me," he groans. "Right in my groin."

My lips twitch, but I somehow manage to maintain my composure.

"Oh," I say casually, though the corners of my lips threaten to betray me as they begin to quirk up in amusement. "Well, maybe you shouldn't stand there."

He mutters something too quiet for me to hear—I'm assuming it was a curse—as I extend my hand out again, higher this time. He grips my hand. I give him a hard yank, and the ward flares to life. A bright blue glow ripples out as Rydian slams into the invisible barrier with a hard smack.

No access granted.

He groans again, and this time, a quiet chuckle escapes me before I can stop it.

"Really?" he snaps, his whisper sharp. "Do you think this is funny?"

I bite the inside of my cheek to stifle the laughter bubbling up. "It's a little funny."

I shrug and then sneak a glance around the corner. Silas still sits just outside the gate, warming his hands over the fire and seemingly oblivious to what's going at the end of the castle.

"I said you have to grant me access by *speaking* it," Rydian hisses. "You can't just fling me through the ward like a sack of salt."

"Alright, alright," I say calmly, holding my hands up in surrender. "No need to be dramatic."

His voice drops an octave. "Would you like for me to show you what dramatic looks like when I finally get inside that room, little fawn?"

His words hang in the air, and for a moment, I can't tell if he's talking about the ward or something else entirely. My face warms, the double meaning sinking in before I can stop my thoughts from going in a dangerous direction.

"Howler got your tongue?" Rydian asks, his tone light. "Now are you going to let me in? Because I don't have all night."

I glare. "Yes, okay. Just… give me your hand." I flex my outstretched fingers to encourage him to grab it.

"If I smack into that ward again, I might actually kill you," he warns.

"Hush and give me your hand."

He finally places his hand in mine, giving me a gentle but tight squeeze when I tuck my chin, wrapping my other hand around his. I hesitate, unsure how to begin.

"Just state your name and who you're allowing inside the walls of Castle Alvonia. Orin said to do that first," he says.

"We don't even know if it's going to work."

"Just do it," he snaps, though the tension in his voice says even he's uncertain. He adds more softly, "Please."

I sigh and give it a shot, but our hope is fleeting as we spend the next thirty minutes voicing different ways to access the castle, leaving us both frustrated. He strides forward again—for the fifteenth time—only for the invisible wall to glow a bright blue, denying access. When he finally steps out of the Veil, his jaw is clenched tight.

I rub my hands together for warmth, the frigid chill seeping into my bones. "Why don't you come back tomorrow and we can try again? It's too cold to stand out here all night."

"You're doing it wrong," he says, releasing a frustrated exhale as my eyes narrow. "Focus. State your name and who you're letting in."

"We already did that," I clip. Yet there's one way we haven't tried yet. We haven't stated where we're letting access—perhaps that's what we're missing. Just as he steps back to leave, I snap my hand out to grip his. "Wait. Let me try one more time."

His brows draw close together before he cranes his neck, checking Silas's location one last time, then facing me with a nod.

I focus my eyes on the invisible wall, hoping that it works because if it doesn't, we're going to have to do this on another day. Or I'm going to end up doing this whole thing myself without help.

I quickly mutter the words, and with a gentle tug, pull him to me and hold my breath. He finally steps through as the ward of Castle Alvonia shimmers gold, rippling around his frame.

A grin lights up my face as I look up at him.

He's in.

21

Shutting the door behind me, I shiver, shaking off the snow that accumulated on my shoulders. I stride to my wardrobe, then hang my cloak and turn to find him inspecting my room. And I've become self-conscious of the area.

It's obviously not as grand as his loft, but I love it regardless because it's mine. The wardrobe clicks shut, and I lean against it, grinning when he catches me staring.

"What?" he asks.

The mantel is not yet lit, giving the room a brisk chill. Although I can't see him in the dark, I can tell he's raising a brow just by how the moon lights up the side of his face.

"How's your groin?" I grin.

He grunts as I walk to the mantel, flicking out a hand to spark the wood, but it's not catching because my hands are practically frozen. *I literally did this yesterday.* I huff, becoming increasingly more frustrated.

Rydian walks behind my right shoulder and throws out a hand, lighting the fire instantly. A blast of heat greets me as it lights the chamber in a soft, orange glow.

"Show off," I mutter under my breath.

"It's not showing off when it's basic magic."

But I stand, dusting off my hands, and startle, realizing just how close he is as I'm met with a hard chest in front of my face. My breath hitches, and I try to recover by backing my way to the whiskey table, looking over my shoulder. I pull the glass cork from my favorite bottle and fill two glasses.

"You need to be practicing," he states.

I turn to find him sitting in one of the settees with his hood down, leaving me to arch a brow. He normally has his hood up, always placing it back on when we're together. I just assumed he was trying to conceal his identity without having to muster the energy to shift his appearance.

His face glows as shadows dance across, giving him a regal, dark look in a way that highlights the auburn tint to the unruly strands. I hand him his glass, taking a sip from my own.

"I *am* practicing. You know that. My hands are just cold."

"That's not it. You just need to focus. You almost took my face off in front of Bess, remember? You had no trouble focusing then." He smirks.

"Because you were being an ass." I set my glass down as he lets out a quiet, amused chuckle.

"Have you tried talking in the Veil without the coin?"

I glare. "Do you think I wanted you to pester me for those two weeks? If I could respond, I would have."

"You can do it," he says smugly, then rises to face me, inches apart. He sets his glass down next to mine. "When you want to talk in the Veil, you focus on the tether connecting you to the person you want to reach. Like for you, you feel... warm and sharp. You're like the crackle of a fire, yet you carry the rich scent of a black orchid." He stares down at me, and the intensity of it makes my stomach twist. He slowly lifts his hand, moving a stray hair out of my face to press a finger to the center of my forehead, right between my eyes. "Now, what do I feel like?"

"I…" My voice falters. I'm aware of how close he is, unable to help the breath catching in my throat. "I don't know."

"Focus. What do I feel like?" His tone is dark with challenge. *"Talk to me,"* he whispers in the Veil.

I narrow my eyes and then quickly close them, drawing in a deep breath and trying not to focus on the way his scent fills my nostrils. I reach out, not with my voice but with my mind, focusing on him as my eyes begin to warm where his finger was. Then I feel him at the forefront of my mind as if waiting for me.

His presence feels cool and heavy, like the pressing of shadows—heavy like condensed fog. There's a crackle of energy to him, almost like static in the air right before a storm. Restrained power, yet his scent is earthy. A deep, smoky richness with hints of amber—oakmoss.

My eyes open only to find him hovering above me, already smirking. I'm certain he feels it too.

"You're standing too close." I smirk, pushing the thought out. I take a step back, but he chuckles and sits back down, whiskey in hand.

"See? Focus on that, and you don't have to listen to me pester you all the time. Now you can reply," he quips. "That should be fun."

I finally sit with an exhale, pulling at the end of my braid, and begin to untie my boots. My hair spills over my shoulder, and I realize that my tunic sits a little low. I forgot I wore one of my green low-cut tops. The kind that hangs off my shoulders, exposing the soft skin underneath.

I glance up to find Rydian's heated gaze peering down at me. My eyes flick to his mouth almost instinctively, and I smirk, knowing he was unintentionally given a show of my breasts.

"Now that you're in the castle, what's next?" I ask.

He breaks his stare to look at the blazing fire and leans into the settee, crossing a leg over his knee before answering. "I think I'll walk through the castle in the Veil tonight. I need to get a layout of everything. I won't be able to Veil in or out if I haven't been in one of the chambers. It might take me a couple of hours but it's best if I do it tonight rather than risk getting caught during the day."

He glances at me, my feet casually resting on the small table in front of us. I lean back, clasping my hands together. "Do you need me to go with you?"

"No need. You've already taken off your boots. I'll be quiet," he says.

"Okay, I guess I'll wait for your return. Be careful though. I caught Ren lurking in the halls last night. I can't imagine you'll be Veiling back to the brothel?" I ask with a raised brow, throwing back the last of my whiskey.

"If you don't mind," he replies warily, assuming he thinks I'll kick him out. "After being Veiled for so long I won't have the energy to go back tonight. I'll need to rest here. What was Ren doing?"

I shake my head. "I don't know. I'm pretty sure he was stealing sweets from the kitchens." I all but snort, choosing to leave out that he caught me. "He was appointed captain when we got back from Sylvanor."

Rydian's eyes narrow. "Have you had a captain before?"

"No. We've always just had our training masters. For some reason, King Elion promoted him because he follows orders, but Ezra told me it's most likely due to him being ruthless. Capable of taking out anyone who's a threat to any of the missions."

He watches the flames. "I'll keep an eye out. Thanks for the warning."

I nod, standing in silence as I make my way to the bathing chamber, already aware that he's watching me.

"See you in a couple of hours," I call out, not waiting for a response.

He growls just as I shut the door with my foot, a smile

already on my face. My chamber door clicks shut shortly after, making me aware of his departure.

I exit the bathing chamber after an hour of soaking and scrubbing, cherishing every ounce of warmth. Even though the fireplace does an exquisite job of heating my chambers, it still has a nasty chill that emanates from the stone walls. I often obtain multiple quilts when winter hits in order to stay warm well into the night.

After pouring another whiskey, I reach for a quilt and wait for Rydian's return, becoming lost in the dance of the flames that wildly flick in the mantel. The amber liquid swirls as I sip, warmth rising in my chest in a way that matches the heat of the fire. The chamber is quiet except for the crackling in the air as my thoughts drift back to the events from today.

Spending the afternoon with Rydian was oddly comfortable, despite our bickering. But the only information I know about him is what he shared with me in his memories.

My eyes glaze over, the flames soothing the edges of my mind. The day finally wears on me after being up since dawn, my eyes drifting closed, the warmth of the fire pulling me in. I don't know how long I sit when my eyes flutter at the feeling of being carried, leaving me to groan.

"It's just me, little fawn," Rydian mumbles.

I'm gently placed in bed, covered by a quilt, when the weight of his presence leaves me. My eyes fly open, and I snap a hand out to grip his wrist in a silent request. His warm gaze meets mine, brows drawing close together as if hesitating.

"Stay," I mumble, my voice groggy from sleep. "Where are you going to sleep, the floor?"

He chuckles and gives me a gentle nod.

The last thing I feel is the bed dipping under his weight, and for once, the comfort of not being alone as I drift off to sleep.

22

——————

My eyes flutter open. I wake tangled in my sheets, quilts, and... I barely move my chin, looking down. A muscular arm wraps tightly around my waist, where a hand is snugly tucked between my ribs and the bed. His thumb lightly grazes the underside of my right breast. Rydian.

His face is tucked into the crook of my neck, breathing deep and soft, strands of my hair fluttering around my face. His chest moves steadily behind me—asleep.

He must have snuck into my bed last night after he returned —I *asked* him to stay. Frustration grips me at the realization.

How could I be so weak? I was supposed to stay awake, waiting for him, and must have fallen asleep in the settee. I remember sitting down before Rydian carried me to bed.

I stir a little, attempting to give myself distance from this... interaction, when he groans, pulling me in tighter. *Closer.*

My eyes flare. I don't need to be *closer.* That's the last thing I need—bad idea.

"Don't go," he mumbles. "You're warm."

A loud exhale escapes through my nose. His squeeze steals

my breath when he finally loosens his embrace, though he still holds me firmly enough to keep me there.

"Why are you cuddling me?" I groan.

My ass lies perfectly at the curve of him, and I can't help but feel the taut muscle behind me, thick and strong. My face heats, and I'm thankful I'm facing the opposite direction.

How is it that I'm always flustered around him?

Other than Ezra, I've never actually spent the night with a male before, let alone shared a bed for *sleeping.* Any time I've needed to get my needs taken care of, I've always gone to the brothel and then headed straight back to the castle after. Never... this.

No, this feels intimate.

"I didn't mean to. It just got so cold last night. You're like a furnace," he mumbles, and my eyes roll so hard to the back of my head that I'm surprised I can't see my skull. I'm tucked so tight into him, I can hardly move. "You asked me to stay, remember?"

"*That* was a momentary lapse in sanity. I was clearly tired. Now are you going to let me go?" I ask.

"Do I have to?"

"It would be wise. Unless you'd like to be stabbed," I say, my irritation spiking.

He chuckles. "I do love your aggression, but I can hear your heart beating wildly. Are you nervous?" he mutters, his voice going down an octave. "Do you want to know what I think? I think you want me here. I think you like it when I touch you and are too stubborn to admit it."

My teeth grind because I know he's right, no matter how much I deny it. Heat reaches my ears, searing its way across my skin as my heart continues to pound. Every breath I take comes out in pants as I grow more irritated by this interaction.

It's maddening—the way he knows exactly what he's doing

to me. Yet the longer I lie here, the more I want to stay. And I hate that.

My frustration bubbles, and I attempt to fling myself off the bed, desperate for an escape. But before I can move, he reacts.

He whirls me back down, pinning me beneath him with startling force as he hovers over me. His body presses into mine, my shoulder wedged tightly beneath his chest, my head resting on his forearm. He traps me in place, pinning me with ease. The weight of him makes it clear that I won't be escaping.

The air thickens in the space between us when his brows lower. Something in his gaze changes when his pupils dilate, swallowing the vivid blue of his irises until they're nearly black. A look I've never seen before, yet I find myself completely mesmerized by it.

His eyes slowly shift to my lips, lingering in a way that leaves me to believe he could devour me right here. I expect my fear to rise, perhaps the need to push him away. Instead, gazing at him only fuels the fire beneath my skin as it roars to life. His eyes lift slowly as if savoring the sight of me.

"Yellow... orange... a morning sunrise," he murmurs after a moment, breaking the silence, but my brows pinch in confusion.

"What?" I ask on a breath.

"I never knew what my favorite color was until I ran into you at the Painted Bird, rewriting everything I thought I knew about beauty," he says quietly, my breath hitching at the confession. "I don't think I've ever seen eyes quite like yours. You quite literally took my breath away." A small smile.

"Are you going to let me go?" I ask softly, but even as the words leave my lips, a small part of me hopes the answer is no.

He lightly brushes a strand off my face, his gaze pinning me in place. After a few quiet breaths between us, his arm lifts, allowing me the opportunity to get up.

But I don't move—I can't.

It's as if all sensibility escapes me while I remain frozen in place. My heart beats wildly in my chest, my mind racing as he hovers over me. I know I should get up and push him away, but I don't, and the desire to kiss him—to pull him back down—claws at me as I struggle with the decision.

Pride keeps me in place.

I'm torn between wanting more and refusing to let him know how badly I want him. Even though I know he can sense it. My breaths become uneven as I decide—kiss him or get up.

His eyes search mine, calculating, as if daring me to make a choice. I hate choices, especially when it comes to emotions. Yet the tension between us simmers, waiting for one of us to shatter it.

But he's right. I'm too stubborn.

My eyes flick to his mouth before I quickly shuffle out from under him, leaving him alone in the bed. He lets out a low chuckle, putting his weight onto his elbow and resting his head in his palm, glancing at me.

There's no mistaking the heat between us. But is that all it is? A spark, something temporary? Or is it more? Perhaps that's all it is for him, but for me—I'm currently pining for the king of Aurelia, and I think that's more terrifying than any mission I've ever been on. *What is wrong with me?*

"Get out," I demand, putting distance between us as my back hits the wall. Then he reaches for me. "Get out," I repeat with more force this time.

I'm not explaining myself because I can't. I close my eyes, urging him to leave before I make a really foolish, impulsive decision. And it's not because I don't want to, but because it frightens me. *He* frightens me.

And although I want to cross that line with him, doing so would feel as if I'm accepting my role as heir of Aurelia.

A role I'm not quite ready to accept yet.

My eyes remain closed when I hear the soft whooshing

sound, the only indication that he's left my chambers. The room feels empty, much colder than it was just moments ago. My eyes open on an exhale, scanning my chambers only to land on a piece of parchment lying on the table near the door.

A black orchid lies atop the paper just as it starts to bloom, the only flower in Elderheim that blooms at dawn during the colder months—deadly and typically found in the castle's courtyard. Or if you're adventurous, the northern woods. It tugs at me, realizing that he must have plucked it when he was walking the castle last night.

I glance down, eyeing what looks to be a sketch of myself sleeping in the settee before the fire. My heart stops at the sight of it.

He somehow caught the warm ambient lighting from the fire, soft shadows casting across my face, my cheek propped against my knuckles. He captured the way my lashes lay, drawing every freckle on my face, even the solo one beneath my right eye. My lips are slightly parted as I hold my whiskey glass in my right hand, resting in my lap. He's captured me, just as a mirror would.

And I look peaceful—beautiful, even.

I find myself wondering how late he stayed up to sketch me before carrying me to bed, feeling guilty for kicking him out. If his goal was to make me feel bad, it worked.

I dress quickly, knowing that I have to find him and mentally kick myself because we need to formulate a plan on how to get into the archives.

Only I wasn't thinking about that when I kicked him out, too flustered at the thought of him being so close. I'm fully aware that he won't come back unless I invite him—not from the wards, but out of respect for giving me space.

As I go to rush out the door, my hand stalls on the knob, remembering that I was able to communicate with him through the Veil last night. I lean against the door with a huff, wanting to try before I decide to travel in the cold. No need to waste precious time if I can reach him through the Veil.

I close my eyes, searching. Feeling for the warmth that accompanies me when I touch the edges of the Veil. Then I feel the coolness of his presence, the earthy scent of oakmoss flooding me as the spot behind my eyes tingles.

"I'm sorry," I say, not knowing if he receives my words, getting nothing back. I bite my lip, fearing I may have been too harsh. *"Can you come back so we can discuss our plan?"*

Agonizing minutes go by. I'm still propped against the door when I push myself off, turning for the knob again when he finally responds.

"Say please," he mumbles and I groan, banging my head against the door. Is he really going to make me beg? *"Oh, come on. I know you can do it."*

"I'm not going to beg like a hungry animal."

"I never thought you would, but I bet you'd beg if I—"

"Please!" I blurt, stopping the train of thought before it enters my mind and ruins me. He makes me want to scream in frustration, but as soon as I blurt the words, a faint knock sounds at my door.

"Let me in," he demands.

I only realize that I've slumped against the door again when my eyes land on the flower and sketch beside me. My stomach lurches, leaving me to frantically shove them into the drawer, my movements rushed. With a scowl tugging at my face, I yank the door open.

He storms past, folding his arms only to stop in the center of the room to stare at me. I mirror him, lifting my brows.

"I already apologized," I say.

He unfolds his arms and walks to the table holding the whiskey bottles, then pulls the corks and sniffs them individually. "For what?"

"Did you discover anything last night?" I ask with a sigh. I suppose that's how the rest of the day is going to go, pretending like nothing happened.

"I did. Are you going to rein in your anger long enough to hear it?" he quips.

"Yes," I say slowly, hands clenching at my sides as I stare daggers at his back. He finally faces me, casually leaning against the table as if it were any other day.

"Good, because I think we'll be able to sneak in fairly easily."

"Really?" I ask cautiously, doubt lining my voice.

"Yes. There are two guards stationed at the archives—"

"There are four," I correct, shaking my head. "Two outside the doors, two inside the archives. You probably didn't stay long enough to see that the two inside the archives change shifts around midnight. They take a break before retrieving the other two guards. I'm not sure if they're supposed to, but after following the two of them, they stop outside to smoke a pipe."

He blinks. "Regardless, it'll be easy to get in. How long is the break?"

"Are you insane?" A disbelieving laugh bubbles out of me when he throws me another blank stare. And then I sigh. "It's a fifteen-minute break."

My brows furrow, and I glower like he's grown two heads. I'd like to know at what point he thought this was going to be easy. Getting into the king's private archives with four guards stationed there at all times will be difficult. With two of them being inside the archives, we'll never be able to get in and look for what we need. It'll be impossible to leave if we do happen to get in.

"Yes, *easy*," he reiterates, taking a seat in front of the mantel and lighting a fire with a flick of his wrist. He must have refilled it with more wood last night, leaving my brow to arch. Silence stretches as he carelessly rubs a hand over his jaw as if lost in thought, clearly planning.

"Here's what we'll do," he says, angling toward me. "We'll

arrive in the Veil just outside the doors and wait for the two guards stationed inside to change shifts. We'll have fifteen minutes to look around before the next two arrive."

"And how would we get in?" I ask because that's the tricky part.

"We'll sneak in the doors when they open for shift change, walking right past them as they leave. Then, we'll Veil out of the archives and into the loft arriving with the map… or a copy of it. See? Easy." He smirks and leans back, his posture reeking of arrogance as his forearms rest against the settee. Like he's had a revelation formulating this plan, though I'm not convinced.

"What if it doesn't work? We need another plan," I say.

I've been in the Brotherhood long enough to know we don't go into missions without a secondary plan and another exit. He has holes, and in my experience, nothing ever comes easy.

He scoffs, looking like I've just wounded his pride.

"Don't insult me. We can Veil out of there in an instant. We'll be fine." He waves a hand like he's shooing my words away with a scowl plastered across his face.

"Okay, so when will we be doing that?"

"Lucky for you, Ivy and Orin arrived just this morning. We can steal it tonight while Orin shifts into the captain. We could use him as a distraction in case something goes wrong. After that, we'll need to visit the Siphon I tracked," he adds, pulling his focus away from the fire and meeting my gaze.

"You want Orin to shift into Ren?"

My stomach drops. I hope that Ren doesn't decide to take a stroll to the kitchens like he did a couple nights ago. He'd have to walk past the courtyard in order to reach them, and as much as I believe we could win in a fight, a small part of me doesn't. Ren's one of our most skilled fighters.

Rydian studies me, a mischievous look slowly forming as he rises, then throws me a teasing wink. "It'll be fun."

23

———

It's close to midnight as I pace my chamber, waiting for Rydian's arrival. We'll be stealing a copy of the map from the archives tonight, but it's not just stealing. We'll have to transfer it to parchment and exit before anyone notices.

My adrenaline is pumping. I've had no problem fulfilling the king's orders over the years, but breaking into his private archives is far different than a simple mission. It puts me on edge.

We decided that Ivy and Orin will remain in the Veil as we search for the map unless we need Orin as a distraction, which I'm hoping we won't.

A faint knock sounds at the door. I find Rydian in all black with his hood up.

He steps in. "Are you ready?"

"No. Are you?" I huff, wiping my damp palms on my tunic.

"When we step into the Veil, you need to hold my hand or we risk you stepping out by accident. Once we get inside and find the map, we can Veil out of there and into the loft," he says and then grins. "Just don't, you know... throw up this time. I'd hate for you to ruin this by vomiting."

After deciding to steal the map tonight, Rydian convinced me to travel to the loft through the Veil this morning, leaving me to run to the nearest basin to keep from hurling all over the floor. Embarrassment floods me, as it wasn't exactly how I wanted to be introduced to Orin.

A frustrated growl escapes me when another knock interrupts whatever insult I'm about to throw Rydian. He only winks, chuckling as he steps aside.

Pulling the door open with a huff, I find Ivy and Orin waiting in my stairwell. I gave them access to the castle as soon as dusk hit, so it's no surprise to find them knocking at my door while everyone sleeps.

Ivy wears a thick cloak like ours, but Orin wears a black tunic rolled up at the sleeves and black pants—similar to Ren's typical wear in the Brotherhood. Luckily for us, Orin is very similar to Ren in height, give or take a couple of inches. Only Orin is actually friendly and not a grumpy brute.

With dark hair and wide-set shoulders, he looks everything like a trained warrior, but also like he would start brawls for entertainment. His shoulders hardly made it through the opening on the stairs at the loft.

My curiosity spikes when a blonde birthmark near the back of his head comes into view, leaving me to wonder if everyone in Aurelia has them. Ivy has a white one resting at the top of hers, but I have yet to see one mixed into the auburn strands on Rydian though.

"Princess." Orin grins as I step aside and stifle a groan. A nickname I'm not fond of *at all*. The room feels ten times smaller with everyone crammed inside.

Ivy's serious gaze collides with mine for a breath. "If you have time, I'd like to see if you could search for anything regarding the army's movements—battle plans if he has any."

"Weapons and armor too," Orin adds, scratching the dark

scruff on his face. "Anything to help gauge where he is on maintaining distance from Aurelia, or if he plans on another war."

Though my face remains neutral, my stomach drops with unease. I only agreed to steal the map to search for my mother, but now they want army movements and battle plans? What happens if I find something?

Ivy's eyes briefly shift to Rydian's as he silently strokes his jaw, but now I'm feeling as if they know something I don't.

All I can do is nod, eager to get this over with.

Rydian and I clasp hands, and within a second, we arrive outside the archives near the two guards stationed at the doors. The Veil is almost weightless, feeling so light it's as if I'm walking on water, yet my head buzzes with energy. An unwelcome curl of nausea rises, leaving me to slowly exhale through my nose in order to settle my stomach.

We remain quiet—not a word is said as I hold Rydian's hand, waiting for the other two guards to exit. At any other time, I might have dwelled on how his hand comfortably wraps around mine, but now would be a bad time to get distracted.

A few minutes go by when the archive doors finally creak open, the two guards deep in conversation as they exit. We begin to move forward on silent feet, squeezing our way in just as the doors begin to shut. I breathe a sigh of relief.

Then, within seconds of arriving, the Veil flickers out, leaving me to whip my head to Rydian's with panic on my face.

"Did the Veil just disappear?" I breathe, my voice trembling with fear. "Please tell me the Veil didn't just vanish on us?"

"Elion must have put a ward in here. It's fine. We'll figure it out," he mutters, if only to convince himself. He's lost in thought as if coming up with another plan at the last minute.

"I told you your plan was flawed!" I say through clenched teeth, and he throws me a glare, clearly not in the mood to argue.

The ward most likely protects Elion's precious archives against anyone with magic. Although I'm trying not to panic, we only have fifteen minutes before the next two guards arrive.

"We need to hurry," he snaps, pulling me from my thoughts.

"I'm going to die here." My words drip with sarcasm, but I move regardless.

Scurrying across the archives on silent feet, I stop at the wall holding every rolled parchment since the beginning of Elion's rule. And it's a lot.

Quickly thumbing through them, I sift over dozens of rolled papers, pulling on the corners for anything that resembles a map. Nothing.

Rydian follows closely behind, going through the other side at record speed. I comb through all of them, yet nothing comes close to resembling a castle map. Just plans for cities, local buildings, and whatever future projects he has planned.

I remain standing, thinking of where Elion could possibly keep the map, especially if he has any hidden locations within it. I realize that he would be actively using it.

With a quick turn, I hurry to Elion's desk, pulling open drawers for hidden compartments. Finally, I flip through parchment sprawled over his desk, scattering papers to reveal anything.

The movement of my hand stalls when my eyes land on a few neatly stacked papers with the duke of Alvonia's name written on it—Ekrin Highcrest, one of his council members.

Ekrin is the only Aetheri duke who hasn't married—every female in Alvonia groveling at his feet because of it. He came into his position roughly ten years ago at the age of twenty-four, making him the youngest Duke in Elderheim. But what does the king want with Ekrin?

Unable to stifle the rising curiosity, I gently spread the papers, quickly scanning the documents when my brow lifts. A small grin tugs at my mouth as I read. Interesting, but not what I'm here for.

As soon as I neatly stack them again, the corner of a rolled parchment comes into view under a slew of disorganized papers, as if it was mindlessly tossed aside. My breath catches in my throat when I see the label written on the back corner— *Castle Alvonia 112.*

Is that the map? What does the number mean? Perhaps it's the number documenting how many have been made over the centuries. I know sometimes they update the castle, so naturally, they'd need to update the map. I peel the corner back, confirming what I suspect.

A rush of relief washes over me before I glance over my shoulder. Rydian quietly rummages through the rolled parchment on the wall—occupied. Then I glance down at my hands as I'm met with a decision and swallow. Dread curls in my gut.

I have to make a decision.

Stealing this map will set in motion a future I'm not sure I want. Is it what I want? A future in a realm I know nothing of, heir of Aurelia—future queen? Or a king's assassin, killing on demand whenever ordered?

This is my *home*, isn't it?

We have minutes before the guards arrive, and I chew my lip, stuck between the tug to stay in Elderheim or wanting something more in Aurelia.

Then something catches my attention out of the corner of my eye, forcing my gaze down. One of the drawers is cracked open, catching shiny sparkles whirling in the low light. My brows pinch when I lean in get a better look, as if it's calling to me—

"Did you find anything?" Rydian whispers, breaking my focus. His steps stride closer, leaving me to quickly fix the king's desk and turn to Rydian with a tight smile. And , I've made my decision.

"I found it. We need to go," I get out.

He hurries to my side when we unroll the parchment, revealing the entire map of Castle Alvonia. Rydian pulls out a blank rolled-up parchment and lays it flat next to the map. He hovers his hand over it, but nothing happens.

"We're going to have to take the original," Rydian mumbles, and my eyes flare at the realization. "I can't access my magic."

My teeth grind. "We can't take—"

The archive doors begin to open, and we share the same panicked look before Rydian begins to roll the map. We silently rush to the doors, and with a sharp intake of breath, hide behind them the moment they swing toward us. My eyes squeeze shut, and I force my breathing to slow as I hone in on my training.

We wait until the guards walk through before stepping out, sliding past the double doors on silent feet. Orin has impeccable timing as I spot him standing across the courtyard, striding toward us, disguised as Ren. His eyes go wide, which means he sees us.

The two guards in the hall slowly begin to pivot our way when my breath hitches, but as soon as our feet touch the hallway, Rydian slams a hand over my mouth. We disappear into the Veil and remain in the hall. They can't see us.

The guards face us when Orin calls out, catching their attention and accusing them of not doing their jobs correctly. Our backs slide against the stone as we calm our breathing.

"Hush, little fawn, we're almost out." Rydian slides into my mind. In a single beat, we're standing in the middle of the loft with the castle's map and breathing heavily, shock settling itself into my core. My frantic breaths heat Rydian's palm as it remains over my mouth. His hand begins to slowly lower to my shoulders, both of us too stunned to speak.

Did we just steal the map of the castle?

With wide eyes, I pivot into him as we step from the Veil, but he hasn't moved. His arm remains tightly wrapped around my chest, and I'm —painfully—too aware of him against my back. For a moment, everything is silent except for the pulse climbing to my temples, blood rushing in my ears from the adrenaline. But also something else I'm too afraid to name.

Rydian's grip briefly tightens, as if he doesn't want to let me go, and the heat of his chest burns through my tunic. The logical thing to do would be to pull away, but the adrenaline rushing beneath my skin has my legs unsteady. His breath gently grazes my temples, and for the faintest of seconds, I catch the way it falters as he peers down at me.

My eyes lift when his heated gaze meets mine, brows lowering as if he's also sensed the rising tension. The urge to say something tugs at me, but the words dissipate before they even get a chance to reach my tongue. Then I part my lips in surprise, realizing just how close he is to my mouth. And how much I actually want him to close the distance between us.

I actually want him to kiss me?

It was just this morning when I hesitated, leaving me to pull away from him, as I was too afraid to cross that line. Yet for some reason, I want it now.

Is it because of the decision I made in the archives? My decision to choose Aurelia over Elderheim?

His gaze shifts to my lips like he's sensed where my thoughts landed, and my breath catches in my throat, thrown from the unexpected tension between us. *Is he going to kiss me?*

The pull of his mouth has me wanting to lean in when the hand secure around my chest lifts to my neck, as if he planned on pulling me in.

Then the sudden *whoosh* from Orin and Ivy's arrival has me jolting back with wide eyes, swiveling my attention to the kitchenette. I nervously rub the back of my neck when both Ivy and Orin's brows pinch, eyeing us, expressions full of confusion. The nervous trembling in my hands forces me to clench them as I realize we were just seconds from our lips touching.

Rydian remains planted when I shoot him a glance, though his heated gaze is already fixed on me. His expression and tightly clenched jaw tell me that he hates the fact that we were just interrupted, and I find myself wondering what would have happened if we weren't.

"Now what?" I ask breathlessly.

24

———

It took us three days to confirm what we thought the map might reveal—all the tunnels and hidden passageways.

We spent the first two days studying where each passage connected, where Ivy marked sections most relevant to where Elynor might be held in. Orin translated sections of old Fae text none of us recognized, while Rydian and I made overlays of the map with the current architecture, using my memory to fill in most of the blanks. While the map looked mostly updated, it's obvious that it's at least twenty years old.

But by today, Ivy and Orin left with a duplicate of the map to report back to Aurelia, leaving me behind to wait. Again. So I do what I always do when I'm left alone—I find something to keep my hands busy.

It takes everything in me not to growl in frustration as I feel this damn wall for the tenth time. My hands scrape over the stone, searching for the spot that moved when I was sneaking back to my chamber a week ago.

Rydian and I will be traveling tomorrow to search for the Siphon in hiding, but he told me to wait for the others before exploring the tunnels, since I'm not good at holding myself in the Veil just yet. But idle hands cause me to do foolish things.

Like feeling this wall at two in the morning.

Yet my frustration bubbles because the moving stone I felt against my back last week should be right where I'm standing. At least that's what it showed on the map.

The only reason I'm here is because I feel like I need to do something—anything. Anything to keep my mind off Rydian and my incessant need to want to touch him. We've hardly made eye contact after stealing the map, refusing to acknowledge the heated moment between us in the loft. And definitely ignoring the curious glances both Ivy and Orin shot at us.

Huffing, I drag my nails across the thick spaces between the stones, hoping for a gap but with no luck. I smack the wall in frustration, resting my forehead against the cold stones, and grit my teeth.

Then the energy shifts as someone steps behind me, and I immediately stiffen, sensing who it is by the way cedar and leather hit my nose. *Seriously? How does he do that?*

"Your stealth is lacking," Ren murmurs. "I heard you from down the hall. Why are you groping a wall at two in the morning and being loud while doing it?"

My stomach sinks with a chilling fear, but my irritation flares higher, surging to the surface. I stifle a growl and whirl around, my smile tight as I'm barely concealing the storm brewing beneath my skin.

"Do you just know where I am at all hours of the day?" I ask quietly, my teeth grinding with restraint. "Is there some invisible string I don't know about that tugs at you and tells you what I'm doing?"

Ren only clenches his jaw, throwing me a cold stare as if I've already annoyed him. "Maybe I'm just good at tracking," he says.

"You tracked me here?"

Gods, I really hope that isn't the case. Regardless, my pulse climbs and my eyes quickly scan the corridor, searching for anyone else who may have joined him. Dim torchlight continues to flicker in the courtyard where the guards remain at the archives. But knowing that does little to ease the curling in my stomach.

I exhale and snap my attention back to Ren just as the corner of his mouth tips into a knowing smirk. He must be joking since there's no way he could have known I wasn't sleeping—not at this hour. The thought barely crossed my mind before I decided to throw on my clothes and slip into the shadows.

Unless he'd been watching.

A chill crawls down my spine at the thought of him keeping an eye on me, but with a lift of my chin, I give him a small smirk.

"You're messing with me," I say casually, then remember that he stole from the kitchens the last time we were in this hall. My eyes instinctively flick to his hands. "Oh my gods, you're stealing again."

"Hush," he snaps.

"Do you have a thing for sweets?" I chuckle as a quiet growl rumbles up his chest.

Again, my eyes dart behind him to ensure we're alone. That the guards at King Elion's archives didn't overhear us. Ren holds my gaze for a breath, then suspiciously squints his eyes.

I fear he'll mention this to King Elion in passing, regardless of him stealing. My stomach twists at the thought. I know that his loyalty is with the king first and foremost, so I decide to give him a partial truth for fear of him doing just that.

"Well, since you're *stealing* again, I'll tell you. The last time we were in this hall, I could've sworn I felt the wall move when I leaned against it," I say cautiously, my eyes shifting to the chain around his neck, spotting what looks like the shape of a ring settling beneath his tunic.

He studies me, not answering right away. Instead, his gaze

drops slightly as if reading the anxious flicker across my expression. Like he knows what's currently running through my mind.

"And?" he asks.

I exhale. "And it felt like a door. I was curious and I'm awake so…" I carelessly shrug, but he glares in silence as if deciding whether or not he should believe me. "But I've been here for thirty minutes and can't find anything, so I'm giving up and going to bed. See you later, thief."

I quickly step around him, eyeing my exit at the end of the hall, and hope he doesn't chase me down or report me to King Elion. Sweat beads my forehead despite the chill in the air. But then a quiet scraping noise fills the air behind me—stone.

Pivoting, I find Ren aiming his palm toward the wall as a stone door cracks open, right where I was standing. Excitement pricks my skin, my mouth falling open when he turns to me with a wicked grin. Then my irritation flares, realizing he just found what I was looking for—for the last half hour—in a matter of seconds.

"Want to explore?"

How I ended up in a dark, hidden passageway with Ren in the middle of the night, I'll never know. But here I am, striding down the darkened corridor, floating an orb over both of us while listening to him bite into one of those tarts he stole from the kitchens.

Despite my chilling unease.

Pushing the orb higher, I glance at the cobwebs that cling to the walls, dust thick in the air. The floor is cracked and uneven, showing how much of the area has been left untouched—unused. But I notice a few empty crates on the ground and how torchlights hang on the wall.

Ren notices where my attention shifts as he flicks out a

hand, igniting the torches. The corridor lights up, each one flickering to life, and I see how far the corridor goes. *Wow.*

I assumed he would have killed me by now. The thought still lingers at the possibility, but the thrill of discovering this tunnel outweighs the logical part of my brain. The part where it tells me to go back to my room and ignore the fact that I'm alone with him in a tunnel.

Rydian's going to be pissed when I tell him.

But Ren pushed out his magic to find the door, encouraging us to investigate it, and I can't help but think that he already knew it was there. With where it's located, the entrance sits directly beneath the ballroom.

"Did you know this was here?" I ask, my voice echoing off the walls. "What is this place?"

His hand grazes the dark stone beside him as if dusting it, and then he wipes his hands on his pants. I listen to the thud of his boots on the ground, but his steps remain light as he reaches my side in only a couple of strides. He throws me a wary side-ways glance, like I should already know, but I brush it off. I never really bothered to learn about the castle anyway.

"This is an old housemaiden tunnel. They used to use this as a way of getting around the castle from the kitchens without being seen. But now that times have changed a little, they aren't really needed anymore. There are multiple entry points in the courtyard, but most are hidden behind the shrubs."

"I think that's the most I've ever heard you talk, brute," I mutter, stifling an amused snort. "But I'm not surprised you know that since you're so familiar with the kitchens. Are you not afraid I'll go sneaking around and cause trouble?"

This could be useful later, especially if Rydian and I end up exploring the castle with Ivy and Orin. But I begin to wonder how much of the castle Ren is aware of and if he knows where everything is. If he does, it could make it a little more difficult to search the castle. We'd have to stay in the Veil if that's the case.

"If I thought you were a threat, I wouldn't have brought you down here."

"That's insulting," I say. "Would you like for me to show you how threatening I can be?"

He huffs out a quiet, disbelieving chuckle. "You could try, but with how loud you are? I doubt you'd be able to reach me before I put you on the ground."

"You're arrogant."

"It's not arrogance when I know your weaknesses. I just know how to use them for my benefit. The rats practically flee in the opposite direction with you stomping around," he grumbles.

My irritation spikes at the insult, and as much as I want to punch him, I hate to admit that he's partially right. Stealth has always been a weakness of mine, and though I'm fairly skilled at remaining quiet, being utterly and eerily silent has always been a struggle of mine.

We reach a sharp left turn, and he lights the torches that line the new hall. I have to glance over my shoulder to ensure he still trails behind me with how silent he is, wondering how the hell he stays so quiet for someone so large. He hardly makes a sound.

Walking down the corridor, I begin to notice the doorways scattered here and there, thinking they may lead to the dungeons below or old servants' quarters.

"I'm surprised you haven't tried killing me yet. Changed your mind, brute?" I grin, throwing him a sideways glance as we reach another sharp right turn. Only this time he doesn't light the torches. He shoots out a palm, urging my steps to slow and muttering under his breath.

"If I wanted to kill you, it would've already happened. You wouldn't have had the chance to know it was coming," he says, his tone unsettlingly sure. A coldness creeps down my spine as I get the chilling realization of how true that statement probably is.

My steps are calculated and quiet as I inch myself forward before he snaps out a hand again, halting me from going further. I glance at him. His expression is grim as he puts a finger to his lips and points up. Tilting my head, I listen as the guards' boots thud above us, hearing whispers of their conversation. Then I peek around him, spotting one of the grated doors that's blocked by shrubbery, and inch closer.

He hovers over my shoulder, looking out as I glance between the leaves, spotting the opposite side of the courtyard from where we just came from. We're by the archives, hidden in plain sight right under the steps.

After a few more tense, quiet minutes, we finally return back from where we came, striding toward the exit. His boots quietly hit the stone beneath us, hands casually swaying before we reach the small stairs leading to the main floor.

As I move to ascend the steps—following him out—he puts his hands in his pockets and faces me, blocking the only exit with a hardened stare.

My eyes narrow, studying him as he holds me hostage.

A dark expression settles over his features. "Do you want to tell me the real reason you've been sneaking around the castle so late at night?"

"What's it to you? Going to turn me in now that you've walked it with me? Or shall I remind you that I know you steal from the kitchens?" I purr, but my tone drops.

He gives me a lazy smirk. "Unfortunately for you, blackmail won't work since eating sweets isn't treason. That's what sneaking around the castle currently looks like, doesn't it? Trying to find new entry points and ways to sneak around undetected? I'm willing to bet King Elion glazes over my snacks for your treason."

"You wouldn't dare," I say, exhaling.

"Are you willing to risk finding that out?"

My chest heaves with unsteady breaths as the silence between us stretches, hanging thick in the air. His gaze never falters, but a sinking realization settles in the pits of my stomach—he would go to the king. And he'd do it with a smile.

The thought of him doing that fuels my anger, and my hands warm as the blaze of magic beneath my skin simmers. He'd probably savor the moment, watching as they hauled me to the dungeon, knowing I'd finally be silenced—no more defiance or retorts that ruin his day. Not from me at least.

He steps down from the last step, getting close. "If you're *curious,* you either learn how to be stealthier or risk having a guard find you in the hall. You're lucky it was me who found you and not one of the others." He gives me a smirk, and if he weren't so cruel, I'd almost find it charming—almost. "But now you'll be running laps this week, and expect to work on your stealth over the next two as punishment."

I exhale, almost in relief, but then my eyes go wide. "Seriously?"

He crosses his arms, glaring down at me. "You should've known I was behind you. I watched you for ten minutes before approaching, and you were loud. I'm shocked those guards didn't hear you, which means they aren't very good either. So you'll be working on that." He pivots to the side, motioning me up the stairs.

Glaring with each step, I shove past him and return to my chamber in silence. I'll take the punishment if it means he won't be reporting me to King Elion.

For now.

25

Ren followed through with his punishment during my training this morning, meeting me in the arena two hours before dawn. I had woken up early only to find him waiting with a menacing grin. The kind of grin that had me stifling a groan.

But I complied without complaint, only because I knew I needed to leave the castle again and didn't want questions flung my way. He didn't say a word the entire morning, only stood by, silently watching until the sun rose before leaving to hand out missions—which are still happening.

Now, I pull my cloak tighter around my chest, fighting off the chill coming in from between the trees as Rydian and I ride further into the forest.

"Where are we going exactly…?" I ask warily.

I've never ventured out this far since there's been no need to. Our missions are typically located in the cities, and the furthest I've gone is Nymara. Instead of going further north on our way into the Twin Valley, we veered east, deeper into the woods.

We decided to Veil into Alvonia earlier to save time and to grab some items from the loft, including the bag slung across my chest.

Though my experience with traveling through the Veil remains nothing short of chaotic. I hoped that after stealing the map, my time in the Veil would get easier.

But I was clearly wrong in that assumption.

As soon as we arrived in the loft, my head started spinning, forcing me to tuck myself between my legs to keep from retching all over his floor. Rydian growled, *"You better get a bucket because I'm not cleaning that,"* which didn't help my nausea.

Better than the first few times, but still.

He was adamant on traveling to the Siphon—whose name is Milena—through the Veil, but I convinced him not to. That if he didn't want me to hurl up everything I ate this morning, we would be grabbing a horse from one of the local stables. I instantly regretted the wording because he did, in fact, come back with a single horse, forcing me to ride with him.

"The Whispering Woods," he mutters finally.

"What?" My brows lower on a growl, leaving me to pivot in the saddle to face him. His eyes dart to mine as a smug grin pulls at his lips, full of wicked amusement.

"Do you know what that is?" I ask, facing forward.

"Are you frightened?"

I only scoff, unable to help the smidgen of fear that rises in my chest. Not that I couldn't handle myself, I'd just rather... not. The Whispering Woods hold the spirits of the realm, but creatures of Elderheim live there as well. Including Grokees, Wraiths, Nightlurkers, and Howlers.

All of which I have no interest in meeting today, and now I'm going in with only a horse and a few knives? King Elion wouldn't dare go into those woods. He doesn't even send the brethren in them, knowing just how dangerous they are.

"I told you that we should have Veiled in," he murmurs. "But you insisted we use a horse. I've already traveled through the area. We should be fine for now."

He mentioned that he tracked Milena soon after we arrived

in Alvonia, having traveled here the week prior. I wondered how he could have tracked her so fast given that she's in hiding. He only told me that it had something to do with Bess, and that she wasn't willing to fork out the information.

"Easy for you to say," I mumble, now hyperaware of every noise and crunch of the branches lining the path.

The dirt road is scattered with the leaves left over from fall, creating a blur of yellows, oranges, and reds. Although winter is in full force, the trees are so thick that the snow hardly covers the road we travel down, sheltering us from the harsh winds.

It's also a path frequently traveled on, given the thick indents in the road, leaving me to wonder who could be traveling to and from the Whispering Woods. Rydian sits snug behind me, and I catch myself thinking about the drawing he left.

"I saw the drawing," I mutter.

"Did you like it?"

"Maybe," I say, fighting a grin. "How did you learn?"

My hood falls, and he pushes my braid to the side, playing with the loose, dark strands that hang off my neck. I stiffen slightly, silently thanking myself for tucking my birthmark within the braid before leaving.

I don't know why I choose to still hide it, perhaps a habit at this point. Regardless, I can't help the rising flush to my neck from his touch. And then he hums to himself before answering.

"Andre's mother, Queen Jhessa, used to take me to the city while Andre was learning how to be a king through his father. We would often travel to the market together, sketching the folks that shopped. It's a nice memory."

"Are your parents still around?" I ask, because even though he mentioned that King Malvain raised him, he never went into detail if his parents were alive or not. He's silent for a moment, as if he's taking the time to think about his answer.

"No," he murmurs softly. "My mother died shortly before I left to live with King Malvain. And my father..." He trails off, then quietly sighs. "He was a selfish male, but he's not around anymore. Andre's family helped shape who I am."

Before I can stop myself, my hand grazes his leg the moment he slips an arm around my waist. My heart skips, unease prickling my neck as an unfamiliar feeling of warmth curls in my stomach, leaving me hesitant.

Almost like the slow realization that I might actually like him. Like he's growing on me—something more than just a simple infatuation. It's sharp and hard to push down, impossible to ignore.

Yet the thought of being the heir to Aurelia plagues me. Can I say no to being queen? What if I don't want it?

If I'm being honest, I'm not entirely sure how I feel about ruling a realm of Fae I know nothing of. Not fully anyway. The history of them has been lost over the years due to King Elion's laws—banning the Shadovar, cursing their name, and punishing the residents of Elderheim who speak of them.

My thoughts continue to spin, but after a couple of hours of riding, I hate to admit that Rydian was right—we weren't bothered while we traveled. Why is it so feared if there's nothing here?

Sable, our mare, plants herself in the middle of the road and comes to an abrupt stop. I glance around, feeling as if we're being watched.

"Why did we stop?" I whisper, gripping the dagger that's secured to my thigh, palming the hilt. I'm confused as to why we would be stopping in the middle of the road when it clearly doesn't end for miles. My stomach twists.

Then he begins to whisper something I don't understand, murmuring under his breath, looking above and into the trees.

I pivot, my brows pinching as I'm drawn in by the curve of his lips while he speaks—precise and fluid. Then a shimmer of what must have been a glamour begins to fade, rippling across and outward, revealing a hidden home.

Tucked neatly into the forest is a unique cottage built into a large tree on our right. With the door being regularly sized, I begin to wonder how someone could live in a place so small.

"We've arrived," he says and hops down, offering me his hand.

I look down and then back to his face as he arches a brow, leaving me to sigh and sheathe my dagger. My stomach flutters. I slip my hand in his and swing my leg over. Rydian's hands slide up my waist to steady me, leaving me to sharply inhale.

"Stay close, little fawn. There are creatures nearby, but don't be alarmed." His breath grazes the shell of my ear.

We walk through the glamour, and then it conceals us like a cloak again. I reach my hand for his, despite feeling ridiculous, and tuck myself into his side. I scowl at the thought of those creatures as my eyes graze the area.

Things creep me out, especially Grokees. After that nasty bite in the Twin Valley, I don't plan on revisiting a wound that took two days to recover from.

Rydian glances down with a smirk, our hands still joined. Scowling, I drop his hand and step to the left, falling into step behind him.

"Where are we?" I mutter under my breath.

"Milena's home. Heavily glamoured to turn away anyone who ventures too close. Bess informed me that once the horse stops and we feel the need to turn around, we've arrived. But I had only gone so far, so I didn't know what to expect."

"She lives in a tree?" I ask.

I'm not convinced this isn't a hoax. Who in their right mind would live in a tree? Stopping just outside the wooden door, Rydian knocks as I look up. And up. It just keeps going.

The tree swallows the sky above us, not a cloud in sight. It's eerily quiet as we wait. The only sound is our breathing and the soft breeze that slips through the trees.

My eyes flick over the area again, searching for anything

indicating a presence. With a glance down, I notice a disturbance in the mud and take a step back, eyeing the footprints beneath my feet.

Massive—easily twice the size of my hands—and I quickly notice a path around the tree. Curiosity tugs at me, eyes fixed on the ground as I move left, carefully trailing the large footprints. My steps remain quiet and light, not daring to disturb the leaves as I begin to round the tree.

"Isa," Rydian whispers, but I brush him off with a wave of my hand. My braid falls to my left as I look over my shoulder, meeting his gaze with a small grin—a look warning me to stay nearby while we wait.

"I found prints," I say on a breath.

Rydian stiffens, shoulders going rigid as his eyes widen, shadows instantly forming in his palms. I halt dead in my tracks, a dagger already in my palm.

I feel it first and then hear it—the hot breath and growl emanating from the creature beside me. Breathing down my neck, blowing pieces of hair across my face with a menacing growl.

I stand frozen, mirroring Rydian as we stare at each other. My eyes squeeze shut. I'm begging the thing to not eat my face off as I inhale, willing my body *not* to run.

Don't run. Don't run. Don't run.

"If you run... I will eat you," it warns me in a tone so low that it raises the hair on my arms. Oh my gods, it spoke to me.

"I see you've met my wonderful companion," a stern female voice says.

I'm too frightened to breathe, afraid I'll cause the thing to lunge for my throat, given its mouth so close to my neck. I slowly turn, facing the creature and the female beside it, eyeing what has Rydian so paralyzed with fear. I'm met with the largest Howler I've ever seen.

One of the ancient wolves, where Grokees originate from.

Only Grokees are sick.

This one still has all of its fur and flesh, somehow making it more terrifying. Its controlled anger chills me far more than that of a Grokee, where I can anticipate its rage and hunger.

The Howler's sharp canines are four inches long, its tongue tucked inside its mouth as it snarls in my face, deep and low in warning. Its fur is a deep gray with a white undercoat, eyes a shade of gold, reminding me of a wildfire.

A raging, angry wildfire.

My eyes graze the female standing beside it, her head reaching the top of its haunches. Fair-skinned with tawny brown hair and hazel eyes, wearing rounded glasses, Milena looks to be in her fifties, indicating that she must be a few hundred years old. She smiles, giving the damn thing a pat—like a hound.

"Sit, Grim," she says.

He calms his growling, allowing me to straighten and wipe the sweat off my forehead, adrenaline coursing hot through my veins. Rydian comes up to my right, slowly nudging me behind him.

"I'm Rydian Vaelborne, king of Aurelia. We came to see if you had any information regarding the last Siphon," he says, getting right to the point, it seems. I smack him for the poor introduction, earning me a glare and a shrug.

"Why are you trespassing?" Milena asks, eyes narrowing suspiciously. She gives us both a once-over, then shakes her head. "Never mind. I have no answers for you, and I want no part in it."

She gives Grim a final pat, sending him into the forest as she strides to the front door of her tree.

Rydian follows, growing agitated. "We just need a moment to talk. We'll be quick. You might be the only one who can give us anything of use, and we would greatly appreciate your help."

"No," she clips.

And I can practically see Rydian growing more frustrated, his jaw clenching over her clipped words. He throws me a hardened scowl as if silently urging me to step in. She finally reaches her door, placing her palm on the frame as three runes light up, unlocking it in an instant.

I step forward. "Please, Milena. I fear someone in the castle has been siphoning my memories. We don't know who else to turn to. If we can just sit down for a minute, we won't be very long. We can pay you for your time—"

"No." She brushes me off, already halfway inside.

"Please, my name is Isa, and I'm..." *The heir of Aurelia,* I almost blurt. My eyes flare as I wonder why I was about to admit that, but her head whips to me with wide eyes.

"Isa?" she whispers.

Does she know me? My brows furrow, but I don't know what else to say so I just stand there. Rydian's stare blazes into the side of my face.

"Just a few minutes," I say.

I don't want to be here anymore than she wants us here, but we need this information, and she's our only lead. If she says no, we'll have to start over and hope we can track the other Siphon. She holds my gaze a moment longer when she finally huffs.

"One hour. That's it!" She steps inside, and I shoot Rydian a grin. "Hurry up! The door won't stay open for long!"

26

Shutting the door behind us, we come into an extraordinarily large cottage that doesn't look like a tree at all, more like another illusion from the outside. My brows are practically touching my hairline at this point.

We're greeted by a wide stone mantel that sits in the far right corner of the room, angled at a small kitchen and a round wooden table with four chairs. Next to that sits a domed window overlooking the forest with a settee large enough for reading and napping.

My eyes slowly graze the area—lining every visible shelf is a lifetime of books. Herbs hang from the exposed beamed ceiling, the earthy, floral aroma hitting my nostrils a second later. Milena heats the kettle on the stove.

"Have a seat," she tells us.

After a moment, she sits, handing us both a steeping hot mug of tea with a tray full of muffins. It tastes of honeysuckle and chamomile with the faintest trace of fresh rain—crisp and sweet.

"You're Elynor's daughter?"

"You knew my mother?" I ask in disbelief.

She flicks her gaze between us. "What is it you need from me? I don't see how I can help either of you."

Rydian leans forward, resting his arms on the table. "You're one of the last Siphons. From what I've gathered, you used to work closely with King Elion, and we would like to know why you're in hiding."

She removes her glasses to pinch the bridge of her nose, then holds her mug and stares. "I might kill Bess for this. It's been so long since I used my magic, afraid the king will somehow track me down for it. But then again, he replaced me almost as soon as I left." She sighs. "King Elion and I disagreed on what was ethical. He wanted me to experiment by extracting memories from the Fae—criminals at first, but then it changed. He had a very specific goal and agenda. Little did I know, it started to pull their essences, leaving them without their magic. I didn't feel comfortable taking the very thing giving our land life, criminal or not."

That explains why I haven't been as skilled with my magic— removing my essence.

"What happened?" I ask.

Milena shakes her head, lost to her memories, thumbing her bottom lip. "He started to obsess over it. I'm not entirely sure why he was wanting me to continue, but it was during the time of the treaty—years after the War of the Veilstone. When Elynor wasn't queen yet. I didn't even know she was a Shadovar until she was sneaking out of the castle, informing me that she could get me out if I wanted. She knew I didn't agree with Elion—I was never quiet about it. She offered to help me go into hiding. We stayed in touch all those years up until her letters stopped coming. I never knew what happened to her." Milena's eyes soften as they meet mine. "You look just like her by the way. I should have recognized it as soon as I saw you."

Rydian stiffens at her words, a small shift.

"You knew my mother and she came to find you... as in, she

was here in Elderheim? What do you mean? How was she in the castle?"

I glance between her and Rydian, confused, because I don't remember anyone mentioning to me that my mother was a resident, realizing that she shared the same walls as me.

"She was sent here by me a few years after the treaty as an informant before she became queen," Rydian explains, eyes locking on me. "At the time, I was Andre's second-in-command, leader of the army's informant operations. I knew her before she married Andre. She had insisted on going to Elderheim since we needed the information on what Elion was planning to do with the Veilstone. She worked her way in as a king's guard, staying around a year."

"*You* sent her here?" I growl.

I'm stunned at the new information that was just revealed, knowing that he could have told me before coming here. Instead, I find out in front of a stranger after almost getting my face eaten off by a Howler.

Milena chuckles. "A king's guard, hah! They had a whole relationship, Elynor and King Elion. She fled shortly after she received her Varethin and took me with her. She was afraid that King Elion would see it and immediately know what she was." She points to the top of her head, where Elynor's birthmark sits.

Elynor had a relationship with King Elion? It's hard to imagine my mother wanting a relationship with the very king who stole my memories. A thousand questions climb to the surface, yet I can't get a single one out. My hand settles on my stomach as nausea consumes me, leaving me to stand and pace —to process. The fire presses against my skin, leaving sweat to trickle down my neck, when my hand settles on my chest, right over my racing heart.

"Impossible. I would have known about that," Rydian hisses.

If my mother was close with King Elion, it would explain his motivation of capturing her after fleeing the castle. Was I captured because I was in the way? Was it revenge? More questions fly through my head when I land on one I don't dare ask in front of Rydian.

Then my curiosity spikes again, my brows furrowing as I recall the term *Varethin*—in Rydian's memories and Milena's description of my mother, thinking of what I saw in Ivy and Orin's hair just a few days ago. Is that common?

"What is that, a Varethin?" I ask quietly, unsure if she even hears me as she scoffs at Rydian, eyes narrowing.

"You wouldn't have known—she didn't tell a soul," Milena says. "The only people who knew were me, King Andre, and whoever else was in Castle Alvonia at the time. From what I heard, Elion was frantic over her disappearance, not realizing that she was Shadovar. He had placed his wards around the castle shortly after he found out what she was."

"You're lying," he accuses.

She leans forward, pointing a finger. "You don't get to show up on my property uninvited, come into my home, and accuse me of lying. King or not, I do not have to help you. Isa's the only reason I'm giving you this information, because of who her mother is. You can take what I tell you however you want, but I am no liar."

I dart my eyes between them, feeling extreme respect for her, especially if she's speaking to Rydian the way she is. Anger flashes across his face, and he scoffs with a shake to his head.

Then she pivots to me with a sigh. "A Varethin is a mark of Aurelia—mate marks. Aurelia's is found in the hair, tying you to someone in the realm by the color of it. Though both realms have their own versions as Elderheim's are typically colorless marks on the skin. Your mother's mark was tied to King Andre, which is why she fled. Where *is* Elynor?"

I blink, masking my shock as my stomach sinks. Does that mean I'm tied to someone in Aurelia—that the color in my hair isn't from birth? If that's the case, it directly ties me to the realm, meaning everything Rydian's been telling me has been true. That I'm from Aurelia and I'm the heir to the throne.

Although he showed me his memories and I can wield Aurelia's magic, I still had my doubts. But now those doubts have been squashed in a matter of seconds. Nausea curls in my stomach at the thought of my presumed responsibility to rule Aurelia, as if it's just now sinking in. I feel as if I have no choice but to accept it, whether I want to or not.

I used to dream of my freedom, slipping from Alvonia—out of the castle—for a quiet life in the woods somewhere. This newfound responsibility is the complete opposite of that. What am I supposed to do, run a realm and throw balls as a queen of Aurelia? That thought alone leaves a whirl of apprehension crawling up my spine.

Rydian stands to pace. "We aren't sure, but we're looking. Elynor was captured during the battle twenty years ago. Do you happen to know where he'd keep her?" he asks, but she shakes her head, and he lets out a defeated breath. "What of the siphoning? You said he was experimenting. How does memory siphoning work?"

His auburn hair brushes against his brows, his cloak swooshing from the sudden movements near the fire that crackles behind him. I lean against the wall near the windows, willing my heart rate to slow as I take it all in.

Milena hums. "As you know, the king is a very powerful Scry, which allows him to see glimpses of his future. Before I left, he was having me place those memories and essences into crystals for his own personal use, telling me it was detrimental to the future. Storing them for what, I don't know. I left before I could find out."

Elion's archive flashes across my mind and what I found in those drawers, my thoughts whirling with more questions.

"Can they be put back? If these crystals... or memories are

found, can they be put back into the Fae they came from?" I ask, hope rising in my chest.

"Yes. If they can be taken out, they can be put back in." She eyes me over her glasses, and a relieved exhale leaves me.

"And can *you* put them back?" I mutter.

"I haven't used my magic in a very long time, but I should be able to. Can you wield any magic at all?" she asks after a moment, brows furrowing.

"Some," I admit. "I used to not be able to do any, but over the last few weeks, it has been growing rapidly."

She points a finger at me. "Don't breathe a word about your magic if you suspect your memories are being stolen. When we pull a memory from someone's mind, it's attached to their very soul—their essence. But over time, you're able to grow some of that essence back. After all, it's ours, regenerating similarly to the blood in your veins but at a much slower rate. It takes a few years to replenish, but once it starts, it grows rapidly."

Her words reassure me of my decision to remain quiet.

But if it only takes a few years to replenish, does that mean my memories have been taken more than once? If my calculations are correct, the essence stolen from me as a child would have regenerated by now. I should have been able to wield magic for years already. Right?

"That's good to know. Do you know who the Siphon is?" Rydian asks, something we desperately need to know.

He's stopped pacing, facing Milena with his arms crossed, somehow making her cottage feel compressed—almost claustrophobic with how large he is.

"Mm." She nods. "I do. It's my grandson, who's now King Elion's second-in-command. He was appointed shortly after I went into hiding."

I quickly recall Rydian's memories of Ivy mentioning that King Elion's second-in-command killed King Andre. But it's me who's confused, knowing that King Elion doesn't have one—not that I'm aware of. I've only ever seen Theron at his side, and as cruel as he is, he's no second-in-command.

"And what's his name—your grandson?" I ask.

"His full name is Witt Dralor, but the last time I checked, he changed his name. He was a sweet boy, but his parents died during the war, leaving me to raise him after. He was pretty much raised in the castle while I worked for King Elion, but when he hit adulthood, something changed," she says.

During the war? So that means that he's been around close to when King Elion took the throne.

She frowns. "He became unpredictable and could switch between moods in seconds, as if he was a different person entirely. He's the last Siphon ever born in this realm and is fully at the king's disposal. He's dangerous, but I'm not sure what he goes by now."

Rydian looks off to the side when a look of revenge hardens his features, his brows lowering. It casts shadows over his eyes, giving him a dark edge, and I swear that I see them moving as he clenches his fists.

The tight line of his jaw reveals someone who's willing to destroy anything in his path. Anything to avenge his king, no matter the cost.

27

My hair catches on the breeze, grazing my lips, and I cast a glance to my left. Rydian has walked quietly beside Sable with his hood up ever since we left Milena's. He wanted to walk to Alvonia and has done so in complete and utter silence. I assume it has to do with the new information we received.

On the bright side, if I were to find my missing memories, I'd be able to get them back. If King Elion even decided to keep them. With my luck, he probably tossed my valuable memories into the nearest river and went along with his day.

That wretched king. All these years he's been pulling memories and experimenting with Fae, and we never even knew it. It's a miracle Milena got out alive when she did, though I can't help but wonder what it was like for my mother—stuck alone in a castle with no allies and a secret heritage. I shake my head at the thought of it being very similar to my current situation and begin to wonder *who she knew.* If she stayed in the castle twenty-six years ago, it's possible someone could have known her at the time.

Unfortunately for Rydian, this new information means that the second-in-command still walks the realm and works for the king. Although I don't blame him for his current mood, I do find myself wishing I had the knowledge of who the second-in-command is if it could give him an ounce of happiness. To soothe the rough edges of his heart, knowing it's why he's remained silent on our trek back. But I don't, and it's just one more missing piece to the never-ending mystery—my memories.

But what else did they take from me? If King Elion only wanted to wipe my past, wouldn't he have left my recent memories alone? Other than that time at the orphanage. I can understand why he would want to wipe that, but everything else?

I find it odd I don't know much about the castle or who King Elion works with. Why wouldn't I know about the second-in-command? Then it crosses my mind—King Elion must want to keep him hidden for a reason, but why?

The saddle groans beneath me as I adjust to the empty space at my back, and for whatever reason, I miss the steadiness and warmth Rydian provided. We keep a steady pace, and I listen to the trees rustling in the breeze as the thick of it finally lets up, the Twin Valley resting in the distance. We've been riding for an hour, meaning we should be in Alvonia soon, spotting the slight left curve in the path ahead. The sun makes its descent in the sky as the chill of the evening begins to settle, wrapping around me like ice. Nighttime quickly approaches.

I didn't realize how late it's getting, but hopefully no one will notice my absence. , a chill snakes down my spine, slow and ominous. I shudder, recalling how familiar it feels as a wave of unease settles over me.

Goosebumps form on my arms and an eerie silence falls, the only sounds in the vast forest being our breathing and Rydian's solid steps, as if every bird decided to sleep at once. Squinting, I scan the open space before glancing at Rydian, watching as he keeps his steady pace on the path, as if nothing is amiss.

I adjust again, squirming on the saddle.

"Rydian," I whisper, and he grunts at me. "Something's not right. We need to hurry."

He keeps his gaze forward and gives me a quiet huff of amusement. "Don't tell me you're scared of a little forest."

"I'm not joking. Something is *off*," I hiss, but he ignores me, letting silence fall between us again for a few breaths. He keeps his leisurely, carefree pace when I kick my boot out and connect it with his back, causing him to snap forward. Sable comes to an abrupt stop.

"Are you even listening to me?" I growl.

Rydian whirls around with a glare, holding tightly to the reins. "There's nothing wrong or I would have noticed it. Though I'm happy to remind you that you're the reason we took a horse today. We're almost to the city—or are you only saying that because you want me to join you on the saddle again?" He gives me a teasing grin, and it takes everything in me not to smack it right off his face. "Just ask, if that's the case."

"Are you always like this?" I snap. "No, I don't want you *back* on my saddle, you snubby, arrogant king."

As soon as the words leave me, Sable shuffles and stomps her feet, leaving me to palm my daggers in an instant. Rydian's expression shifts, the hard lines of his jaw feathering as he scans the area in a slow circle, palming his own daggers. Sable becomes increasingly more agitated, throwing her head up and down. I throw Rydian a menacing glare just as she enters my mind.

"The air is different here," Sable says, huffing.

"I fucking told you," I tell Rydian, quietly hopping off the saddle to meet him at his side. "Do you believe me *now*?"

"We don't know if it's anything yet," he says casually, but the way his body is rigid and taut tells me he doesn't believe his own words. That he's only trying to calm my unease.

But it's not working. I've felt this type of unease before, and that was in the Twin Valley with the Grokees. I wouldn't be surprised if more creatures venture out and into the Whispering Woods. We're close enough to the valley that it could be possible.

Evening creeps in, leaving a nasty bite in the wind as clouds of my breath form around my face. A dense fog settles at our feet, winding through the trees as hues of blue and orange cast a soft glow across the forest floor. Then a light crunching sounds to our right.

We whirl toward the noise, but after a few minutes of waiting, nothing happens. I grip Sable's reins to keep her calm when I catch Rydian's smug smirk peering down at me, and I roll my eyes.

"See, it's nothing," he says.

Then , a loud screech pierces the air and something crashes into both of us, throwing us forward and into Sable with a hard smack. I cry out as my face connects with the edge of the hard leather. My right cheek stings just as Sable throws her head back and whinnies, rearing on her back legs, front hooves slicing through the air.

"No!" I shout.

Rydian grunts behind me, and Sable's sudden movement has me grappling for the reins. Without warning, a sharp sting travels down my left calf and I cry out, losing my grip on Sable. Then she's gone, galloping down the path, leaving me to hope she finds her way back to Alvonia.

Whirling to face the creature reaching for me again, I dart back from its shocking appearance. It's nothing I've ever seen before.

It's gaunt and as large as any Fae, looking as if it used to be one with its pointed ears. Only this one is pale with milky white eyes. It looks as if it's been starving its entire life by its thin appearance, razor-sharp claws, and tattered clothes. Skin is missing in places, exposing bone along its arms and jaw.

Just like the Grokees.

Its thin lip curls into a snarl, screeching again, the sound slicing through the air. I wince, fighting the urge to cover my ears. My breath catches, and I scramble as it begins crawling toward me on all fours in a blur of frenzied speed.

Oh my gods, why is it crawling?

It throws me off guard, but I quickly twist, barely missing its claws and sharp teeth as I lunge forward to stab it through the temple before it reaches me.

"What the fuck?" I pant as it slumps on the ground, and then I whirl to find Rydian fighting off three more. On instinct, I quickly throw a dagger, hitting one in the eye as he cuts down one and then slices through the other with a pained cry.

"Are you okay?" I exhale, stumbling toward him.

He pants, breathing ragged, but when he turns to me, I notice the raw, jagged gashes marking his shoulder and fore-arm. Blood drips to the ground in uneven splatters. My eyes go wide as I assess him, and that's when I feel the pain throbbing in my leg, forcing myself to ignore it. The wind howls in the distance, the orange glow of the sky continuing its descent. Evening has made its final appearance.

"We need to get out of here," I say.

He gives me a slight nod just as another ear-piercing screech cuts through the air behind me, eyes going wide with fear. I pivot in time to watch as the creature flies toward me, right for my face.

Within a breath, I'm yanked into his chest.

Everything goes black as nausea rises, my stomach twisting in a whirl of movement as we enter the Veil. But before I can make sense of what happened, we both land near a small cave by a river with a quiet groan and a loud thud.

Rydian holds me tight against his chest, but the weight becomes unsteady when he releases me, stumbling back to brace himself against the stone of the cave.

His skin is pale, breathing labored. I glance down—his right shoulder and forearm are shredded, leaving his clothes bloody, hanging off him in pieces.

Gods, it looks terrible. And as if the emotion is involuntary, panic rises in my chest, and I bend down to meet his gaze, inspecting him. Even though I know that he can't die, I find myself mentally praying to whatever fates who listen that he lives through it. My heart skips as I realize that I would be devastated if he died.

"Rydian," I get out, gripping his chin to hold his gaze as my other hand attempts to stabilize him. "Where are we? We need to get you to a Healer, and we need to do it now."

He only shakes his head, closing his eyes. "I just need… rest. We're near Arcan."

"What do you mean?" I grind out. "Why didn't you take us to Alvonia or the loft?"

Arcan is south of Alvonia by almost two days, which means he's landed us in an entirely different location in the middle of the woods. *Great.*

I stand, giving the area a quick scan. The river roars behind us, flowing at a steady pace, so we'll have plenty of water. Surrounded by trees, firewood is no issue, but we might be without a decent meal besides what I have packed in the bag that's now slung across my back. He groans again, and I glance down to meet his stare.

"I'm injured… which drains me," he mumbles, taking a deep breath. "Which also means that… the location I originally aimed for when traveling through the Veil didn't quite line up… and instead, landed us here." He groans again, pushing himself off the wall, cradling his arm. "I'm afraid we're stranded until I heal, unless you want to give traveling through the Veil a shot?"

A groan escapes me, and I turn from him with a shake of my head, knowing damn well I won't be able to muster enough magic to risk traveling with both of us. *We're stuck here for the night.*

"That's what I thought," he mumbles. "I've been here before, though. This cave is empty so we can stay here and Veil back in the morning."

"Fine, but I'm still inspecting it in case it's not. Just stay here. I'll be right back," I mutter and attempt to walk away but the adrenaline has worn off, leaving me limping. I bite my lip to keep from crying out when Rydian grips my wrist, gently pivoting me toward him.

"You're injured," he mutters. "Why didn't you say something?"

"I'm fine," I say, pulling my arm away.

28

A fire crackles in the middle of the cave, small enough so that it doesn't smoke us out but large enough to boil water and heat the cramped space. It's unnervingly cold—bone chilling even—and even though a fire quietly roars in front of us, I can't help but shiver. Perhaps it's the injury that has me so cold, or maybe a storm is rolling in.

Luckily, since Rydian has been here before, he previously moved large stones in varying sizes into the cave, used as chairs. He claims to have come across the location a few years ago when meeting an informant in Arcan. He didn't go into much detail about it other than that it was a peaceful spot, enjoying the river when he passed through.

We've just finished cleaning our wounds, taking turns soaking strips of my torn sleeves with the boiling water. Now we sit in silence around the fire.

"Are you hungry? I have some dried meat in my bag." I shoot a glance to my right, catching the hard line of his jaw as he clenches it, but he gives me a small nod anyway. Stuck in Arcan for the night isn't exactly what either of us had in mind, but we'll have to make it work. I can only hope that no one comes knocking on my chamber door over the next few hours.

Lifting the flap and digging through the canvas material, I quickly find the meat, offering him a few pieces when I notice something shiny at the bottom of my bag. Reaching in, my hand grazes a small metal tin, and I pull it out to find the leftover salve from my trip to Sylvanor.

I grin. Ezra gave me the first tin after he replaced it just in case I needed it on my ride. I rise to my feet, limping to stand in front of Rydian just shy of his knees.

"Take your shirt off," I say, motioning for him to lift it with a flick of my wrist. He lifts his gaze to mine with a raised brow and a wicked smirk.

"Naked so soon? I figured you would've held out longer," he says and I groan, exhaling through my nose.

"Just let me put this on you."

His eyes finally dart to the small tin in my hand when he gives me a nod and begins to peel off his shredded shirt. He pulls his left arm out and inches it above his head with a wince, so I reach over to help with the remaining pieces. The movement forces me to hover over him as I peel off the torn fabric stuck to his arm. He hisses in pain, and I pause, catching his gaze.

"I'm fine," he growls, shaking his head.

My brow arches. "You're not, but it's good to see you're at least well enough to throw out your usual charm," I mutter, opening the salve with a quiet *pop*. "This isn't like your injury in Sylvanor. How come you're healing slower here?"

Stepping between his legs, I motion for his right arm. He silently lifts it, but I catch the way his breathing stalls as he meets me with a heated stare in a way that forces my eyes to focus on his arm instead of where I'm standing. His warmth radiates off his muscled chest, and I feel it heat the space around my hands despite the brisk chill in the air. I slowly work the salve into the cuts when his voice goes low.

"I was at full power in Sylvanor, but whatever that thing was, its bite slowed my healing. It's worse than any damage from a blade, which is usually a clean cut, but the longer I'm in this realm, the more it dampens my power."

I gently hold his arm, lightly grazing the paste over the four jagged gashes that reach from his elbow to the top of his wrist. He's at least stopped bleeding, but the fleshy wounds remain open.

"Have you seen something like that before?" he asks.

"No," I murmur, the fire crackling behind me. "But they remind me of the Grokees we encountered when we tracked you to Sylvanor. One left a gaping wound on my shoulder after knocking me off Bjorn. The healing took me a couple days to recover from." I glance up to catch him staring before I shift my gaze back down. "Their torn, decomposing skin looked the same. They also had a very similar scent, and the feeling I got…" I shudder, shaking my head and remembering the chill that went down my spine before he realized we were surrounded. "I could almost sense them. I don't know. It was odd."

His soft breathing brushes the hair over my face, and I realize then just how close we are. Eager to focus on anything else but his mouth, my thoughts land on the hidden birthmark in my hair, pulling me back to what Milena said.

"My mother had a Varethin mark in her hair. Milena mentioned she received hers in the castle—does that mean they're not born with it?" I ask quietly.

He hums, a puff of air escaping his nose. "The marks of Aurelia are often acquired later in life. Most don't get theirs for many, many years."

"Do a lot of Fae have them?" I ask as my fingers graze his wounds again, drawing a low groan from him.

"It's not uncommon," he gets out between clenched teeth.

"Most spend their lives trying to find their connected soul, oftentimes marrying when they do."

I nod, thinking. "And if someone has one of these… marks. Who's to say it's not just a birthmark?"

He chuckles softly. "That would make life easier, wouldn't it?" he mutters almost to himself. "To believe it was only a birthmark. No need to wonder if there's a mate somewhere in the realm only meant for you."

My fingers slow their movement. "So you're saying it's not possible for something like that to only be a birthmark?"

"No, I've never heard that before," he mumbles. "If you have a streak in your hair—of any color—it's a mark. And it means you have a mate in Aurelia that's bound to you."

I have to pull my hand back to hide the trembling in my fingers. All my life I believed the color in my hair was a birthmark, and if what he says is true, why don't I recall getting it? Unless King Elion wiped that part of my memories, but if he did, why?

"So, what makes you worthy of a mate mark in Aurelia?" My finger dips into the tin again as he shifts his shoulder forward for me to reach. His eyes graze mine, a small grin tugging at his lips before shifting his attention to my hands.

"I'm not sure, but I know that the Fates don't make mistakes with their marks. Some Fae wait a lifetime for theirs to arrive, while others don't receive one. Some even believe it's because their mates aren't born yet, or perhaps they just don't have one. But if you *do* get one, it can be a… lonely life."

"Lonely?" I frown. "How so?"

"If a mark appears, they spend a lot of time searching for their mate, often turning down future partners in hopes of connecting with their mate at some point. But it's never guaranteed," he murmurs.

"How would they know who their mates are?"

"By the color and the location. They align in the same spot, and then there's… that feeling. The connection, they say, and a couple other details like claiming them during a ritual," he says.

Interesting. I already know about the mate-claiming rituals, but his words force me to pause, turning them over in my head. The color and location? Would that mean it has to match mine? Truthfully, I'm not sure how I feel about being connected to someone else, but his words leave me curious.

After dipping my finger in the tin one last time, I pivot to rub the salve on the rest of his shoulder when he catches my hand right below the scar on my wrist. My eyes narrow, meeting his gaze, but he shakes his head.

"There's not enough in there for my shoulder but there's enough in there for you," he murmurs, grazing his thumb over the top of my hand, then gives me a lopsided grin. "It's your turn. Take off your pants."

I find myself chuckling with a shake of my head, his eyes gleaming with amusement as I wipe the remaining salve back into the tin. "I'm not taking my pants off. Nice try, Your Majesty."

He chuckles. "Fine, leave your pants on, but you're getting the rest of it."

He guides me to sit on his left, pivoting me so that my legs drape over his lap, giving him access to my calf. I put weight into my palms when he takes out one of his daggers. I attempt to sit up, but he pushes his hand against my ribs with lowered brows, halting the movement.

"Relax. I'm just going to just cut the fabric at the knee. It needs to breathe." He throws me a sideways glance, and I catch the way his mouth quirks as if he's fighting a grin.

"I like these pants."

"Well, they're useless now."

I groan as he cuts and rips the fabric off with a rough tear, exposing the torn flesh, leaving me to wince as it brushes against the wound.

"Sorry," he murmurs and then falls silent as he rubs the salve over the back of my calf in soothing but gentle strokes.

The fire flickers, lighting up his face, leaving me to notice how his auburn hair falls to his forehead while he leans forward.

My eyes snake down the left side of his neck, landing on his bare chest, where swirls of dark ink stop right above his nipple. My gaze travels farther down, noticing the hard lines of his stomach. I find myself wanting to lick the area right above his pant line. *Dammit.*

My face flushes at the filthy thoughts bouncing around in my head, feeling too hot even though it's cold enough for ice to form. A soft breath escapes me, and I quickly close my eyes. I drop my head back, forcing myself to focus on savoring the gentle touch of his callused fingers instead of how he looks while putting it on me.

The salve is cool on my skin, then warms almost instantly. I sit for a few breaths, losing count as I listen to the sounds of the crackling fire, my neck rolling to the side as the earthy smoke fills my nostrils. My body relaxes, an involuntary quiet sigh slipping free.

"There... all done," he murmurs, and I slowly open my eyes to find him staring at me. I blink, my lips parting as he holds my gaze, then gives me a slow, lazy smirk. "Are you going to remove your leg from my lap?"

I glance down to find his hand has stopped moving without realizing, and my face heats, leaving me to yank it off. He chuckles, the sound deep and throaty as he tosses the empty tin near my bag on the ground with a clink. But I can't help but notice that the throbbing in my leg has gone away.

"Thank you," I mumble.

"Now go lie over there. We need to rest for our travels in the morning," he demands, nodding to where our cloaks lie side by side near the fire, and my face heats again. Just the thought of sleeping next to him has me flustered. It's one thing for me to suggest it when I'm half asleep. It's another when I'm agreeing to it *fully awake.* Was that only four days ago?

"Last time was a moment of weakness," I say with a tight smile. "We're not sleeping next to each other."

He huffs a sarcastic laugh. "We are if you don't want to freeze."

I roll my eyes and toss another few sticks into the flames, ignoring the fact that it will be dropping to a freezing temperature sooner rather than later. "Isn't that what the fire's for?"

"Yes, but unless you want more unknown creatures finding us while we sleep, we'll be putting it out before bed. Not to mention you're still shivering, so yes, we'll be nice and huddled up to stay warm for the night," he quips.

I straighten, my hands flying to my hips. "No."

His brows lower a fraction as he stands—clearly annoyed— meeting me near the fire in one large step as a tense silence hangs in the air. His gaze meets mine, though I catch the way his eyes briefly dart to my lips before he speaks.

"Now why are you being stubborn? Don't pretend like you don't like my demands, because I can smell it on you—how much you like it. Tell me something..." he says quietly. "Were you going to meet me that night at the brothel? Did you plan on coming back to see what we could do together?" A silent beat passes between us. "You know, if you had waited another five minutes to knock on my door, I wouldn't have been at that inn —I would have been at the brothel waiting for you."

Oh gods, he was going to go back.

His question makes my chest grow hot, my skin warming under his gaze because I *was* going to go back. I wanted to see him again, despite knowing that I shouldn't.

Then he takes the smallest of steps into me and his fingers lightly brush my chin, tilting my head back and forcing me to hold his gaze. A breath catches in my throat as a burning need shivers down my legs and settles right between my thighs. It takes every ounce of control I have not to groan.

His mouth hovers over mine, inches from me, his breathing shallow and uneven. We're so close we're practically sharing breaths. So close that I can almost taste him as his fingers linger on my chin. His eyes flick to my mouth the moment I catch the intoxicating scent of him flooding the cramped space. It feels way too small for the both of us.

Yet I really want to graze my mouth across his, like it's pulling me in similar to how waves answer to the moon—involuntary.

Call it a moment of insanity, but within a span of a single breath, I'm planting a quick, impulsive kiss to his mouth. So quick that he immediately stiffens, his breath completely halting in his chest as he stares at me, frozen.

I quickly dart back with a gasp, eyes wide with shock as my hand rises to my lips. Did I just kiss the king...? Oh my gods. I have never done that before—never.

What the fuck is wrong with me?

A heavy, awkward silence stretches between us. His chest rises with deep breaths, leaving his lips to part on a sharp inhale as if he's trying to maintain his control. Or perhaps stifle his anger?

Then his brows pinch with a flicker of confusion as he silently watches me, stunned speechless, and staring. Something changes in his gaze, something close to matching the flames of the fire beside us—heated.

Dread crawls up my spine, realizing that maybe I misread the energy between us and crossed a line. I know he was teasing before, but perhaps he didn't want me to kiss him. I find myself mindlessly backing up as he inches forward with lowered brows. I can't read his expression.

"Fuck, I'm sorry. I shouldn't—" I say quickly, words halting in my throat the moment he growls.

His good hand shoots out, fingers curling at the back of my neck as he yanks me to him. The jolt of his strength catches me off guard, leaving me to gasp right before his mouth crashes into mine with desperate intensity.

And before I can comprehend it, his tongue slips past my lips, stealing the breath right from my lungs. He tastes me—devours me, as if he were drowning and I'm the very air he needs.

An involuntary breathy moan escapes me, my entire body melting into him like his mouth was always meant to be on mine. Stars fill my vision—gods, I've never been kissed like this before.

The scent of him floods my senses when his hand slides beneath my ear, deepening the kiss, as if it were his last day in this realm.

He groans and bites my lip, leaving me to gasp at the sharp pinch of pain the moment my back hits the stone behind me. The force of his kiss is not gentle—it's hungry and eager, and all it does is send a roaring heat between my legs. His hips drive forward, flush against mine, when I feel the hard length of him across my torso. *Fuck, I want him.*

Without a second thought, my hands are reaching for the rim of his pants, eager to feel him just as his other hand rises to my face as if to pull me closer. Then he hisses in pain, leaving him to break our kiss and jolt back, like the pain in his arm brought him crashing into reality.

"Isa," he breathes, almost like a warning—regret, maybe.

That definitely sounded like regret. But I don't want to look at him and squeeze my eyes shut, leaning my head against the stone as disappointment rolls through me. Heat sears my skin, but it's not from the nearby flames. My breaths finally slow as I focus my attention on the scent of the smoke and the crackling fire. I don't think I've ever wanted someone more.

"Are you in pain?" I ask finally, but when he doesn't answer, I open my eyes to find his heated gaze still fixed on me. Yet I can't help but think he regretted it with the way he jolted back like that. "I'm sorry. I didn't mean to—"

"Now's… not the time," he says quietly, so low it forces me to step forward with furrowed brows to hear him better.

"What?" I ask.

He takes in another sharp inhale, slowing his own breaths. Watching him makes me realize that it wasn't regret I saw—he's trying to maintain his control. *Oh.*

"You have no idea how badly I want to strip you of every article of clothing right here in this cave," he says finally, and my lips part in surprise, heart thundering in my chest. "But if I'm going to fuck you, I'm going to be at full power so I can spread those legs myself without worrying about being in pain. And when I do, I fully expect my name on your lips when you come around my cock."

Oh gods, I forgot how to breathe.

"Stop looking at me like that," he growls.

A breath of air leaves me. "How am I looking at you?"

"Like you'd enjoy fucking me," he says quietly, flicking his tongue over his bottom lip.

Tension hovers between us, frustration rolling over his rigid shoulders, bare chest flexing in the dim light, as if this entire situation has him flustered. I almost laugh at being the one to fluster the king of Aurelia until his next words leave his mouth, dropping my grin.

"Now do as I say and lie down before I make you," he clips. "I can't promise that if I do make you, it won't escalate into… well, something else. My self-control is good, but not that good, and we need each other for warmth or you'll freeze. Got it?"

My eyes narrow at the sudden switch that squashes any lingering arousal in my blood in a matter of seconds. "Fine, but I'm going outside first unless you want me to relieve myself on you for added *warmth.*"

I quickly snatch my cloak off the ground and pivot for the exit. His deep chuckle echoes across the cold walls just as my feet touch the hard ground outside, leaving my teeth to grind.

As soon as the cold air beyond the cave hits my cheeks, I realize very quickly how much I wanted our kiss to turn into something else. I find myself wondering when I began to care about his feelings toward me.

And how much I want him to like me. That perhaps I could allow someone to shatter the walls I've built around myself for the first time in my life.

29

Over the last several days, Ivy has taken the time to teach me how to hold myself in the Veil now that my magic has been consistently growing.

I'm thankful no nausea plagues me anymore when it comes to the Veil, but the more days that pass, the more I feel the power beneath my skin itching to escape.

The magic frequently shifts between the warmth of the sun and the icy temperatures of the mountain, and I often find myself in a whirl of confusion when it surfaces. It's most likely due to not having magic for the last twenty years, so I've just slowly learned to embrace it, even if it feels odd.

"Where's Rydian?" I ask finally, pushing the thought to Ivy and hoping my tone doesn't sound too desperate for information.

She quietly walks beside me in the Veil as we inspect one of the castle's hidden tunnels. Two tight braids cascade down her shoulders, resting on the cloak that barely brushes her ankles.

"King Rydian and Orin are meeting with an informant up north. They'll be back in a few days," she says, feeling the stone wall beside us before throwing me a sideways glance. My brows

shoot up at the information she willingly gives me. A grin tugs at my lips. I want to test how much she'll give me.

"Who's the informant?" I ask, keeping my face forward.

Ivy only chuckles, the sound light and amusing. *"I can't tell you that. But King Rydian and Orin have been working with the same one for the last three years—the longest an informant has lived in Elderheim. It's best if it stays that way."* She wipes her hands, and I let out a defeated huff—it was worth a shot.

It's dim, leaving us to navigate the dark corridor with nothing but our instinct as our hands graze the cold, dingy walls. So far, we've only inspected a few, but she offered to come with me while Rydian and Orin were away. I just assumed it was to keep an eye on me.

I was annoyed at first, only because I had plans to sneak back into the king's archives while Rydian was gone. Was it risky? Yes, but I know I can do it without getting caught, as I need to put the original map back before Elion notices.

Not to mention, what I saw sitting on Elion's desk is something my mind—and curiosity—refuses to let go of. I just need to get back in to look at it.

"He seems to be... fond of you," she says warily.

My eyes narrow on her tone, as if being fond of me isn't a good thing, but maybe she's curious. Or perhaps I'm reading into it, as I still don't completely trust her yet, especially after wanting me to pull army information for them. For whatever reason, it felt wrong at the time.

"I'm sure I'm no different than any other female in Aurelia," I say, recalling what he said in the stables about someone in Aurelia he liked. As if I have no control over my emotions, an unexpected stab of jealousy shoots through me, leaving my teeth grinding.

After what happened in the cave, he practically spends his time avoiding me. I assumed it was because of his injuries at first. Then two more days went by, leaving me to believe that it's definitely me that he's distancing himself from.

Her chuckle infiltrates my mind. *"Did he tell you there was someone in Aurelia?"*

"Is there not?"

She chuckles again, the sound almost filled with disbelief. *"No, definitely not. Not after he got his—"*

Her words are interrupted by the guards echoing through the grates above us, leaving us to halt our walking. A musky dampness hangs in the air, reminding me of a wet cave as we stand in silence for a couple of minutes.

With a few slow breaths, I shoot her a glance when she nods toward the exit, and we quietly walk back to where we came, entering the castle from below. It's getting late, meaning the guards that do shift changes in the archives are about to arrive at any moment.

Sneaking through the castle has been much easier with the ability to use the Veil, walking the darkened corridors, right past a few lingering guards posted on the corners of his private indoor garden. We quietly inch ourselves toward the front of the castle—toward the kitchens—careful not to disturb the air as we stride by.

"I think I'm done for the night," I finally get out, eager to be left alone. *"I'm quite tired."*

Not a complete lie, but I'm hoping she doesn't question it as I quickly shoot a glance toward the king's archives where the two original guards remain posted. I may have a little time left...

We turn the corner toward my stairwell before she finally answers. *"We can pick back up tomorrow."*

"Perfect." I give her a small grin. *"See you tomorrow."*

Within seconds, she disappears, leaving me alone near the door to my stairwell and the door to the commons. A sudden burst of adrenaline shoots through me, sending my pulse to climb to my temples.

Yet for a few seconds, I hesitate, struggling with another decision. I remain in the shadows with an impulsive thought, my instinct pulling me toward the archives. But also a tug urging me to my room—to leave it be.

Then a flicker of light catches my attention, forcing me to shift my gaze to the door that leads to the commons. Someone in the Brotherhood must be awake.

I find myself quickly stepping out of the Veil and pulling the sleeping hall door open, the commons brightly lit from the mantel near the back. My feet quietly thud against the stone, but just as I reach the end of the hall, Ezra steps around the corner.

"Ezra." I exhale, quickly glancing around. "What are you doing awake?"

He's fully dressed, clad with his fur cloak and thick boots. Clasping the cloak at his collarbone, he gives me a quick scan before throwing me a grin. "I just got back from a mission and couldn't sleep."

"I couldn't sleep either. I was coming in for something to eat. Was there anything left from earlier?" I quickly lie, knowing he's probably realized I'm fully dressed too, wondering why I'm lurking the halls this late.

"I was actually planning on going to Alvonia for a drink. Want to come? We could get something to eat while we're there." He throws out the offer.

I hesitate for a moment as the memory of Elion's desk flashes across my mind, but Ezra's warm grin and the way he's looking down at me makes my resolve waver a fraction. And before I know it, I find myself throwing him a grin.

"Yes," I say, following him out the door, through my stairwell toward the side of the castle near the rise. "Where was your mission this time?"

"Went to Arcan again. Apparently there's been more Shadovar sneaking in," he says, and I stiffen at the word.

I feel my heart race, knowing that I'm one of those Shadovar.

He just doesn't know. No one here knows, but what would he think of me if he did? I'm unsure if it would be something I could tell him at all, and the thought of not being able to causes my chest to ache. Our boots crunch against the gravel as we exit the rise of the castle, leaving us to raise our hoods to ward off the chill. He flicks his wrist, summoning an orb.

But even as we catch up on missions and walk toward Alvonia beneath the orb that glows above us, I can't help the way my stomach sinks, knowing I just ruined my plans for sneaking back into the king's archives.

I'm dreaming.

I know this just by the way I'm looking down at myself, tossing and turning in bed as a cold sweat beads across my forehead. No fire roars in the mantel as the full moon casts pale streaks of light across my face. My brows pinch.

I'm pulled deeper and deeper into the depths of sleep as I watch myself, and it's odd. I know I'm asleep, yet I can't seem to wake up.

My body hums, the sensation building and consuming me as tingles slowly spread across my skin like static in the air. The warmth radiates behind my eyes, causing my breath to quicken.

I'm thrust from my room in a chaotic whirl of movement, my surroundings shifting so fast I can hardly comprehend it. Then I'm standing in a dark, unfamiliar chamber.

The distant sound of wind whirling against the windows sends a shiver down my spine, and within seconds, I know exactly where I've ended up. Because I've been here before—in my dreams.

My heart pounds against my ribs as a chilling realization washes over me. It's always the same dream.

Only this time, I'm in the dark castle, as I would recognize it from anywhere, although I've never actually been inside. I've only ever seen it from a distance—rolling, lush hills, damp air, and a dark ocean nearby.

I'm standing in what looks like a grand bedchamber—a king or queen's room, perhaps.

"How do you always seem to find me?" Rydian asks.

Why is he here? I groan, rolling my eyes as I face the king of Aurelia. I haven't seen or talked to him since Milena's cottage five days ago. Not since we were stranded in that cave. Ivy claimed he needed to meet with an informant, but I feel like it was an excuse to put distance between us after what happened. Our kiss.

Yet finding him in my dreams isn't all that surprising with how I've come to miss his incessant pestering. My head has become unnervingly quiet over the last few days, and for some reason, I find that odd.

His auburn hair grazes his forehead, missing the cloak he typically wears. He's in a loose dark green tunic, the long sleeves rolled up to his forearms with a pair of dark pants. He strides forward, and I realize I really like this view. Looking down at myself, I'm in the same slip I put on before bed—light in color and loose but still hugging my curves as it sits right below the crease of my thighs.

I scoff. "I didn't find you. You're invading my dreams. You just show up at the most inconvenient times."

The floor is made of a dark marble, cool to the touch, but my eyes land on his whiskey table. It rests by what looks like the main chamber door near the mantel, but I'm not too sure. Taking my finger, I run it down the length of it as I look around and then halt my steps. I turn and lean against it, pinning my hands behind me.

I throw him a grin. "Is this your chamber?"

He lets out a breathy laugh, flashing me a grin, none like I've seen in Elderheim. It's vibrant and full of life, as if he's genuinely happy to be here.

"It is. Do you like it?" he asks.

He stands in front of me, tugging lightly on the end of my braid, and pulls out the tie, freeing my wild hair. I stiffen as he's loosened the mark from its hiding spot, then quickly remind myself that it's dim and only a dream. Regardless, I scoff, and shove it over my shoulder.

"I love your hair," he mutters, eyes meeting mine for a moment. "You should leave it down more." I remain quiet, as it's something I find myself unable to reply to. He intently scans my face. "It's beautiful, like you."

My breath catches when he steps closer, sliding his hand to the back of my neck. Yet for some reason, I let it happen.

"You could be wearing rags, and I bet you'd look amazing in them," he murmurs.

I chuckle, shaking my head, though my head tilts back to study him, and I pull my lip between my teeth. I study the soft curve of his mouth, the scar resting at the top of his lip, and his jaw flexes.

"You shouldn't hide yourself from anyone," he says, his words soft. "I prefer your hair not tied. It's wild, just like you. You're a wildfire and need to be set free."

"Wildfires are destructive and unpredictable. And since when do I care about what you like, Rydian?" I smirk, though my eyes instinctively dart to his lips again as the memory of us in the cave comes crashing back.

"Wildfires are necessary for new growth," he counters, expression serious before his lips tilt. "And you don't, but I'd be disappointed if you did."

He catches where my eyes have focused, stiffening as if he's aware of the thought brewing in my head. His brows lower a fraction, a hunger flashing in his eyes, and he slowly leans in. Like he's testing the waters, unsure if I'll run the moment we touch.

But I step into him, my pulse racing as I tip my head back, anticipation humming in the air. He pauses an inch from my lips, his breath warm against mine as oakmoss fills my senses. A scent I've started to yearn for in his absence.

His right hand remains steady at the back of my neck, his left hand slipping around my waist, pulling me tightly against him. Our lips finally meet, firm yet soft, though I can't help but softly moan into *him, lips parting. It starts slow and tentative, then quickly turns hungry as he deepens the kiss—devouring me—his tongue exploring mine. My hands slide to the back of his head, my fingers tangling in his hair, noticing that a section at his nape feels shorter than the rest.*

He groans, the sound rumbling deep from within, sending a thrill through me as the realm fades, leaving only the two of us. With a gentle pull back, he breaks our kiss.

I groan in frustration, our foreheads touching.

"Isa," he groans, as if it pains him to stop just as much as it does me. "As much as I love hearing you whimpering for me, we should stop before we do something we might regret."

"I wouldn't regret it," I say, my words speaking the truth, because I wouldn't. But what would it mean? Does it mean I'm accepting my role as heir to the throne? What does it matter? It's only a dream.

He leans down, his lips brushing the shell of my ear. "If that's true, then I won't be taking you in the Veil. Wake up."

What was a kiss seconds ago is now me sitting up in my bed, panting heavily and finding my chamber bathed in darkness once my vision clears. The loss of his touch has me feeling empty, traces of his scent somehow lingering in the air. I didn't want it to end, now aching and aroused.

Fucking typical.

Anytime something good happens, *something* has to ruin it.

Smoothing my hair away from my face, I glance out my window. It's still dark. The moon streams in like it did earlier but is now a little farther across the room—a couple hours after midnight.

I rise, reaching for my water as my racing heart calms. A few seconds go by before a faint knock raps at my door. Setting the glass down, I grip one of my daggers, striding cautiously toward it and wondering who could be knocking at such a late hour. Maybe it's Ezra.

Cracking the door just wide enough to peek out of, I find Rydian panting in my stairwell, out of breath. My stomach flutters at the sight of him. He rubs the back of his neck and faces me, dressed in the same loose plants and dark green tunic from my dream.

My brows furrow at how familiar this feels and his appearance at my door so late at night. I thought he was still gone on his trip with Orin. Perhaps I was wrong.

Without a word, he pushes himself through the door, our lips colliding.

30

The force of it steals my breath as our mouths crash together, leaving my dagger to fall from my fingers and land near my feet as it clangs against stone.

He steps forward, guiding us further in as he kicks the door shut, my back landing against the bedpost. His mouth consumes mine when my lips part on an eager groan, deepening it like he did in that cave. The fabric of his tunic bunches in my hands, pulling him to me as I inhale him like he's the last breath I'll take.

A ferocious aching consumes me as my hands reach the back of his head. He releases a soft, hungry groan, and I'm reliving what my dream was just moments ago.

"Do you want me?" he growls, traveling a scorching path of his mouth to my jaw, then grazes his teeth down my throat. "Tell me you fucking want me, Isa."

I gasp—*fuck, yes, I do.*

His hand squeezes my neck in silent demand for my answer as he works his way to my collarbone. Yet I can't seem to find the words as I gasp for air. *Is this really happening?*

Granted, I've thought about what he'd feel like between my

legs since our first interaction at the brothel, but I never truly expected… *this*. Actually, I never expected it to happen given my future role in Aurelia.

"Answer me." He pushes the thought out, but it's forceful and icy, pulling me back to reality with a sharp inhale through my lips. I force myself to focus on forming words rather than how his hands are currently lifting my night slip over my bare hips. An unbearable ache grows right between my thighs.

"Yes," I say finally, eager to feel him as my hands graze the edge of his pants again, grazing the hard length of the king…

Realization runs through me, and I quickly push him off with a gasp, putting distance between us and grappling the bedpost behind me. He growls, shooting me a hungry glare, his tongue flicking over his swollen lips.

"What are you doing?" I get out, but my voice trembles, the words rushing from me.

I know damn well this isn't a dream. This is real, and the intensity of the moment has me flustered and aching all over. But he's the king of Aurelia. I can't—

"Do you want me to leave?" he asks quietly, studying me.

Do I want him to leave? The question of the century. Now would be the time to tell him to, as it would be the logical thing to do because he's the king of Aurelia.

And I'm just… an assassin. My stomach drops, dread curling in my gut because I know that's a lie—I'm a princess. A princess of Aurelia, future queen.

Yet my chest heaves with quick breaths, and against my better judgement, I find myself wanting him to stay. Wanting to feel his skin flush against mine like I wanted the first night we met. My heart skips. I know that if I say yes, I would be opening a door with him that I wouldn't be able to close.

Still, I hesitate as my thoughts whirl, realizing that perhaps I want it to open. And for the first time in my life, I'm eager for something more.

His eyes dart to my lips, and he inches forward, a low, throaty chuckle escaping him, as if he can sense my decision. It's almost sinister, and filled with dark promise.

"I want you to stay," I say finally.

Agonizing seconds pass, my heart pounding in my chest, when I'm squeezing my legs together. A growing heat reaches the apex of my thighs. My chest rises and falls in uneven breaths as he stalks forward until there's no space left between us. Then his hand slides to the back of my neck, forcing me to tilt my head back.

"Good. Because I've been wanting to taste you since that damn brothel," he murmurs, leaning in. "Are you going to let me taste you, Princess?"

Awareness prickles my skin as he peers down at me, a look full of an unyielding hunger. Just the scent of him sends a flood of arousal down my body, leaving my lips to part as a quiet breath of air slips out.

Rydian growls at the sound before our mouths clash together again, quickly becoming entangled.

Within seconds, he lifts me by the backs of my thighs, my legs wrapping around his waist. He tosses me on the bed, forcing the air out of my lungs as our mouths collide again. I arch into him, and his tongue slips into my mouth.

I whimper, gripping the edge of his tunic, frantically lifting to reveal the hard muscle beneath. But before I can sit up on my elbows to glance at him, he yanks me to the edge of the bed by my knees with a hungry growl. Then without warning, his head is between my thighs, grazing his nose toward the very center of me.

"Fuck," I gasp when he grazes my thigh with his teeth, my hand flying to his hair.

"Just what I wanted." He pushes the thought out, groaning against my skin. *"To spread these legs with my own two hands, feeling you soaked for me. Is this what you wanted—me on my knees*

with my head between your legs?"

He quickly reminds me of what I said at the brothel when we first met, and good gods, I love every second of it.

"I thought that..." I pant, grasping at his auburn hair, "kings didn't kneel for anyone."

He chuckles, the throaty sound vibrating against my core when his hands travel up my soft thighs. He spreads me wider, his grip tightening as my night slip inches over my hips to reveal myself completely bare and soaking wet. He groans, his mouth so close to the spot I need him as the warmth of his breath caresses my skin.

"Are you surprised that I'm kneeling for you?" he asks just as his tongue swirls over my clit, leaving me to cry out and drop my head. I lose all sense of reality as my world tilts.

Then his whole mouth is on me—devouring and sending stars of pleasure across my vision. My hips drive up, grinding against his mouth as sharp moans slip out, unable to restrain myself. His hands grip my thighs, pinning me, leaving me to growl in frustration as I chase my release.

"Look at me," he grumbles, my eyes flicking down. His gaze finds mine in the dim light, watching from between my legs as his tongue swirls over me. A simmering heat scorches my blood when my hips grind into him again, my mouth parting on a gasp. *"Fucking beautiful,"* he says. *"But I want to hear you cry for me."*

My heart races, tight pressure coiling low—too fast. I'm teetering on the edge of my release when he pushes in two fingers, driving them into me right before he curls—oh, fuck.

Legs trembling, I cry out, the sound sharp and wild as my release explodes from me. He straightens, leaving me no time to recover when his fingers slide out. Towering above, he watches me pant for breath before sticking them in his mouth, tasting me.

Heat sears across my damp skin, slick with sweat as I watch

him lick me off his fingers. With eager eyes, I finally get a good look at him. *Breathtaking.*

His skin ripples in the moonlight, revealing the hard lines and taut muscle beneath, as if he were carved by the Stone Shapers themselves. Swirls of dark ink travels down the left side of his neck and onto his chest, and I quickly notice that his injuries have fully healed from earlier this week.

My eyes rake over every inch of his body. The lingering high of my climax heats my skin, escalating to a frightening level. A flash of hunger forms in his eyes, and then they narrow slightly, darkening his features as a menacing grin plays on his lips.

"I bet you feel just as good as you taste," he says.

His fingers work the ties of his pants before they flutter to the floor, leaving my lips parting when my eyes land on the hard length of his cock.

Long and thick, a vein runs down the length of him. Oh gods. I've been with a few males, but I haven't been with any that looked like... *that.*

My breath hitches in anticipation when he steps forward, settling himself between my legs, leaving my core clenching. His hands grip the collar of my night slip, my heart stopping the moment he rips it right down the middle, freeing my breasts from the thin material. He reaches forward, taking my breast in his hand before pinching a nipple, leaving me to cry out in surprise.

"Do me a favor, little fawn." He lifts my hips, pushing the head of his cock against me when he rolls his hips—teasing. "Try not to scream. I'd hate to wake the castle." And he drives his hips forward.

"Oh gods..." My mouth falls open as a pleasurable, shocking cry passes my lips, forcing my head back from the pressure of him stretching me. *What the fuck?*

"You're fucking perfect," he pants, his chest rising and falling in a frantic rhythm, as if battling for control.

His hands glide up my body before grabbing the crook of my shoulder, just above my collarbone, and he thrusts once more—slow yet sure. Savoring. His eyes squeeze shut, his lips parting on a moan like he's soaking in every bit of me gripping him. The pleasure shooting through me is so intense, it's intoxicating.

Yet he sets the pace, slow and controlled, pulling out only to deliberately drive himself into me as I adjust. But slow and controlled isn't what my body is begging for right now—I need more.

"Are you going to fuck me or make love?" I ask, a mocking grin lining my mouth.

He shoots a hand out, gripping my neck. I let out a shocked gasp before he scoops an arm beneath me, pushing us further onto the bed.

As soon as I hit the pillows, he flips me over, pulling me up by a fistful of my hair. My back rests against his chest—on my knees, legs spread for him to enter from behind as I hover right above his cock.

"I thought you were going to behave for me tonight," he mutters in my ear, pushing my hair aside. "You're an impatient little thing, aren't you?"

"When did I ever give you the impression that I was going to *behave?*" I bite out.

"You didn't," he mutters, then forcefully pushes me down. "I guess that just means I can fuck it out of you."

My face hits the pillows on a gasp as his hand rests on the middle of my back, holding me in place as if he's inspecting me. Then a moment later, his head is between my legs again, tongue swirling.

"Fuck." I grip the sheets when he slides in two fingers. I pant for breath and the trembling in my legs begins—pleasure consuming me.

He grips my hip with a hand only to snake the other around, rubbing my clit and driving his hips forward at the same time.

My whimpers reverberate off the walls as he thrusts into me again and again, giving me exactly what I want.

He releases my hip to grip my hair, pulling me back into his chest. "You're doing so well for me, but tell me... why aren't you begging?" His teeth graze the inside of my neck before he bites. I moan as he guides my hips back. "Do I need to make you cry for me? I bet you'd look so pretty if you did."

"I'll do..." I pant in between breaths. "Anything you want. Please, please just..."

A pleasurable hum leaves him as he thrusts into me—faster, less controlled. Frantic, even. His fingers swirl around my clit, his needy touch causing the pressure between my legs to form again.

My breath catches, feeling as if I can't breathe.

And I whimper, over and over as every thrust becomes too much. My muscles tighten from the pressure, deep and low, as I begin to crest the wave of my climax.

My back is slick with sweat, sticking to him as my gasps brush the air mingling with whimpered cries.

"Rydian. I can't..." My eyes slam shut, words escaping me as I cry out, the pressure building between my legs.

His breath quickens, and then he releases my hair, steadying me by my hips as he drives into me from behind. He pushes deeper, filling me in such a way that I can feel every thick inch of him inside me.

I'm almost there. Please, gods, don't stop.

"You're going to come for me again, aren't you? Say my name when you do or you're not going to enjoy what happens if you don't." He pants. "Come on me like you want to claim me— show me how wild you are." He breathes against my temple, my head resting against the crook of his shoulder. His cock firms.

"Rydian—fuck, I claim you. Gods, I fucking claim you. Just... don't stop," I get out, though his words and the pressure—it's too much. Way too much. *Oh gods, I'm coming.*

Pleasure bursts from me as I cry out his name, as if a golden thread has tethered me to this very moment, stars shooting across my vision. My body trembles as I pulse around his cock, but then he pushes me forward and grips my hips, frantically driving into me as he loses more of that control he claims to have.

"Oh, fuck," he says, his moan laced with quiet shock as he loses himself completely. He grips me tighter, driving his hips— once, twice—and then spills himself in me with an exasperated groan, his pace slowing.

My own breathing eases, leaving me to blink in the darkness as I grapple for my composure. Yet for some reason, I feel lighter. *What was that?*

He rests on his side, turning me so that I'm pulled into his chest, gently kissing me below my ear as he pushes my hair to the side.

But his fingers linger for a breath, as if studying the strands, when the movement of his chest stalls behind me. Too tired to decipher what he's doing, a contented sigh leaves me as I settle on my side.

"Go to bed, little fawn. You need your rest," he mumbles, though it doesn't take long for the featherlight touches down the side of my neck to lull me to sleep. A quiet sigh escapes him. "The fates sure do have their jokes, don't they?" His quiet, mumbled words brush the shell of my ear, spoken as if they were meant for himself before I finally doze off.

31

My eyes flutter open, only to find Rydian tangled around me with a leg pushed between my thighs, tucking me into his chest. I fit into him like a mold, as if I was perfectly crafted for him.

The warmth of his body forces me to snuggle deeper as he wraps around me like a quilt, too exhausted to put clothes on.

Last night was not what I expected, but perhaps it's what I needed. I've spent years going to the Painted Bird to indulge and satisfy whatever wild urge I had, but it was never like this. Heat and desire. Like he wanted me, not like I was seeing someone to service me—like it was their job.

Thinking about last night has my stomach fluttering, sending desire straight through me—burning from the inside out. My face flushes at the utter filthiness, recalling every little detail. Lustful and needy.

Rydian stirs, as if he's just waking.

Yet I have a feeling he was already awake given his fingers resting in my loose, unbound hair. It doesn't take long before the scent of his arousal floods my senses—sweet and earthy, followed by the hard length of him. The scent of him floods me in a wave of pure heat, leaving me to aching all over again.

"You're distracting," Rydian mumbles.

"I haven't even moved," I exhale, and he tightens his arm around my waist.

"I can smell you, rich and sweet like a deadly black orchid. So yes, you're utterly distracting. I wanted to sleep a while longer, but now… mm, now I want to…" He trails off just as his hand travels below my navel.

My breath catches in my throat, and I close my eyes, my legs instinctively falling open for him. His breath stalls when he kisses my neck, groaning into my skin.

"You're already so wet for me," he says, rubbing me in taunting strokes. He slowly pushes in two fingers, his thumb swirling against me, causing my back to arch and—

A faint knock at the door interrupts, forcing us both to freeze at the sound of it, and I almost groan—*every fucking time.*

I pivot into him with wide eyes, catching Rydian's stare when he cautiously shakes his head.

"Don't say a word. I'll quietly get dressed and enter the Veil to stay here with you." He pushes the thought out.

I'm hoping that whoever stands outside doesn't scent Rydian on my sheets while he waits in the Veil. But I might kill them before they get the chance to.

"Isa! Open the door," Ren calls out.

I groan—*he ruins everything.* For a moment, I entertain the idea of not opening it at all before my stomach sinks to the floor. *Ren is now captain.* I either have a mission or he's turned me in.

Shit. I fly out of bed, searching for…. my night slip—ripped right down the middle from last night. Double shit. I lift it, shaking the tattered clothing in front of Rydian.

"You ripped my only night slip!" I say, but his laughter rumbles in my head just as he disappears into the Veil, dressed at record speed.

"I'll get you a new one so I can rip that one too," he says as Ren pounds on the door again.

"Hold on, you impatient brute!" I call out and rush to my wardrobe, quickly throwing on a tunic and pants.

With a heavy breath, I finally open the door only to find him dressed in black and armed to the teeth, every weapon of his in sight and missing his cloak. *Is he not cold?*

He looks terrifying as he towers over me, standing a few inches taller than Rydian. His black hair is raked back as he glowers at me with gray eyes, the color of stone.

"What took you so long?" he grumbles, pushing himself into my chamber. I try not to panic when I stumble, easily pushed to the side. He's never been in my chamber before, and he just pushed open my door with ease, as if I were a mere insect and not a part of the Brotherhood.

Rydian's irritation flares across my mind, growling in my head at Ren's forcefulness to push himself in without so much as a warning. But he should know better than anyone that Ren's ruthless, especially after Sylvanor.

"If he touches you, I'll kill him," Rydian warns, sending a wave of burning heat through me.

"I hate you right now," I reply, throwing Ren a tight smile at his back. *"But I guess now would be a bad time to tell you he caught me searching for a tunnel?"*

"What?" His growl echoes in my thoughts, and I wince, the sound reverberating across my mind.

Ren turns to me when I spot the king's seal on a white envelope, but then he pauses with a subtle sniff to the air, and I catch the small scrunch of his nose.

"What?" I snap, knowing exactly what he's *smelling.*

"Are you alone?" Ren knits his brows.

"Yes, I'm alone. What do you want?" My words are laced with pure annoyance, but his expression shifts into something between confusion and amusement.

"Are you sure? You don't smell... alone."

Heat flashes behind my eyes, my hand moving to rub the inside of my wrist where the ache pulses, but I catch myself, forcing my fingers to still. The small movement draws his attention anyway, his gaze flicking to my hands.

"Who I have in my room is none of your business, *Captain*," I bite out, emphasizing his title with sarcasm. "I'm alone now. Can I help you?"

"Yes, actually. There's a mission you need to attend with me. It's in Nymara, and we leave in a few hours."

"Nymara?" I repeat, my irritation flaring. "That's a four-day trip."

Meaning I would be gone for eight days, pushing us back from searching the tunnels and finding my mother. Time we can't afford to lose. And I would be separated from Rydian. After last night, I'm not sure I *want* a mission. My fingers curl into fists, and I give him a tight smile.

"Which is why we'll be leaving shortly." Ren smirks, crossing his arms. "And here I thought you'd be happy about receiving a mission."

I force myself to relax, even as I mentally groan because he's right. I should be happy for a mission, but I'm not. All it does is stir up more questions. Who are we sent to kill, and why? I've never dared to ask—fear of Theron's wrath keeping me silent—but ever since I learned who I've been killing all those years, the questions only grow.

My eyes narrow. "I want a mission without you tagging along. Where's Ezra? You seem to be giving him everything anyway. Let him go with me. I'm just shocked you're giving me anything at all. Plus, I thought I was being punished. Can't punish me if I'm not here." I smirk.

He chuckles, looking off to the side when he spots my torn night slip. His brows pinch as a question forms on his face, but he doesn't ask. "You weren't my first choice, but Ezra is still gone on his mission. He won't be back for another few days. King Elion wants to use your *excellent* infiltration and disguise skills. But you can count this trip as a part of your punishment. What better way to train your stealth than to do it on a mission with me?"

Gritting my teeth, I roll my eyes so hard I'm surprised they don't fall out of my head. "Glad to know I'm such a valuable asset when no one else is available. I've had weeks of nothing. Training, sitting around, and twiddling my thumbs," I say sarcastically.

"Don't you think that's why I'm here?" he snaps finally, tossing the envelope on my bed. "I'm giving you something, but you already know that it's not up to me—Elion gives the final say."

I clench my fists. "Gods, you frustrate me."

"Good. I'd hate to be boring and easily forgotten," he bites back. "Now get dressed. We leave in two hours."

"Fine. I'll meet you in the stables," I mutter under my breath, turning away with a shake of my head.

Ren strides to the door, then stops, pivoting to me as he grabs the knob. "Oh, and Isa?"

"What?" I ask, not bothering to hide the frustration in my voice as I reach for a glass of water.

"Take a bath. You reek of sex." He quietly chuckles just as I throw the glass at his face before he quickly slams the door, glass shattering against it.

"Ugh!" I scream, hands clenching. *He's infuriating.*

, I'm not so sure he'll make it back from our trip in one piece. I might leave him out there and return alone. Then I remember —the ground is frozen. Burying him would be too much of a hassle. Perhaps I'll just leave him out in the snow.

Rydian steps out of the Veil, dragging me from my dark thoughts. He's fully dressed, and I realize that I prefer him without clothes. There's nothing to see now, no glimpse of the body I had my legs wrapped around just last night. Still, I stare, hoping that his clothes will just… vanish. My eyes drag over him in silence.

"Stop looking at me like that, little fawn, or we'll be doing something other than get ready for this journey," he says.

I blink, registering his words. "No, not *we*. You're not going."

"I'm going. And I won't be waiting around while Ivy and Orin are in Aurelia."

"Then meet with them in Aurelia if you need to. Study the map while I'm gone. You can't stay in the Veil for eight days, remember? I'll go with Ren to finish this mission and meet you at the loft after. This will give you enough time to plan with Orin and check in with Ivy. I'll be here when you get back. I promise."

Yet as I say those words, my chest tightens. I don't want to go on a mission, and I definitely don't want to be without Rydian for so long. I sigh, knowing that this is our best option even if I don't want it.

He strides to me, cradling the back of my neck. "I don't want to leave you alone with him. I can't tell if he's in love with you or if he wants to kill you. Regardless, I don't trust him." He sears me with his intense, possessive stare.

I've been a trained weapon my whole life—sharp and efficient. Yet for some reason, the way he approaches this feels different. Like something in him shifted between last night and this morning. Softer. Warmer. And I can't quite put my finger on why.

"You think everyone is in love with me," I scoff, thinking of what he said about Silas, leaving me to believe he's jealous and doesn't want other males near me.

"That's because they are. If they aren't, they probably enjoy male company rather than that of females," he mutters.

A sharp laugh of disbelief escapes me. "I'll be fine. Ren may have trained me when I was younger, but I'm far more agile than he is. I can handle myself." I step away because he's distracting, and I need to bathe.

He rubs his hand over his jaw, lost in thought. Then he nods after a moment. "Fine. I would like to test the distance of the Veil now that you can travel."

I halt mid-turn, slowly pivoting. "What did you say?"

"You can travel in the Veil. Last night when you were sleeping, you met me in the Veil at the castle in my chambers, don't you remember? Why did you think I showed up when I did?" He furrows his brows, and then a sly grin slowly forms on his lips at the realization.

"That was real?" I ask in disbelief. Embarrassment coats my veins at having thought it was a dream. "How is that possible? I was asleep but ended up in the Veil with you? I thought we couldn't travel from realm to realm unless we crossed the border."

He smirks, crossing his arms, as he realizes I didn't know I wasn't dreaming. His cloak flares, revealing the dark tunic underneath, spread thin across his muscled chest.

"There are different ways to access the Veil. We can do it through communication like we do when we talk to each other. Then there's the physical and not physical aspect of it—allowing us to access it in a dreamlike state. Like last night, we can continue to stay in one location while we visit another in sleep. It's still very real, just not there physically. Think of it as a state of in between. But this means that your power continues to grow, and I want to test it while you're gone."

The dark castle must be where Rydian lives, near the ocean, and I was *in his chambers,* somehow traveling to Aurelia without knowing exactly where I was.

"It's fine," Rydian says, mouth tipping into a lopsided grin as words continue to fail me.

"I literally kissed you in the Veil," I get out.

"Is that all you got from what I just said?" he asks, his scarred lip slightly rising, certainly amused at how flustered I am.

"That doesn't explain how I ended up in the castle if I've never been there." My brows lift.

"It does because technically you grew up there, which means you've already been in the realm. The chamber you ended up in used to be King Andre's. Subconsciously, you could have just been pulled there out of habit without knowing where you were going."

"Oh. I don't… really know what to say to that," I admit because for some reason, his words leave me speechless. My hand rests on my forehead as I rack through the information and let out a sigh. "I'm going to bathe. I'll see you soon?"

His brows lower as a seriousness crosses his face, all prior humor dissipating when his gaze locks on to mine, intense and unwavering. He strides forward and without a word, he cups my face, pressing a searing kiss to my lips. *Oh, fuck yes.*

"I'll see you in eight days." He pulls back, my eyes dazed as his gaze locks with mine. He steps into the Veil a moment later.

It feels way too cold in the chamber without him, though a fire roars from across the room. A large plate of food waits for me by the door. I notice that he lit a fire and brought me something to eat.

Dread settles in my stomach, hands curling into fists at the realization that I'm going to miss him—more than I care to admit—and it's going to be a long eight days without him.

32

Gods, it's fucking cold.

I sit shivering in my cloak despite it being lined in thick fur. Even though my scarf covers half my face, I'm absolutely freezing from the biting wind, waiting for Ren to start a fire.

Too frightened to use my magic for fear of being caught wielding more power, I suffer in silence. Although we've traveled farther south, it's still unbearable this time of year in the dead of winter.

It's been three and a half days, meaning we should be arriving in Nymara tomorrow afternoon and leaving us one more night to camp before arriving in the city close to the Aurelian border. We stopped in little towns along the way, long enough for the horses to be watered and given fresh hay, only staying in one of those towns to sleep. The rest of our time has been spent camping. I shiver again.

Ren briefly discussed our mission, something that's a little different than our previous ones. Instead of killing this target, we're to bring him back to the castle unharmed, which I find odd.

We're to break into the home—where I come in—and bring

him back in one piece. I assume he'll be bound and gagged by Ren, as it's his specialty because he's a ruthless ass. I'll just leave him to do that part by himself.

"It's not that cold out," he grumbles behind me, grabbing logs for the fire and throwing them on the pile in front of us. He finally lights it, and I let out an incredibly loud, exaggerated sigh, pulling my scarf off my face to bathe in the heat.

I throw him a glance and scoff. "Sorry, I don't have a beard on my face to keep me warm."

A short beard, but a beard nonetheless. He throws a rabbit at my feet, blood coating its white fur.

Although I'm exceptional at hunting, occasionally going with Ezra, it's not my specialty. I have no desire to go tromping around the forest, leaving Ren to do that. Not that I can't do it, I'd just rather not waste my energy. Plus, he has no problem leaving me alone in the cold while he does it, voicing that he doesn't want to hear me complain about it. He's better at tracking anyway.

"Thanks," I mutter.

My hands work the pelt as I skin it from its feet to its neck. Ren tosses me his kill with a devious grin, silently asking if I can skin his rabbit as well. His grin widens when I glare, but I can't say no, not after he found us a meal, so I just huff and skin his next.

After finishing, he shoves a sharp stick through the length of his rabbit and holds out his hand, urging me to hand him mine so it can cook over the fire.

Ren has been surprisingly decent, mostly remaining silent during our travels. Or perhaps I'm just too cold to throw him any snide remarks. No sign of the mean brute I usually see.

After placing the rabbits above the fire, Ren pulls out his knife and carves into a block of wood like he did in the valley. Only this time, it looks like he's about halfway done carving a fox. I sit across from him, bundled in my cloak.

"Why am I here again?" I ask.

He lifts his brows. "I already told you, the king wanted to use your skills."

"I don't believe that." I squint my eyes, smoke clouding my vision as I lean against a tree. "Luke is just as exceptional at disguise and infiltration—he could have used him instead, or you could have just gone alone."

Luke *is* exceptional, if not more talented than I am, yet I was sent here with Ren, who hates me instead. So although it could be a believable story, I don't believe for one second that I was King Elion's or Ren's first choice. Not after these last few weeks of not having any missions.

"I just find it odd that I'm back on the list for missions when it was clear I was being punished. What changed?"

He huffs a sigh and stops carving, like I've already annoyed him with my observation. He forgets that I'm in the Brother-hood. I'm exceptionally skilled at *everything*.

"Fine, do you really want to know?" he grunts.

"Well, that's why I'm asking."

He looks off to the side as if he's too afraid of my reaction to meet my gaze. "I was supposed to bring Luke, but he's a prick and he never shuts up. For the most part, you keep to yourself and are far better company than he is," he mumbles as if he can't stop himself from the confession.

I blink in stunned silence for a moment, trying to decipher if he's messing with me or not. A few seconds go by when he begins carving again, not waiting for me to respond. I realize that he's probably telling the truth.

Then I smirk at the thought that crosses my mind—the horrible idea I just had, causing me to chuckle as something sinister forms in my chest.

"Is that a challenge?" I tilt my head, forcing him to lift his gaze at my tone. He just admitted that I'm better than Luke, telling me that I haven't been unbearable enough this trip.

"Isa," he warns, brows lowering.

He knows that look—we all share it—but I can't help myself. In an instant, I'm flipping a dagger in my hand, catching it by the tip, when he stands, mirroring me over the fire. A vicious grin pulls at my lips as I hone in on my training.

"Isa, don't..." he growls.

Aiming for his head, I barely miss him when he jolts to the side, landing in the tree behind him with a low thud. He whips his head back around with narrowed eyes.

"I give you a compliment, and your response is to throw a dagger at my face?" He sits again.

"What can I say? I love a challenge." I cross my arms with grin and a shrug, sitting back down.

"You missed. I taught you better than that. You should've hit me." He scoffs, insulting my aim, then grabs the rabbits off the fire with a hard yank.

"You did teach me better than that. If I wanted to hit you, I would have," I bite back with a tight smile, snatching the rabbit from him.

I ignore the fact that I just confessed that I didn't plan on hitting him. I just wanted to make a point: don't get too comfortable around me. After a few minutes, I catch the faintest of grins pulling at his mouth before he hides it, silently finishing the fox carving in his hands.

Shortly after eating, I find myself entering my tent, bidding Ren a good night, which results in a few inaudible mumbles. With my body secure under my thick quilt, cloak and all, I rest on the pack beneath me.

Over the last three nights, Rydian has consistently met me in the Veil while we slept. But the farther we travel apart, the more the connection falters, stretched thin by our distance across the realm.

When we do find each other, it's as if the world stops for a few minutes with the way his hands brush my face before his lips meet mine, like he's afraid to let me go. Then it flickers out, leaving me feeling cold and empty in the middle of a tent.

Now, as my head rests on my pack, I begin to feel Rydian the moment I drift off to sleep, as if he's been waiting for me in the Veil all night.

We arrived in Nymara earlier this afternoon.

All morning, Ren kept stealing glances at me like he was trying to solve a complex problem, probably due to the dagger I threw at his head last night. I just ignored him, hoping to complete this mission and head back.

Since we'll be breaking into someone's home, we know we won't be needing an inn tonight—let alone rest—so we set up our horses outside the city. Getting our target back to Nymara is going to be... challenging. We've never had to bring someone back to the castle before.

We learned our target's name—Theo—after reading through our missive, mentioning that he went by the nickname *Smudge* around the local metal forges. So that's what we did earlier: spent the day questioning locals to track him down. Eventually, we ended up at a forgery near the docks.

When we arrived, only the owner was there, and we quickly realized that Theo had already left. Ren took it upon himself to distract the owner, and without a word between us, I slipped past them and found Theo's workspace, stealing a pair of his gloves.

Tracking him by scent proved to be more difficult than we thought with the ocean nearby, as it gives off an intense fishy aroma. It's midnight now as we head into the city—my hand tightly gripping the glove marked with his nickname on the edge of the leather.

Nymara is set up on cobblestone, greeted by large towers

that extend for miles before reaching the outskirts of the city. Built near the water, the salt from the ocean drifts by on a breeze as the waves crash in the distance.

We finally reach the edge of the neighborhood, where homes climb the hills in narrow rows, stacked side by side and sloping away from the ocean. Thankfully, streetlamps are out for the night, allowing us to remain hidden in the shadows.

With a quick glance around and no words spoken between us, we pull our hoods up. My mask covers my nose, shielding me from the cold bite of the wind as our feet pull us toward Theo's home. Ren nudges me, nodding at the lone house on the corner.

On silent feet, we approach Theo's home. Ren quietly lingers behind me as the crescent moon casts a dim glow, just enough for me to find a way in. With a quick inspection, I find the home warded with three protection runes.

My palms press onto the wooden door, eyes closed and tuning into the energy. The runes are simple—easy to counter. I quickly etch a sigil onto the frame, stepping back as it glows briefly before the others begin to fade. With my hand on the knob, I twist and gently ease it open on a soft creak, pivoting to find Ren inches from my back. I jolt, not having sensed him there.

"How do you do that?" I whisper, eyes narrowing over my mask. Ren ignores me with a blank stare, swiftly motioning for us to split, and I go left. My adrenaline pumps, but I force my breathing to slow as I take calculated steps inside the home.

My eyes land on the shoes and clothes scattered near the windows before darting them from door to door and quietly striding down the hall. It smells like a bakery.

I gently ease open the first door—just a closet. A soft creak breaks the silence as I shut it and move to the next. The kitchen. A sigh slips past my lips, but that's when I spot the last door across the hall.

My back presses into the wall as my hand grazes the knob, twisting it. My breath catches as I peek around the corner, finding a figure asleep inside the dimly lit room. Only one window near the bed.

On nimble feet, I quietly slip into the room, inching toward the bed just as Ren appears beside me. He throws me a curt nod —this is our target.

I tug back the quilts and immediately freeze. A jolt of adrenaline surges through me as my head whips toward Ren. His eyes are just as wide as my own. Our gazes lock.

"Did you know about this?" My tone is hushed, yet frantic and sharp.

His eyes meet mine as he slowly shakes his head, stunned. I've never seen him like this—shaken by the sight of the male lying before us.

It's not a male but a boy, no older than ten, with wild, shaggy brown hair strung in all directions. He sleeps deeply, his chest rising and falling in a steady rhythm.

We certainly can't take a boy from his home, away from his parents. Whom I *know* he lives with just based on the larger shoes and clothes by the entrance. My breathing becomes erratic, the realization of it setting in. Taking a boy in the middle of the night—it's wrong.

"I won't do it," I say firmly.

Ren grips my arm and silently leads me into the corridor, his voice low and firm as he whispers, "We have to take him. The king is expecting us to bring him back, and if we don't, there will be consequences. You know that. Please don't fight me on this. Not now." He scans the area one last time as a lone, unexpected tear slips down my cheek, hidden by my mask.

"How?" I whisper, my voice cracking with disbelief. "How are you okay with this? You don't question what the king does and now you're just—just taking a boy while he sleeps. What about his parents? How do you even know this is our target?"

Ren doesn't answer right away, his jaw clenching as he steadily holds my gaze. "I know it's not right, but I also know what happens if we don't obey King Elion. We don't have time to question it, but he matches the scent. We can ask questions after we leave."

"We were orphans once, or have you forgotten?" I murmur.

His brows knit, but he doesn't look away. His gaze holds mine, almost pleading, as if he's silently begging me not to fight him. That we'll somehow find answers. And I want to believe him, but I can't. My head shakes with disbelief, but still, I swallow the lump in my throat as resolve settles over me. I give him a curt nod.

"Fine." I silently shove past him.

We'll wake the house if we were to argue in their hall, so I remain quiet, refusing to meet his gaze over the quickness in which he's able to accept his orders. We were orphans once and now, all of a sudden, he's just okay with snatching a child from his home.

Stepping back into the room, we find the boy still breathing deeply when Ren pulls out a sleeping draft, pouring a few drops into his mouth, if only to ensure he remains asleep. *Was that always his plan?*

Ren cradles the boy in his arms, leaving me to gather a few of his clothes. I pause long enough to scribble a note on parchment, hoping the words will bring his parents some measure of comfort. That they won't come looking for him. A quiet sniffle slips from me as I finish writing, leaving it to rest on his pillow.

The walk back to our horses is both achingly silent and unbearably loud. My tears dry, but the furious storm in my chest only grows as our steps continue. My eyes are fixed forward with a hard clench to my jaw, and I refuse to speak to Ren on the way back.

I'm furious at the king. Furious at Ren for doing whatever

Elion wants—no questions asked. We're nothing but tools to Elion. Yet here we are, doing what we're ordered to do.

But wasn't that me just a few weeks ago? I surely wasn't questioning my missions, but this is a boy. That changes things.

The night's chill has eased, replaced by the heat of my fury and betrayal wrapping around me like a second skin.

When we finally arrive, I yank my mask down, eyeing Ren as he gently settles the boy inside the tent, pulling a quilt over him. But the moment he steps out, I shove him hard—my rage no longer being held back.

"How could you?" The scream tears from me before I can stop myself, then my angry fist connects with his nose. He recovers quickly, gripping my wrists, pulling me to his chest with a snarl.

"You don't know *anything*," he growls, dark hair falling messily to the sides of his forehead.

We're deep into the forest when I finally break—raw, broken sobs tearing free. Tears uncontrollably stream down my face as I struggle in his hold, trying to pry myself free. He only tightens his grip, pinning me against him as if letting me go isn't an option.

"I would rather die at the hands of Theron than take a boy from his parents." My eyes frantically search the hard lines of his face.

"Would you?" He chuckles, then finally releases me with a shove as he frantically begins to pace—like he's in distress— whipping around with a scowl. "You're not the Isa I knew from a year ago—not even a month ago. What happened? Why are you questioning it now? Did something happen?"

"I'm not, because *you* don't know anything. You're a fucking coward," I get out.

"Me?" he snarls back, storming toward me.

Fury consumes me as betrayal grips my heart, refusing to let go. Rage surges beneath my skin, so sharp it almost steals my breath.

Everything from the past few weeks flies across my mind—the secrets, the lies, the harsh truth that my life was never really my own. Stolen memories and the betrayal of a realm I called *home.*

This was supposed to be my home.

I'm unable to think straight—unable to contain it any longer. A golden orb bursts from my palm, slamming into him, sending him sprawling into the clearing next to our camp. His eyes go wide as he sits up on his palms.

Yet my rage crackles like a fire beneath my skin as it comes to the surface—power. Raw power.

My body hums as it ripples from my shoulders down to my fingertips. A dull, throbbing ache forms behind my eyes, head pounding with pressure. I can't control it—the fury.

Or my sudden need for blood.

Ren braces himself on his hands, eyes widening as I stalk him like a predator. Snow drifts down.

"Isa, stop," he blurts.

His voice doesn't reach me though. Not as my vision blurs, glossed over as I stride forward, my gaze locking on him.

"Isa, stop!" he shouts again as I reach the edges of his boots.

My hands blaze a bright white, joining and swirling in wisps of darkness as if the moon and sun meld beneath my skin, crashing together in waves of shadow and light. Power pulses through me as I slowly lift my eyes to him, a dark, menacing smirk curling my lips.

He stands with palms raised, his words slow and calculated—carefully chosen words meant to soothe my rising fury. "Isa, I know more than you think."

"You know nothing!"

"Yes... I do," he says cautiously. "I know the king has been doing something secretive for many years."

My chest heaves as his words register, pulling me from the energy I've summoned, and I tilt my head with panted breaths. "How do you know that?"

"I know that they did something to you, right? I think they hurt you, and I think you know that now. But you don't remember it, do you?"

"How do you know that?" The shadowy glow of my hands falters and then flutters out completely a second later. "What do you know? Tell me!"

He steps toward me, a hand extended. "Calm down, and I will explain…"

The energy shifts, like static hanging in the air. A raw surge of power vibrates around us, stealing the breath from my lungs at the presence appearing in the depths of the shadows a few feet away.

Rydian.

33

"Lay a single finger on her, and I'll tear the hands right off your useless body." Rydian's voice is a low, vicious growl. Ren stiffens, steps halting as his eyes go wide.

Rydian strides out from beneath the shadows of the trees— not the trees, *his* shadows. My breathing stalls.

I always knew he was king of Aurelia, but I never truly grasped the extent of his power until now. It's absolutely terrifying.

His cloak swirls around him, billowing like a storm with his hood drawn low over his brows, hiding all but the faintest trace of his features. Every step he takes seems to make the ground tremble, as though he's bending the realm to his will. He strides forward and then smirks, the small curve of his scarred lip tipping up ever so slightly.

Chills snake down my spine.

If this is his power in Elderheim, it must be absolutely shattering in Aurelia. I shudder at the thought. But Ren makes a grave mistake and reaches for his blades, lowering his brow and widening his stance.

Good gods, he's preparing to fight.

Before I can blink, Rydian thrusts out a palm and slowly curls his fingers, lifting Ren clear off the ground as if he's a child's doll and not like the six-foot-six male that he is. Rydian dangles him in the air from an invisible force by his neck.

The king of Aurelia has made his appearance.

Ren scrambles his hands across his throat—gasping for air—as he kicks his feet, looking for purchase. Yet for a reason I can't quite explain, panic surges beneath my skin.

"Rydian, stop!" I shout.

My feet pull me to him, at his side with a hand clawing at his chest. Frantic eyes dart between the two of them as I shake his arm, attempting to gain his attention. He glances down, furrowing his brows.

"Are you hurt?" he asks.

"No. Now please, put him down. He knows something. I'm okay, I promise." I beg him to stop.

"Say the word, and I will end him right here," he vows. *"No one lays a finger on the princess of Aurelia, mark my words."*

And I believe every word he says. If I told him to, he would kill Ren without a second thought. But I don't want Ren to die, not today anyway.

"I don't want you to. Please, Rydian. There's a sleeping boy in the tent behind you."

He holds my gaze a moment longer, then drops Ren to the ground with a hard thud. Wrapping an arm around my neck, Rydian pulls me to him, watching Ren collect himself all while he holds me, as if he's claiming me as his. I can't help the relief settling in my chest.

Ivy and Orin step out from the shadows, lifting Ren to his feet only to push him toward the fire, sitting him down as it roars to life. I begin to follow when Rydian gently tugs my hand back. He searches for any signs of injury, then cups my face, tilting it from side to side—inspecting me.

"I'm fine." I meet his gaze, but I can't help the sudden wave of exhaustion settling over me. Whatever I did to Ren, it took a lot of my energy.

"What happened?" he asks.

"We tracked our target to his home but when we got there, he was sleeping. A boy no older than ten. I don't know why we're bringing him back to the castle. We shouldn't have taken him in the first place, and I fought Ren on the issue when we got back. Things got... heated."

His expression darkens, his usual calculating demeanor cracking, revealing the raw anger forming behind his eyes before quickly masking it.

"How did you find me?" My brows pinch. He shouldn't have been able to find my exact location without setting foot on this side of the realm first.

His gaze locks with mine, features softening as he studies me, then smirks. "I told you that I would always find you, no matter where you are. But if you really want to know, I felt you first. Your power is growing rapidly. I assume it's because you haven't told anyone about the magic growing in you, but I can't be sure. I'm afraid others may have felt it too. It... tugged at me, and I followed it. I brought Ivy and Orin with me."

I'm quickly reminded of the moment right before Rydian stepped through the Veil, when my hands glowed in a mix between light and dark shadows. My entire body hummed with it.

"Ren knows of my power now, so we need to figure out exactly what he knows and find a way to keep him quiet," I say.

"I know one way to keep him quiet," he mutters, and I throw him a scowl.

More snow falls, blanketing the clearing in a soft powder. I quickly peek my head inside the tent, checking on Theo, only to find him still snoozing from the sleeping draft. I close the flap, walking in Ren's direction.

Ivy and Orin stand on either side of Ren as he sits near the fire on a large log. We halt on the other side of the fire when Rydian finally tugs his hood down. His hair barely touches the slight points of his ears, the auburn waves curling around the edge. The hard line of his jaw flexes, arms crossed over his chest as he eyes Ren from over the fire.

Ren's expression is close to what seeing a spirit would look like—the color draining from his face, eyes darting between the two of us. No doubt recalling the memory of what he saw at sixteen when Rydian came for me the first time, right outside the orphanage.

"It's you." Ren exhales, staring at Rydian with wide eyes. He attempts to stand but Orin pushes his shoulder down, preventing him from reaching his full height.

"It's best to just sit there," Orin says.

"What do you know?" I ask Ren, his attention shifting to me.

"Where do I begin?" he asks.

"Maybe the orphanage when we were children? What happened that day?"

"You remember that?" His eyes grow wider.

"No, that's why I'm asking. Have you known about my stolen memories this whole time?" I say.

A lingering silence falls over us as he processes my question, brows knitting close together before he clenches his jaw. His eyes dart back and forth, as if he's piecing together information I'm unaware of, tightening the tension in his face.

The only sounds around us are the soft crackles from the fire as the wood burns. Small sparks gather in the air as the smoke travels up, hiding his hardened features behind the haze.

"Answer her," Rydian warns after a moment.

Ren sighs, shaking his head, tone even. "I know nothing of your memories. I don't even know what that means. What I do know is that I saw *him* at the orphanage when we were children. He was attempting to take you, and you were upset over it. *That,* I remember. But after you came running back—with me being your instructor at the time—both of us were taken to the king to explain to him what happened. You were my responsibility. I never lied when I told you that we used to be close, Isa. I instructed you when we were younger, yes, but we were also very close friends..." He knits his brows and looks off to the side as if calculating his words. "When they took us to the king and you came back, you acted as if I hardly knew you. You stopped talking to me. You were cold, distant, and were convinced that we hated each other. Ezra was assigned as your training partner after that, and I kept my distance. After a while, I realized that whatever happened, you didn't recall anything— not our friendship, not even when he showed up." He gestures toward Rydian, his voice flat.

For a moment, the words hang heavily in the air before they fully register. My pacing halts as the anger simmering beneath my skin ignites into a full-blown storm. I glare, the weight of his admission hitting me like a slap to the face.

"You *knew* they did something to me?" My tone is sharp, cutting through the silence. "And you said nothing."

His eyes widen slightly before his voice drops, disbelief in his tone. "What was I supposed to do? You acted as if it never happened. I didn't understand, but as time passed, I realized that something was wrong. That the king was involved in something far beyond what I could understand. I was worried they would continue to do whatever they did, so I chose to stay silent for fear of them doing it again. I only did it to protect you. You never would have believed me anyway."

Rydian glances at me, entering my mind. *"Do you believe him?"*

"I don't know." I stare at Ren, processing his words.

"What of the boy?" Rydian asks. "Can you tell us anything about why you're bringing him back to the castle?"

"We were only given a location, workplace, and a name. Nothing of his age or why we were to bring him back, just that we were to bring him back alive and unharmed," Ren says, and Rydian's eyes flick to me. I nod, confirming what Ren says to be true. We know very little about our target.

"I'd like to help," Ren offers, causing both of us to snap our gaze to him.

Rydian's lips curl into a snarl. "We can't trust you. Why would we even consider it? You could betray us the moment it benefits you and Elion would know everything, including Isa's power. You're a liability."

Ren stiffens, but his voice remains steady. "I won't. I'm captain now. I can help with whatever you need. Whatever they did to Isa, I don't want to be a part of it. My loyalty has always been with her, anyway, more so now than ever." His eyes flick toward me. "Let me help."

His confession hangs between us as I study him, wondering when he has ever vowed loyalty to me. Then I realize that if there were a time that he did, I probably wouldn't have known about it.

Rydian sneers. "Loyalty. How convenient for you to remember where your loyalties lie, so forgive me if I'm not easily convinced. I don't trust you."

"You're forgiven." Ren smirks, but his gaze never leaves mine as we stare at each other.

Rydian turns to me. *"What do you think? Can we trust him? You know him far better than we do,"* he asks, and I scoff at the question, not knowing how to answer it.

Because can I?

All this time, I believed Ren was against me, but now I'm wondering if I was wrong. If what he says is true, that we were both taken to the king, then perhaps there's a small chance that his memories were also stolen. But he remembers Rydian, so I'm unsure. We could make this work. Using him would allow us access into parts of the castle we wouldn't typically have without him.

"I don't know. I know him, but not as well as you think," I mumble. Ren's brows furrow at my response to a question that wasn't spoken out loud. But I've made my decision.

I walk around the fire to stand in front of Ren, gesturing for Ivy and Orin to lift him to his feet. The point of my dagger slowly trails from his chest to his chin when I lean forward. A knowing smirk plays on my lips as my head tilts back, my voice lowering.

"If we allow you to help us and you betray my trust, I will gut you in front of the entire city," I mutter.

Ren's dark hair falls over his brow as he smirks down at me, scanning my face with his eyes. "I would expect nothing less from you. Kill me however you wish. My life is yours."

34

"No, we're not doing that."

"We have no choice! We need to bring him back to the castle."

"Well, we need to come up with a different plan because the boy stays."

My eyes shift between Rydian, Orin, and Ren as they argue over the large oak table in the loft—papers are scattered, showing how much Rydian's been working. I rub my forehead with both hands at the raging headache that's formed between my eyes.

We've been discussing what to do with Theo, who sleeps downstairs in the spare room. I'm shocked he hasn't woken from the amount of yelling we've done over the last day, leading us nowhere. We arrived a day early, pushing the horses to their limits in order to give us extra time to figure out a plan before heading back to the castle.

And we're running out of time.

Ivy offered to take Theo back to the loft through the Veil to make our trip easier, while Ren and I pushed our horses to get here in time. Rydian tagged along, of course, still not completely trusting Ren with me after our argument in the clearing, but we managed to make it in one piece.

"If we don't deliver that boy, we're dead," Ren grinds out.

"I'm the king. The decision is made."

"You are *not* my king."

The air turns cold, and just as Rydian's lip curls into a snarl, Ivy interrupts, breaking the tension.

"We don't even know why King Elion wants him. We need to figure out why first before we just drop him off," she says, hands resting on the hilts of her swords.

A thought crosses my mind, and I lean forward, releasing a loud exhale that causes each male to swivel their head toward me in confusion.

"If we can wake him up, maybe you could use your only Vision Walker in the room to get information?" I ask.

Silence follows. Rydian doesn't bother to hide his smirk, dipping his head toward the map on the table when a chuckle breaks free. It should have been obvious, but of course they'd rather argue than notice what's right in front of them.

"Couldn't have said something sooner, Princess?" Orin chuckles, and I internally cringe at the nickname.

"I'll go ask Bess if she has anything to wake the boy," Ivy says, her boots hitting the steps a moment later.

Orin and Ren are quick to follow, though my gaze remains locked on Rydian with my elbows resting on the table. He runs his hand over the short stubble on his face, exhaustion from travel settling in. That makes both of us.

"Are you okay?" he asks.

"No, if I'm answering honestly," I mutter. "Unfortunately, I agree with Ren."

Rydian slowly tilts his head, studying me as if I've grown a second pair of eyes.

I sigh. "If we don't deliver Theo, the king will come looking for us. If we want to successfully find my mother, we have to deliver him to the king—we have no choice. Let's find out what King Elion wants with him first. I'm sure Ren could find a way to keep tabs on him since he's captain. But we need to find her, Rydian."

"I know, but I don't like it," he says.

"Me either, but we have someone close to the king offering to help us. Let's use him to help us search the castle." A grin tugs at my lips.

He walks around the edge of the table, pulling me to my feet to tilt my chin up. He grins and silently pulls at the end of my braid, freeing my hair.

"Okay," he says under his breath. "If you think that's what we should do, then I agree."

I groan. "Gods, it was that easy the whole time? I should have said something sooner."

"Yes, because I care for you," he says with conviction, and then his tone goes so low it's almost a whisper as he studies me. "Ask me to burn the world for you. Ask me to shatter the realms, and I would. You know, I don't think you understand how insane you make me—you quite literally set my world on fire."

His words have my breath stalling, unable to form a simple reply—not even a retort to diffuse the rising emotions in my chest as I hold his gaze.

His eyes soften. "I would happily destroy the realms if you asked, and I would do it without a second thought. The grip you have on me..." His hand gently pushes my hair aside, a thousand words playing on his face. "I wouldn't be able to let you go, even if I wanted to."

His eyes dart across my face as if he has something more to add, but he chooses to stay silent. I nervously swallow because I know he means it. And I begin to wonder at what point I became something more precious to him because that's what it feels like—*something more.*

A throat clears at the top of the stairwell, and we turn to find Ren as he glances between the two of us. A flicker of shock crosses his features before he masks it, and I step away from Rydian.

"Bess is here, and Ivy has the waking serum. She's woken the boy and is talking to him," Ren says.

I nod, watching as Rydian makes his way down the stairs after giving a light squeeze to my hand. But Ren silently eyes me from where he's standing.

"You really don't remember anything?" he asks quietly.

I shake my head. "I'm hoping to get some of it back though. We were friends?" I ask finally, still shocked at the two of us ever being close. It's created an awkward tension around us, unsure how to behave around the other.

"We were…" He trails off, looking as if he's running through his memories before pulling his gaze back to me with a pinch to his brow. He scratches the back of his head. "As close as you and Ezra."

I hum, letting it soak in, when a thought crosses my mind. "If we were as close as you say we were, why did you always act like you hated me?"

His hands go in his pockets as he studies me, a small smirk forming on his lips, but the way he does it has my heart stopping. It's… charming. "It was the only way I knew you wouldn't be able to forget me, especially if you were angry."

I blink, registering his words. "You're the worst, you know that?" I mumble, but all this time he just wanted me to remember our friendship. "But I'm sorry."

I'm at a loss for words because what *can* I say? I had no control over my memories being stolen, but I can't help but feel utterly guilty over a lost friendship I knew nothing about. Wouldn't he at least try to help me remember?

"It was never your fault—don't apologize," he says and turns for the stairs, preventing me from asking.

I collect myself and follow, spotting Bess by the fire with a glass of whiskey. The sight of her has me catching my breath, though my feelings for her are nothing more than that of a close friend.

"Bess." I grin as she turns to me. Her hair spills over her shoulder, and she throws me a friendly smirk with a kiss to my cheek.

"Isa, darling. How are you and how is your male friend?" she asks quietly—about Rydian. And just like that, we're old friends again.

I snort. "Maybe later, when there aren't prying male ears."

"It was good." Her mouth falls open, a devious grin tugging at her lips.

"Stop." I chuckle quietly, throwing a glance over my shoulder at the others lost in conversation. "I missed you. I had no idea who you were all these years—I just wish you would have told me."

"I know, me too. But I want you to know that I still care for you deeply," she says.

"You know, I was worried you were angry with me when I showed up here."

She gives me a soft, knowing smile. "I admit, I was at first. When Rydian asked for my help, he discussed what you were doing for the king... I just didn't know that it was *you* in the castle. It took me by surprise. But I know that everything King Elion had you doing in the Brotherhood wasn't your fault. What he does still angers me, but you didn't have a choice—not really."

"Why didn't you say anything?"

She chuckles, tucking her hair behind an ear. "Because I knew that what I was dealing with didn't have anything to do with you. King Elion is controlling and will find any way to exploit you. If he found out who I was, he'd raid my entire brothel just to kill me. But it wouldn't be only me, it would be every one of my willing courtesans. I offer a lot of them safety—jobs where they wouldn't be able to work otherwise." She looks down to her glass.

"He would do that?" I ask.

She lifts her chin. "He would, and he wouldn't hesitate. You know firsthand how cruel he is, but I hope this doesn't change anything between us." And then she pauses, opening her mouth as if calculating her next words. "King Rydian is a good king, Isa. What he's done for Aurelia is… well, I can't really put it into words."

"I know," I reply as Rydian's eyes meet mine from over my shoulder, then face her again. "And it doesn't—change anything between us, I mean. I swear. Do you want more whiskey?"

She nods, but before I can refill our glasses, Ivy steps out, her gaze meeting mine from across the room. I quickly break away when she motions me over.

"He's scared, so take your time. But he's agreed to let you use your ability to see into his mind," Ivy says.

I nod, entering to find him huddled in the corner of his bed, scared half to death. Despite the warm air in the room, he shivers.

"It's okay, Theo. I promise I won't hurt you. I just want to see why the king would want to take you from your parents. Is it okay to touch you?" I ask.

He chews on his lip, hazel eyes scanning me for a solid minute before finally giving me a small nod. As I sit at the edge of the bed, he whispers in a small voice, "Will it hurt?"

"No," I reassure him with a soft smile. "But you might feel a little warm, maybe even a tingle here." My finger settles between his eyes. "I've been told I have the scent of a black orchid, so try to focus on that. I won't see anything you don't want me to."

His lip quivers, glancing down. "I'm scared."

My heart shatters as I try to maintain my composure,

forcing myself to take a deep breath. But I take my hand and lift his chin, speaking calmly. "I know. If any of it feels wrong, you tell me to stop. You're in control, okay?"

His hazel eyes search mine before he takes a deep breath and nods again. I take his hands and place them on my face near my temples, letting the warmth spread over me as our connection forms. He feels light and soft—something fragile and innocent as I catch the scent of salt, reminding me of the ocean he lived near.

A series of memories pass through my mind, vivid and raw. Voices whisper, faces quickly passing by. Then the sensation of magic being drained and refilled fills my mind. His hands leave my face, taking all of five seconds to know why King Elion wants him.

As I step out of the room, shutting the door behind me, the sound of mumbled conversation greets me. Everyone is huddled around the mantel, Bess taking charge of the conversation.

I lean against the door, the weight of Theo's memories fresh on my mind, pressing heavily on my chest. Guilt churns in my stomach, realizing just how far Theo was pulled into all of this, and I can't help but feel as though it's my fault.

The room grows quiet as they begin to notice me leaning against the door, wringing my hands together. Their expectant gazes wait for me to reveal the real reason he's here.

"He's a Siphon," I say finally, my voice low.

The silence that follows is deafening as it settles over the group in a chilling realization. From behind me, the door creaks open and Theo's small voice drifts in.

"What's a Siphon?"

35

After arguing for what felt like an eternity, we finally came to an agreement, sticking with the plan I mentioned to Rydian and spending one more night at the loft.

Ren and I just delivered Theo to King Elion this morning, and now we walk down the corridor from the throne room, completing our mission as if it were any other day. No questions asked.

My hope is that King Elion won't hurt the boy, given that he's one of the last Siphons in existence. I reassured Theo that he would be well taken care of if he agreed to work with the king. I imagine Theo would be bribed if he served him—at least that's what I cling to, hoping that Elion won't harm him if it means aiding with whatever he needs.

So I told Theo to openly agree to whatever King Elion wants if he wanted to stay out of the dungeon. Yet even as I did so, it didn't help the incessant guilt that rose in my chest from delivering him this morning.

Our boots lightly thud against the stone on our exit, the sun peeking over the mountain as we descend the steps of the castle.

Ren quietly walks beside me as we walk to my chambers, stopping just outside my door before breaking the silence, turning to me.

"Does he know?" he asks quietly. I assume he's speaking about Rydian.

"About what?"

Ren throws me a wary sideways glance. "Your power. What I saw in the clearing was—"

"Don't." I shake my head, stepping into my chamber. He follows, quietly shutting the door behind him.

"He doesn't know, does he? The extent of your power."

"Are you going to say something?" I challenge, crossing my arms with an arch to my brow.

He only scoffs, shoving a hand through his dark hair. "Not unless you want me to. He may be a king of Aurelia, but my loyalty is with you."

He declares his loyalty to me for the second time in just mere hours, causing me to intently search his face. He's telling the truth. "You mean that, don't you?"

He holds my gaze for a moment before giving me a curt nod. I quickly come to the conclusion that there's more to Ren than I originally thought, and if he's willing to keep this to himself, it must mean something.

I find myself wondering why he would vow such loyalty to me, and it kills me not knowing anything of my past—my memories. Memories of a friendship I know nothing about. Curiosity pulls at me, wishing I knew more.

I frown. "Would you be willing to share some of your memories?"

But he steps back, darting his eyes across my face, slowly shaking his head. "I hope you understand, but I'm not ready to share that with you," he mumbles and I nod, feeling foolish for asking.

"When you're ready—if you're ready," I stutter, allowing him to hold on to whatever memories he keeps of his past. And I can't help but feel guilty, especially after all the harsh things I've said to him over the years.

After a couple minutes, Ren leaves without another word, just the soft click of my door closing behind him being the only thing to break the silence.

I stand for a few breaths, biting my lip as exhaustion settles in from the last few days. Then a sigh leaves me, knowing that I don't want to crawl into my own bed but Rydian's as he told me to come back to the loft after we dropped Theo off.

The tug that pulls me to him feels involuntary, like a thread between my eyes, though I know he's probably already asleep.

With a couple of slow breaths, I close my eyes and envision the loft, taking a step once I feel the Veil—now that I can do it myself. The weightlessness of the Veil consumes me, and within seconds, I'm standing in the middle of the loft as if I never left.

Rydian is sprawled across the bed, tangled in the quilts. His auburn hair is tousled, brushing across his brows, lips slightly parted as his head rests against a muscled arm. Even in sleep, he's striking to look at.

He hasn't been able to recover properly from using so much of his power after his appearance in Nymara and has had very little sleep since then, so I let him rest. With a quick glance around, I realize that Ivy and Orin are nowhere to be found— either back in Aurelia or with Bess somewhere. I'm alone.

But instead of my feet pulling me toward the bed, I find myself striding into the kitchenette for tea and walking up the stairs, careful not to wake him. The weight of my curiosity presses in as I think about the magic humming in my veins— what I experienced in Nymara with Ren.

Setting my mug down, I head to the shelf where I previously noticed a row of books and titles that spoke of tradition, legacy, and ancient customs. Rydian brought them from Aurelia since nothing like that exists here. Reaching the shelf, my fingers brush the spines, pausing on one specifically.

The Threads of the Fates - Lineage and Customs.

After pulling it out, I settle myself at the table. As I turn the pages, I notice records and rituals created to keep balance, including that of both realms. How the bloodlines were created and how to continue the bloodline, even if you're not born as one of the originals the fates made, passed down by the royal essence. *Interesting.*

I find myself rereading a few passages detailing the customs shared between realms—unspoken rules, ceremonies, and the unions of power and tradition.

I exhale, leaning back as a flicker of realization hits me. I softly close the book, my thoughts swirling. Another book catches my eye, but even as I read, my mind continues to land on my missing memories and what I lost—what I want back.

Hours go by, quickly turning to evening as it settles in from the skylight above the mezzanine. I'm stacking my notes when I peek over the railing to find Rydian still asleep, assuming he'll be sleeping until the next morning.

My idle hands and impulsivity have me recalling the original map that I still haven't returned to Elion's archives yet, and if Rydian's asleep... well, now is the perfect time to return it.

Over the last couple of weeks, I've spent what free time I've had learning the patterns of the guards standing outside the archives. After careful consideration of sneaking back in, I'm quite pleased with myself knowing that this time is much easier than the first time we did it.

Unfortunately for the guards' sakes, they're quite awful at their jobs—remaining completely unaware to who trails in after they leave before the Veil flickers out. All they'd have to do is watch the doors when they open to find me standing there as soon as I step in, yet they don't.

Luckily for me, the extra stealth training Ren had me doing has begun to pay off, as not a single speck of dust is disturbed once my feet touch the floor. Even though adrenaline courses through my veins, a smug grin plays at my lips as I release a relieved exhale.

Getting back out is the tricky part.

It's dim in the archives, save for the flicker of sconces along the stone. Long, dark bookshelves line the back wall behind his desk. The air feels thicker here, like there hasn't been a draft of air since it was built. Which isn't all that surprising since there's not a single window in the chamber, assuming it's to keep others out. Extra security.

I've begun to realize just how paranoid King Elion is. The thought has me holding in an amused snort at the irony of me infiltrating his archives in the middle of the night. He brought this on himself if you ask me.

My boots quietly thud against the floor as I stride toward his desk, careful not to disrupt the stifling, musky air. I only have fifteen minutes, so I delicately place the map back in its previous position beneath the slew of papers on his desk, hoping Elion hasn't noticed.

I'm assuming not, considering there hasn't been a single word about it—no rumors among the castle. No new gossip, not even orders in the Brotherhood. A good sign.

Yet as always, my curiosity gets the best of me when my eyes land on those documents of his council members. Each stack has its own information for each member, scattered among the realm—from Arcan to Nymara to Eldryn, then Alvonia. I've never been one for political gossip. Yet for some reason, I find myself itching to learn what Elion's currently digging up. The elite are the ones responsible for placing all those requests in the Brotherhood anyway... but then a thought crosses my mind.

Are they placing those requests, or is that what we were always told? My instinct tells me it's the latter.

It wouldn't surprise me if Elion lied all those years, if only to take out his greatest enemy under the guise of blaming it on his council members. It's something he would do.

For the next few minutes, I only stand, carefully reading through the documents as I wait for the doors to reopen, so as to not infiltrate his chair with my scent. Though the smell of me should be gone by morning, so I'm not worried about it.

Whispers float in from beneath the doors, leaving me to snap my head up and quickly fix the papers along the desk— back to perfection as if they were never touched. A rush of adrenaline rushes up my chest, my heart racing, as they'll be open at any moment.

Just as I'm about to dart for the doors, my eyes snag on his desk drawer again, and I recall what I saw within his belongings among a slew of other tossed aside items. Something that caught my eye the last time, like it was calling to me.

My pulse continues to climb when I internally groan and pull the drawer open, unable to stop myself. The boots of the guards thud against the stone as they get closer.

Fuck, they're opening.

My hand quickly shoots out, gripping the item to inspect later and shoving it in my pocket. With a smooth motion of my hand, the drawer quietly slides shut as I rush for the double doors and hide behind one as they creak open. My breath catches, too afraid to breathe.

The guards are deep in conversation, clearly unaware of my presence as their conversation doesn't falter. Just as they step through, I quietly slip into the hall and into the Veil, all within a span of a few seconds. The two guards outside don't even turn, leaving this adventure a success.

A grin tugs at my mouth right before it falters as awareness prickles my skin at the feeling of being watched. My eyes flick across the corridor—across the courtyard—as I remain in the Veil, too afraid to suck in a breath for fear of being overheard by the two unaware guards in front of me.

Nothing catches my eye, though, leaving me to quickly travel back to the loft and crawl into bed with Rydian.

36

Rydian stands beside me, concealed beneath the shadows of his hood with Ivy and Ren hovering nearby. Four weeks have passed since we stole the map. Still, we haven't found a single passageway that could lead us to my mother.

"You're sure there won't be any guards tonight?" Rydian asks.

Ren stalks forward with a glare, shoving his dark hair away from his face only to stop a few feet away. The throne room is bathed in complete darkness except for the dim orbs floating above our heads, only bright enough to view our expressions.

King Elion left the castle today, leaving us four days to walk the passages. It makes me wonder where he could be going that requires his presence so often.

And tonight, we'll be breaking into his private chambers after Ren confirmed that the only wards there are the ones similar to his archives. A chilling unease crawls up my spine, but we should be in and out within ten minutes.

Orin waits outside—concealed in the Veil—watching for anyone coming in through the front, while Ivy and Ren are to guard the doors in the throne room.

Ren's deep voice quietly echoes in the chamber. "Yes, I'm sure. I just did a perimeter check. They're mostly focused on his archives right now, but there will be two posted in his private garden near the path you'll walk down. If you stay in the Veil, they won't be a problem."

Ren pivots, holding his palms out in front of him, and the stone on either side of the entryway creates a solid wall over the throne room doors, sealing us inside.

"What are you doing?" I ask quietly.

"I must admit," Ivy mumbles, stepping to my right, "the Stone Shapers are incredible. I've never seen anyone actually use it before though."

"Don't feed his ego," I mumble, leaving her to chuckle quietly.

"I'm just making sure that no one comes in and discovers us. I'll reverse it once we're done," Ren explains, a hint of amusement lacing his tone before he faces us with a controlled expression, eyeing Ivy. "If that impresses you, you should see what I can do against a wall." He smirks, gray eyes briefly darting to mine. My brows shoot up and I glance at Ivy, who has her arms crossed.

"Not interested," she clips, turning sharply.

Ren chuckles, moving his gaze away from me, and strides to the back of the room. The door sits to the left, the one Elion uses to get to his chambers, only now it's sealed shut. I flick my wrist, the orbs dying, leaving us to adjust to the darkened space once again.

My heart lurches to my throat when I'm gently tugged back by my wrist. Rydian gazes down at me, a soft smirk playing on the corner of his mouth before leaning down, brushing his lips against the shell of my ear.

"Is there a reason you're avoiding me? I've missed you..." he says quietly, pulling back just enough to read my expression.

"I haven't… been avoiding you," I say, the words tumbling out.

Then my face warms with embarrassment because I have been mildly avoiding him. Even though I've comfortably shared his bed almost every night since we arrived from Nymara—drawn to him like static in a storm.

But my emotions remain locked up, away from him, regardless of us frequently tangled in his sheets as the days go on.

I'm afraid I'm only setting myself up for failure, though, after realizing just how much he makes my chest ache. It leaves me no choice but to put distance between us… emotionally.

Something he's seemed to notice.

Only because whatever's building in my chest—the way I feel about him—is different. Different than what I typically feel for males of any race, which is pretty close to nothing. I don't know exactly when I began to feel this way but I did, and I can't seem to stop it from growing.

King Elion would use it against me, slicing through me in every way possible to get me to yield to him. I'm not entirely sure I could live with myself if something were to happen to Rydian, and it makes me want to flee from Elderheim. And that terrifies me.

But Rydian's warmth toward me hasn't wavered—steady and calm in a way that's both admirable and incredibly frustrating.

"No? Then what is it?" he asks, amusement flashing in his eyes before they turn heated, certainly distracting me from whatever I'm about to say.

"We just… just need to find my mother," I exhale, scrambling for the right words, but it's true. My focus is on her. "That's all."

He holds me firm at the low part of my back and softly pushes my dark braid over my shoulder with a low, disbelieving grumble. My breath catches in my throat with how close his lips come to mine, and for a moment, everything disappears.

"Well, I'll be here when you're done avoiding me. We're in this together, remember?" he murmurs, sliding his other hand behind my neck, tilting my head up. Still, I find myself stepping out of his embrace with a frustrated scowl, inching back.

"Stop looking at me like that. We need to hurry. Now's not the time for… whatever that is," I grumble, pointing to his heated, hungry gaze before turning on my heel.

But not before his hand shoots out, his fingers curling at the base of my neck to forcefully tug me into him again. A gasp leaves me, and within a single beat, his mouth crashes into mine, devouring every part of me as if he's been starving and nothing has satiated his hunger until now.

The dim heat that was consuming my body before is now a full-blown fire as I melt into him—*fuck, what is he doing to me?*

His tongue slips past my lips, his taste so consuming that it alters my reality. A small, breathy gasp brushes the air, leaving me to ache all over again. Then an unfamiliar longing forms at the base of my neck before I finally come to my senses, realizing that we currently have an audience.

"We… need to get going. We don't have long," I mutter, my breath coming out in shallow pants.

"I'm inclined to agree. I need more than five minutes to worship you. How do you want it tonight? On my knees, taking my time over every inch of you, or wrapped around you, reminding you exactly who you belong to?" He gives me a small grin. Yet the way he says those words has my core heating.

My mouth falls open, but when I don't respond—unable to form a single word—he places a gentle kiss on my temple with a light chuckle.

"Later then," he mumbles in the Veil before releasing me to join the others, leaving me to close my eyes and catch my breath. My poor attempt at finding any sort of control before following him to the door where Ren and Ivy wait in silence.

But I don't miss how Ren looks when I approach—a flicker

of annoyance passing between us as he clenches his jaw, straight to Rydian. He quickly composes himself, hiding whatever was there behind his perfectly trained mask. I know he's not fond of Rydian—only here because of me—and the tension between the two of them could be cut with a knife.

It's stifling.

Ivy steps forward, standing near the large steel door, then faces me. "When you get inside, see if you can find any more passages that could only be accessed in his chambers in case they're not on the map. Look for hidden documents or even a journal if you can, anything that could lead to Queen Elynor."

This feels like stealing the map all over again, but I nod anyway and glance at the door, noticing two counter runes etched onto it. It counters the five locking runes going up the edge of the frame. That should give us at least an hour in case we need it, but I suspect Ren will clear it before we leave.

Rydian turns to me, making sure my cloak is secure. My face heats when his fingers brush against my collarbone. "I'll go first in case there are guards in the corridor, so stay behind me. I don't want you getting caught in the middle of it in case something goes wrong," he says.

"She'll be fine," Ren grumbles.

Rydian's eyes narrow, giving the captain a deliberate once-over. Ivy's brows shoot up, and then she glances between us before sighing with a shake of her head, walking off to subtly peek out the windows.

"You think I don't know that?" Rydian asks, voice low in warning. Ren only scans him with a smirk, as if he's sizing up the king to fight. *Did he forget about what happened in the clearing?*

"You act like you don't. Why don't you cut the protective king act and stop hovering? She's capable of doing what she needs to." Ren's words are smooth, almost casual, as he remains expressionless. I find myself wishing I could hear what he's thinking or what Rydian's not saying in the silence that follows.

Rydian straightens, glancing down at me. "Do I hover, little fawn? Do you feel like I'm being overprotective?" he asks in that low, heated way of his, and I can't help the flush that rises on the back of my neck, flustered.

"No, now stop. Both of you. Now's not the time to argue," I grind out, throwing them an icy glare. "We need to hurry before someone catches us."

"See?" Rydian replies. "I'm not hovering."

Ren chuckles, a low, menacing sound that echoes off the walls, but I catch the way his eyes gleam with something he's clearly choosing not to say. I glare, holding my breath, but he refuses to meet my gaze. I'm praying to the Fates they don't start a brawl in the middle of the throne room. That's the last thing we need.

"I don't think she needs you questioning what she can or can't handle. She's a trained assassin, not a helpless *little fawn,*" Ren mocks quietly, then opens the door for us. "Stop treating her like one. It's insulting."

"To you or her?" Rydian asks, striding toward the door.

"I'm literally right here," I groan, knowing that whatever I say won't stop either of them from bickering. There's nothing like putting two rivals in a room together, and the only thing keeping them from killing each other is an heir to a realm she's not even familiar with.

Although Rydian holds his tongue, I know Ren's mocking tone annoyed him by how thick the air became in a matter of seconds. He steps inside the darkened corridor with a smirk on his face, walking past without so much as a second glance.

I face Ren. "We can't afford to argue, not when we have a mission to complete. Can you cut it out until we can figure out where she is?" I sigh, clenching my fists. "I don't want to be here anymore than you do."

His only response is staring down his nose in complete

silence, then breaking his gaze long enough to nod to the door, urging me to leave. Silence.

It takes everything in me not to groan in frustration, knowing that I have to remain quiet as the door sits open. I turn sharply and brush past him.

"Isa," Ren says quietly, and I pivot. "Be quick. Be quiet."

He orders like the captain—*like my instructor.* But I study him for a moment before reluctantly nodding, disappearing in the Veil a moment later.

The steel door quietly slides shut behind us. We move in silence, our steps light as the corridor bends left. The air is cooler here, with the heavy scent of damp stone as I follow inches behind Rydian. We're halfway down the corridor before we hear quiet chatting to our left, spotting the entrance to the king's private garden. My hands hover over my daggers as we inch by.

"Stay close," Rydian says as we move past in swift silence, his fingers lightly grazing mine. *"Looks like the captain is on edge."* Annoyance coats his tone, and I can't help but stifle a grin.

"Can you blame him? We're sneaking into the king's chambers. If Elion were to find out, he'd kill all of us, not to mention you're both from different realms. It's best to just ignore him," I say.

"Are you speaking from experience?"

I grin. *"As a matter of fact, I am."*

The guards don't even pivot in our direction, and then we're at the back entrance to King Elion's private chambers, quickly approaching the arched stone foyer and steel door.

Rydian stands behind me, eyeing the corridor as my hand instinctively hovers over the door frame, revealing similar runes to what was found in the throne room. I make quick work and etch two counter runes, hearing a soft snick and silently pushing it open, praying that the old door doesn't make a sound.

"We're in," I say and he follows me inside, but the Veil doesn't

disappear, and I arch a brow. *"I thought Ren said the wards were the same."*

"He must've been wrong. This one feels slightly different. I can still access the Veil somehow, but I can't touch my magic. Can you?"

I realize the warmth in my hands is gone, then shake my head—no magic. Luckily, if we can still access the Veil, that means the king won't be able to scent us.

Walking down a short hall, I see a private mantel sits to the left with many dark crimson and gold chairs pointed at it. The royal chamber opens to a vast area, and I immediately spot the four-poster bed centered in the middle of the room, right beneath a large *L* shaped mezzanine. I quickly scan the space, noticing more bookshelves and a large table sitting directly across from his bed. There's a lot.

"Search his items on the mezzanine, and I'll search down here," I say.

We make swift work of the space, checking for hidden nooks and stone hiding places. I find myself rummaging through the stacks of books left on his table, doing my best not to misplace anything.

A thick brown ledger sits at the bottom of the pile. I flip it open. Names—pages and pages of them.

Many names I recognize from the Brotherhood, others I don't. Scrawled next to them are numbers, including mine. Tallies or ranks? A shiver crawls up my spine.

I wonder if he's keeping track of who he has serving him. What do the numbers mean?

But beneath the ledger is a scrap of parchment with jumbled, frantic writing. Hardly legible, making little sense—clearly not Elion's writing. Or perhaps it is. It's hard to tell.

The script is written in multiple lines down the page, and I realize it must be some future he's seen as a Scry. I begin to wonder if this is a part of his motive for the Veilstone.

The book closes, leaving me to quickly place the parchment

back beneath the ledger as if it were never touched. Then Rydian brushes his fingers against my shoulder.

"I inspected the walls. No hidden passages in his chambers except for the two separate doors leading into the courtyard and his archives. I did find this though," he says, handing me a letter.

My stomach dips at the signed signature near the bottom. *"It's signed by Witt Dralor, his second-in-command."*

37

I've been trembling since I woke up an hour ago, clenching my fists as the quiet, frozen forest greets me with an icy breeze. But the tremors consume me. She told me they would eventually go away and that I just need to rest, but I can't get them to stop. I don't even know what to think.

Perhaps coming here was a mistake.

I should be back at the castle by now, having been gone two days longer than I originally planned. Yet here I am, turning to wave goodbye before the sun fully rises.

And although I feel sick to my stomach, I close my eyes and visualize my next step. Veiling to different locations has become easier and easier over the last two weeks, the wave of nausea non-existent except for now. Yet the sickness I feel now has nothing to do with the Veil.

In an instant, I'm back at the castle and in my room. I breathe a quiet sigh of relief, entering the familiar space just past my door, but I'm exhausted. My head pounds, feeling as though every part of my body is aching.

Looking across the room, I see Ire perched outside, the window cracked open. My stomach drops, and I hope that

Rydian isn't looking for me. I told him I was on a mission for the next few days.

I still have a day left.

"Good morning, Ire. Do you have something for me?" I ask casually, draping my cloak across one of the settees, fully expecting him to answer.

"I don't think he does." Ren's voice resonates behind me, and I whirl to face him. "Considering I've already spoken with him."

He stands cloaked in the shadows near the door, casually leaning with a foot braced against the wall, hidden from sight as the sun hasn't quite lit up my room yet.

His large form fills the space, the chamber feeling smaller than usual. He pushes himself off the wall and steps forward, the scruff on his face cut close to the skin, highlighting the hard line of his jaw. His gray eyes come into view as he strides forward, his boots hardly making a sound. He's eerily silent.

"What do you want? Why are you in my room?" I snap, flustered as he gives me a slow, lazy once-over.

"Where were you?" His tone is sharp and accusatory, but I casually cross my arms in an attempt to hide the trembling that refuses to subside.

"I was with Rydian."

"Don't lie to me," he says quietly.

"I'm not lying."

He tilts his head, narrowing his eyes. "Do you forget who trained you? I know when you're lying, Isa. I know more about you than I probably care to." His words drip with irritation, though he steps closer. "But that's not how I know—I just saw Rydian yesterday, and you weren't there."

My hands clench against me as the shaking persists, and I can't help the breath that catches in my throat.

"What did you say to him?" I ask.

He crosses his arms, posture casual but unrelenting as he studies me. "You first. Now, where were you?"

I step back in an attempt to put space between us only to hit the bedpost behind me. Then my chest tightens, eyes closing as I will my thoughts to steady. My eyes finally open, but my face heats and the trembling in my hands has become obvious with how his gaze flicks down.

"I can't tell you," I say quietly.

He growls in frustration, pacing before he stops, his expression shifting with understanding, clenching his jaw. "You found something, didn't you?"

"It was nothing," I mutter, glancing out the window. Ire remains perched on the roof, no doubt memorizing every word exchanged between us.

"It wasn't nothing. You're pale and shaking. What was it?"

"I said it was nothing." I grind out the words, refusing to meet his gaze. It's not something I can discuss, not with him... or anyone.

He presses, stepping forward. "Does it have anything to do with how you can speak to animals? The last time I checked, Shadovar couldn't communicate with them. Only the Aetheri can. If you're from Aurelia, you should be—"

"Drop it, Ren. I won't tell you." My head snaps to him as he comes eerily close to figuring out what I suspected weeks ago. And I realize that whatever he discussed with Ire, it somehow revealed my ability to speak to animals. "Please, I just... can't. Now what did you tell Rydian?"

Ren eyes me for a moment, clenching his jaw, and then perches himself on the top of the settee behind him before sighing. "I was looking for you and went to the brothel yesterday. Then Rydian mentioned your mission, but I knew I didn't give you anything. I realized you weren't there and that he probably didn't know where you were either. I just told him that I wanted to schedule a time to walk the castle after inspecting the map again."

My breath catches as I realize that he didn't say anything

about not giving me a mission even though he had no idea where I went. *Why didn't he say anything?*

"Okay." I breathe a sigh of relief, rubbing my eyes. "But why are you here?"

"I was worried."

"Well, don't be. I'm fine." Though I feel anything but fine at the moment. He only scoffs, shaking his head as if in disbelief.

"I brought you this." He leans forward, handing me a white envelope—a mission. My brows pinch in confusion. "So you don't have to lie to him."

"Oh," I mutter, guilt gripping me. "What's the mission?"

"Well, there's no killing. You just have to steal documents from Ekrin Highcrest."

My head snaps up at the duke of Alvonia's name. "Ekrin, why?"

"There's suspected treason. King Elion wants to make sure Ekrin is obeying the law. The documents could possibly contain evidence of that and must remain sealed so he knows they haven't been tampered with. The location of the documents should be in the orders. He's offered to throw in extra money for the trouble."

I huff, gripping the envelope. Elion has never offered more money for any mission. It's either you get it done or get beaten, so whatever he wants to find out now must be important—yet my thoughts land on what I saw on Elion's desk a couple weeks ago. I raise my head to the sound of Ren standing.

"Thank you," I mutter. "For doing that. I just—"

"Don't," he interrupts. "You're right, I don't need to know. The less I know, the better. But whatever you're planning— because I know you will eventually—just make sure it's good and don't get yourself killed over it." All I can do is nod.

Not only did he *not* say anything, he gave me a mission so that I don't feel like I have to lie to Rydian. He gave me an alibi.

And now he trusts me enough to go along with a plan I haven't even created yet.

A knot settles in the pit of my stomach when a knock sounds at the door and I frown, shooting Ren a wary glance. Who's outside? Ren nods in its direction, silently encouraging me to answer it.

In an instant, I cross the threshold and crack the door open, finding Ezra fully dressed for training.

"Hey, are you ready?" he asks, eyes bright and eager, clearly rested. I almost groan. *I need sleep.*

I completely forgot about meeting with him. We planned on training when he got back from his most recent mission, but that isn't supposed to be until tomorrow, giving me extra time with Milena if I needed it. He's a day early.

I've somehow managed to calm the shaking enough to give him a soft smile, composing myself. "Yes, but I got a mission today so I can't go hunting like we wanted to. We can train though." I chuckle. *Not that I mind.*

"Oh, okay. Well, get dressed, and I'll wait out here then." He gives me a once-over, noting how I'm not dressed to train.

I chuckle again and shut the door, expecting to find Ren waiting on the settee, but I return to an empty room, the middle window slightly ajar from his departure.

"He's busy," the guard growls, standing outside King Elion's archives. "You can wait just like everyone else."

After rising this morning, I was met with Theron at my door, summoned by King Elion to meet in his archives. My stomach dropped, but I know it isn't for anything other than the documents I stole last night. He's eager to see what I have, and hopefully we're only meeting in his archives for privacy.

I glance to my left as the second guard widens his stance,

clinking the armor he wears. I almost laugh at his confidence, as if he could hurt me. But I know that Elion has some of the best fighters and that includes his guards.

I have no doubt he would be an interesting opponent to fight. One hand rests on the hilt of my short sword, itching to reach for it, while the stolen documents from Ekrin Highcrest are held firmly in the other. My gaze flicks back to the mouthy guard on my left, giving him an icy grin.

"Is swinging that sword all you're good at, or are you compensating for something else?" I ask casually, darting my gaze to the lower half of his body.

He's on me in an instant, but not before I have my dagger pointed at his throat, forcing him to halt with a sneer on his face. The other guard inches forward a step.

"Try it," I murmur. His hot, putrid breath hits my face, and it takes everything in me not to wince from the smell. "Honestly, your fighting skills might be good, but I think your breath would kill anyone before they even got to you." The guard grunts as I twist my face in disgust. The archive doors open.

"Isa." Ezra walks out.

I straighten, flicking my gaze to Ezra, who's armed to the teeth and wearing a thick dark gray cloak, his hair windblown.

"Were you summoned too?" I ask, flinging my dagger back into its position at my waist, stepping away from the guard who's returned to the edge of the door.

"I was. I didn't get the chance to update him yesterday." His gaze drops to my hands, and then he raises a single brow. "Documents?"

"Isa!" Elion calls out.

"I have to go—he's been waiting for these. Let's train later," I get out and Ezra nods, watching me enter the archives.

My pulse races, and Elion's yellow eyes stare back at me as I approach, stopping just shy of his desk. I hold my composure with a lift of my chin, leaning in to hand him the documents.

"Your Majesty." I bow.

"It would be wise of you not to keep me waiting. What do you have for me?" Elion asks.

"The documents you requested. This is what I found last night, still sealed like ordered."

"Good. Did he notice you?"

"No," I say curtly. "I did eavesdrop on his conversation with a male named Kon. They mentioned something about meeting in a few weeks, though I'm not sure who he is, but he seemed important to Ekrin. I stole the documents shortly after they finished up."

He looks off, clearly lost in thought, and then eyes me from across the desk, the silence stretching for a beat.

"You did well," he says, and I realize that this must have been a test somehow. It takes everything in me to keep my expression neutral, my hands lightly clasped behind my back. My stomach flutters at the unexpected praise, throwing me off because that's as close to a compliment as I'll ever get from King Elion.

"You are the only female in the Brotherhood, are you not?" he asks, his tone firm.

"Yes, Your Majesty," I reply, wondering where this is going.

"There are some..." He trails off, stroking his white beard while casually leaning back. "Perks to that. I'll be throwing a ball at the castle next week and need you to attend as a guest."

A guest? What kind of guest and what does he mean by perks? Perks for him or for me? It's hard to decipher the meaning as I've never attended as a guest before. Usually when I go to one of King Elion's balls, I'm attending as another guard. He likes to increase his security when festivals or balls are held, typically around the perimeter to eavesdrop. To watch the dukes and duchesses of Elderheim, but no one seems to notice us.

"As Sensa Blackwyth. You'll be going as one of the Blackwyths' long-lost nieces, and since they are so far from Alvonia, no one would question your appearance. All of Elderheim's high-ranking citizens will be there for our yearly Aurorafest. It will be the perfect excuse to attend since none of them have any familiarity with you."

"And what of the Blackwyths?" I ask.

"The Blackwyths will not be attending. You will be able to do what you can that night because I need you to get close to Ekrin Highcrest. I need more information from him regarding the rumor that's been floating around. A rumor that he's been sympathizing with the Shadovar, and I need to confirm whether or not that's true. I want you to do it for me," he says, and I mask my shock.

Kiev and Selphira Blackwyth are the duke and duchess of Eldryn. Last I heard, they haven't been attending any of the balls given they're so far north, making it hard to travel due to the rocky and snowy terrain. King Elion hasn't seemed to mind though, but now I can understand why, especially if he wants me going as one of their nieces. *A niece I know doesn't exist.*

Elion eyes me cautiously, as if watching to see how I'll respond to this new mission. A mission directly given to me by the king himself. Although alarming, I remain steady as an icy grin begins to form at the corners of my mouth.

"I'm always happy to serve you, Your Majesty. How shall I dress?" I ask.

His expression remains the same, but I catch a gleam of amusement in his eyes before he answers. "I'll send you to Karina the day of. The ball is in six days. You'll hear more about your mission from Captain Demaris," he says dismissively, but as I begin to bow, he leans forward. The air thickens, his gaze locking on to mine, forcing me to straighten. His voice goes low in warning. "I've spent years perfecting my guards and making sure they are loyal to me—their training is just as important as yours. It would be unfortunate if your sharp tongue was found on the wrong end of one of their blades. Count this as your only warning from me. I'd hate to lose someone so... skilled, and I hope you're wise enough to avoid that mistake again."

He must have either seen or heard me outside his archives with a knife to his guard's throat. My mouth goes dry, but I nod firmly. "Of course. I apologize, Your Majesty. It won't happen again. I'll be ready in six days." I bow, and he waves a hand in dismissal, then rips open the documents.

My stomach flutters as I exit, breathing a quiet sigh of relief for the catastrophe I just avoided.

But now I have a new mission.

38

I pinned my auburn mark before seeing Karina, the castle's seamstress, in her workspace this afternoon. My black hair is elegantly pulled away—half up—with a few wavy strands framing the sides of my face.

Karina dressed me in a mesmerizing two-toned cream-and-gold gown that cascades to the floor. The bodice fits snug at my chest, hanging just off my shoulders and dipping to the swell of my breasts.

I expected to learn more of my mission from Ren like King Elion mentioned, but all I got was a missive shoved under the door with an extensive backstory on Sensa Blackwyth. I haven't seen Ren since he caught me sneaking back into my own chamber last week. I just figure he was searching for any information regarding the second-in-command without being obvious.

Karina opens the massive white door with a soft smile. "I'll send someone tomorrow to retrieve the items from your chamber."

My grin widens as I stride past before stopping short. Ren

pushes himself off the wall across from me, eyes grazing mine with a disinterested stare.

"What are you doing?" I ask just as the door quietly clicks shut, leaving us alone in the hall.

"I'm your personal guard for the night," he says, slowly scanning me from top to bottom before meeting my eyes, expression unreadable.

"You're my what?" That's when I notice what he's wearing.

Dark pants are covered by the long cream-and-gold colored tunic with a matching cape, elegantly draped from his shoulders, a golden clasp securing it at his collarbone. His arms are gloved, matching the dark belted sheath secured at his waist holding a golden sword with an emerald jewel nestled at the top —matching the one at my throat. My cheeks heat at the realization of him matching me.

He looks like a royal guard.

"If this were a few years ago, you would've been delighted about me being your personal guard with all the chaos we caused." He fights a grin, but I can't help but throw him a glare as he offers me the inside of his elbow.

We silently walk through the courtyard and up the steps near the kitchens, as the ballroom sits right across from it. Music flows into the corridor as every door remains open. Extra guards are posted nearby, and I spot a few from the Brotherhood disguised as more royal guards.

"How many weapons do you have?" I mutter.

The ballroom is nothing short of exquisite. Vaulted ceilings draw you in with the gilded chandeliers that drip with fine crystals, casting speckles of light across the polished white marble floor. Lively but soft music weaves through the conversations, laughter filling the air as couples spin gracefully across the room, the quiet rustle of gowns brushing against the floor.

"All of them," he says quietly, then glances down, lifting his scarred brow. "How many do you have?"

A smirk plays on my lips. "All of them."

He chuckles, leading us toward the edge of the room where guests mingle around clusters of chairs and tables. Spiced mead lingers with the scent of savory treats behind us, enticing more guests to filter in from outside.

I quickly scan the room. Only the finest dressed dukes and duchesses trail in with their family and close friends. Then I spot King Elion sitting on the raised dais toward the back with Xane, Luke, Ezra, Malrik, and Theron—all disguised as royal guards. All dressed similarly to Ren, flanking King Elion, behind and in front of his elegant table.

"It's going to be quite interesting watching Rydian hear about this later," Ren mumbles, and I glance up just as a smirk tugs at the corner of his mouth.

"Stop provoking him," I grumble.

Ren huffs a quiet laugh. "It's entertaining watching him unravel at the thought of you being unprotected or touched by someone else. He can't seem to control himself."

A frustrated sigh leaves me, wondering why Ren thinks that. Rydian seems to have plenty of control when I'm around him.

"He doesn't unravel," I say. "Technically, I'm not unprotected. You're here, aren't you?"

"You don't need protection. I made sure of that. He just needs to be humbled a bit," he says, and I catch the tightness of his jaw.

"And you don't? All you males do is argue. The least you can do is get along for a few weeks until we find my mother, and then we'll leave."

His gaze swivels down to meet mine. "Trust me, I've been humbled for the last four years." He scans the room again. "You're going with him."

"I don't know yet," I say, even though he said it like a statement. But I know that going with Rydian is the deal I made before we agreed to search for my mother. I'm just not sure how

Ren will take it now that I know we used to be friends. "Afraid you'll miss me?" I ask.

He only sighs. "You won't be a thorn in my side anymore, and I'll finally be able to sleep without worrying about what you'll do next."

My eyes roll. I figured he felt that way. He'll probably rejoice the day I leave, knowing I won't be a problem anymore.

Guests twirl in and out in mesmerizing movements, my stomach fluttering—not from being hungry or my current mission, but from realizing that I might have to dance. I swallow, my face heating as my pulse climbs, unsure I'll be able to complete my mission without making a fool of myself.

"What's wrong?" Ren asks.

"I don't even know how to dance."

Ren lowers his gaze, clearly fighting a grin. I can tell he's holding back what I'm sure would be an amused chuckle if we weren't in such a highly trafficked area.

"Are you panicking?" he asks with a blink. "I've never seen you panic before."

"This isn't funny," I snap quietly, grappling for composure. I pivot to face him, my gown brushing against the floor. "I'm sure Ekrin is going to want to dance with me, and I have no idea what I'm doing."

"Yes, you do," he mumbles, almost in annoyance, forcing my head to snap up in confusion. "You know how to dance. I'm sure that's the one thing you didn't forget because we're all taught ballroom etiquette in the Brotherhood. Just... follow your instinct."

"I have no recollection of ever learning these dances—" My retort is cut short when Ren's composed mask slides into place, nodding toward the center of the room. I realize then just how good he is at that.

My attention shifts to King Elion striding toward us with Ekrin Highcrest at his side, guests parting down the middle.

The next thing I know, I've become Sensa Blackwyth, high-ranking niece to Kiev and Selphira Blackwyth of Eldryn.

He's just as I remembered from my mission last week: tall and dark-haired with pale green eyes. Only this time he wears an elegant black-and-gold colored tunic that covers his dark pants. His outfit complements his light tanned complexion, complete with a matching high collar cape that clasps at his neck. Too bad his arrogance drips from him like a fine wine.

They finally meet us, coming to a stop just shy of our feet. Ren and I bow to King Elion.

"Your Majesty," I say, cautiously eyeing the duke.

"Ekrin Highcrest, this is Sensa Blackwyth, niece to Kiev and Selphira of Eldryn. And this is Ren Demaris, our current captain and her assigned personal guard during her stay. Sensa is currently visiting the castle for the next few weeks and has never been to the Aurorafest. I'd love for you to show her around," Elion says, clasping Ekrin on the shoulder and gesturing toward me. "Please, get acquainted!"

King Elion meets my gaze before leaving to greet the other dukes and duchesses approaching him nearby. I give Ren a nod and he steps back to hover behind us.

I face Ekrin with a soft, convincing smile. "It's nice to finally meet you. I've heard many wonderful things." I extend my right hand. He gently lifts it to his mouth, inhaling as he places a soft kiss to the top of it. He eyes me, slowly releasing my hand, then gives me a charming smirk.

"I doubt that, but I am interested to hear exactly what you heard. Care to walk with me?" His voice is smooth like honey, and I quickly understand the allure to him.

A soft laugh slips free as I wrap my hand around the inside of his elbow. "You're right, I've heard many wicked things, but I think you might have to pry them out of me."

He chuckles. "Tell me, Lady Sensa, what brings you to Alvonia?"

The ballroom walls are lined with arched windows, draped in shimmering cream-colored curtains that lead into the courtyard. Housemaidens glide around the room with practiced ease, passing out drinks to guests who continue to mingle. There's a palpable energy to the room—a blend of excitement and curiosity.

"Well, Duke—"

"Please, just Ekrin."

"Well, *just* Ekrin." I grin, and he returns it with an amused gleam to his eyes. "We received an invite to the Aurorafest. King Elion offered to allow us to stay for a few weeks, but as you know, Eldryn makes it very hard to visit. I begged my mother and aunt Selphira for so long they finally agreed to let me visit until the spring. Childish, I know, but it's stifling there, and I couldn't wait to visit any longer."

"Mm." He hums his understanding. "And your family couldn't visit with you? I would have loved to meet the infamous Duke and Duchess of Eldryn." He chuckles, leaning into me. "And no, it's not childish. I understand all too well what that's like."

I glance at him, then sheepishly avert my gaze. "They couldn't stay, not for that long anyway. Once coming down from the mountains, it's almost impossible to travel back up in the dead of winter. Kiev and Selphira needed to stay in Eldryn, but I'll be back up there in the next few weeks once the ice melts," I explain with a sigh.

He pauses our walk. "And you don't want to go back?"

"Gods, no." I laugh, tucking the loose strands behind my ear. Ren stands a few feet behind us. "Don't get me wrong, I love my family very much, but we remain isolated in the mountains. It's beautiful here and much warmer than the freezing temperatures up north. I'm afraid I've been struck with the incessant need to stay in Alvonia."

"I see," he mutters, then quickly grabs us both a glass of

wine from one of the housemaidens passing by. "Here's to running away when life sucks." He holds up his glass, handing me mine.

His brazen words catch me off guard, and before I can stop myself, a genuine, carefree laugh escapes me. With a grin tugging on the corners of my mouth, I raise my glass and clink it against his. His eyes widen slightly, watching me with curiosity. A flicker of something unreadable passes through them before he takes my empty glass and hands it off to another passing housemaiden.

"Would you like to dance?" He scans my face, extending a hand for mine.

A nervous look is thrown over my shoulder, finding Ren's annoying smirk from behind me, and I clench my jaw as he gives me a curt nod. He's clearly *not* saving me from what's going to be a catastrophic embarrassment on my part. I finally turn to face Ekrin, who patiently waits for my answer.

I sigh. "I'm going to be honest—I haven't danced in a long time. I'm afraid I'm not very good." He only grins and grasps my hand anyway, tugging me behind him as he walks toward the center of the ballroom.

"I'll teach you. I won't take no for an answer," he says over his shoulder.

He elegantly twirls me, and I quickly end up in his arms while he clasps my hand, the other resting on his chest as we fall into an easy rhythm. The music is soft, yet loud enough so that others can't hear our conversation should they pry, which I gather they'll do given how many are staring.

"I hope this isn't too forward," he mutters, gazing down at me. "But... you're incredibly beautiful. Especially your eyes— they're mesmerizing. It's no wonder your aunt and uncle hide you in the mountains."

A genuine flush reaches my cheeks. "And *I'm* sure you've said that to many of the ladies in Alvonia, but don't think I haven't noticed how you've hardly even spoken about yourself. What's it like being Duke of Alvonia?"

His brows lower, a grave expression settling over his features as he thinks about his answer.

"Honestly?" he asks, and I nod. "I hate it. My parents had me toward the tail end of their life, and after they died, the title was immediately passed down to me. It was a responsibility I knew was coming but secretly hoped wouldn't."

I frown, finding myself thinking about my abrupt responsibility to Aurelia. How I've had this unwavering feeling of wanting to flee in every direction, but also toward it. It's been a struggle, knowing I should go while also having this urge to remain in Elderheim... until recently. Now the feeling of wanting a life with Rydian tugs at me, even if it means claiming Aurelia as mine.

"I know the feeling," I mutter. "How do you do it? How do you go into something you're unsure you want but know people are counting on you to claim it?"

"I don't. Not really, anyway. I manage by tucking myself away in my studies with my head down, doing as King Elion wants," he says and spins me again. "I thought you said you weren't good at dancing."

"You make it easy." I smile, realizing that he's right because I haven't tripped once. "Is that why you haven't married, because you've been busy with your studies?"

"So you've heard. Not surprising, I guess." He chuckles, his chin grazing the edge of my temple.

"It's hard not to, given how the court talks," I reply. "But I can't help but be curious as to why someone as striking as you hasn't married yet. You're a male in power and have so many ladies groveling at a chance to be your duchess, yet you remain unmarried. Or have you just been blissfully unaware of how everyone stares at you tonight?"

He gazes down at me. "They're not staring at me."

My face heats as I glance around the room again, realizing that most gazes are fixed on me dancing with the duke of Alvonia, including King Elion. He twirls me back into his arms again, catching Ren's hardened stare from across the room.

"Have you ever been in love?" I ask.

"I have, though that relationship is long gone. We were young, but she was also my first love at the age of thirteen. When the ban was put in place, she was forced from the realm," he explains, and my breath catches as I realize that she must have been Shadovar.

"I see you've heard the recent rumors," he says, pulling me closer by my waist, mumbling under his breath. "I'm curious, though. Do you know what power I hold, Sensa?" His voice is low. Knowing he speaks of the Aetheri magic, I shake my head. "I'm an Herb Weaver. As you know, Herb Weavers have this intense connection to the land and the plants that thrive in the realm, but with that comes my overwhelming, heightened sense of smell. It's much stronger than most, allowing me to detect poisons and unfamiliar scents—blood, even. My familial line does, anyway. The Highcrest line."

"I didn't know that," I mumble, wondering where this is going.

"Surprisingly, not many do. It's fascinating, especially when I come across something I've never scented before, like the rich black orchid I got off of you," he explains, and I stiffen against him. "So, you can understand my surprise when I realized it was you who stole those documents out of my study."

39

____

We transition into another dance, easily swaying as if nothing interrupted us. I find myself sliding my eyes up with a soft smile, hoping that I've masked the fiery storm brewing beneath the surface. I didn't count on him scenting me in his studies.

I glance to my left, catching Elion's stare, who's then distracted by Ezra. He leans down to murmur something to Elion, and I take advantage of the reprieve.

"I'm not sure what you mean," I purr.

A broad smile. "I must admit, you are quite convincing. I have no doubt that you belong in this royal gown, but I don't believe that you are Sensa Blackwyth as you say. But now I'm intrigued, and that's a dangerous thing for me to be. So who are you?"

I hold his gaze, my thoughts racing as I carefully calculate my answer. The music fades, marking the end of our second song before Ekrin dips me low, arms holding me steady around my waist. He hovers close with a wide, mesmerizing grin.

"Tell me whose blood it is that smells of Shadovar, but also of royalty? Such power you hold," he whispers the moment I plant my feet onto the marble, my eyes flicking across the room for any sign of someone overhearing.

Ice coats my veins. "If you breathe those words any louder, I'll gut you in the middle of the floor while Elion watches."

A menacing gleam shines in his eyes, as if seeing me for the first time, and then he grins. I find myself facing off with the arrogant male I suspected he was just moments earlier—he's as arrogant as I thought.

"Then why don't we find somewhere private to discuss this," he mumbles, guiding us to the balcony overlooking the courtyard.

We stop at the railing and face each other. Ren follows but hovers by the glass doors with a wary look on his face, remaining far enough away to not overhear our conversation.

I hold Ekrin's cold stare when he leans in. "I've been wondering if it was a coincidence that you stole the wrong documents with a fresh seal, or if you're just really bad at your job."

My elbows lean against the railing, a knowing grin lifting the corners of my mouth. I knew that what I stole is nothing important. *Not really.*

Nothing other than a stack of marriage proposals from women waiting in line for their chance at being a duchess. I placed them into a new envelope with the duke's wax seal, knowing that what I *did* find is enough to get him killed.

What can I say? Curiosity is a weakness of mine.

"And what if I did purposely steal the wrong ones, choosing to leave behind what was so bravely left out on the desk? A duke should know better, don't you think?" I tsk with a smirk.

"Then you have my full attention, because why would you want to steal marriage proposals knowing that what I had lying around was incredibly incriminating?" he asks.

I face the courtyard as he steps beside me. He's so close that I feel the warmth seeping through his tunic, but I know if we were farther apart and arguing, someone would relay that to King Elion. Ekrin pivots, angling his body toward mine.

His cold but curious gaze meets mine, keeping my voice down. "I spent my time doing what I could to find out why King Elion had me steal those documents before I even scouted your estate. You'd be surprised by what you can find out when posing as someone looking to leave the realm," I mutter, and he clenches his jaw. "You can imagine *my* surprise when I learned that Duke Ekrin Highcrest has been smuggling out the Shadovar half-breeds and into Aurelia right under Elion's nose. Or is that Eldryn?"

"What do you want?"

"Answer me this and I'll tell you. Why do you do it?" I ask, and his gaze softens for a breath before scoffing.

"Because I watched him *murder* my parents for caring about their half-blooded staff and their Shadovar friends years after he placed the ban. They made the mistake of keeping the knowledge of their Shadovar friends a secret and were then labeled as sympathizers. I watched his eyes glaze over with madness as his guards cut off their heads. He made me stand there, begging for him to stop, and said he used them as an example in case I had any ideas as a new duke. I decided to help those who want to flee from this realm after witnessing everyone I loved die, and I'll continue to do it until my own head is rolling on the floor."

For a moment, my heart stops as I hear one of the many senseless acts King Elion committed all because he was angry with my mother. Was she really the reason he snapped or was it always bound to happen? Silence passes between us before I give him a small nod.

"I'll keep your little secret to myself if you keep mine, and I'll agree to be there should you need it if you do the same for me. Now that you've sniffed out whatever it was through that nose of yours."

Because now I have more than who's necessary knowing what blood runs through my veins, and I can't risk Elion finding out that I know through a duke. Ekrin could be beneficial if I were to use him in the future, for whatever plan I decide to brew later. Who knows how far my mother's mission will go, but I have to prepare for anything.

"I don't like to repay debts," he warns.

"It's not a debt..." I glance over my shoulder, finding Ren leaning against the frame with a scowl on his face. "Call it even."

Ekrin chuckles, yanking me to his chest, my lips parting in surprise. His mouth hovers over my ear.

"You want an alliance? Fine. I'll even keep to myself how someone of such royalty lives under the roof of her largest enemy, or—" He stops himself, and I stiffen. "Should I say more? There's *so* much I discovered just by scenting you. Your blood is rich and dark, yet light as the air we breathe. It *hums* with power. I wonder what that mate of yours would do..." He casually glances at guests who continue to dance inside, seemingly unaware of who stands on the balcony.

My eyes go wide as I reach back, feeling the mark in my hair to ensure that it's secured beneath my thick waves. His brows pinch. *Did he see the mark of Aurelia?* He couldn't have—it's hidden.

"I don't have a mate," I mutter, stepping out of his hold.

He tilts his head with a smirk. "I guess that means you're available then. If that's the case, I would like to formally ask for your hand in marriage, Sensa Blackwyth. *If* that's your real name."

A small grin tugs at my lips. "I'm already spoken for."

"Are you? I don't see a ring on your finger, and you're clearly *not* mated." He narrows his eyes, assessing me again before briefly glancing at the doors. "Why not create the best alliance through a marriage bond? We could change the world."

"You're only interested because of what runs through my

veins. Nothing more," I say, and his pale green eyes narrow in assessment, as if I'm a prize to behold—something precious.

"That would be a perk, wouldn't it? Though that's not why I ask, because I have a feeling you are incredibly.... important. But out of everyone I've met, you are by far the most captivating. And although you're really good at lying, you're the only one that has ever given me such an *interesting* conversation. And that really intrigues me. You'd be an incredible asset, and we could make the perfect team since you clearly sympathize with... them, don't you think?" he mutters, refusing to say those specific words out loud. "I have a thing for the mean ones. It's always been a flaw of mine."

"I'll take that as a compliment," I purr, giving him a once-over. "I got it from my mother."

He gives me a slow smirk, and the way his pale green eyes hold mine—like he *knows*—makes my smile falter. My breath catches in my throat. He couldn't know just by scenting me... could he?

"Just think about it," he murmurs, casually tucking his hands back into his pockets.

"I don't need to. I'm not interested," I say cooly, somehow managing to hold my composure as I walk toward Ren, my dress sweeping across the cold stone. My side grazes him before looking over my shoulder at Ekrin, who leans against the railing with a hungry, knowing look on his face.

"What did you do?" Ren asks quietly. The look on his face tells me that he's heard at least some of our conversation—but how much?

"I just formed our first alliance."

The next morning, I chose not to wait for Karina to send someone up to my chambers. Already awake, I secured my weapons to my waist, gathered the borrowed items, and took them to her.

Now, as I step into the hall, my attention is quickly drawn to King Elion and Ren striding past with Theron closely behind. Elion's eyes land on me. He halts a few feet away and motions for Theron to remain at the corner of the hall. The gesture is clear—he intends to have a private chat with me. Ren remains silent behind Elion's left shoulder.

I bow. "Your Majesty."

"Isa, I just sent Theron to your chambers, but you weren't there. I'm curious, what did you find out last night?" he asks.

Looks like we'll be discussing this in the hall, but okay.

I lift my chin. "I believe the rumors being spread about Duke Ekrin Highcrest have something to do with his previous childhood relationship with a Shadovar. But once the ban was put in place, it was clear to me that he remained no contact with those of the other realm. He even expressed great interest in finding a duchess of Elderheim, mentioning the most recent proposals he's received from all over the realm."

He grunts, stroking his jaw for a moment. My hands remain clasped tightly behind my back, steadying myself under his piercing gaze.

"I agree," he mumbles. "That would explain why he asked for your hand in marriage, which came as a shock to me, but that just told me you did your job correctly for once."

I straighten. "He did?"

Elion smirks. "Yes, but I told him you were already spoken for by a selected match from your aunt and uncle in Eldryn. He was quite... enthralled with you. He even offered a hefty payment, which was more than enticing, but Captain Demaris made an excellent point—you're exactly where I want you to be for the moment."

My blood turns cold at the double meaning, and I realize that both Ren and King Elion had time to discuss this already.

Yet I can't shake the fury rising in my chest at another choice being stripped from me. By *Elion*.

Despite that, I only respond with a small nod. "My wish is your command, Your Majesty. Anything for the realm."

He gives a small wave of his hand, catching Theron's attention before giving me one last glance, accompanied by a cold smirk.

"Anything for the realm," Elion murmurs, then walks past.

Ren remains in front of me, and I wait until King Elion is out of earshot before I speak.

"Why?" I ask, but he looks past me, refusing to meet my gaze.

"Because a male like Ekrin Highcrest wouldn't know what to do with you."

"You made that choice for me," I snap quietly.

I never would have agreed to it because of Rydian, but the option—the choice—was stripped from me just like every other time. After spending my life with choices taken away, it feels like a violation. Bitterness coats my tongue as I glare with a lethal calm when he finally meets my gaze.

"We both know Ekrin is not where you need to end up," he says so quietly, and I quickly realize the true meaning behind his actions—he speaks of Aurelia.

He knows that if the king decided to marry me off, I wouldn't be leaving with Rydian by the end of this mission— whenever that is. One way or another, I won't be tied here much longer, and Ren just secured that for me.

I blink, registering his words, and give him a curt nod before King Elion calls for him down the corridor.

40

I lean against the bookshelves with my arms folded, watching as Rydian makes another *x* across the map, crossing out one of the tunnels. We've discovered five, including the one by the kitchens near the ballroom that I happened to discover when running into Ren.

Ivy and I Veiled into the tunnels a couple of hours ago, remaining quiet and unseen. Although I've finally been able to hold myself in the Veil for extended periods of time, it quickly drains me. We just completed our seventh walkthrough, unable to find anything.

But something is missing. We just can't figure it out.

"This one," Ren says, pointing to the map, dark hair falling over his brow, "leads to the dungeons, but those were empty. No need to keep anyone in there when he has us do his dirty work." He scratches the back of his head.

"What about this one?" Orin asks. "Maybe there's a hidden entrance to another location in the tunnel behind the throne."

Ivy sighs. "We checked. No matter how many times I'm going to feel up one of those dingy walls, there's nothing there." Her voice drips with irritation.

We're all frustrated, and after having the map for a little over a full month, we still haven't found anything regarding my mother's whereabouts. I'm almost convinced she's not there— but the feeling in the pit of my stomach tells me my thought is wrong.

She's in there, but where?

Rydian leans forward on his hands, then drops his head, defeat and exhaustion coating his features. He sighs. I shake my head and push myself off the shelves without a word, turning for the stairs. If we're going to sit around, we might as well have some tea or something.

Starting the kettle, I grab a couple of mugs when I feel Rydian step behind me. My breath hitches at the closeness.

"Talk to me," he says quietly, brushing my hair off my neck, and I freeze at his touch. It's as if he knows the mental turmoil going through my head. "You've hardly said anything since you and Ivy arrived. What's wrong?"

I shake my head, placing the mugs on the counter as the porcelain clinks against it. He grips my shoulders and forces me to face him, tilting my chin up. He studies me, then slides his hand to the back of my neck before leaning down, softly grazing his lips against mine. A question.

And against my better judgment, I welcome it.

My fingers graze the hair at the base of his neck, leaving him to let out a soft groan. Over the last week, I've intentionally stayed at the castle and have chosen to keep my distance— emotionally and physically. Especially after what I discovered.

"Talk to me," he repeats, his voice warm and inviting.

I sigh and step back, my frustration bubbling over. "I just —I know she's there, Rydian. I can *feel* it. Something is missing, and I'm getting impatient. What else are we going to do? We're working, yes, but we have nothing to go off of. *Nothing,"* I say firmly, turning to snatch the kettle off the stove.

"I know," he mutters. "I'm frustrated too. We'll figure it out. We just have to be patient a little longer."

He says his words so confidently, and I'm reminded that this is the closest he's ever gotten to discovering the whereabouts of my mother. After twenty years of searching, his eyes continue to spark with hope.

"How do you do that?" I ask, and his brows knit together. "Remain hopeful. After all these years, you still search."

His gaze only softens. "Because my *hope* led me to you, and I refuse to give up on your mother. She deserves that, don't you think?"

I study him and find myself nodding because he's right. She does deserve that, and if it weren't for him, I would never know how crooked King Elion is. I walk past and up the steps again, reaching the top only to find Ivy rolling her own copy of the map with the updated marks.

"Orin and I will head back to Aurelia to study the map further with the council now that it's updated. We can be back in a few days to continue the search. Maybe we can discuss the options of searching outside of the castle. Find out if King Elion has any private locations that only he has access to."

Then Orin clears his throat. "Wayd and Kaeda are becoming... impatient. What do you want me to tell them? They offered to help."

My brows furrow when Rydian's jaw clenches so tight it looks like he'll shatter teeth. Like the sound of those two names already irritates him.

"Tell them if they step foot in this realm, it'll be the last time they do it. A little longer," Rydian says, but Orin only chuckles and nods. "I'll see both of you in a few days. Send Ire if you discover anything while you're there."

They nod, Veiling out of the loft, most likely already at the border. Our gazes swivel to Ren standing at the other end of the table, hands in his pockets. A sudden wave of awkward tension passes through the air, and I find myself fighting the urge to fidget.

Ren has remained quiet about both my power and my past whereabouts since he caught me almost two weeks ago, and I don't know what to make of it. His knowing gaze meets mine.

"I think I'll head back to the castle," Ren says finally, stepping around the table.

"I can Veil you in," I say, placing my mug down.

"No need. I want to walk."

With my back to Rydian, my eyes narrow. Whether it's intentional or not, Ren leaving me alone with Rydian is surely a bad idea, and he knows it. *What is he trying to do?*

Ren smirks, catching my expression. "You know, I think the chill air is just what I need to cool down. See you tomorrow."

I fight a groan, watching as he descends the stairs, when I have the sudden urge to chuck my mug right at his head. Within seconds, he exits the loft, and I face Rydian in silence.

"I guess we're done for the night. I'll need to go back to the castle—I have training with Ezra in the morning."

Rydian narrows his eyes slightly, stepping into me and closing the distance. "Are you lying to me, little fawn?" *Gods, does he know?*

"No." I swallow, eyes locking on him.

"I thought Ren said Ezra left the castle?"

Oh. I exhale and let out an uncomfortable laugh. "I must've forgotten. Still, I should go back tonight and keep up with the routine. I wouldn't want anyone searching for me, let alone King Elion."

"You're avoiding me." His gaze flicks to my lips. Then he crowds me, slowly walking forward, forcing me to stumble into the table. He reads me like a damn book. "Why don't you stay tonight? I can light a fire, and we can have a glass of whiskey— relax. You need rest, especially after spending so much time in the Veil earlier." *I hate it when he makes sense.*

"I don't have any change of clothes," I say.

"Who needs clothes?" He chuckles again just as my eyes snap up. "Relax, I'll lend you one of my shirts. You can have the bed if you want. I'll sleep on the settee."

And although I smirk, the composure I'm barely holding together almost cracks under his stare. "Fine. I'll stay if it means you'll *get out of my face.*" I lift a brow.

He steps back, hands up in mock surrender with a smug grin. "I'll be in the bath. Come down when you're ready." He grabs both our mugs, then stalks past, descending the stairs.

I frown at the thought of him not sharing a bed with me, listening as he places the mugs into the basin below with a clink. His boots thud against the brick floor before entering the bathing chamber below.

For a moment, I chew on the inside of my lip as the weight of everything begins to press down. The silence in the air feels heavier somehow, and I hate where my thoughts go when I'm alone.

My mother. Who we've continued to search for, yet everything we could find has led us nowhere. I shove down the dull ache forming in my chest as it's easier than admitting defeat. Because that's what it's starting to feel like.

And Theo. Ren has kept tabs on him since he was given to King Elion a month ago. Thankfully, I was right in my assumption of how Theo would remain unharmed... for now. Last we heard, he was working in the kitchens with the rest of the staff while also training with some of the orphans in the Brotherhood.

My thoughts begin to spiral, leading me down an endless path of chaos whirling in my head. Breath catches in my throat, feeling as though I can hardly breathe. With a shaky exhale, I find the courage to saunter down the steps even though my turmoil continues to simmer.

My steps remain light as I walk to the kitchenette for water, just past the bathing chamber. That's when I notice the door was left slightly ajar.

I arch a brow with a hum, curiosity getting the best of me when I slow my pace. A quick glance through the small gap in the door has my steps faltering, falling silent as I'm captivated by the massive king before me.

Dammit, I shouldn't have stopped.

My lip pulls between my teeth as I study him. With his back to me, he rinses in the tub before dropping his head. His arm reaches across his back, scrubbing himself.

I can't help but stare, practically breathless, as the muscles feather and ripple with each movement. I'm captivated by every strong muscle on his body in the soft lighting of the chamber.

Ink snakes up his neck, and I can't help but become dazed at the sight of him. My eyes drift when I notice it—just beneath the damp strands of his dark auburn hair, located at the nape of his neck.

Is that what I think it is?

My breath hitches, freezing at the sight of it.

But he must sense me because his movements come to an abrupt halt, stopping mid-scrub.

The stone wall beside me hits my back, hiding me as I clamp my eyes shut. My chest thumps erratically, adrenaline shooting through me even in my attempt to control my breathing. Only it's not slowing.

Water sloshes, hitting the floor in loud splatters, probably due to him standing.

"Isa," he calls out.

My eyes fly open, and I force myself to grasp any sort of composure while I remain against the wall. Slowing my breathing, I grasp the mask of the assassin beneath the surface and turn the corner. A forced, tight smile lines my mouth just as he wraps a towel around his waist. Water drips down his muscled chest when I meet his gaze.

"I didn't mean to leave the door open… What did you see?" he asks warily, scanning my face for any sign of recognition or betrayal perhaps.

Because that's what it feels like at this moment—betrayal. He chose not to tell me. Not that he owes me anything, but after what we've shared together these last few weeks… it hurts a little.

His eyes narrow slightly, as if he's bracing for the worst possible reaction from me. Water drips from his lashes, landing on the curve of his scarred lip. Though I remain silent, unable to form the right words.

My eyes flick behind him to the mirror, spotting the black patch behind his right ear, confirming what I saw just a moment ago. I realize that all this time I've never truly seen the back of his head, not really.

Not to mention, it looks as if it was cut shorter than the rest of his hair, like he was intentionally hiding it.

His *mark.*

41

My eyes shift back to his face, heart racing, keeping my expression neutral. Though I'm not sure I'm doing a good enough job as my pulse pounds in my ears. He frantically reaches for his tunic, but I'm already bolting for the door.

"Isa, wait! Please, I was going to tell you."

"Tell me?" I whirl around, and he skids to a stop, pulling on his pants. "Tell me what, Rydian, that you have a mate mark? Who does it belong to?"

I attempt to view the right side of his neck when he shoves my hands away and then smirks, causing my anger to rise to a frightening level. My hands heat, power surging.

"Are you jealous, little fawn?" He laughs. "You won't tell me how you feel but you're jealous of my *mark*?" He shakes his head, like he has any right to be angry.

"I'm not jealous."

"No? What is it, then?"

Shock tears through me. "You could have… told me when we talked in the cave. When we talked about them, but you didn't. Before we started whatever this is between us—"

"It wasn't important at the time. And what of your mark? Were you going to tell me about yours?" he snaps.

A shocked breath leaves me. He saw the auburn mark in my hair? Realization flickers through me—he must have seen it when we shared my bed that first night together, recalling how his fingers lingered in my hair.

Regardless, I feel as if our situations are not the same, because if he already has a mate in Aurelia, I want to know about it. Then guilt grips me, knowing he's just as blindsided with my own secrets as I am by his.

A flicker of wariness—perhaps confusion—flashes in his eyes before he turns to light the mantel. It roars to life when he straightens and scratches the back of his head, brows pinched. "What do you know about mate marks?"

I blink. "Just... what we discussed."

Which is true—I only know as much as we discussed. But just as I go to ask, a breath of air escapes him, a sound of disbelief right before he shakes his head. Like this is all... amusing somehow.

He glances at me, then slowly inhales, hair dripping. "Are you going to tell me how you feel?"

"Why would I, when you have someone waiting for you in Aurelia? There's no point," I snap.

Anger flashes in his eyes. "You think there's no *point* in telling me how you feel? Would you like to know *my* point or how I feel about *you*?" He stalks toward me, stopping a foot away to get in my face. "Because you haven't asked, nor have you seemed remotely interested in finding out. You've been avoiding me for weeks and until tonight, I didn't even think you wanted me, so I've kept my mouth shut."

"Well, you're right. I don't want you."

"You're a liar," he growls, snapping a hand out to grip my jaw, forcing me to look at him. "You can't tell me that you don't want me when I can literally smell it on you. But let me tell you something, little fawn. I've wanted you far longer than you think." His voice is so low it causes the hair to rise on my arms. The words hang between us, his gaze never leaving mine. "I've been in love with you ever since you captivated me at this damn brothel. No one—and I mean *no one*—has ever made me feel the way you did that night. You took my breath away. And when I found out it was *you* who was there that night, I..." He trails off, searching my face. His intense gaze pins me in place, and , the room feels smaller.

"You what?" I ask quietly.

The crackling of the fire pops and hisses, filling the void of the silence between us. My breath falters, the rich scent of him consuming me, making it almost impossible to see reason. His lips inch closer, and the soft brush of his breath against my cheeks causes my hair to stir.

"I knew you were mine," he mutters, his brows pinching as if he's become confused. "Can't you feel it? Tell me you can feel it."

For a heartbeat, time stops, as if the realm is holding its breath, waiting for me to recognize what this is between us. My pulse climbs, pounding in my ears as I struggle with the weight of his words. His eyes search mine, waiting for something— anything from me—when it becomes too much.

Then it dawns on me—I'm in love with him. *And he feels the same.* What I feel isn't mere affection. It's more.

How did I ever let it get this far?

I pull back, stepping out of his embrace with a shake of my head when his expression falls. Why would he ever want me? I'm broken and lost and confused. I don't even know who I am anymore. He shouldn't want me because I'll never be enough for him. I will never be enough, especially not now.

"You don't mean it," I say, hating how my voice wavers.

I pivot, storming up the mezzanine for my items, but Rydian's on my heels. I'm almost to the table when my arm snaps back, forcing me to whirl around when his mouth slams into mine with such force that it knocks the breath out of me.

But then I find myself melting and clawing at him, my knees weak as he devours me. He backs me up, my feet stumbling, and I hit the edge of the table before he frantically lifts me, setting me on the edge. Papers rustle beneath me.

He breaks our kiss only to start trailing his nose down my neck, small sounds slipping past my lips. He growls right under my jaw, pulling back to look at me, and then his hand grips my hair at the base of my neck.

"Does this feel like indifference to you?" he hisses, fierce and unflinching. "You don't get to tell me what I feel, not when every damn part of me is already yours. I would burn the world for you. Don't you understand that?" He lands another hard, claiming kiss to my mouth.

I instantly grumble into him, and somehow, the sound of it forces him to pull me in as if he can't get enough. His mouth claims mine while his hands explore, finally landing at the rim of my pants and undoing the button.

And fuck, do I want him.

I'm fully dressed one moment, and in the next, clothes are being tossed aside. I gasp, scrambling for his tunic, lifting it in a frenzy, then work his pants down, dropping them to the floor.

Our mouths clash again, his hands pulling my hips to the edge of the table. They slide down my legs, forcing me to wrap around him just as he pushes his hips forward, and I feel his cock brush against me.

A whimper. "I need you, Rydian. Please."

My voice trembles with urgency as something dark and exhilarating begins to form, coiling at the very center of me. His answering growl vibrates against my skin.

"I know." His voice is rough, but he doesn't stop. His grip only tightens, hands trembling as if trying to hold himself back. "Do you have any idea what you do to me?"

His head dips, lips trailing a scorching path down my neck and onto my chest. My hand flies to his hair when I feel him begin to work between my legs, rubbing me in tight circles.

Then he groans against me once he feels how soaked I am. The pressure has already begun to coil low, aching for my release as he rubs and slips a finger in, curling. My hips begin to rock against his hand, urging him to continue, when he takes away my pleasure, halting the movement.

"Wha–what are you doing? Don't stop." My eyes flutter open.

I ache and attempt to guide his hand back down, but he holds it firm on my hip, leaving me to groan in frustration. He gently guides me down so that my back rests on the table, continuing to graze his mouth down my stomach, grip firm on my hips. He straightens, his tongue trailing across his fingers—tasting me—and I watch his muscles twitch with restraint.

"You look so beautiful when you beg," he mumbles, eyes slowly raking over my body. "Do you know what I love?"

A whimper escapes when I shake my head, my tone unrecognizable as I continue to grip his hips with my knees. I begin to quiver and my back arches, the movement involuntary as the pressure becomes too much.

With a groan, my hand dips between my legs to relieve some of the tension, but he snatches both of my wrists and holds them above my head, pinned between him and the table.

"Not until I say so." He leans over me, a possessive glint in his eyes as he holds my gaze. His head dips, biting my bottom lip, and I writhe beneath him. "I love it when you beg," he growls. "And I love it when you're mine."

He forces my legs apart, spreading wider as he lines himself up, a small grin forming on his mouth. Then our mouths instinctively part, collectively moaning when he drives his hips forward and finally—finally the pressure subsides. With gasped pants, we hold each other's stare as we savor the moment. And then his hips begin to move.

"Fuck," I get out.

My eyes fall on his expression as he hovers, my hands still tightly secured under his grasp. He drives into me with the perfect rhythm and without restraint, his gaze never leaving mine when his brows knit.

"Nothing—no one—will take you from me," he breathes.

His movements become frantic—hungry. The table rattles beneath us, scraping across the floor as papers scatter to the ground.

He releases my wrists, pulling me up so that my arms clasp around his neck. My head drops back, my release already forming with a sudden quickness, leaving my legs trembling. Our moans collide, the sounds echoing in the loft as if they were always meant to meld in the air together.

Then he wraps an arm around my waist, pulling me in and somehow pushing himself deeper, forcing a breathy cry to rush past. My clit rubs against him as he pushes into me over and over, and somehow, it's the right amount of—

"Rydian, gods!" I tremble, my body too weak to hold myself upright, but he holds me in place before devouring my mouth.

His cock tightens just as he thrusts his hips forward, once, then twice, before he's spilling himself in me. Satisfied groans fill the air.

We pant, holding each other as we slowly crawl back to reality. My forehead rests on his shoulder, slick with sweat, when he leans down to kiss the top of my head with a soft chuckle. Then his lips brush mine, though a grin tugs at his mouth.

"I'll bring you water and something to clean you up," he says, vanishing, then appears with water and a rag. I brace my palms against the table with a smirk, taking the glass from him and sipping, arching a brow. After taking the time to clean me himself, his gaze meets mine, and he straightens.

"In case you didn't hear me earlier—I love you," he murmurs, his voice steady but intense. I lean forward with pinched brows, my gaze softening as my own doubts come flooding back.

The emotions—the fear of never being enough for him. I part my lips in an attempt to speak, but he interrupts, his voice firmer this time.

"Truly, Isa. I love you." He studies me, tilting my head back as a swirl of emotions threatens to consume me. "Not the idea of you. Not just the pieces of you that you're willing to share but everything. Even the secrets you keep from me, and I know you have a few." He tugs at the end of my hair. "I love your wild spirit and the way you try to hide your embarrassment. The way your eyes flicker when something angers you, or the way you rub your wrist when you get nervous."

My secrets. "I—"

"I want you to tell me when you're ready, but I just wanted you to know," he interrupts, then leans down for my clothes. He dresses me in silence, and I watch as he pulls his pants over his hips. "Let's clean up." Rydian smirks. "The others will be fully disgusted if they find us all over our research."

I snort, bending to grab papers to begin placing each one back in their original stacks, sorting through the notes and relabeling everything. Gods, we made a mess.

"Remind me not to fuck on our research again," I mumble, smoothing out the wrinkled map and flattening it only to lean in again. "What the... oh my gods." My eyes flare as realization dawns on me.

I'm bracing myself against the table for stability as I take a deep breath, willing the nausea to subside. I can't help the bile that rises in my throat.

"What is it?" Rydian rushes to my side. His eyes meet mine over my shoulder.

"Do you see that?" I ask, pointing to the edge of the map, and he furrows his brows.

"That's the map of the castle."

"This," I say slowly, "is the edge of the king's archives. This is not his archive, or the correct one anyway. I was there a couple of weeks ago when he summoned me and got a good look at the inside. What is on this map is not correct. It's wrong."

"What do you mean?" he asks, though his face goes white as he registers my words.

"The map. It's wrong." I reach across the table, unfold the corner of the parchment, and point to the title. "Look at the title, here. It's not just a numbered document. We misread it."

A dark, unamused laugh escapes me. I *knew* it meant something. I just didn't know what it meant, but now I do. But how did I miss that before?

"It's not a number. It's a slash. Castle Alvonia one out of two. Meaning this map is the first one and we're missing the other half—the rest of his archives. I'm willing to bet it's what we need."

42

"Are you sure?" Rydian grinds his teeth, anger palpable across his face.

"Yes, I'm sure. There are two maps. *I know it*. The other one must be for the passages in his archives. I can feel it. I know I'm right." I pause for a moment, holding his gaze. "I think we should get it tonight."

Considering I've already done it one other time by myself, I believe we could slip in and out without getting caught. He just doesn't know that yet.

Rydian walks around the table, and I lean in on my hands, attempting to read his expression. His face twists with anger, mind whirling, as if he's racking through every possible outcome.

"We can't confirm that just based on your intuition. I know you're eager to find your mother, but we can't go in there based on a feeling," he says.

"We have to at least try," I press.

My mother is in that castle somewhere, I know it. And then we can leave for Aurelia—I can leave with him because I know he's who I want.

"I'm not saying I don't agree with you. I'm saying let's wait until we can get Ren and Orin here to formulate a plan. We can break into the archives to see if we can find the other map in a few days. It's too risky to do it by ourselves."

"We can't wait—we should do it tonight. Please."

"No, we shouldn't. Don't be impulsive. We need to wait for the others," he clips, though he's not doing a good job of convincing me.

"If you don't go with me, I'll be going by myself. Either you join me or not at all, but I'm going tonight whether you like it or not," I sneer, instantly regretting my words.

He straightens and lowers his brows, a dark shadow spilling across his face, reaching my side of the table. I regretted the words as soon as they left my mouth, but I couldn't stop myself. Shame runs through me, and even though I realize my mistake, I stand my ground with a lift to my chin. A gasp slips from me when he grips my jaw, dragging me closer to him. Although firm, he doesn't hurt me.

"You think you can threaten me, Isa?" He scans my face. "Do you think I'm going to allow you to leave? You've clearly misjudged my affection for you."

I only chuckle at his words. "I'm going. Please don't make me fight you—or beg you, as much as I'd love to right now." I smirk, but he doesn't take the bait.

His eyes remain fixed on me, sharp and unyielding, while the war inside him plays out across his face, as if struggling with his decision with a shake of his head.

"Please, don't do that," he whispers, his forehead resting against mine, stealing my breath.

"Do what?"

"Don't force me to do this. Your safety comes first, and I can't risk us going in there without a plan."

"I'm not forcing you. I'm asking you to go with me. Please. It's better if we do it together, wouldn't you agree? We'll do what we did last time, only now we know there are other wards there. We'll be careful," I whisper.

His expression shifts, brows drawing close together as he searches my face, flickering with something raw—fear, I realize.

It's brief, barely there before he masks it, but I see it, and , I *feel* the struggle he's trying to hide. It's stifling and raw, settling at the edge of my temples, filled with an emotion he forces himself to bury. He's wrestling with the guilt and pain of losing me not once, but *twice.*

The realization hits me hard as my chest tightens, my breathing impossible as his memories of the battle come flooding back to me. As easily as if I pulled them from him myself. My breathing stalls, images and emotions flying across my mind in a whirl.

I felt it then just as I do now.

"It wasn't your fault," I whisper, forcing him to look at me, his jaw tightening from restraint. "What happened at the battle wasn't your fault. It was an impossible situation. But if we steal the map tonight, I'll leave with you. For Aurelia. We can continue the search from Aurelia if it's what you want because it's what I want. I want that with *you.* I want to be with you, no matter the cost."

His blue eyes find mine as he searches my face again. Only this time his expression is softer, with more understanding before he drops his head. He nods on an exhale, and without a word, his grip loosens, and he takes a large step back to study me before turning for the stairs.

"Then we'll leave tonight. We only have a few hours left so we better get going. Grab your weapons. We leave in ten minutes."

Ten minutes go by when I whirl to the front of the archives, cloaked in the Veil. It's like second nature to me as my essence continues to grow, feeling it become a part of my body as if it never left. Conjuring my magic up is as easy as a thought, my hands warming at the thought of it while we wait.

We should be in and out in a matter of minutes. Two stand in the hallway, guarding the doors near the edge of the stairs that lead down into the courtyard. One on each side and far enough away that it would take them a moment to become alerted of the doors being opened.

Standing in the Veil allows me to see anyone in it, as it's like sharing the same space. I look at Rydian now, who's armed to the teeth, hood drawn low over his brow. But his jaw is firm as he glances at me, still wary of doing this tonight. He can't shift in the archives, so he has to stay in his true form.

"We've been here for ten minutes with no shift change," he says.

"A few more minutes," I plead.

We came to the agreement that if there was no shift change, we would leave and wait for Ren in the next couple of days to formulate a plan. I agreed only because I was determined to get the second half of the map tonight.

Then the doors begin to open. The two guards from inside the archives walk out, leaving us just enough space to squeeze through without alerting the two in the hall.

Rydian's gaze meets mine as we silently walk at a quick pace to catch the doors right before they close—we're in.

A sigh of relief escapes me just as the Veil flutters out like the first time we came, leaving us out in the open. I share a look with Rydian when he nods.

Striding to the back once again, I see large bookcases line the entirety of the wall, spotting the section holding the rolled parchment off to the right. Rydian goes straight for them.

"No, not there. I found the first map on his desk. I think it will be over here," I whisper, and he quickly nods, meeting me at the edge of King Elion's desk as we quietly go through it. I spot the first map we made a copy of and push it aside, pulling it up to see if anything else lies under it, quickly spotting its twin.

The second map—I gasp at the sight of it.

"Here, it's right here. I found it," I mumble.

I knew there was a second one. Relief shoots through me, and a second later Rydian begins to roll it up. I glance down at the drawers again and begin to dig through them when I spot a chest nearby. I open it, and my eyes flare wide at what's inside.

"We have to hurry," he warns, and then my stomach drops at the sound of a door opening, only to find that the archive doors are still closed. Worry etches my face, and I frantically glance around when a low chuckle sounds from behind us.

"Look what we have here," he drawls.

Rydian's head snaps toward the sound coming from the shelves, and I realize that it's a door, a hidden passageway, when I turn to face the voice.

A voice I recognize.

43

Ezra—what's he doing here?

Relief washes over me for a moment, but then I see his expression. It's nothing like the Ezra I know, but someone far more sinister than that of my best friend. I knew he was loyal to King Elion, but I never expected this. I scan his face, searching for the friend I grew up with.

His features are sharper, like a mask of someone I don't recognize, but a deep part of me knows that this must be his true personality. He walks toward us, each step calculated—predatory. My stomach drops.

This isn't the Ezra I know.

Rydian pushes me behind him, his hood lowered over his brow, casting a shadow over his features. He slowly tucks the map beneath his cloak unnoticed.

Ezra's expression becomes darker, and a slow, unsettling smile begins to creep up the corners of his mouth, but there's no humor there. The warmth that once defined him as my friend has been replaced by something far more chilling. The air becomes thick, and my pulse races at the new threat in front of us.

His voice drops, his posture reeking of earned arrogance. "I see you've been busy."

"Ezra." I smile cautiously, slowly grabbing the daggers at my waist. "What are you doing here?"

"I could ask you the same question."

His eyes graze us as if assessing his own threat, leaving my body screaming at me to run, but I know we can't escape—we can't access the Veil. Rydian can't even shift his appearance, leaving us no choice but to confront him.

"I thought you were on a mission," I say.

"Who is this?" Ezra asks, tilting his head.

His attention swivels to Rydian, his eyes darting to him—studying—as if he's finally seeing who stands at my side.

"Just some drunken fool I forced into coming here tonight. Are you jealous?" I smirk, but my stomach dips before stepping out from behind Rydian.

"And why *did* you come here tonight, Isa?" Ezra asks.

"Why do you want to know? Just let us walk out of here and we can forget all about it. The king doesn't have to know, does he?"

With my shoulders back, I step forward, forcing his attention to remain on me. He slides his gaze away from Rydian.

A slow, eerie laugh emerges from Ezra, causing the hair to rise on my arms. "And why would I do that when I can just take your memories?"

No. My stomach twists, nausea curling the moment his words pierce the air, and I rapidly blink as images fly across my mind. Milena's warning about the Siphon passes through me.

My face drains as I hold myself steady, his confession sitting on my chest like a weight. *I can't breathe.* Rydian stills beside me, growling under his breath.

I feel betrayed—our friendship built on a lie.

It was Ezra stealing my memories and essence, but why? He

disguised himself as a trusted friend, taking what was mine. But that means he's King Elion's second-in-command.

He killed King Andre.

Witt Dralor, Milena's grandson. Never the Ezra who I was raised alongside—he was always the second-in-command, replacing the Ezra I once knew. I would have known if he was working with the king, right?

My mind runs through scenarios, wondering if he touched me without my knowledge, pulling precious memories.

"What do you need with my memories?" I ask.

"So you know." He sighs dramatically. "I guess it was only a matter of time."

"Of course I know. Do you think I wouldn't figure it out? You underestimated me. I thought we were friends," I get out.

His features darken. "Friends. What a... *peculiar* word. No, we were never friends, Isa." He tsks with a low, eerie chuckle. "I was forced to be your shadow after that event at the orphanage when you were a child. Ordered to make sure you knew nothing of your past. It was quite exhausting. Pretending to be your friend and enjoying... well, *you*," he mocks, exaggerating the wave of his arms, and circles both of us—calculating. But his words slice through me, leaving pain in their wake. My heart shatters.

"Oh, but the king wanted me there," he continues, "making sure you behaved—that you remained unaware of your marks. That your magic wasn't *refreshing*. But it has been, hasn't it? I can feel your power even from here. I should have known, but it won't matter soon. We'll kill your little friend here and start fresh, just like the last time. Do you remember when I took them? You never told me who they belonged to."

Nausea rises, and I feel my stomach drop over his cold words, unsure of what he means. His eyes flicker to my face with an expression I can't quite place before it's gone, his chin dipping, assessing us over his brows. He inches closer when I notice the daggers in his palms. He must not recognize Rydian, or he would have said something by now. *Wouldn't he?*

I know how Ezra fights. I know he could probably take both of us, especially without the use of our magic. He's one of the most skilled fighters here, and if he's the second-in-command, he's capable of killing any king.

"You can't," I blurt. "King Elion wouldn't allow you to pull my memories without his knowledge. You're his second-in-command, are you not? Which means you must take me to him before doing so. If you pull my memories, he'll have questions as to why certain things are missing from his archives. You wouldn't want to be caught accused of stealing, now would you? That would be treason."

He halts his steps, eyes darting from me to Rydian as if struggling with the decision to steal my memories or take me to King Elion.

His features twist back into someone who's relaxed and uncaring. As if we didn't just have a heated conversation. His face lights up, hiding the cold expression he was just wearing, and he assesses me again. Then he strides to the archive doors to bang on them.

Ezra's personality would make him the most excellent second-in-command with the ability to detach from his feelings. This must be the switch Milena mentioned. I've never seen anything like it.

Rydian and I exchange glances, his face twisted in anger, realizing that he's the same one who killed King Andre. A low rumble escapes him, fists clenched at his sides. I know he's using every ounce of his control to keep it together.

Four guards storm inside, immediately flanking Ezra as their features line with shock at the sight of us. *Do they know he's Elion's second-in-command?*

In a flash of movement, Ezra pivots to his left, pushing his blade into the throat of the closest guard. The guard crumples to the ground, a pool of blood quick to follow. Then he smiles, the chilling expression sending a shiver down my spine.

What the fuck?

"Take this as a warning for not doing your job correctly. We'll be escorted to the throne room. Find someone to fetch the king, will you?" he commands.

There's no sign of the menacing Ezra we saw moments ago. He graces us with the casual male I've known for years.

"Follow me." He begins walking down the corridor, urging us to follow. Once I step into the hall, my magic immediately warms my hands.

"*I thought the king was gone,*" Rydian says. "*We can Veil out of here. We can fight.*"

"*Me too. But we'll lose the upper hand if we vanish. We need to see what the king says, and if it turns for the worst, we'll find a way to leave together. We'll go to Aurelia—gather the army,*" I say, and he shoots me a wary glance and reluctantly nods.

Two guards follow closely behind, one walking a step ahead of Ezra as he leads us to the throne room. The sun begins to rise, casting a soft pink glow over the horizon through the windows of the castle.

Our steps create an echo as we thud down the stone corridor, stopping twenty feet from the throne. The two guards following behind us grab Rydian, pulling him off to the side. Rydian pulls back, kicking one in the chest as dark shadows form around his hands at the surge of magic.

"*No! Please, Rydian. Please, don't fight them. They can't know who you are,*" I beg, my stomach lurching with unease.

He immediately halts, his head swiveling to me, allowing them to kick his knees in, and he drops to the ground. Rydian kneels before the throne of Elderheim, arms pinned behind him.

Ezra stands to my left, and after a few minutes, King Elion steps from behind his throne, followed by Ren and Theron. Ren freezes at the sight of us, his gaze locking with mine. I give the faintest shake of my head, a warning to remain silent.

Please, please just go along with it.

Elion pauses once he notices me below the dais and then silently surveys the chamber. But I don't bow—I refuse to give him that respect.

"Witt, what is this?" He throws out a flat smile, using Ezra's real name, but I have a feeling he already knows. Elion eyes Ezra and then narrows his gaze as it lands on Rydian kneeling a few feet from me.

"I'm sorry." I push the thought to Rydian, knowing exactly where this is going. He throws me a concerned look.

But I was too afraid to tell him sooner. I knew we would be taken to King Elion if we were caught. I just hoped I wouldn't have to do this tonight, especially after finding out about the second half of the map.

Now I have no choice.

"I found these two digging through your desk. I'm happy to siphon for you, Your Majesty, should it come to that," Ezra says.

Elion only chuckles, stroking his beard. "We've been waiting for your return." He pauses long enough to look at me. "Did you think we didn't know? With the wards I have in place, I know when someone *new* steps into my archives. Then I saw something very important to me was missing." My stomach drops. "Tell me, Isa, which memories did you find?"

Rydian's stare blazes into the side of my face, but I remain forward, though I know what masks his features now—betrayal. But I couldn't say anything as a precaution to myself, not until I was certain of the truth.

And I didn't want him to know yet.

"Isa, is that true?" Rydian asks, voice straining with hurt. *"Tell me it's not true."* But it is.

A white crystal with swirls of yellow was calling to me,

buried deep into Elion's desk when we searched the first time. Then when I went to return the first map, I stole it.

The moment the crystal touched my skin, it sent a thrumming power surging through me, and I knew then that it was mine. I finally found the courage to go to Milena two weeks ago, confirming my suspicions. She successfully placed my memories and essence back in their rightful place.

"Only the important ones," I say, tilting my head to study the king.

"And who is that friend of yours?" He nods to Rydian, whose hood is drawn low.

Asking about Rydian only confirms that he remains unaware of who he truly is. And if we have access to our magic, Rydian should have been able to shift. I can only hope that he did.

I scoff. "He's just some drunken fool I coerced into coming here tonight. Kill him if you must." Elion chuckles at my response, almost as if he's proud.

My eyes mistakenly flicker to Rydian, finding his head turned toward me, but the shadows of his hood conceal his expression. Although I know what's there because I can feel it at the forefront of my mind, right between my eyes—pure outrage. His magic remains tucked away, no sign of his shadows.

I return my gaze to Elion, realizing that he just revealed he's been waiting for my return. He knew we were in his archives, and nothing happened. Yet, he didn't mention anything about his chambers or the map we stole.

Is he lying about the wards? Did he actually know we were in there, or did he only notice my missing memories?

I study him, realizing that I must use every ounce of my training in the Brotherhood if I want to get us out alive.

"What do you know, Isa?" Elion grumbles, a bright white power crackling at his fingertips in warning. Only he doesn't scare me—not anymore.

"*Isa*," Rydian says.

A laugh escapes me, a slow smile playing across my face as I step forward. "I know that you've been stealing my memories, but I'm ready to step into my role now."

Within seconds, I wear the mask of the skilled assassin he's raised me to be, slowly tilting my head up. Locking my gaze with his, I continue to take slow, calculated steps forward. A mask of indifference slides into place as my smile turns cold.

Ezra moves to intervene, but I hold my hand up, fingers outstretched and freezing him in place. Not because he wants to, but because I make him. Fear spreads wide across his face like a wildfire, his feet slowly coming off the ground.

I could end him right here if I wanted to.

My hands burn from the heated surge through my veins, wild and unrestrained, eager to be unleashed. With a ferocious quickness, my body hums with power, and I close the distance, each step calculating. My gaze locks with King Elion when I stop just shy of the dais.

Elion grins, eyes glinting with something between pride and malice. The drumming of his fingers ceases as he leans forward, watching me with amusement, as though he's been waiting for this moment.

"And what role is that?" His voice is smooth, dripping with curiosity.

I put it together shortly after speaking with Milena, but it was when she spoke of my mother that I began to question it. The depth of my magic was undeniable with how fast it was coming in despite my essence being siphoned—power strong enough to shake the realms, and I just *knew*.

I have only seen power like that a handful of times in my life —only royalty is able to obtain such strength.

Only bloodlines chosen by the Fates.

I smirk. "As heir to Elderheim, Father."

EPILOGUE

TWO WEEKS PRIOR

The moment I grabbed the crystal from King Elion's desk, a heat of energy surged up my arm, and I knew it was mine.

Yet even after taking it, I couldn't bring myself to have that conversation with Rydian, knowing he would scold me for being reckless—sneaking back into the archives by myself.

But after a week, I wanted to confront Milena about the relationship my mother had with King Elion in private, believing she had the answers I was searching for.

Like who my father is, because I had the suspicion that it wasn't King Andre. And King Elion's physical similarities with me couldn't be mere coincidence.

Not with the power surging through my veins, humming constantly, begging to be unleashed despite my essence being pulled out. Shifting from a burning heat to an iciness forming at my fingertips.

I only planned on being gone today, having told Rydian I had a mission. And so I Veiled out of my chamber and into the woods first thing this morning.

Crisp leaves fly across the wet ground, forcing me to pull my cloak a little tighter across my chest as I follow Grim further into the trees—leading me to Milena.

The Howler is as terrifying as he is beautiful—dark gray with a white undercoat, fur thick for winter. His haunches reach the tops of my shoulders, making the top of his head near my total height. He makes me feel small.

His bushy tail barely grazes the frozen ground, brushing my ankles as we walk further into the forest. After a few silent minutes, we arrive just outside what looks to be a den made solidly of stone. The ground is covered in a light layer of snow, and I look up. It's easily as tall as I am, if not a little bigger.

"Milena is inside," he grumbles.

My brows pinch. Why not just meet in her cottage?

Warm light flickers across the stone and although cold out, it's surprisingly warm inside. The ground is covered in an array of leaves as the scent of pine and earth fill my nostrils.

Grim steps aside. Milena kneels near a dark ebony-coated Howler as an orb floats above them, as she has just given birth to seven pups.

Milena glances over her shoulder with raised brows, glasses halfway down her nose, hair messily gathered into a loose bun. With a huff and a glare, she returns to the Howler as if this was any other day.

"I wasn't expecting you," she says.

The female Howler opens her eyes, lifting them to mine as if she just realized my presence, and growls. I step back, my eyes darting back to Milena, who's focused on Grim, tilting her head as if having a silent conversation.

"You have a crystal, and you're here to see if it's yours?" Milena asks me.

I swallow and nod. "I also have a few other questions to ask you, if you have time."

She shoots a glance down, furrowing her brows. "Well, Nisha just informed me that she birthed her last pup a few minutes ago. I guess I'll leave the new parents to tend to their pups."

Straightening, she grabs a linen cloth. She wipes her hands and ushers me out of the den as Grim settles himself next to Nisha.

"I didn't know there were more Howlers nearby. I've never seen something so beautiful. Seven pups?" I ask as Milena pushes her glasses up her nose, then lays the rag over her shoulder.

"Yes, and I'm shocked Grim allowed you in the den. That's his mate," she says, and we reach the door to her cottage. "I suspect he trusts you, and that says a lot. With new pups, Howlers are incredibly territorial. And with the female being in such a vulnerable position, the males become quite aggressive."

She opens her door, urging me to sit at the table, and washes her hands. The fire from the mantel floods my senses and I sit, shrugging off my cloak. She brings two mugs of tea to the table.

"Nisha has been his mate for twenty years now. It's still considered a new pairing," Milena says.

"And they're born in the winter?" Most animals would have a litter in the spring or summer when it's warm.

She hums, nodding. "They're the only kind to have litters in the middle of winter. A survival test. Pups who survive winter are privileged enough to live, forged in the harshest conditions. By the time spring arrives, they are no longer pups but survivors."

"Have they lost any?"

"They're the first pairing to have every pup survive winter, making them the strongest living pair for the last 200 years. Howlers have pups once every two, but this is the fourth litter

I've helped them birth. It's a privilege to be accepted as one of their own. I've been in these woods long enough, I guess." She chuckles quietly.

I find myself wondering what it's like for Milena to be isolated from others for so long—to live in solitude with only the Howlers for company, the loneliness stretching over the years.

I wonder how she met them and if she ever longs for something more. Does she ache for the people she's lost? Does she ever wonder if the world has forgotten her as much as she was forced to forget it? The thought unsettles me, and for a moment, I understand a fraction of what it means to truly be alone.

Yet… a part of me envies her. The quiet—*the freedom.*

A life untethered from the expectations that come with being part of a realm that demands too much from me. And out here, in the silence, there are no lies to unravel, no hidden secrets, no duty to fulfill. *Could I live like this? Would I want to?*

"Don't worry, I like being out here, and they make my time in the woods much more manageable," she says as if sensing the question on my face. "Show me what you have."

I glance down and huff. "First, I have a question about my father." She eyes me warily, but I force myself to hold her gaze. "Is King Elion my father?"

She's silent as she sets her mug down with a soft thud against the table, rubbing her thumb over the curve of the handle before looking at me.

My eyes narrow. "My mother was in contact with you all those years, and she didn't tell you? Please, I need to know because the power surging through me isn't just from Aurelia, and I need to figure out how to control it before it gets out of hand. How can I talk to animals if I'm from Aurelia? How can Grim communicate with me? It doesn't make sense."

She takes a long sip, eyeing me over the rim. "I've been waiting for that question since you arrived. King Elion is your father, but I was sworn to secrecy by Elynor, and with me being out here alone in the woods, who am I to tell?" She chuckles again, but then her face falls at my reaction.

I fucking knew it. A laugh of disbelief brushes the air as I stand to pace, tears threatening to fall. All this time, I've been living in the castle with my father. My *real* father. I'm not a priority because I'm a female or skilled—I'm his *daughter.*

A daughter he's trying to punish for what my mother did to him. Yet every mission I received wasn't because of my potential, it was to take out *his* enemies as I killed off my own kind.

Bitterness threatens to consume me, rising in my chest. For years I served King Elion without questioning the missions he gave me, yet he said nothing. Instead, he was stealing my memories and forcing me to believe the lie he's spun.

Milena's brows pinch. "You carry the royal essence of both bloodlines, Isa."

My stomach drops. "How? What does that mean?"

"Truthfully, I don't know," she mumbles, but my heart skips with dread. "Your mother didn't tell King Andre about the pregnancy until after they had already completed the marriage ritual for her to become queen of Aurelia. Until she herself had the royal essence, which means you carry the royal essence of the Vaelborne bloodline." But also the royal Aethralis bloodline.

I'm heir to both realms.

What's Rydian going to think? If he knew about this—my real father—would he still want me? I might be considered heir to Aurelia, but would he allow me to accept it? But what if he already knows? He would tell me if he did, right?

My thoughts spiral as I think of the king I began envisioning a life with, but now... now I'm not so sure. My future feels uncertain, my stomach curling at the thought. Rydian just became an enemy.

Maybe not in my eyes, but I would be in his, especially if my father is King Elion. Rydian would expect me to take Elderheim, not Aurelia. Elynor wasn't even a Vaelborne.

He'll never trust me, regardless of how I feel about him. He'll always see me as his enemy. *Gods, I feel sick.*

"Please sit, Isa," Milena says quietly, but my chest tightens, feeling as if I can't breathe. Frowning, I close my eyes and take a deep breath and sit, but my legs begin to tremble.

"What do I do?" I ask. Panic threatens to take hold, because what *can* I do? I have no one to confide in.

"You pretend that you don't know. He's cruel, and if there's anything I've learned from working with him, it's that you need to stay one step ahead. Keep it to yourself and use it, because he will use you and he will not apologize for it."

I bite my lip as my thoughts continue to whirl, sitting with what she's advised. I know deep down what she says is true, so I'll keep it to myself. Which means I can't tell anyone, not Rydian or the others—not even Ezra.

Gods, I want to tell Ezra. He would know what to do, wouldn't he? But I'll form a plan and stay one step ahead.

Milena extends her hand. "I need to see what you have."

Sucking in a long breath, I grab the crystal from the inside of my cloak. A bright yellow glow whirls wildly within the crystal as if trying to escape.

Her eyes go wide, lost to the sight of it. "How did you get this?"

"That's not important. I just want to know if it's mine or not," I say, hoping she doesn't ask for more information.

She glances at me before closing her eyes, taking a deep breath and hovering a hand over the crystal. She's feeling it— the energy.

I'm silent as she hovers her hand between us, watching the yellow frantically swirl around like it's aware. She yanks her hand back, eyes snapping to mine, and nods.

Relief washes over me with a rough exhale. "What now?"

"Well, do you want them back?" she asks cautiously.

I pause. That was the plan—getting them back.

But I find myself hesitating if only for a moment before nodding, realizing very quickly that I *do* want them back. I want the past that was stolen from me, something that should have never left me in the first place.

"How does it work?"

"Placing them back or taking them?" she asks, and I realize she has only given us the very basics of what it takes to siphon memories. Curiosity tugs at me, and I find myself wanting to learn more.

"Both," I say.

"Do you want more tea?" she asks, and I nod. "When Elion first started experimenting, I didn't know what to expect. I went in blind, as it was something no one had ever tried before. I wrote everything in a notebook as I worked, writing down anything significant—good or bad." She sits across from me again.

"And what did you discover?"

Her brows pinch. "I discovered that us Siphons can't see the memories, but what we can do is feel them based on your essence. Think of your memories as a web tied to your specific essence signature. Each memory is connected to this web through shared experiences, emotions, or people. Through that signature, we're able to pull memories tied to those emotions or experiences. They act like markers in a way, allowing the Siphon to identify and target clusters of memories without seeing them."

"So there's a chance that whoever took my memories hasn't actually seen anything?" I don't know why, but I'm relieved that no one was able to see my stolen memories—whatever they are.

"Yes, that's correct. They must know what to look for. All we can feel is a signature tied to that event or emotion, so it's likely that when they took something, they took everything regarding that moment."

Like my parents. Aurelia. My childhood.

"And how do you place them back? Will it hurt?" I ask.

A wave of fear grips my chest at the thought of my lost memories being put back, and I take a deep breath.

What if these memories bring back a wave of emotions I don't want to deal with? What if I find out something about myself that I'm better off not knowing? I nervously rub the inside of my wrist, lost in my thoughts—my worry. She tracks the movement, furrowing her brows before I shove my hands under the table.

"You may experience… mental turmoil, but it will not hurt you when placed back. It will feel as though you are receiving a lost piece of you, like filling your lungs with air you didn't know you were missing. As far as your power goes, you may get a surge of energy, but it should subside after a day or two."

She places our mugs into the basin as I chew my lip. "Okay, let's get it over with."

"Alright, I'll have you lie down on the settee over there." She gestures behind me, and my brows furrow. "Just as a precaution, I would rather have you lying down. I will act as a pathway for your memories to move back into you. The energy will pass through my arms and exit out of my palm. Can you manage to lie still?"

I nod. A second later, I'm lying down, staring out of the window. Grim stands guard at the mouth of the den, snow falling lazily from the sky. Milena sits near my head, placing a palm on my forehead while gripping the crystal.

"This will take a few seconds, but it will be over before you know it. I haven't done this in quite some time, so give me a moment to feel it," she explains.

Just then, she closes her eyes as the crystal begins to frantically swirl again. After a few seconds, the yellow swirls slowly drain down the length of the crystal, her palm glowing as it travels up her arm.

I slam my eyes shut, terrified of what I'll receive. The uncertainty has my breath coming out in shallow pants as I begin to tremble. Then my forehead warms, a slow, tingling heat spreading through me. Pressure builds, deep and insistent, like diving too far into an ocean, losing sight of the surface.

A moment later, the world around me tilts, as if I'm falling, and images slam into me, fragmented and disjointed, yet impossibly vivid. My breath catches as overwhelming emotions surge through me—fear, longing, sorrow.

And then, as quickly as they come, everything goes black.

I wake abruptly, sitting upright as my breaths come out in shallow pants, feeling as if my throat has been dry for weeks.

Gods, I'm thirsty. Swallowing feels like eating sand, my hair plastered to my forehead in a sweaty mess. I'm in a small room, lying on a bed covered in multicolored quilts, when the door to my left creaks open. Milena walks in with a glass of water, round glasses resting high on her nose.

"Oh, you're awake! Thank the Fates," she says.

"What happened?" I croak, reaching for the glass and gulping it down. I groan as the cool, crisp water slides down my throat.

"After placing your memories, you went in and out of consciousness without realizing. I assumed it was the surge of power you gained. It was a lot of energy and drained me quite a bit. You don't remember walking back here?" she asks warily, and I shake my head. "Mm, I'll have to add that to my notes."

"How long have I been asleep?" I lean forward as she walks to the foot of the bed.

"A day and a half."

"What?" My disbelief echoes across the room.

Gods, I hope Rydian and Ren aren't searching for me. The last thing I need is to explain where I've been, especially if I'm to remain quiet about who my real father is.

"Sit for a while longer and you can leave. It's best not to rush it if you're tired. How much do you remember?" She fixes the corner of the bed, patting the quilt.

A rush of images flew through my mind so fast I couldn't quite catch it all, and then everything went black, rendering me unconscious.

I frown, attempting to recall everything. "I—I'm not sure. I remember bits at the orphanage, when Rydian tried to bring me back, and then..." I touch my lips with wide eyes, a small gasp leaving me as broken pieces of memory flood me. *It can't be.*

"Don't worry," Milena says. "You will slowly start to remember things as they come in. Some moments will trigger a memory for you, and then , you'll realize it was one you were missing. It's common for them to come in slowly over time, especially if there were a lot." Then she places a gentle hand on my shoulder, squeezing. "Take a deep breath. Take a few days to process if you need to, but the most important thing you can do is rest and stay quiet. The shaking will subside."

How is that possible? My fingers tremble as I brush the auburn mate mark behind my ear. But I stare at my wrist, my breath catching in my throat, eyeing the scar there. The one I never truly questioned.

But it's not really a scar—it never has been.

It's a mate mark of Elderheim.

ACKNOWLEDGMENTS

I want to thank my husband for always encouraging me to chase after whatever crazy idea comes next, for believing in me when I doubt myself, and for being my constant source of support.

To my family for always hyping me up and for reminding me why I started this journey because without their support, I wouldn't have had the courage to finish it in the first place. To my sisters who listened to my endless ramblings about plot twists and character arcs and for believing in my story.

To my kids, who are the source of who gives me life, filling every moment of it with love and laughter, inspiring me to dream bigger and work harder. I hope this inspires you to chase after your dreams.

And finally, to every one of my readers—thank you. This books exists because of people like you who believe in the magic of storytelling.

ABOUT THE AUTHOR

C.J. Blaire was born and raised in Texas, where she developed a love for storytelling when she just couldn't get it out of her head until she wrote it. With a creative background in wedding photography, she has always been drawn to capturing moments —both through a lens and on a page. When she's not weaving wild, intricate stories, she enjoys reading, sewing, and staying active. A wife and mother of two with lots of animals in tow, she finds inspiration in the quiet moments of her everyday life.

https://www.threads.com/@author.cjblaire